I0547054

the BRIDGE to WICKMORE

a novel by

Larry Cunningham

Copyright © 2020 Larry Cunningham - The Bridge to Wickmore
Second Edition
All cover art copyright © 2020 Larry Cunningham
All Rights Reserved

No part of this book may be reproduced or transmitted in any form or by any means, electronic or mechanical, including photocopying, recording, or by any information storage and retrieval system, without permission in writing from the author.

Publishing Coordinator – Sharon Kizziah-Holmes

Paperback-Press
an imprint of A & S Publishing
A & S Holmes, Inc.

ISBN -13: 978-1-951772-51-2

CHAPTER ONE

Boston

Sam Prescott's life changed forever one evening at a school dance. Girls screamed and the band stopped playing, adding emphasis to his defining moment. An alert chaperone dialed 911 for medical assistance. Two police officers assigned to spend the evening sat in a squad car at the entrance to the school–Ashcroft Academy–an exclusive prep school for boys. The officers heard the 911 call and rushed up the front steps where the panic-stricken headmaster beckoned. He led them quickly down the hall toward an elaborately decorated ballroom. Both officers glanced up as they entered beneath a gilded banner reading:

ASHCROFT ACADEMY
SPRING COTILLION

The cops paused briefly under the banner, then shoved through a murmuring crowd of well-dressed teenagers toward the middle of the dimly lit ballroom. The center of attraction appeared to be a young man encircled by three campus security officers; all well past sixty; all underpaid and quite content to wait for city cops to handle the trouble. Two young men lay writhing on the polished dance floor, the surface now splattered with their blood.

"That's him, officers! Arrest him!" a matronly chaperon shrieked, pointing toward the towering teenaged boy hovering over the moaning victims. The boy was still breathing heavily, fists clenched.

The officers analyzed the scene quickly, exchanged wry smiles, and then relaxed. Corporal Nat Winkler, a supple, athletic black woman nearing forty, clucked disapprovingly, unsnapped a pair of handcuffs and stepped forward, eyes locked on the boy. Her expression suggested disappointment rather than displeasure.

"Well, well, if it isn't little Sammy Prescott. We meet again. Okay, you know the drill, kid. Turn around." She dangled the cuffs toward him. "Don't mess with me."

The boy glared, weighing his diminishing options, eyes jerking from Winkler to her gigantic partner, a six-foot-five, 250 pound, hatless, head-shaven white man circling behind. Most of the cops at precinct knew the officers, both married, not to each other, spent occasional dead-time hours at Mentone's Motel, compliments of Alvarez Mentone, the illegal alien proprietor.

No one in the gawking crowd of teenagers moved or spoke, still stunned by the violence, half expecting another explosion. The current of tension suddenly flowed from the room like a punctured balloon, collapsing into an undertone of nervous whispers as the cornered culprit, anger checked, escape alternatives depleted, capitulated. The boy sighed heavily, turned his back to Corporal Winkler, gave a resigned look toward the ceiling and extended his wrists.

The corporal clapped the cuffs on, nodded her partner toward the exit, shoved the boy gently and said, "Let's go, kid." Her authoritarian voice boomed, "Okay, that's it people! Show's over!"

As the officers cleared the area with their captive, the ballroom once again swirled with action, this time featuring activities of a party breaking up: chaperons herding boys and girls from the scene; paramedics surging through the crowd to assist the battered casualties. The hired band packed to leave, pocketing a full evening's pay for less than an hour's work.

Three chartered busses pulled into Ashcroft's parking lot to collect the girls, many still with tear-streaked faces, for the return trip to Halstead, a finishing school for cultured young ladies. Most of the girls had never encountered such primitive violence during their sheltered lives, and probably never would again. The excitement and mayhem that ruined their evening had taken place immediately after the two bleeding boys taunted Sam Prescott about his mother's choice of employment: she worked for an escort agency, furnishing unconditional affection to anyone who could pay for it.

* * * * *

The grizzled duty sergeant at precinct headquarters, Dan Kinnegan, veteran of thirty years, crippled somewhat by a bullet through his knee, grudgingly looked up from a pile of paperwork, then frowned as the corporal steered Sam toward his desk. "What have we here, Corporal Winkler? Looks like an old friend."

"Same ol' thing, Sarg. Ashcroft's finest still fightin' about his momma."

Kinnegan carefully placed his drugstore Ben Franklin's on the desk. "I see. Right up here, Master Prescott. Let me have a look at you." The sergeant stepped down and limped around the elevated desk to examine the boy's injuries. After a brief inspection, he said, "Evidently not that much worse for wear." He jabbed the ornate Ashcroft coat of arms on the boy's blazer with his trigger finger and said, "Any damage I can't see, Lad?"

"No, Sir," Sam said, eyes straight ahead. Kinnegan's inspection continued. "I see. Well then, what about the guy he hit, Nat?" This directed to the corporal, once his partner.

"Oh, he hit two of 'em this time, Sarg. One ain't talkin', but that's only 'cuz he can't. Pretty bad shape. Real bad. Medics pumpin' oxygen down him like a flat tire when we left."

Kinnegan shook his head sadly, muttering under his breath, "Well, that's just great." He stepped nearer, his nose drill-sergeant close to the boy's face. "Why? And this better be good." The entire precinct called Kinnegan "Professor." He needed two more classes at Boston U to complete his doctorate in Medieval History. He planned to retire and become an academic with one more semester to go.

Sam straightened defiantly, chin up, eyes ahead. "They called my mother a whore. In front of everyone. They started it."

Kinnegan stepped back. "Right. And I bet you didn't do anything to spur their anger."

"No, sir. Just dancing with a girl."

Kinnegan's eyebrow lifted. "Ahh! Possibly someone else's girl? Hmmm?"

"He doesn't own her. She could have said no."

"I see. Well, it all sounds pretty juvenile to me." He returned to the desk, replaced his glasses and started writing. A few moments later, without looking up, he said, "And I take it you took issue with what they said about your mother?"

Sam, now fighting back tears but still defiant, said, "Look, I know what she.... They don't have any right to...." He clenched his teeth. "They asked for it!"

The sergeant, still writing, nodded agreement. "Maybe. Maybe not. Doesn't much matter, though, does it? I expect you can remember what the judge said last time, right?"

Sam looked contrite for the first time, eyes beginning to glisten, forming tears dethroning his air of cockiness. Oh, he remembered.

Kinnegan aimed his pen at Corporal Winkler. "Okay, Natasha, we have to keep him. Put him in juvenile. Call his mother." He waved her away and returned to his notes. "And take those cuffs off, Nat." He looked up at Sam. "We don't need them, do we?"

"No, Sir."

Winkler started to object. Kinnegan cut her off. "Just do it, Nat. He won't be a problem."

She flounced off shaking her head, grumbling, "Yes, Professor. Yes, Sergeant." She stopped and glared back at Sam, still standing at the desk. "You comin' or what?"

* * * * *

The phone rang three times before Elena pulled the velvet sleep mask up and switched the bedside light on. She appeared to be in her late thirties, hollow-eyed, exhausted, red welts the shape of fingers glowing on both sides of her neck. The room reeked of cigarette smoke and whiskey. She squinted at the clock, then picked up the phone and growled, "Before you say anything, the damned answer is, no!" She listened for a moment before saying, "Well, it better be damned important. It's two in the friggin' morning." She listened again, obliviously wadding up two torn condom packages on the night stand before tossing them on the floor. "You asked that already. Yeah, that's my name. So what?" A moment later she flopped back on the bed moaning, "Oh, God. Not that damned kid again. Why me?" More listening. "No, dammit, I will not come down to the stinking police station again–not ever again. You people deal with him any way you like. I'm out." More listening. "I seriously really don't give a damn what you do." She slammed the phone down and turned out the light. After a prolonged fit of screaming rage, she flopped back and wept bitterly.

* * * * *

Another phone rang in the darkness fifteen-hundred miles west of Boston. The bedside clock read 3:11A.M. A physically fit, rugged man of about forty flipped on the light. He literally radiated masculinity–the alpha of alphas. Enough women found him attractive to suit his needs; most men steered clear of him. He squinted at the glowing clock and thought, This won't be good. After fumbling for the phone, he growled, "Prescott," threw the covers off, sat up, feet on the floor and listened, brows creasing deeper by the moment. At length he said, "All right, honey, just calm down. I'll be there as soon as I can. Probably tomorrow–next day for sure." He listened again, fingers running through his short sandy hair. "Don't you worry. I'll take care of it." More listening. "I don't know, but I'll think of something. Get some sleep, Elena. I'm on the way." He hung up, sat thinking for a moment, then packed an overnight bag and left the house within ten minutes. Three hours later he parked at the St. Louis airport. He arrived in Boston in mid-afternoon and took a cab straight for a meeting with Ashcroft Academy's headmaster.

* * * * *

Welborne Buckley, Ashcroft's very proper headmaster, met Wes in the Academy's stately wood-paneled waiting room. Buckley sported an English accent developed in acting school before spending twenty years as a public school principal in Cleveland. He extended his hand along with a solemn smile and said, "Ah, Mister Prescott. Wesley, isn't it?'

"It is. Call me Wes."

"Very good. Wes it is. Well then, we meet at long last. I have looked forward to this for years. Terribly sorry about the circumstances. Sorry, indeed." The headmaster placed his hand on Wes's shoulder, gave a consoling pat, then led the way to his office, cautioning his secretary as they passed, "No calls, Miss Kelly. None at all."

He directed Wes to a straight, stiff leather chair in front of his desk–a chair deliberately chosen as insurance against any visitor becoming too comfortable–then sat and leaned back, hands on his stomach, fingertips forming a steeple. The two men observed each other long enough to become ill at ease before the headmaster cleared his throat and sat up. "Well, all right then. I wonder how much do you know about last night?"

"Enough. My sister called. I also spoke to the police."

Buckley nodded, his facial expression a performance of almost sincere sadness. "I see. Well then, where do we begin?"

Wes leaned forward, demanding eye contact. "Let's just start with first things first. Does the boy have a future here?"

The head master swiveled his chair to gaze out the window at the splendid view of the ivy-covered campus. When he spoke moments later, he still had not turned back to Wes. "No future whatsoever. I am afraid Sam has been expelled." He spun back to Wes. "I hope you can understand our situation, Mister Prescott. The Board of Directors had much difficulty with the decision, particularly after all you have done for Ashcroft financially, but their decision, I am sorry to say, is final. There is no appeal. For my part, Sir, I am sincerely sorry."

Wes sat back and exhaled explosively. "Well, no surprise, is it?"

The headmaster felt relieved. "And we had such high hopes for the lad. No student at Ashcroft has ever possessed as much raw ability as Sam." After recognizing there would be no scene, he devoted himself to softening the blow. "Sam is a brilliant student, and by far the greatest athlete who ever crossed our threshold. His overall potential is unlimited, if only...." He gestured helplessly, sighed dramatically, then said, "Ah, me. If only."

"Yeah, if only. Well, I wish things could have turned out better. Thanks anyway." Wes stood and offered his hand.

Buckley said, "Sam's things are packed and stored. I will hold them until you call." He picked up a folder from the desk. "Here are his records and final grades. The school year does not conclude for two weeks, but Sam has certainly done well enough to advance without finals exams. He obviously needs something we have been unable to supply. Once again, I am terribly sorry."

* * * * *

The next morning Wes met juvenile judge Marta Walcott at her court office.

"Mister Prescott, is it?" She didn't wait for a reply. "What can I do for you?" The judge, a statuesque black woman in her early fifties, literally oozed confidence and authority.

"I came to see about my nephew, Sam Prescott." Wes fidgeted with his hat, wondering if she would ask him to sit.

"So, you're here about Sam. Well, I'm glad someone is." She opened a folder; all business; no smile. "I'm afraid Sam has exceeded the boundaries of polite society again. His predilection for violence has become a serious problem. I have decided to assign him to the juvenile detention home for problem adolescents. Two years, I think." She closed the folder, engaged Wes with another disarming smile and said, "The sentence could have been much longer if the boy he hurt so badly pressed charges. Lucky for Sam he didn't. Please, have a seat."

Wes took the only chair available and said, "Detention? Is that a reform school?"

"Same thing. Just sounds more politically correct."

Wes gave his most sincere expression and said, "Your Honor, I think I can help that boy."

She sat back, studied him carefully for several moments, then said, "Was that, I think I can? Or was that, I can?"

Wes saw the opening. "I can. I want to."

She smiled, stood and took off her jacket, hung it on a rack at the back of the office, then returned to settle into her chair before saying, "All right. Start by telling me about yourself. Please be concise and complete. What we decide here may well determine Sam's future. And, by the way, I'm pleased you're here, Mister Prescott. Very pleased. Now, let's see if we can do business." The ensuing conversation lasted an hour. Wes told her about his life, his finances and ability to care for Sam.

"Good. I needed to know all of that, but what about Sam's mother? Tell me about her."

Wes stared at the floor between his knees, shaking his head sadly, then spoke softly in a voice subdued by shame. "Elena. My sister. Elena got mixed up with a bad bunch in high school. Some of them were already out of school. She was about fifteen." He held both hands out palms up, frustrated. "We lost her. She turned against us. Hated my folks and wouldn't listen to me. We tried everything, even a psychologist, but in the end we lost her. Damned drugs. She got hooked. Stole from us and rebelled against us. She ran away a couple of times; got in trouble with the law–

stealing from stores and selling drugs. Elena was awaiting trial when she left home. Possession with intent to sell. She didn't finish high school."

Wes looked down, took several deep breaths attempting to control his emotions. When he spoke again the judge had to strain to hear. "That's not the worst part, though. The worst part is...." He cleared his throat. "Excuse me. This is tough." He took several more deep breaths, steeling himself, then said, "Elena was driving. She had a car wreck. A terrible wreck. Didn't hurt her too much–some deep scratches, some bruising, but...." He looked directly into the judge's eyes. "But the wreck killed my folks and twelve-year-old brother."

He got up and paced back and forth across the office in front of the desk before sitting again. "Elena was high on drugs at the time–totally under the influence according to the sheriff, and she had drugs in her purse. Enough to sell. She came home from the hospital a day after the funerals, and then disappeared the next day. I looked for two years before finding her here in Boston. I think she wanted me to find her. She used a credit card. Easy to track. Anyway, Elena came to Boston for no reason other than to get as far from home as possible. She worked at a restaurant for a few months until Sam was born. She wouldn't talk to me. Refused my help until the boy started school. I knew by then that she was working as a call girl. I thought the boy would be better off at a boarding school–away from her lifestyle. She agreed to the boarding school and that worked out pretty good. She didn't see him much during those years. When he was ready for high school, I made the arrangements for him at Ashcroft. Elena went along with the idea. I have been able to keep track of her and the boy through a private investigator. Anyway, I'm pretty much up-to-date on Sam, and I know all about my sister's life. I would like to help him."

"I'm terribly sorry to hear about your family, Mister Prescott. What happened is sad, but unfortunately not all that uncommon. Now, let me tell you what I know: Sam has fought at least five times, always about his mother. Law enforcement has been involved three times. I had him tested by a psychologist after his second encounter with the law."

Wes said, "He should have done better."

She selected another folder and opened it. "I agree. Listen to this. His IQ is nearly 150. He is a brilliant student, if somewhat aloof. I discovered during my talks with the headmaster that Sam may be the best athlete in this entire state. He won the state high hurdle championship as a sophomore. He's a one man track team. That may be his problem–one man, never part of a team. He is extremely defensive about his mother." She looked up. "Possibly some of his anger is from conflict created by loving his mother on one hand and hating her on the other. He has not been to see her in three years. Did you know that?"

"No. I don't know much about his personal life. Just general information."

"He won't permit her to come to the academy to visit. Do you know why?"

"I have no idea."

"Let me tell you. Last year the police ran a sting operation involving exclusive call girls. The sting caught some important men–police–city government–a couple of well-known clergymen. Huge news. His mother's picture made the newspapers and television. Apparently a student at Ashcroft remembered seeing her visit Sam at the academy, and now.... Well, I suppose you can fill in the blanks. Children can be very cruel."

"Seems like he had good reason to fight."

"Oh, I don't disagree, entirely. I dismissed charges against him the first two times. Let him go with a warning. No real harm. But now?" She engaged Wes with a piercing gaze. "I hope you recognize this pattern of violence is serious."

He nodded. "I agree."

She sat back. "Good." She frowned and sighed, pointing to the report. "Says here he is not close to any student at Ashcroft." She looked up. "That's not good. And he reacts more violently each time someone mentions his mother." She snapped the folder closed. "I think, in a way, he may be deliberately self-destructing." She put the folder in a portable file and placed it aside. "Anyway, I'm willing to try to work something out. How about you?"

Wes nodded and sat up straight. "I will do anything I can. Absolutely."

She smiled. "That makes us co-conspirators. I have some ideas. We need to have a nice long talk. Get comfortable."

* * * * *

Wes arrived at precinct headquarters just after noon and spoke with Sergeant Kinnegan. The two men liked each other immediately.

"Tell you the truth, Mister Prescott, I wish he was my kid. I don't much blame him for what he did, except he's done it too many times. The boy may be just a tad too proud. I hope he doesn't fall through the crack, though. That would be a great loss." He glanced around the room, then almost whispered, "Would it be okay if I say something personal?"

"Sure. Go ahead."

"Well, Sir, about your sister. I don't think...I mean...." Kinnegan rubbed the back of his neck, wiped his mouth, groaned, and then said, "Oh, the hell with it. Fact is, I don't think she's all that good for him. I think your sister is his problem. Know what I mean?"

Wes nodded and said, "In fact I do. I've kept track of my sister and the boy over the years. Now, I need to talk to him."

* * * * *

Sam sat at a table in the visitor's room, smoldering with anger. His eyes didn't waver from the door, watching for his mother, indignant that she had taken so long, that she had not been to see about him since the arrest. Two nights and nearly two days. He noticed, but quickly dismissed the tall man dressed in western clothes walking through the door to the visitor's room. Sam didn't pay attention until the guy took the chair opposite and slapped a Stetson hat on the table. He glared at the country rube for a moment, then turned away.

"You Sam Prescott?"

Sam's face wrinkled, exposing annoyance from what he considered to be a jerk dressed in cowboy costume. "What if I am?"

"Well, if you're Sam Prescott, then I'm here to see you."

Sam's expression altered from vexation to outright scorn. "Look, Tex, I'm waiting on someone. Bother someone else." He watched the older man appraise him coldly, adding to his irritation. He looked to the guard, back to Wes, then said, "Look, cowboy, I don't want to be bothered with you. Why don't you just–"

The visitor leaned forward suddenly and slammed his palm on the table. "That's enough!" He paused, glaring, daring a retort.

Sam sat back and didn't respond. Wes waved a hand, dismissing the incident, and then said, "Never mind that. Answer me, Are you Sam Prescott or not?"

"I am. So what?"

"All right. That's a start." His eyes didn't waver from Sam's. After a long pause he sighed and said, "I want you to listen carefully to what I'm going to say, boy. Your mother is my sister, and, like it or not, I just may be your last damned chance." He waited. Sam looked confused. "Your mother called and asked me to help with you." He watched Sam's expression alter from annoyance to astonishment. "Now we don't have much time, so pay attention." He scanned the area out of habit, and then said, "As I see it, you have only two options left. The first option should be obvious. You are going to jail for a long time. The second option, depending on what you decide, is that the judge might release you in my custody." He leaned forward and said without a trace of humor, "Frankly, I don't know which option is worse."

Wes stood. "You will see the judge tomorrow morning. I spoke with her and made the offer to take you. If she decides to send you with me, there will be some strict rules, and I will make damned sure you follow them. If you decide not to come with me, she's going to lock your ass up for two years. Wes picked up his hat. "But I think she's going to offer you a deal: Me or jail." He smiled for the first time. "Hell, kid, most things work out. Think it over." He turned to leave.

Sam couldn't believe it. *My uncle? This is the guy Mom wouldn't talk about? This is the family she ran away from? And I'm supposed to go with him?* He stammered, "Wait! This is all too weird. I don't know you. Why would I go anywhere with you?"

Wes turned back, chuckling to himself. "Well, I sure as hell can think of one real good reason. To stay out of jail, maybe?" He stopped smiling in an attempt to look sympathetic. "Listen. If the judge releases you to me, I have a place for you. I know you don't know me, but I don't see a better option. I don't know you, either, but I'll do my best."

Sam scoffed. "Your best? Was that what you did for Mom? Your best?"

The comment caught Wes off guard. He started to answer, paused to think, and then said, "I don't know what your mother said about me, but that doesn't matter right, now does it? You need to stay focused on what does matter. Option one or option two. If you decide to come with me it won't be a some spoiled kid picnic. Just so you know."

Sam stood and turned his back. A moment later he faced Wes again. "This is ridiculous. What would I do? Where would I go to school?"

"Didn't your mother tell you anything about me; where I live; what I do?"

Sam's voice rose, "She hated you! Why would she talk about you?"

The older man's eyebrows lifted. "Well, there may be a little inconsistency here, don't you think? If your mother hates me so much, why in the hell would she call and ask me to see about you?" He waved the comment off. "Don't answer. It doesn't matter. Anyway, I'll be back tomorrow. I hope the judge lets you come with me, but the decision's not mine." He walked out.

* * * * *

Corporal Winkler came for Sam the next morning, with handcuffs. Upon arrival at the court building, the bailiff escorted him to the judge's office where Sam fidgeted in front of her desk while she spoke on the phone. He scanned pictures on the walls, including a black man wearing a Boston Celtic basketball uniform. He recognized the player, Ardis Walcott, then remembered reading her name on the glass door. *Judge Walcott? Is she related to Ardis Walcott? Wow! All-Pro, All World.*

The judge replaced the phone and stood. "I wish I could say it's nice to see you again, Sam."

"Sorry, Ma'am."

"This won't take long. I expect you have met your uncle, is that right?"

"Yes Ma'am."

"Well, that must have been quite a surprise?"

"Yes, Ma'am, it was."

"Did he tell you about the arrangement we are considering?"

"Yes, Ma'am."

"I would like your input on the matter. What do you think?"

"I don't know enough about him to think anything, Ma'am."

"I see. Well, I like your uncle very much. If you're agreeable, I am seriously considering placing you on probation and releasing you to him. Would you be okay with that?"

He shrugged. "What choice do I have?"

His answer angered her and she bristled. "What choice? Young man, let me make this crystal clear. Either you gratefully and respectfully go with your uncle or I will send you to detention for two years. Is that plain enough? Now, are you okay with that?"

He didn't have to think long, not after yet another sleepless night pondering his future. "I guess I'll go with him, on one condition."

She stood suddenly and leaned forward, hands on the desk, the chair rolling away behind her. "Oh, no you don't! There will be no conditions. None. Now, try it again."

Sam decided to end it. "I am fine with it, Ma'am."

She retrieved the chair and sat. "Good thinking. All right. Then I'm going to make your uncle legal guardian, giving him full authority as a parent. I am also going to release you with the condition"–she glared fiercely–"and I *do* have the right to prescribe conditions, Master Prescott, that you graduate from high school without another altercation. No more fighting! Is that clear?"

"Yes."

"Yes, what?"

"Sorry. Yes, Ma'am."

"Good. If there is another incident of fighting during the next two years I will have you extradited–brought back–and you will do the two years in detention. Is that clear?"

"Yes, Ma'am."

"Also, if your uncle tires of you, he can call me and I will have you brought back." Her sudden bright smile brought an abrupt end to the proceedings. "All right then. Looks like we have reached an accord. However, if things ever get too tough and if you decide detention would be better than living with your uncle, here is my number." She handed Sam a business card. "Now, I expect great things from you, and I happen to think your uncle is a gift from providence. Don't mess up this opportunity." She studied him for a few moments, pensive, seeming concerned. "Before you go, let me ask a question. Your answer might provide direction for the remainder of your life. What would you ask for if you could ask for only one thing?"

Sam sat back and pondered the question. "Just one thing?" She nodded. More thought. "Okay, I would like a permanent place. A real home."

She nodded. "That is a good answer. Everyone needs roots. Good for you." She waved him away. "Go now. I have work to do and you have a life to live. Good luck."

Sam turned to go, then hesitated and turned back. "Excuse me, Ma'am."

She looked up. "What is it?"

Sam nodded toward the pictures. "Ardis Walcott. Is he...?"

She smiled. "Yes, Ardis is my husband. Do you know him?"

"Oh, not really, Ma'am. I get to play ball with him sometimes. He stops at the playground next to Ashcroft. Pick-up games, you know."

She seemed genuinely pleased. "Yes, he mentions that. He seems to enjoy those games now that he is retired. Run along now."

* * * * *

Wes saw his sister the moment he walked into the diner that evening, sitting alone in a corner booth. *God, she is so hard looking. Way too thin.* She still hadn't noticed him. Her face was smothered beneath layers of pasty cosmetics. His heart sank at the sight of her. He took a deep breath and closed the distance. She saw him and stood as he approached. Wes stopped short of the booth, unsure of himself, uncertain what to expect from her. She tried to say something. No words came. She rushed into his arms and burst into tears. Wes felt tears welling in his eyes and choked them back. He held and comforted her until she finally pushed away to look at him wistfully, and then said, "Some things never change, do they? I always cry, don't I? I'm such a mess."

They ate and talked in hushed tones for almost an hour. Wes told her about his agreement with the judge, and then reached into a vest pocket and extracted an envelope. "The judge wants you to sign these papers making me Sam's legal guardian. Is that okay with you? If not, we can try something else. I'm not pushing, but I don't think there is anything else."

"No, it's all right. I think you might be the best thing for him." She took the folder and scanned it without reading anything. Wes pointed out the appropriate blanks and she signed.

Wes said, "I hope we're doing the right thing." He folded the document and placed it in his jacket. "Do you think he'll get along with me?"

She had given up wiping the mix of tears and mascara streaks from her cheeks. "I really don't know, Wes. Maybe." She looked defeated. "I guess I don't know him well enough to say. Sam hasn't talked to me in such a long time. He asked me not to visit his school. He doesn't approve of.... Well, you know." She couldn't look at him.

Wes placed another envelope on the table. "I know you will try to refuse this, but take it. For me. You can use it for emergencies, or don't use it at all. I don't care. Just take it. Please take it, Elena. It will make me feel better." He nudged the envelope toward her.

"No. I'm doing all right. I don't—"

He shoved it across the table. "Take it, dammit! Just don't use it for drugs. If you ever need more, just call."

She gave in, as they both knew she would, and put the envelope containing five-thousand dollars in her purse; she didn't look to find out how much until later under a street light, alone. "I won't buy drugs with your money. I promise." She looked up at him, pleading with her eyes. "Take care of Sam, Wes. He's a good kid. Really. Teach him what he—"

He covered her hand with his. "I know, I know. I've kept an eye on him over the years. I know, honey."

"I never told him you gave the money for his school. I should have, but—"

He waved a hand dismissively. "Doesn't matter. No matter. Money isn't important." He gazed at her thoughtfully, and then said, "You are, though. Why don't you come home, Elena? It's time. Don't you think you could—"

"No!" Her voice came as a whispered scream, taking Wes by surprise. Elena glanced around to see if the outburst attracted attention, then leaned over the table and whispered passionately, "No, Wes! I'll never come back. I don't want to. Too many bad memories. You know that. Just take care of Sam for me. I can't do it. I just can't." She started crying again.

They left the diner after she regained control of her emotions, walking opposite directions, both tormented and depressed about the way things turned out, one with no hope, the other with a demanding challenge that would alter his life forever.

CHAPTER TWO

Back to the Future

Wes wasn't surprised that the boy slept on the airplane from Boston to St. Louis, not after having spent three sleepless nights in jail. After landing, Sam followed his uncle through the terminal; a reluctant player trailing behind still smarting from events in Boston; still defiant and unwilling to communicate. Wes had tried to engage the boy several times but received no encouragement. He decided to bide his time, figuring the kid had enough problems sorting out the drastic changes in his life. *We'll have plenty of time. He'll come around.*

At Saint Louis, they located the mud splattered, foul-smelling flatbed pickup Wes left parked at the airport. He threw their bags onto a layer of hay and half-empty feed sacks cluttering the bed.

Sam stood back surveying the scene, visibly perplexed. "You have got to be kidding. Are we actually going someplace in this?" He backed away, spun and walked a few steps, then turned back to glare, arms folded.

Wes leaned against the truck, laughing at what he perceived to be Sam's contrived astonishment. He didn't understand the boy yet. Sam really couldn't believe anyone could take so little pride in appearance.

"Yep, this is it. Hell, boy, it's got every modern convenience, and enough chewing tobacco on the dash to get us both all the way home. And, as luck would have it, the heater and both air work. Let's go. Mount up." He didn't try to hide his amusement, grinning broadly, watching Sam inch back toward the truck, clearly disgusted.

Sam stopped again, still repelled by the vehicle. "Jeeze, don't you ever clean it? What's all this goo? Did someone puke on it?" He pointed to the door.

Wes opened his door, flipped the seat forward, retrieved a 30-30 rifle from its hiding place, hung it on the gun rack in the rear window and got in. "That? Oh, Cotton John chews some. He might occasionally dribble a little spit out that side. You'll probably get to know him. He is one of my hired hands. Get in. Let's be went."

Sam eyed the gun suspiciously. "A gun? Why do you need a gun? Is someone after you?" Wes didn't answer. Sam tried to get in without touching anything, wiping his hands on his trousers. "God, something smells terrible. What is it?" He looked at his hands like something unspeakably disagreeable had defiled them.

"Oh, just a little cow crap and chewing tobacco most likely. Nuthin' that won't wipe off."

Sam went to sleep shortly after they left the city heading west on I-44. Wes stopped at a McDonald's two hours later and ordered three cheeseburgers, a large shake and two Cokes; woke Sam and drove on. Sam consumed everything but one of the burgers and part of the last drink before Wes snatched the Coke from his hand. He took a sip from the same straw, noting the look of revulsion on the boy's face.

"What? I guess you thought you were the only one who needed something to drink?"

"I drank from that straw. Aren't you–"

"Oh, hell! You got some gawdawful disease or something?"

"No. It's just...." Sam shrugged and turned away, unwilling to be drawn in by his uncle's easygoing familiarity.

Wes kept his eyes on the road and the straw in his mouth. "Well, drinkin' after kin don't bother me none, if they ain't contagious. Anyhow, we may as well get used to each other. Sure lookin' like this is the way things are going to be for quite a spell."

Spell? Sam had noticed his uncle's language deteriorating by degrees as they drove west. He thought Wes was roleplaying; breaking out in country vernacular. After a long silence, still staring through the side window–anything to keep from looking at Wes–he said, words dripping with annoyance, "Would it be asking too much to know where we are going?"

Wes slapped the steering wheel and exclaimed, "Well, I'll be daggone. I been awonderin' if you would ever register any interest at all. High damned time." He looked at Sam and smiled, pleased by the question, taking it as a sign the boy's defensive wall might be crumbling.

"Well, sir, if things work out the way they should between us, you are headed toward the beginning of the rest of your life. That's where."

He didn't say more until Sam rolled his hand to indicated he thought there had to be more. "All right, then. I live near a little town named Wickmore, boy. A town so small and so far down in the hills it's hard to find on a map." He noticed Sam's questioning look. "Yep, I'm serious. Actually, come to think of it, Wickmore is just a dot on a secondary gravel road. Didn't your mother ever say anything about home?"

The question clearly annoyed Sam. "No, I told you she never talked about her past. I asked, but she–

Wes interrupted, anxious to fill in the blanks. "You mean to tell me she never said anything about her folks or me? Where we lived? What we do? Nothing?" He tried to make eye contact but the boy turned away to stare at the blur of passing farms and trees.

Sam eventually said, "No. She never said much. Only that you all were responsible for ruining her life, that's all." He fixed Wes with a fierce glare.

Wes's brow wrinkled. He drove on, wrestling with what he could only assume Elena told the boy. Finally he said, "Did she actually say I ruined her life?"

"No!" Sam's voice rose, revealing his short temper. "I said," he dragged the word out for emphasis, "you were all re-spon-si-ble. Got it?"

Time passed. Wes finally nodded and said, "Well, I suppose I was part of it." He thought for a long time. "Did she ever say what happened just before she left home. About her folks and little brother?" Wes knew the question was loaded and kept his eyes on the road and away from the boy, waiting to see if his suspicions would be confirmed.

After a long silence, Sam said, "She had a little brother?" He turned toward Wes to see if he was serious.

"Yep. He was twelve. Died in the wreck with Mom and Dad."

Wes glanced at the boy to watch for signs of surprise. "Didn't she ever say anything about the wreck?"

Sam could not have looked more surprised. "Wreck? She never.... Wait. What wreck?"

Wes stared straight ahead, jaw muscles knotting. "I wasn't there. Just the four of them." He drove on before adding, "Your mother was driving."

Sam's eyes rolled and he reclined, head on the seat back. "Okay, that's history. I really don't care." A moment later, the matter dismissed, he said, "When are we going to get to...wherever?" His voice emphasized sarcasm.

Wes breathed a sigh of relief, glad to let the conversation drift away from old ghosts. "About another hour. We got to stop in Springfield first to get some outfits for you." He nodded toward Sam. "You won't be worth a lick where we're going dressed like that."

Sam sat up, horrified. "There is nothing wrong with my.... Wait a minute! Outfits? Like yours? Forget that! No way I'm going to dress up in some cowboy costume."

Wes smiled mischievously, enjoying the boy's panic-stricken dismay. "Nah, nothing like these. These are town clothes. Just some work trousers and shirts, maybe a couple of pair of tough shoes. You can pick 'em." He glanced over. "You do wear jeans?"

Sam scowled, folded his arms and looked away again, sullen and angry with himself for getting caught up in the banter.

They stopped to buy clothes at a Springfield shopping mall late that afternoon. After entering Sears and locating Men's Clothing, Wes found a chair near the dressing room and said, "I'll just wait here. Find yourself enough work clothes for a change every day of the week. I live by myself, and I damned sure hate doin' laundry. You'll need at least one pair of waterproof high-top boots. Also, if you buy shirts that are gonna need ironing, you'll have to iron 'em yourself." He checked his watch. "We've got another hour yet to drive, and I want to be there before dark, so move it." He closed the conversation with a dismissive wave, leaned back and pulled the Stetson down over his eyes.

Thirty minutes later, Wes asked the elderly blue-haired clerk how the boy was doing. She looked down her nose at him and gestured over her shoulder. "That your boy is it? Well, he's still in the dressing room." She snorted. "Seems mighty particular to me." She huffed scornfully and went about her business, mumbling, "Yessir, mighty particular."

Wes located Sam standing in front of an array of full-length mirrors, angled to present front and side views He stood beside him and they both noticed the same thing at the same time, and the revelation slammed home hard enough to stop their breathing. They glanced from one image to the other. Sam could easily have pictured himself in twenty-five years, just as Wes saw in Sam the boy he used to be twenty-five years ago. They were both spellbound, stunned by the kinship panorama unfolding before them, transfixed by the striking similarities: sandy-haired six-foot-four clones a generation apart. Wes checked the expression on Sam's face to see if the boy also recognized the similarities. The puzzled look on Sam's face revealed the answer.

Wes cleared his throat to break the spell. "Well, I expect we ought to be on our way, boy." He forced his eyes from the mirrors and stepped back, still dazed by the sight, but secretly pleased. He hoped the boy also recognized the vivid evidence of their relationship. Neither spoke during the next half hour, driving south while still digesting the sobering vision in the mirrors. The road progressively narrowed and the hills loomed higher, hazy grey in the waning sun.

Sam noticed the bullet scarred sign reading END OF STATE MAINTENANCE just before the road downgraded from asphalt to gravel. To his dismay, Wes didn't slow. Dust clouds boiled behind the truck leaving a terrestrial contrail in their wake. The entire region suffered in the clutches of an unusual spring drought. Dried up withered grass, trees and nearby homes, everything lay smothered beneath a thick veneer of dust from the road. As they sped southward, roadside homes deteriorated progressively in appearance from neat, prosperous farmsteads to well-kept modular homes, and then to tumble-down doublewides with jacked up cars and pickups in cluttered yards, yards from which dogs materialized to run and bark beside the truck. On Wes raced, by a series of ancient abandoned homes nearly submerged in seas of last year's weeds. Everything seemed to be the same shade of dead. All road signs, some with homes in the immediate background, sported bullet holes of varying caliber.

Twenty minutes passed. They sped down a steep hill, though a dark tunnel of overhanging tree branches, lurching and bouncing, braking to slow at the bottom while preparing for a sharp turn onto an old steel bridge.

Wes stopped and pointed ahead. "The bridge to Wickmore," he announced, grinning at the boy's startled expression. "The only decent way into and out of Wickmore."

Sam looked distressed. "Decent? Is it safe?"

"Oh, it just looks rickety," he said as the truck inched out onto the wooden deck, "It's over a hundred years old, but the school bus still makes it so I doubt it falls in with us." He stopped in the middle. "A bunch of vigilantes hung two of the Hurd boys right under us back in the fifties. Hung 'em for messing with a Presley girl. Those families still live around here, and they still hate each other."

Sam leaned forward to gaze at the span overhead. "Don't they ever paint it?"

"I don't remember ever seeing a drop of paint on it."

Sam's attention returned to the wooden decking. One lane and extremely narrow.

Wes said, "Most of the cross boards on the deck are rotten, so they nail two rows of boards over them so there is something solid to drive on."

The warped and worn planks, all separated by at least an inch of space, permitted Sam to see through to the river fifty feet below. Wes inched the truck forward, smiling, listening to a familiar symphony of popping, clanking noises. The bridge's planking rattled against the rusty steel girders. The clattering din intensified incrementally as the truck neared the middle, there to be joined in concert by the screeching discord of vibrating support rods.

Wes looked over at Sam, grinning mischievously. "Kinda like cheating death to cross this thing, isn't it?"

After the bridge, Sam's consternation increased as the countryside degenerated even more into run-down ruins and neglect. They passed a cedar sawmill that provided jobs for local men willing to do backbreaking, low-paying work. He shook his head and lost interest in the dusty countryside, scooting down in the seat, arms folded over his chest, staring straight ahead. Then, as they crunched by a squat cinder block building sitting in the middle of a dirt playground surrounded by a field of unmown grass, Wes pointed and said, "You might want to take a peak a this." Sam looked. Wes added, "That right there is going to be your school."

Sam sat up, disbelieving. His brow furrowed as he watched until the bleak, forbidding structure passed from sight, obliterated in the angry cloud of dust raging behind. "That's it? That's the high school?"

Wes smiled, enjoying the boy's alarm. "Nope. That's the whole shebang–all twelve grades. Maybe a hundred kids. Might be some shy of that this year."

Sam studied his uncle's face for signs of mockery. He knew by then that Wes enjoyed teasing. "No way." He looked back. "You have got to be joking."

"Nope. Maybe six to ten kids in each grade. Won't take no time at all to learn all their names."

Sam was astonished. His amazement skyrocketed a mile down the road as they passed yet another bullet-scarred sign and a cluster of squat buildings.

WICKMORE
POP 237

Wes gestured to the sign. "Wickmore. That's your new home of record, boy." He sped through town without speaking, passing through a short block of empty buildings with broken windows, racing by the city limit sign again on the opposite end a scant twenty seconds later. Five teenaged boys wearing letter jackets stood near a pickup in the dusty parking lot of a gas station, yelling and laughing, middle fingers extended in a welcoming salute.

Sam looked back repeatedly, his face an exhibit of confusion and disbelief. "A gas station, two stores and a bunch of dumb hicks? That's it?"

"Hell, what more do you need? A place to eat, a place to get a tire fixed and fill up with gas, and a place to get liquor and rubbers. Everything a man needs." Wes glanced over and noticed the boy's face contorted in creases of disbelief. He added, "About five minutes to go." A mile later he waved his hand from side to side and said, "All this land on both sides of the road is on the ranch."

"What ranch?"

Wes was dumbfounded. "Hell, you mean to tell me she didn't even tell you about the ranch?" He shook his head. "Jesus H Christ! Okay then, from square one, then." He waved his hand again. "This is the Prescott ranch. Prescotts have always ranched and that's what I do. I'm a rancher. I run cattle. Lots of em. This here is Prescott country. All of it. Every damned tree, every cow you see, everything as far as you can see. All Prescott."

Sam couldn't absorb it fast enough. "All this?"

"Yep. Bout fifty-five-hunert acres, give or take. Best cattle ranch in the state." Three miles later he steered off the dusty gravel county road and said, "This is it." He turned onto a neat single lane asphalt road running between two uniform rows of stately poplar trees.

Sam noticed the grounds were manicured immaculately. Nothing could have been more irreconcilable than the private paved road compared to the rough county gravel roads of the past thirty miles. His interest in the surroundings returned and he sat up. The road ahead disappeared into what appeared to be a wall of trees.

Wes slowed as they approached a gate, an enormous edifice that Sam would later regard as the first line of defense separating the ranch from the world–from Wickmore in particular. Wes pressed the remote hanging from the sun visor and waited as two massive wrought iron gates suspended between fifteen foot high rock monuments swung open. An ornamental wrought iron sign reading PRESCOTT RANCH curved twenty feet overhead, crowning the imposing entrance. The truck bounced across a chrome-plated cattle guard gleaming in the evening sun and the gates closed automatically.

Sam recognized the paradox between the wretched poverty of the Wickmore community and what even he considered to be an ostentatious show of wealth. They drove several hundred yards through thick woods before bursting out to a scene he would never forget. He was ill-prepared for the spectacle of his uncle's marvelous home located just over the eastern crest of the hill ahead; the highest hill for miles. Wes later explained that his father built it there to preclude wind damage from tornadoes coming from the southwest. Sam eventually concluded that the home had been located strategically in sight of the county road–probably a deliberate effort to generate envy and resentment. It was a palace compared to the hovels along the road. The locals could view the Prescott home, shining in magnificent isolation, from a clearing in the trees along the dusty county road a mile north of the ranch's main gate–a clearing created by trees cut down for no other logical reason than to provide the view.

The house featured an exterior of natural rock–soft worm rock settlers once used for foundations and rock fences. Pioneers labeled the stones *worm rock* as they contained fossilized traces of prehistoric worm tracks and holes. The house epitomized ranch style architecture: one story, close to the ground with four foot overhanging eaves. The sweeping structure spread laterally in an L shape, conforming naturally to the contours of the hill. It had two levels on the downhill side to the rear, including a substantial wraparound deck supported by columns of natural rock. The huge deck commanded the entire rear of the house, overlooking a beautiful valley sloping gently away to the east, blending in perfect harmony with a grove of huge oaks. Rock wall landscaping, stone steps, wooden shingles, all added to the scene of country elegance.

Wes braked to a stop at the front door. "Grab our things, will you, and go on in. I'll be along directly. I need to check in with the foreman."

As Wes drove away, Sam turned toward the house and stood gazing at the ten foot high polished oak double doors. He didn't move for several moments, engrossed by the scene, wrestling with the stunning turn of his circumstances: from Ashcroft, to jail, to court, to the backwoods of America. *And now this? A downhill spiral all the way, and now this?* Once inside, the sound of muted classical music flooded the house from concealed wall speakers.

Sam dropped the luggage and tried to take it all in. The foyer opened into an enormous living room, warm and inviting, breathtaking, even to a seventeen-year-old boy. Floor-to-ceiling windows all around, overlooking the deck and picturesque valley. Enormous hand-hewn beams secured by wooden pegs swept overhead between walls of solid wood, all stained and polished in western lodge decor.

Sam noticed the lack of anything feminine. Everything in the house was massive. His uncle's choice of furniture reinforced the rustic theme, complementing floors of refurbished oak planks salvaged from a turn-of-the-century cotton mill. American Indian rugs and paintings of country scenes added to the aura of rugged western permanence.

As Wes stepped in, Sam turned to study him intently, almost like seeing him for the first time.

"What is it, boy? Something wrong?"

"No," Sam said. "So, you are her somebody."

Wes looked puzzled. "Her somebody? What the hell does that mean?" He picked up the luggage and started down the hallway toward his bedroom, but stopped when Sam responded.

"You are her somebody. When I asked Mom where she got the money for my school, she always said, Don't worry about it. I know somebody.'"

The comment stopped Wes. He didn't say anything, just stood stock still for a moment, the boy's comments boring in. After a moment, he shook his head and without looking back and said rather sharply, "Your room's here on the left."

Sam never managed to get Wes to admit that he provided financial assistance for Ashcroft, or the long list of other advantages he always wondered how his mother afforded: expensive summer camps, up-scale clothes, two trips to Europe with wealthy classmates, and spending money. The closest he ever came to an answer from his uncle was an angry, "Hell, boy, money is not an issue with me, and it sure doesn't matter anymore, now does it? So drop it."

Wes disappeared into his room. Sam walked to the living room windows and stared out for several minutes, eyes glazed, jaw muscles working. He wasn't looking at anything, just staring, thinking, letting events of the past three days settle like a smothering fog. For the first time in his life, Sam Prescott suffered torment over his willingness to accept benefits without question; suffered over his lack of concern about how much distress his mother must have felt worrying about him. Everything about his past seemed superficial: a seventeen-year-old preppy with nothing substantive to show for all the blessings of an incredibly fortunate childhood. He now knew that Wes had financed everything and despised himself for the years of taking what he assumed to be his mother's money. He detested himself for being indebted to a man his mother hated enough to run away from. *I just took the money. No questions asked. Should have known it could not have been hers. What a jerk.*

He dragged the luggage to his room to be alone as the humiliating, condemning truths of his life boiled and surfaced. Sam disliked himself for being dismissed from Ashcroft, but more for being there in the first place. *I didn't deserve it.* The fights; the lack of concern for his mother; his entire life haunted him, but most of all his casual acceptance of privilege coming from sources he never questioned. His thoughts congealed into censure. *And now a dusty, run-down backwoods town a hundred years back in time. I might as well have gone to detention. At least there would be other people. This place is a prison.*

CHAPTER THREE

Camp Prescott

S am avoided his uncle for days, brooding in his bedroom; exploring the outlying buildings and grounds by himself; staying out of sight. He grudgingly spent a few minutes a day with Wes during meals. Any encounter with his uncle reminded Sam of his mother's bitterness about life in Wickmore, and her resentment of the family. Sam connected Wes to his mother's life choices–all bad–and held him at least partly responsible. His stubbornness saturated every moment with Wes. He resisted conversation. If Wes asked a question, his reply seldom amounted to more than one word. Sam never asked questions.

His uncle became more of an enigma as the days passed. Sam's judgement that Wes was responsible for his mother's downfall slowly began blending with reality. Wes, in real life, did not correspond to the redneck, hillbilly persona Sam had assigned to him in the beginning. He began to wonder if the coarse, unrefined qualities of his uncle's speech patterns might be a facade, or possibly reflected growing up in Wickmore. His uncle became a puzzle.

Wes spent three or four hours every afternoon in his office making phone calls, working with a state-of-the-art computer. He had the *WALL STREET JOURNAL* delivered daily, though he could get it on the internet. Book shelves surrounded his office on three walls, all the way to the ceiling, and all filled with mostly classics titles, titles Sam recognized from school. He thought Wes probably kept the books for show.

One evening at supper he said, "You have some great books."

Wes nodded. "I enjoy reading almost more than anything. It's okay if you want to read them. Just put them back, and in order."

Sam smiled, unable to control his cynicism. "Yeah, like you read all of them."

Wes fixed the boy with a deliberate gaze. "What makes you think I haven't?"

Sam avoided answering. He eventually discovered that Wes would not put a book on the library shelves that he had not read.

He changed the subject. "Is there any way I can keep your choice of music out of my room?"

Wes placed his fork on the plate and sat back to consider the boy. "So, you don't like my music? All right, we'll handle music by alternating days. Pick some music you like the next time you make it to town." He wiped his mouth on the back of his wrist, stood and said, "No music after nine, though, and no louder than I play it." While carrying dishes to the sink, he said, "And, by the way, there's a volume knob on the wall in your room."

Wes tolerated the boy's sullen hostility as long as he could–several days beyond his usual tolerance of temperamental people. After yet another in a series of silent meals and unremitting demonstrations of hostility, as Sam abruptly got up to leave the table one evening, he said, "Keep your seat, boy."

Sam paused, eyeing him suspiciously. "Why?"

"Why? Because I think it's time we had a talk." He nodded toward the chair. "Sit down."

Sam, as had become his practice, didn't answer and flopped heavily and waited, gazing out the windows, avoiding eye contact, as usual.

Wes waited for the boy's attention, finally gave up and said, "All right then, let me make a couple of observations."

Sam, childishly petulant and clearly annoyed, sat back, arms folded, staring at the ceiling, a teenager waiting for the inevitable adult harangue.

Wes tapped his fingers on the table, waiting, harnessing an almost overwhelming urge to lash out and then said, "You just sit there. Give me a minute." He got up and cleared the dishes before taking his seat again, using the time to suppress the surge of anger.

Sam detected an ominous change in his uncle's demeanor after Wes returned to the table.

"This won't take long, boy." He waited for Sam to make eye contact before continuing.

"All right then. I hoped it wouldn't come to this, but I've taken about all of your moodiness I can stand." He inclined closer. "I have waited a week for you to get your act together. You are miserable damned company, you know that?" His eyebrows raised for emphasis. "And I can't see any good reason for your conduct." He sat back, surveying the boy. "I think maybe it's time we both got some relief. Truth is, I'm wearing thin waiting for you to come around. You, sir, are screwing with me, and I don't take lightly being screwed with." He paused to watch for any indication that he was getting through. Nothing. No reaction.

"Okay. Let me identify the problem as I see it." He gazed at the boy thoughtfully, then pointed his forefinger at Sam, letting his thumb fall like the hammer of a pistol. "You. You are the damned problem."

When Sam smirked, Wes slammed his hand on the table. "Dammit, boy, if you're so miserable around here, maybe we both might be better off with you in that detention facility in Boston. If you're making an effort to work things out with me, I sure as hell can't see it." He sat back and relaxed. "Anyway, that's it. If you want to leave, I'll make the arrangements with the judge." He got up and took his hat from the rack before returning to stand by the table, measuring the boy, detecting, finally, the token of alarm he hoped for. The boy actually looked concerned.

Sam knew he was facing a fork in the road but didn't say anything, still uncertain of his uncle's full intent. He unfolded his arms, wiped the sneer from his face, and slowly sat up straight.

Wes noticed the signs of unease and said, "That's better. Now, I been holding back on purpose–giving you time to adjust. Maybe that was a bad idea. Maybe I should have said something sooner. Anyway, here's the deal: If you want to stay, that's fine with me. I'll be glad to have you, but I will not accept your disrespect and moodiness. From now on you need to act decent, and you're going to need to do your part around here. If not, I guess the old saying applies: Either shape up or ship out."

Sam scowled, thinking of a witty retort, but caught himself and managed to keep his expression neutral, and then infuriated Wes by saying, "My part? I didn't know I had a part." His customary sneer of contempt returned.

Wes noticed. He placed the Stetson on the table and sat down. "You haven't offered to do one damned thing." His eyes bored in. "But, hell, that's not hard to understand, is it? Up to now, your entire life has been a free ride. Damned spoiled city kid. Well, you earn your keep from now on. You can either be part of things around here or leave. That's the deal. I'm dead serious." He sat back and waited, eyes locked on Sam.

All evidence of scorn disappeared from Sam's face. They sat silently, watching, waiting, each hoping the other would break the silence.

Sam couldn't take the tension and spoke first. "What would I have to do?"

Wes nodded, acknowledging the break. "It's not about what you have to do, boy. It's what you need to do; what you should do."

Sam shrugged, barely able to subdue the urge to make another sarcastic comment. "All right, what?"

"Good. Begin by following me around for a couple of days, just to learn the ropes, and then start helping me out some. But let's start with your room. Clean it. I know you didn't live like a slob at Ashcroft. No different here. Keep your room up. I make my own bed and clean up after myself. So do you."

Sam shrugged again. "I can do that." He began to relax, thinking the encounter at an end.

"I know you can." Wes was relieved by the boy's change of attitude. "All right. We begin tomorrow morning. Set your clock for 6:00 every morning from here on. You fix breakfast every other day. We'll take turns with all house chores."

Sam looked confused. "Cook? I can't cook."

Wes nodded. "Well, you can damned sure learn. Breakfast is at 6:30. As you know, Janey Compton comes over to clean house on week days. She fixes lunch and supper during the week. Make friends with her." He smiled. "She can whip any man in the county arm wrestlin', so don't mess with her. But we always have to fix our own breakfast and do the dishes after supper. We do all the cooking on weekends." He stood and stretched. "Well, that's a start. See you about 6:15 in the morning. I cooked tonight, so you do dishes." He studied his watch for a moment, clamped the worn brown Stetson over his head and stepped to the door. "I got to go see a man about a horse. Turn out the lights when you go to bed." He walked out smiling secretly to himself, pleased with the boy's reaction. The showdown had gone much better than expected.

The next morning Sam dutifully, if not willingly, watched as Wes prepared scrambled eggs. "Nothing much to it. Break about six in this little bowl. Mix 'em up like this. Pour in a dab of water to keep 'em fluffy. Just a dab. Turn the stove top on–not too hot." He took a pocket knife out and scratched a mark by the dial. "Right about there. Then a little cooking oil, like this. Butter works just as well."

He taught day by day, teaching about hot cakes and waffles, sausage, bacon, biscuits and toast, oats and grits. Sam not only learned about cooking and housework, but followed Wes around the ranch learning about cattle, machinery, and the layout of the far-flung cattle operation. He opened and closed what seemed like hundreds of gates as Wes drove over the land, checking cattle, doctoring sick and injured animals.

After breakfast a week later, Sam approached the pickup to find Wes seated on the passenger side. "You drive, boy. Take me over to the old Horton place."

"I don't have a license. I never learned to–"

"Oh, hell! Get in, dammit! High time you learned. Let's go." He grumbled and bitched as Sam learned, but for the first time since arrival, Sam appeared to enjoy something. He also discovered that his uncle's grumbling meant nothing–just his way. Wes complimented him a few times during their first days together, generally over some small achievement. Sam felt pride but hid it. At first he wanted the praise, proof that Wes underestimated him, but as time went on, and without intent, he longed for praise because it felt good. He would never admit it, certainly not to himself, but he wanted to please Wes.

One morning Wes said, "I want you to run into Wickmore and get that tractor tire fixed. You know, the one we took off the big John Deere last night. Take it to the gas station. B. J. knows you're comin'."

Sam eyed his uncle suspiciously. "Wickmore? I don't have a license."

"Hell, don't worry about that. Here, take this. You earned it."

He stuffed a twenty into Sam's shirt pocket.

Sam threw up his hands. "Fine, I'll go, but what about the cops?"

Wes laughed. "What cops? All you have to worry about is being run over by some twelve-year-old driving eighty-miles-an-hour. Now git. I need that tire."

Sam drove away with the window open, elbow hanging out, feeling powerful, independent and filled with purpose, his metropolitan sensibilities content with the mud and cow manure on the truck. He dropped the tire off with B. J., a wiry little man with tobacco juice streaming down his chin and tattoos covering every bare spot on both arms, and then stepped into the store to buy a drink. He paused to appraise his surroundings, like John Wayne entering a hostile bar. His inspection stopped at the girl behind the counter of the gas station/general store. Pretty, he thought, possibly a nice figure from what he could tell about the fullness of her breasts. Her clothes looked like they came from a Salvation Army thrift shop–way too loose, like something a much older woman would wear if she didn't care how she looked. The girl wore no makeup. Sam picked out a snack and drink, slapped the twenty on the counter, and said hi.

She made change slowly, checking him out without looking directly at him. "I hear you're working for Prescott?"

Sam nodded, a little surprised that anyone knew he existed, and even more surprised at his status in the community. *So, I'm just a hired hand. She doesn't know who I am.* "Yeah, I guess that's right."

He thought about her many times during the following day, wondering how much she was hiding beneath the baggy clothes, berating himself for acting so damned cool, for not at least attempting to get acquainted. He also thought it odd how quiet the men sitting and standing around the card table in the back of the store suddenly became after he walked in, and how their eyes followed him, and how the noise of their conversation picked up again as he walked out.

Sam's next visit to Wickmore took place a couple of days later, with Wes. He again noticed the men at the table playing cards, and others standing on the periphery watching, loitering in the middle of the day. The men looked dirty to Sam, clothes and baseball caps greasy and tattered. Most of them needed haircuts and beard trims. The laughing and conversation ceased as the Prescotts entered. Sam again felt like the center of attention.

The largest man, a hirsute, tattooed giant in bib overalls, stepped forward and spoke to Wes. "See you got yerself a new hired hand there, Prescott."

Wes barely looked up from the tobacco shelf. "Something like that, Hurd." Wes never called a local man by his first name. He selected a pack of chew and turned to face the observant gathering. "Any of you boys looking for work?" No one spoke. "Doubt you find much of it here." His gaze drifted slowly from man to man, taunting them, defying and belittling.

They shifted uncomfortably, then someone said, "Deal the damned cards, Virg."

Wes turned to Sam and said, "I got to check with B. J., boy." He nodded toward the girl intently watching from behind the counter. "That ought to give you a few minutes to say hello to Cynthia there. She's in your class."

Sam deliberated over snacks and a drink before approaching the counter. Cynthia took his money, this time apparently interested, coolly appraising him. "I hear you're staying at the ranch," she said, looking him in the eye.

He tipped his cap back, almost swaggering. "You heard correctly. My name is Sam. What's yours?" He noticed the card players stopped talking in the back of the store.

"Cynthia Roush. Sam what?"

"Prescott. Sam Prescott." He knew by then the name carried weight.

She leaned back and looked up at him suspiciously. "As in, Prescott? Are you related to the Prescotts?" She seemed more amazed than surprised.

He laughed at her reaction. "That would be me. I am one. Why? That okay?"

She blinked, puzzled, pondering the news. "So, you're a Prescott. Hmph" She shoved his change across the counter and stepped back, arms folded.

Sam understood something about body language and decided not to linger. He didn't know what to say, pocketed the change, smiled unconvincingly and said, "Guess I'll see you around." He pulled the bill of his cap down and departed.

His uncle's antagonistic bearing toward the men and his own awkward encounter with Cynthia left much to think about. He wanted to question Wes, yet after two weeks at the ranch, he still would not go out of his way to promote a friendly relationship. They got along well enough, but no one would mistake them for friends. He no longer dreaded each day, though, enjoying the work with cattle and machinery.

Sam noticed a van, WHUPASS FARMS painted on the door, parked in the drive one mid-June morning. "Whose van is that out front?"

"Oh, that's Cotton John. He helps out some during hay season. He's probably out in the machinery shed with the baler. That's his job. Cotton once had white hair before losing it. And he once had some teeth before losing them to chewing tobacco. He lives with his two fat sisters, and, as word around has it, he sleeps with both of them on occasion."

"Whupass Farms?"

"Oh, yeah. Ol' Cotton raises fightin' chickens. Names all his best chickens Whupass. He's up to about Whupass number two-hundred by now, I expect."

Sam's mouth hung open. "He actually fights chickens?"

"You bet. Has the best chickens around these parts. Has to sneak 'em into Oklahoma now. Missouri made it illegal. He's a legend. Makes fair money at it."

Wes assigned Sam the task of operating the hay rakes. Wes cut the hay; Sam raked it; Cotton John baled it. Sam hauled it all in with a tractor, usually at night, a big round bale on the spike on the front loader, and another spike on the three point hitch behind.

Wes instructed, "You have to maintain your own equipment. Keep the tractor serviced and the rakes greased and in good shape. I want you to service them ever morning. I'll show you."

They worked day and night for almost six weeks, ending with a week of baling little square bales to put in the barns.

After watching the boy work, Cotton John told Wes, "That there is shore enough one good kid. Damned good hand."

Wes nodded. "Yeah. He's doing okay."

"Works hard."

"Yep. Like you said, he's a good kid."

"Surprised hell out of me, workin' like he does."

"Yeah, me too."

"Damned good kid. Couda fooled me."

Sam didn't spend time with Cotton John, nor did he want to. He asked Wes, "Does he ever take a bath? He smells like a rancid garbage can."

Wes looked up from his work. "I doubt he's taken a bath in years. Why?"

"He's disgusting."

Wes stopped working, stood and faced Sam. "Now just a danged minute. He's the best at what he does, and he doesn't need the work. He was my daddy's friend when my daddy needed a friend. And now he's my friend. So you don't need to be judging him. If you can't stand his smell, then stay the hell away from him, but I don't want to hear you downing a friend."

Sam worked at least fifteen hours almost every day. Wes complimented him often, assigning ever more demanding tasks; always expecting more.

"I pay six dollars an hour for straight labor," Wes said, handing Sam a check after his first week's work. "You're doing a good job. Well, okay, for a city kid."

Sam didn't mind hard work and took pride in his ability to keep up with Wes. He gained weight and endurance, but thought of ranch life much like the summer camps he attended throughout his childhood–just something to do while waiting for school to start again.

One day while eating lunch in the field, Sam asked, "What should I call you?"

Wes had wondered when the subject would come up, or even if it would. "My name is Wes. Why? Do you need to call me something?"

Sam shrugged. "Not really. I just thought.... Never mind."

Wes flopped back on his elbow. "No, I expect it's a good question. The two of us don't have tradition to fall back on, do we? So it really doesn't matter. Wes works for me." They continued as before. Sam didn't call Wes by any name, and Wes called him boy.

Wes left the ranch twice the first week, late in the evening, driving off in the glistening new pickup he kept in the garage but never used for ranch work. He often didn't return until the next morning after breakfast. Wes always announced his departure by saying, "I got to go see a man about a horse." Sam knew by then his uncle didn't ride his own horses and speculated about his outings, but wouldn't ask.

When Wes left the ranch, leaving no duties, Sam explored. He learned almost everything about ranch geography within weeks–every cave, every spring, the good swimming holes along the crystal clear spring-fed creek running through the ranch. He knew where deer and turkey hung out and most of the game trails. He hiked and ran for hours, until he could find nothing new to discover, and then settled into a routine of jogging to a rock ledge two miles into the interior of the ranch; a picturesque overhang six feet above a deep hole on the bend of the creek.

One abnormally hot early August afternoon, upon return from the swimming hole, dripping with sweat, standing in the yard under the garden hose rinsing off and cooling, he noticed something move at the corner of his eye. He turned cautiously and saw a woman leaning against a front porch column watching him. A very attractive, shapely woman dressed seductively in a low-cut blouse exposing enough cleavage to bring any seventeen-year-old boy to a full stop.

They inspected each other for a moment before she said, "So, you're the kid." She sauntered toward him, twisting sensuously.

The tone of her voice could not have been more condemning. "The kid." She might as well have said, "The problem".

Sam started for his clothes. She deliberately moved into his path, smiling mischievously. He recognized her intent and tried to act nonchalant. "Excuse me. What did you say?"

Her eyes ranged over him indecently. "I said, You must be the kid Wes talks about."

Surprised by her presence and embarrassed by his near nakedness, and her overt interest, his self-confidence suffered. He cleared his throat. "So, what can I do for you?"

"Oh, nothing," she said, looking past him toward the garage. "I'm just a friend." Her eyes snapped back to Sam. "All right, where's Wes?"

"I'm sorry. He didn't say."

She snorted. "Yeah, I'll bet. And you don't know when he's comin' back?"

Sam decided to be indifferent. "No. Really, I have no idea."

She scoffed. "Yeah, right. Well, you tell ol' Wes for Kate, that he better call me. Can you do that?"

Sam said he would.

She examined him shamelessly, and then said, "You are looking good. I suppose you come by that naturally, though." She turned and promenaded toward an old convertible, sashaying across the yard, waving a hand over her shoulder. "Ta Da."

When Wes returned late that night he found Sam seated in the office reading in Wes's favorite chair. Sam jumped up and stood aside. Wes sat down and opened the newspaper.

Sam paused at the door on the way out. "Oh, some woman named Kate said you should call her."

Wes, thinking she had probably phoned, didn't look up from the paper. "Did she, now."

Sam shrugged, and conforming to precedent acted like he didn't care and left. Kate returned two days later. Sam figured out by then that she knew the punch-in combination to the gate. He saw her sitting on the front steps as he jogged into the circle drive. *Oh, man, her again. Too late to turn around. Damn.*

She stood and met him half way down the sidewalk, feet apart, hands on hips, daring him to pass. "You didn't tell Wes I called, did you?"

He stammered, "Yes, I...." *Screw that. I don't owe her anything.*

She flipped a lighted cigarette on the grass. "Never mind. Where is he?"

"I really don't know."

She eyed him suspiciously. "You wouldn't lie to me, would you? You mean to stand there and tell me he didn't tell you where he was headed?"

"That's right. He didn't say. Just said he had to see a man about a horse."

Her expression hardened, eyes narrowing. "Is that so? Well, you can tell ol' Wes for me, one of his horses is gettin' damned tired of bein' ignored." She flounced away, tossing her hair, then whirled suddenly to face him again. "And just in case you forgot, sonny, this here horse is named Kate!" She yelled her name.

Sam watched her leave, smiling to himself. *Ah ha! Suspicions confirmed.* He had already formed a hunch about Wes and his horses–horses being women. Sam started picturing his uncle in a new light, as more than just an interesting riddle and more than a man who read good literature and newspaper comics and listened to classical music and sang country tunes and spoke in the vernacular of a redneck and belonged to a literary society and owned half the county and dealt with wall street brokers daily and chewed tobacco. Wes also, apparently, consorted with more than one woman. Sam casually mentioned Kate's visit at suppertime, then added, "Just how many horses do you have?"

Wes stopped eating, holding the fork of food at the ready, brow furrowed. "Well I'll be damned. Guess I'll have to change the gate combination." He shook his head. "Hmmm. I'll be." He didn't eat, just sat there thinking, fork at the ready, then said, "How many horses? Well, I sure as hell ain't no danged saint, if that's what you thought." He ate the bite, still lost in thought, empty fork poised, then closed the topic by saying, "Women. Women are just part of the equation, that's all." He looked at Sam, an impish twinkle in his eye. "But they make a hell of a lot better friends than any man I ever knew."

Wes didn't tell Sam he was going to see a man about a horse after that, substituting, "I have to go mend a fence or two." Sam figured some of his uncle's fences could use mending, particularly one named Kate. Wes stayed out overnight often, but never talked about women, and never left a phone number.

At breakfast the next day, Wes tossed a state driver's license manual on the table. "You probably ought to study that. I'm headed to the county seat tomorrow. You need to come along and get some clothes for school and take your driver's license test while we're in town."

Wes watched Sam idly flip through the pamphlet and said, "Then, I expect it's high time we get you settled in school."

Sam looked perplexed, dreading the thought of school at Wickmore. "School? Do I have to do anything, like register?"

"Nah. Gettin' into school at Wickmore won't amount to much. I'll have to take you, though. Part of the deal with the judge. You know, the suspension crap–all that."

Sam frowned and groaned. "Oh, man. Can't we just–"

"Nope. Judge's rules. I have to tell the superintendent what the deal is. You may as well be there to hear it just so everyone starts out on the same page."

Sam looked distraught and flopped back in the chair. He desperately wanted a clean start. "Come on! This isn't fair. Can't we just forget–"

"No, dammit! The superintendent has to mail a letter to the judge to confirm the meeting. Anyway, it's just between us and the superintendent. Hell, don't fret about it."

Sam went to town with Wes and passed the license test. On the way back to the ranch he asked, "How did you get the money for the ranch?"

The question pleased Wes. The first time Sam asked much of anything about ranch history. "Well, sir, my granddaddy started the ranch nearly a hundred years ago. He bought the first four little farms, but my daddy was a better farmer than his daddy. He bought several more spreads to add to the place. I just came along and took over where they left off."

"Have you lived here all your life?"

"Nope. Believe it or not, after high school I went off to college. Then I played pro baseball for a couple of years. After baseball, and after Dad died, I came back and took over."

Sam could not have looked more surprised. "Baseball? Professional baseball?"

"Yep. Little bit."

After a skeptical frown, Sam said, "You actually played professional baseball?"

Wes laughed at the boy's disbelief, pleased by his interest. "I did. Played almost three years on scholarship at Vanderbilt University, then two years as a pro. Pitched mostly. Made it all the way to the bigs. Just for a moment before I ruined my arm. Had to give it up."

Sam stared at his uncle, astounded by the disclosure. "You made it to the big leagues?"

Wes nodded. "For a few weeks. Rooky. Went five and one. Doin' good when the arm blew. Only twenty-four at the time. That ended it."

Sam thought for a long time. "Man, that's amazing." He studied his uncle for a few moments before saying, "Doesn't it bother you? I mean, thinking about what might have been?"

"Nah. Hell, that's life. Anyway, I met Angeline at Vanderbilt because of baseball, so I couldn't hardly count it as a loss. And I got a great signing bonus." He glanced over. "That bonus had a lot to do with the size of this ranch. I invested most of it in the stock market. Made good money and got out at the right time, which is almost as important as getting in at the right time. I made some other business deals along the way, mostly real estate. Always managed to come out better than I went in." He looked over at Sam and smiled. "I got a real knack for it."

Sam had much to think about. He stared ahead as the miles passed, then said, "Wow. That is really is amazing. Pro baseball. Now, what about Angeline?"

Wes grimaced. "Some other time. I need to work here."

CHAPTER FOUR

The Nemesis

Wes and Sam arrived at the superintendent's office on Monday. "Mister Roush, this here is Sam. Elena's boy. Sam Prescott."

The superintendent, middle-aged, pink, soft and paunchy with the carefully coiffed hair of a television evangelist, didn't get up or extend a handshake welcome. He studied Sam disapprovingly, brow wrinkled, then said, "Didn't know Elena had a kid."

Wes didn't prolong the exchange by elaborating. "He's Elena's boy. He will be coming to school here this year." He turned to Sam. "This is Edwin Roush, the superintendent."

Sam offered his hand, held it at the ready for a moment, then let it drop as Roush ignored the gesture. Sam glanced at Wes, puzzled by the affront. Wes's indifferent expression and shrug not only let Sam know that he noticed, but in effect said, Let it go.

Wes handed Roush a folder. "These are the boy's records. He's got a good academic background as you'll see. Took the SATS last year. Great score. Upper ninety-ninth percent." He put his finger on the score. "Took all advanced placement courses. You won't have trouble with him."

Roush flipped slowly through the folder, his expression a picture of disinterest that slowly altered to dissatisfaction. "Only one problem I can see is," he said, snapping the folder closed, looking up at Sam. "Is why would you leave such a good school to come here?" The question sounded more like an accusation.

Wes held up a restraining hand before Sam could answer. "This is the reason, Roush." He passed the envelope with police records and the judge's decision. "I've been appointed his legal guardian. I really don't see much wrong with what the boy did. Damned sure wouldn't a made any difference around these parts."

Roush studied the paperwork. "Says here I have to contact some judge."

"Yep. She just wants to know you got the information, that's all. Her numbers are all there. I expect you noticed the boy can't be a problem to you or she'll vacate his suspension. He won't be a problem. I guarantee it. Has to finish school. She was pretty clear about that."

Roush sat back, looking from one Prescott to the other. "Well, well. I'd say we got ourselves an easy problem to solve, if there ever is a problem." He fixed his gaze on Sam. "There will be no fighting while you're here. That understood?"

Wes patted Sam on the shoulder and said, "Step outside for a minute, boy. I need a word with the superintendent. After Sam left, Wes closed the door and turned to Roush, his face set hard, a neon billboard of anger. "He's a good kid, Roush. I don't want to hear about him getting a bum deal. Know what I mean? You be fair. That's all I ask." Roush maintained a tightlipped stare. Wes placed his hands on the superintendent's desk and leaned close. "Don't screw with him just because he's a Prescott."

"That a threat?"

Wes's eyes narrowed. "You know damned well I don't make threats, particularly to you, and I don't use idle words." His eyes narrowed and bored in. He slapped the desk and walked out.

After Wes departed, Sam waited several minutes in the front office before asking the annoyed elderly secretary, "What am I supposed to do?"

She shoved a folder across the counter–a list of available courses. Sam selected humanities over shop and agriculture. The superintendent finally came out of his office, looked over Sam's chosen classes, then said, "Follow me."

They walked down a narrow hallway, past Mrs. Garrison's third and fourth grade classroom on the right and Mrs. Brooks' fifth and sixth grades on the left. Sam learned later that the first and second grades met with Miss Gardner in a mobile home behind the school. Roush opened a door without knocking and stepped into the dimly lit history classroom. Everyone looked up.

Eight students.

"Okay, people, this is Sam Prescott. He'll be joining us this year." With that, Roush walked out. Sam smiled and waved. The students just stared–no smiles, no friendly gestures–nothing.

His attention turned to the elderly teacher squinting at him from behind her desk. She motioned him forward. "Mister Prescott, is it? Step up here so I can see you."

Mrs. Holder appeared to be at least seventy-five, wearing a sweater in the middle of hot weather. She fumbled through a desk drawer looking for a text book. Sam eventually learned that she had taught at Wickmore for forty years and couldn't see more than ten feet away. She also suffered from Parkinson's and couldn't hold chalk to write on the blackboard. She squinted at him and asked, "Where are you coming to us from, young man?"

"Boston."

"Oh? Bolton? Isn't that up near Kansas City?"

"Um, no, Ma'am. Boston. Boston Massachusetts."

"Really? Oh, that Boston. Well, you just take a seat anywhere."

Sam disappeared from her vision into the mist of the classroom with the tattered book and selected a knife-scarred desk next to the side wall. The other students sat in near darkness in the last two rows. No one had bothered to turn on the lights. He counted five boys and three girls. The fourth girl, he learned the next day, was Cynthia Roush from the store. Cynthia attended class only when her mother didn't need help with the store.

Sam spent the rest of the week alone. No one spoke to him except teachers, and they spoke only when he introduced himself in the beginning. He tried several times to engage different students in conversation, only to be snubbed. Sam sat across from a senior boy at lunch and said hello. The boy picked up his tray and moved to another table. He didn't just feel like an outcast, he was an outcast. After a week of being ignored, he gave up and remained by himself. Compared to the snubs and slights of school, the ranch and humane fellowship of his uncle started looking pretty good.

"So, how's school going?" As usual, Wes didn't look up from the daily paper when asking routine questions.

"Okay, I guess. Sure an unfriendly bunch."

"Made any friends?"

Sam snorted. "That a joke? No one talks to me. You would think I puked on their shoes or something. The school's a joke, too. Nothing to learn. I already had everything back in the seventh grade. It's ridiculous. I mean it–seriously ridiculous."

"Well, hang in there. Things may perk up."

Sam found the little country school an academic waste of time and his social prospects a complete wipeout. His studies may not have provided a challenge, but his surly classmates did, particularly Clyde Townsend and his gang of clowning followers. Clyde's crew started mocking and baiting Sam by the end of his first week. Little things at first, mimicking his eastern accent and courtly finishing school manners, holding pinky fingers up, giggling behind his back. Townsend, after encountering no resistance from Sam, became openly disrespectful.

"You want a chew, Prescott?"

Everyone laughed.

"It'll sure enough kill stomach worms."

More laughter.

"You got stomach worms, Prescott?"

Hilarious laughter.

Wickmore's boys sat in class with baseball caps on, dribbling chewing tobacco juice into empty pop cans; talking to each other during lessons; interrupting teachers with silly questions that had nothing to do with the subject matter; making vulgar comments to the girls. The girls didn't seem to mind and the teachers didn't interfere.

Three of the five senior boys, including Clyde, would turn 21 during the year, and none of the five had passing grades, but the administration would, as tradition had it, let them graduate, not only to forestall retaliation, but to be rid of them.

Sam, becoming more open and friendly with Wes, confessed during the second week of school, "I don't think I can take the crap at school much longer. They are really pushing me."

Wes's eyebrows lifted and he put the newspaper down. "Okay, I expect maybe you better tell me what's going on."

Sam reviewed conditions at school, ending by saying, "I'm serious. I don't think I can put up with it, particularly this Townsend guy. I'm ready to blow. What can I do?"

Wes nodded. "I know who he is, and I can sure sympathize. In your shoes I would probably damned sure whip his ass–absolutely–and that might be the right thing to do. But you, my friend, are screwed. I can't help you except to remind you what the judge said. You can't let Townsend get to you." He thought a moment before adding, "Why don't you skip a day every now and then. I'll send an excuse. That help?"

Sam didn't have to think. "How about Tuesdays and Thursdays?"

Wes raised the paper again. "Done. Just don't sit around out here and rot. Do something productive."

"Thanks." Sam left, but returned a moment later. "You got a minute?"

Wes looked over the top of the paper. "Sure, what's on your mind?"

"Why do you think they despise me so much?"

Wes folded the paper and placed it aside. The question deserved a sincere answer. "Sit down. Guess it's time to fill you in." Sam sat. Wes said, "What's happening to you at school really doesn't have much to do with you personally, at least not yet. It's all about you being a Prescott." Wes scooted the chair back and propped his feet up on the desk. "People around here have strong opinions about the Prescotts, and I expect they have pretty good reason. Bad blood goes way back here in hill country, and I doubt being a Prescott with that Boston accent of yours is going to make you a local favorite any time soon."

"Not much I can do about that."

"Nope, and I'm not saying you should. Anyway, my granddaddy started all the animosity with the community. Your great granddaddy. He could whip any man in the country, and he did, more often than not just for the hell of it. He was a badass. That's about all I know about him, other than he put some little farms together to start the ranch and he's buried in that little cemetery out behind the old home place.

"He was the number one Prescott. My daddy was number two. He added more land by hook or crook. The ranch grew. He figured out some pretty slick ways to get what he wanted. He could also whip any man in the county, and I know for a fact he did because I saw him do it. Didn't take much to set him off, either. So, another Prescott badass.

"Then I came along. Prescott number three. I have added nearly three-thousand acres to the ranch, some by conniving and scheming just a wee bit. Nothing illegal. Using go-betweens a time or two, such like that, when folks didn't want to sell to me. And I have taken my turn at whipping an ass or two."

He let his feet slip from the desk, grinning mischievously. "I always kinda liked to mix it up a little." His eyebrows raised. "Then there's this thing about women. None of us Prescotts were ever all that careful about relationships with women, and that brings us to Prescott Number Four, bud. That's you."

Sam's eyes rolled. "Oh, man. I am so screwed."

Wes chuckled. "Yup, in a way. What the hell, it's just a game. You'll get used to it."

Sam sat on the floor beside the desk, leaning against the wall, settling in, curious and wanting more. "Did you know your grandfather?"

"Nope. Never met him. Ma wouldn't let me around him. He was a mean, foul-mouthed drunk. Didn't like little kids."

Sam flipped his wrist. "Okay. So much for him. What was your father like?"

"Oh, decent enough sort, I suppose. Tough on me, but that's just the way things were. I always kinda admired him. Tough old boy, but he sure needed to be. Kinda asked for trouble."

Sam didn't say anything, letting the information sink in, staring at the floor between his knees. When he looked up, he said, "All right. Why did he need to be tough?"

"Oh, probably because he always took what he wanted. Mostly the two things most other men are unwilling to give up: land and women. I expect the community was pretty disappointed that I came back and took over after he died. I'm no great favorite around these parts–little too much like the Prescotts before me. I haven't been working all that hard at it, either." He reached for the newspaper. "And that, sir, is your legacy. Like it or not, you're a Prescott and people are damned sure going to hold that against you." He paused and cocked an eye at Sam. "I suppose the question is, Would you rather be a Prescott or one of them?" When Sam didn't respond, Wes assumed the conversation finished and opened the paper.

"So that's why everyone in the community walks circles

around you."

Wes laughed to himself, but closed the paper again. "Oh, there's way more to it than that." He studied Sam, collecting his thoughts. "You see, none of the Prescott women came from around here, so naturally the community never accepted them. My mother came here from college. Taught science and social studies at the high school for a spell, then married Dad. The school board objected when she taught theories. You know, Big Bang theory, Evolution and sex education. They ordered her to stop. She went ahead anyway. They fired her. She sued. To make a short story long, the courts put the school on academic probation; Ma got her job back and no one around here ever got over it. But she wasn't through with them. Oh, no. Not Ma." Wes paused, shaking his head."Religion. The damned superintendent posted the Ten Commandments all over school—on his desk, in hallways, on the walls in the cafeteria. He held prayer service on the intercom at the beginning of every day and before special events. Ma complained to him, and then the board. They ignored her, so she sued him again. ACLU got into it and he backed off. Everyone from Wickmore backed him. Hell of a mess. No one around here ever forgave Ma for that." He snapped the paper open again still looking at Sam. "And then there's the ranch. Plenty of jealousy around these parts about the size of this ranch. That's about it."

Sam understood more about the prejudices of his peers and steered away from trouble, mostly by avoiding Clyde Townsend. He never corrected anyone, or cringed, or displayed a sign of contempt when they said, "I ain't done it," or "I ain't got no." He learned, to his amazement, that several members of the faculty and both administrators commonly said "ain't" among other grammatical lapses.

Everything about Sam antagonized his classmates: his too dressy taste in clothes, his long, preppy hair, the Boston accent, polished manners, studious habits; everything he did or said separated him from the locals. He heard the not-so-subtle whispers:

"Who does he think he is, some lord high professor or somthin'?"

"Yeah. Always puttin' on airs. Snooty bastard."

Clyde Townsend and his band of cronies never relented, but the other kids tired of mocking Sam, primarily because he avoided and ignored them.

Another of Sam's string of life-defining moments happened one autumn afternoon after the last bell as he walked across the gym heading for the bus. Clyde threw a basketball with all his might at Sam's head. He saw it coming and caught the ball with one hand.

The gathering of players at half-court laughed and jeered.

"Shoot it, Prescott!"

"Yeah, show us what you got!"

The boys laughed and slapped high-fives.

Sam held the ball for a moment, started to throw it back, but changed his mind. With book still in hand, he loped toward the goal, jumped, slam-dunked the ball and walked away.

Noise from the huddle of jeering boys imploded, eyes wide, disbelieving. No one on the team could dunk a ball, let alone wearing street shoes with a book in their other hand. Sam left the gym without looking back. The incident changed everything.

* * * * *

The TV station floor director cued Tad Rollins, long-time sportscaster for the leading Springfield television station. Rollins, aging, revered expert of local and regional high school basketball, read a few baseball scores, talked about the coming baseball World Series, and then delivered his annual high school basketball forecast. He finished by saying, "And last but not least, my prediction for best small school team is, and you probably won't believe this–the Wickmore Ravens. Folks, twenty-five years have passed since their phenomenal, almost three consecutive year unbeaten streak, but I think the Ravens are back. Oh, sure, they may be undersized, but this bunch of boys, like the championship teams of yore, have played together all their lives. The Raven starting five is back after winning twenty games last year. I look for great things from Wickmore.

* * * * *

"Dammit! What the hell has he been drinkin'! Damned nitwit." The outburst came from Tommy Johns, star player from the great Wickmore team of the past.

A circle of men sat with Johns watching the television set attached to the wall at the HANGOUT café in Wickmore. The HANGOUT, located across the dusty road from Roush's General

Store, served greasy sandwiches slapped together by Reba Wirth. Reba, a corpulent woman with a perpetual cigarette hanging from the side of her mouth, squinted through the smoke, red-eyed from the constant cloud of grease and tobacco smoke. She served beer without a license to almost anyone, including the on-duty sheriff and his deputies. Reba drew the line on age, though, "I ain't servin' no snot nose kid no damned alcohol."

"Hey, Tommy, what makes you think ol' Rollins ain't right?" One of Tommy's old team mates slapped him on the back and laughed. "Ain't he generally pretty good at pickin'?"

Johns, now a hefty two-hundred-and-fifty pounder, stomach hanging over his belt, beard over his chest, stood and growled, "Hell!" He spit toward the spittoon by the door and missed. "Oh, they'll probably win a bunch of games, but they ain't never gonna beat no team with good big kids and a smart coach. Hell, we cain't shoot outside worth a crap. We cain't make no long shot. You know that."

Reba joined the men at the table, sitting heavily, collapsing like an overstuffed pillow, gushing smoke and noise, and then said, "Yeah, but I hear tell Clyde Townsend's gonna play again this year. That ought to make some difference."

Johns opened the door, preparing to leave. "Nah. Hell! You otta know bettern 'at. That damned Townsend is useless. Done quit school two years in a row. No countin' on him for nuthin'." He spit outside, and then recoiled. "Whoa! Sorry there, Mitch. Didn't see you acomin'. "He stood aside as a sheepish Mitch Gervin stepped in, wiping spit from his sleeve. Everyone laughed.

Reba nodded. "Maybe. But Roush is sure enough countin' on him."

Johns stepped outside, holding the door open. "Yeah, well I don't like it much–Clyde goin' on twenty-one and such. That ain't no good for the younger kids. Damned outlaw. I don't like it. Anyway, we'll damned sure see tomorrow, won't we? They got a practice game over to Atley. Ought to tell us if that nitwit Rollins knows anything."

* * * * *

Late the following evening, Wickmore's team filed off the bus after the game, spilling onto the dusty parking lot of Roush's store. Some got into their parent's cars and went straight home, others hefted athletic bags and headed across the street to the café. One of the five boys crossing the road pointed to the array of pickups surrounding the café and said, "Crap. Hell to pay. They're already here." The boys stopped, eyeing the trucks.

"Yeah. Just waitin' on us. They'll be ahootin' an ahollerin', won't they. Damned jerks."

"You comin' in, Clyde?"

Clyde Townsend, big-boned, body of a full-grown man, sporting a heavy shadow of whiskers left unshaven in an attempt to appear menacing, stopped and studied the pickups. "Hell no. I don't need their crap."

"Screw 'em, Clyde. Don't let 'em git to you."

Clyde didn't answer, but turned away, climbed into his pickup and slammed the door violently, ripped the truck into gear and spun out, throwing gravel across the parking lot.

The gathering of men in the HANGOUT, all returning from the game at Atley, sat silently, glaring as the sheepish file of boys entered. No one said anything, eyes following the beaten team. The boys kept eyes straight ahead, circling as far from the table of contemptuous men as possible on their way to the counter.

Finally, Johns spoke loudly, "Reba, git them boys somethin' with some damned protein in it, will ya! They sure as hell need somethin'." The men laughed and turned away.

Mitch said, "I wonder what ol' Tad Rollins would have to say about that performance, Tommy? Think he still believes they're number one?"

Johns snorted. "Hell no. They cain't shoot. We ain't got no chance."

* * * * *

Clyde Townsend, from age seven, had lived alone with his father in a run-down shack south of Wickmore on a bluff overlooking the Stocking river. Several year's accumulation of garbage and trash flowed like a waterfall down the bluff and into the river from their back yard.

Clyde's mother abandoned ship without saying good-bye, fleeing during a tiny window of opportunity in the middle of a winter night. Clyde's drunken father had staggered into the house the night before, beat her viciously for no reason, then forced himself on her. Most seven-year-old boys would be devastated by the loss of their mother. Clyde Townsend couldn't have cared less. He led a fairly normal life before she left, discounting the scars of extreme poverty and lack of parental guidance. Clyde never saw his mother again.

Patsy Townsend had a long list of reasons to fear for herself and the little girl. Her husband's new interest in her daughter's breast development finally prodded her into action. Anyone who knew anything about her living conditions also knew she stuck it out longer than anyone with an ounce of intelligence would have.

The grade school principal, Mrs. Kingsley, appeared in Clyde's classroom the day after Patsy disappeared. "I need to see Clyde in the hall," she announced to the teacher, beckoning to Clyde with her finger. She had to physically escort the recalcitrant boy out of class.

"I didn't do nuthin' wrong," the boy protested indignantly as the principal hustled him down the hall to her office.

"The bus driver told me you slugged Molly Francka."

"He's a damned liar!"

Kingsley's stern facial expression didn't soften. "Molly said you did it. Is she a liar?"

"She's a damned liar, too!"

"You watch that mouth! I won't have such language in this school. You sit there. I'm going to call your mother."

The boy smiled like he knew a secret. "She don't live with us no more."

Kingsley paused, digesting the information. "Well, then, where is she?"

"Don' know. Jus' picked up and left. Done took Betsy along, too."

"I'll need to see your father, then. I will write a note to take home. I'll check, so don't forget."

"He won't come. He don't care." Clyde smiled triumphantly.

Clyde's mother was fifteen when she married Homer Townsend, seventeen years his junior. He was a violent drunk, battering Patsy and the children. He treated women and cattle alike. "They been placed on earth to be owned and bred. That's all they're good for." He took great pleasure in broadcasting his chauvinistic philosophy to anyone who cared to listen. Homer Townsend, according to his own account, was a cattle trader by profession. The people of Wickmore knew he occasionally appropriated cattle without trading but couldn't catch him at it. He usually swapped at local auction barns with a few cronies who smelled of cow manure. None of them made a decent living.

After Patsy deserted, Homer reared Clyde the same way he raised cattle. "Just kick the crap out of 'em when they gits in the way." Clyde flourished physically despite the treatment, and contrary to good sense, he idolized his father.

Homer lost fifty pounds from a near fatal encounter with tick fever during Clyde's sophomore year.. One dreary winter day he yelled at the boy, "Git yer lazy ass out there and fetch some damned wood. It's freezin' in here."

"You fetch it. I been–"

Homer struck the boy with the back of his hand as he always did when Clyde exhibited signs of independence. Clyde struck back savagely, changing the Townsend family pecking order forever. The bout with fever had weakened Homer and he couldn't protect himself from the strapping adolescent. Clyde took full advantage of the situation, beating his father until he lay in a bloody heap on the linoleum kitchen floor.

Clyde stood over him, breathing hard. "You had that comin', old man. Now, if you want your damned firewood, fetch it yourself from here on."

The community of Wickmore, with its good 'ol boy code of conduct, also played a major role in Clyde's persona, but he transcended the community's country way of life and became a classic creation of outlaw redneck ignorance. He became a maverick, an outcast, a dangerous and sinister version of his father, courting trouble and defying authority.

Clyde quit school for the first time after the Christmas vacation of his junior year and took up cattle trading. Wickmore's school administration didn't object or pursue the matter, content to leave well enough and Clyde Townsend alone. They simply passed him on to his senior year. He came back for the beginning of school for the next two years, only to drop out after a few weeks of disruption and insubordination. Now, at twenty, he had one final opportunity to graduate before turning twenty-one; after that he could no longer enroll. Clyde loved basketball. Even after dropping out of school, he showed up for pick-up games at the gym. The coach, Edwin

Roush–school superintendent and basketball coach–also happened to be Clyde's kin, an uncle two or three times removed.

Shortly after school began for Clyde's final attempt to graduate, the new high school principal stopped by the store and complained to Irma Roush, "That Townsend kid is really something, isn't he? Does he give you any trouble?"

"Oh, sure, all the time. Steals me blind."

"He's a loud mouth, bragging about poaching deer out of season, dynamiting and electrocuting fish, killing hawks, cranes, dogs, cats, anything else that moves. Do you think there is anything to it?"

"I expect he does all that and more. He's into about everything. The sheriff asked me about him the other day. He's always in trouble with the law."

Clyde needed more than the excitement hunting and fishing provided. He discovered tobacco and alcohol before age ten, and changed to marijuana and meth by fourteen. Drugs were far more entertaining than hunting or fishing. He hung around town listening, stealing little things from Irma's store and any unlocked vehicle. He possessed a canny understanding of how to circumnavigate authority, always operating on fringes of the law.

"He isn't like the other kids. Clyde's in for trouble," Irma told one of the local farmers after he complained about Clyde cussing him out and spitting on his truck.

"Nope, he shore ain't like any kid I ever knowed. That boy's a damned outlaw. He ain't nuthin' but trouble. Gonna git hisself kilt–either that or throwed in the pen."

Homer had schooled Clyde well in the intricate workings not only the cattle business, but women. Perverse as the old man's ideas were, Homer Townsend did have a way with women, or so it seemed to the impressionable boy. Clyde would tell everyone that his dad was a "stud horse." He was too young to recognize that his father's women were pitiful castoffs.

Anson Cader, Homer's traing crony, a man so hidden in a bush of tobacco stained whiskers that only his nose and eyes peeked out, laughed and said, "Ol' Homer only gets the skinny, potbellied culls nobody else wants."

Three months after receiving Clyde's beating, Homer discovered a mentally retarded runaway girl at a truck stop and brought her home. She was pretty in an unsophisticated way–dirty, freakishly voluptuous, totally ignorant, and already pregnant–although Homer didn't know it–and only sixteen.

"Homer, he is soooo cute," she cooed the moment she laid eyes on Clyde.

"Aw, he's just a snot-nose kid. You stay the hell away from him now, you hear me?"

She kept at it with Clyde, touching and flirting. Homer made immediate arrangements for Clyde to spend the remainder of the winter and most of the coming spring with a recently widowed woman living two farms east.

Homer didn't hang around long after dumping Clyde on the widow. He said, "She'll treat you right if you do good work. I'll check on you in a week or two." He drove away and Clyde turned to find the widow surveying him, a playful smile teasing at the corner of her mouth.

"So, it's just the two of us now. Well now, Clyde, I'm sure glad you could come over to hep me. I need a good man."

Even though Clyde's adolescent juices were raging, he wasn't interested in a fifty-year-old woman. "Wasn't my idea," he said, watching his father's truck wind down the dusty road.

That evening at supper, her eyes never wavered from him. "Do you like girls, Clyde?"

He couldn't look at her, aware that her eyes were locked on him. "Oh, they're okay, I guess."

She licked her lips, smiling mischievously. "You know what I think? I think you don't know anything about girls, that's what I think." She leaned forward, exposing creamy, full breasts, unencumbered by a bra, watching his eyes stray to the billowy panorama, then jerk away, then return.

"I get along with girls."

"Uh, huh. I'll just bet you do. Well, that's good. I think you and me, we are sure enough going to get along just fine." Her eyes sparkled with suggestion, hinting at enough to make Clyde squirm.

He awoke later that night with a start as she crawled into bed with him. "What are you doing?"

"Shhh. You just lay still, honey. Let me take care of everything."

He stopped resisting the moment her hand reached his crotch.

"Oh, you're so nice," she cooed. "You're going to do just fine. Here, let me help you get these shorts off."

Her insatiable carnal appetite challenged Clyde's adolescent stamina. They spent more time in bed during the next two months than at work. He didn't need to learn how to make love to a woman. She gave him no reason to perfect his sexual skills beyond whorehouse lust. No thanks necessary. The widow once told him, "You know, honey, I worried a little when your daddy told me you was only fifteen. I thought you would be just another skinny teenager with a cigarette dick, but this," she exclaimed, fondling his erection. "This is better than candy. This is better than my old man's tool by a mile."

Clyde traveled through life after that believing himself endowed with an extraordinary device for pleasing women. He never understood that Mrs. Kelly's aged husband had been impotent for fifteen years before dying, or that her randy demands had at least partly precipitated the old man's condition, or that her husband suffered deflating performance insecurity for he, in fact, did have a cigarette dick.

Homer came for the boy that spring after tiring of the truck stop girl. He lost interest after she started wearing loose clothing to hide a pregnancy he wanted no part of. Homer loaded her up, and despite her wailing and begging, dropped her off at the truck stop where he found her, then retrieved his son for the summer's work.

Clyde returned to the widow's place often. His ideas about sex had come from a father who abused women and from a woman who demanded nothing from him except animal lust. He had never kissed her–not once.

Homer didn't fully recover from the thrashing at Clyde's hand, or the ravages of tick fever, and died within two years. At seventeen, Clyde had unbridled freedom–an old truck with a foot of cow crap in the back and a forty acre farm mortgaged to the bank. He defaulted on the farm loan and then did the only thing he knew to do–moved back with the widow Kelly. Their relationship deteriorated rapidly after her craving for sex switched to food. She turned fifty-four that year, ballooned out of her clothes, lost all pride in how she looked, and became obscenely obese.

"I'm lonesome, honey," she complained to Clyde. "You don't do it any more."

"Hell! I don't even want to think about some fat old woman. That's more than I can stomach."

Clyde began looking for other sources of entertainment. He traded the pickup for a worn out two ton flatbed hay truck and made enough money hauling hay to buy drugs. That year also marked another milestone in his life–a symbiotic alliance with the Appleby boys.

Tom and Charlie Appleby's father drove them from home because he couldn't afford to feed them, let alone the other seven mouths clamoring at his kitchen table. The Appleby boys hooked up with Clyde. He needed a hay crew and they needed a place to live, and guidance. Charlie was mentally slow but could control Tom who was seriously retarded. They were fraternal twins but favored each other in almost every way– clumsy, oafish farm boys much too strong for their limited intelligence. Both boys stood well over six feet and weighed more than two-hundred pounds. They occasionally hurt themselves and others during chaotic horseplay. They weren't mean. They just couldn't help themselves, but they were an excellent hay crew.

The Appleby boys were sheep in need of a shepherd until Clyde took control of their lives. They followed him around like clumsy puppies, walking behind subserviently, holding doors and gates for him, doing his bidding. Tom and Charlie fell over themselves trying to anticipate their master's every command, following without question or hesitation. Clyde soon recognized that he could really be someone with the twins as subordinates. He could be someone dangerous to contend with; someone powerful and frightening.

Clyde moved the Applebys into the widow Kelly's home where they remained for many years. The widow began drinking because the three boys drank and soon turned completely to alcohol, lost weight, regained her lost hunger for sex and evolved once again into a grateful hand maiden.

*****

One evening, after drinking heavily, Clyde badgered the twins to have sex with her.

"You boys ought to try her on. Go ahead. I don't care."

"Naw, that's okay," Charlie said, blushing and giggling.

"Hell, you don't even know how, do you?"

Tom and Charlie ducked their heads, embarrassed by the thought of "doing it."

"Gracie, you're just going to have to show 'em how. These here are good boys. Go on. Show 'em what to do. You first, Charlie."

The widow objected weakly but Clyde pressured and she capitulated, taking the boys one at a time into her bedroom After that night, the Applebys wouldn't leave the widow alone and Clyde refused to touch her again. He had too much pride to share anything that personal with the twins.

Clyde commandeered the widow's farm operation and traded the herd of brood cows without her knowledge. Years of experience observing his father was a valuable asset. He made a few insignificant mistakes in the beginning, but became a shrewd, hard-bargaining cattle jockey.

Clyde followed the rules for nearly a year before finding little ways to cheat. Simple things at first: switching cattle, falsifying weights, lying. He enjoyed cheating; the excitement and easy money provided entertainment and thrills. Cheating opened the door to the next step: cattle rustling. The Widow Kelly's farm became the repository for baby calves the neophyte thieves found sleeping too close to isolated farm roads. Sometimes they snatched two or three a night.

*****

Clyde Townsend soon drifted into Sam's domain and provided the impetus that changed his life forever.

CHAPTER FIVE

Basketball

Jim Denning, assistant basketball coach and physical education teacher, had just leaned over to tie his shoes at the opposite end of the gym the day Sam dunked the ball. Denning had played basketball four years at college and could recognize the sound of a slam dunk. He looked up in time to see the ball bouncing beneath the goal, the boys on the team staring, and Sam Prescott walking away.

The next afternoon, a week after Wickmore's poor showing at the Atley practice game, as Sam passed Denning's office the coach yelled, "Yo, Prescott! Got a minute?"

"Yes, Sir." Sam liked Denning. He wasn't like the other teachers; he interacted, joking and talking with the kids. Sam enjoyed the PE class.

"Prescott, I want to see you after school just for a minute. Be here!" He winked and punched Sam on the shouldeand trotted down the hall toward the gym.

"Yes, Sir." Sam watched the coach, puzzled by the encounter, wondering what could be so important. After school, he edged through the coach's partially open office door. Denning stood, stepped around his desk and held out his hand. Sam responded hesitantly. No one from Wickmore had ever offered to shake his hand.

"You got a way home, Prescott? If not, I'll drive you. Don't worry about the bus."

"Yes, Sir. I have wheels."

The school bus took too long to wind through the back roads and Sam was the last off in the evening and the first on in the morning. He persuaded Wes to let him drive an old truck if he get it to could get it to run. Wes agreed, never thinking Sam could fix it. Sam had it running in two days.

"Okay. Answer me this, Prescott, did you or did you not dunk a basketball yesterday in my gym?"

Uh oh, Sam thought. Trouble. "Um, yes, Sir." He expected a reprimand for being on the gym floor in street shoes.

Denning nodded, suspicions confirmed, then broke out in a broad smile. "I thought so. Why aren't you out for the team?"

Sam shrugged.

"You dunked. You ever play any basketball?"

Ashcroft Academy had not sponsored sports teams other than track and field. Sam often joined pickup games with black kids on an outdoor court at the city park two blocks down the street from the campus. He played every time he could get into a game, learning basketball from some of the best players in Boston, even, on occasion, professional players.

If I say yes, he'll pressure me. "Some, I guess. Not on a team. Just fooling around. Pick-up games."

"Why aren't you out for the team? You must be at least six-four."

"Just never thought about it."

"Won't your parents let you play?"

"I guess. If I wanted to." *Parents*?

The coach leaned over his desk, glaring playfully. "Do you mean to tell me you don't want to play? That's un-American."

Sam shrugged again. "I'm really not interested, Coach. Anyway, I don't think it's a good idea. Not for me."

"Really! Why not? You're a better athlete than anyone on the team. I've watched you run and jump. You're a natural. You could play some ball and we can sure use your height."

Denning, a new hire at Wickmore, drove more than an hour each way from his home in Springfield and didn't know much about Wickmore, or Sam's station within the community.

Sam felt uncomfortable about facing a new problem. He knew Denning didn't understand his dilemma. "Is that all you wanted?"

He turned to leave.

The coach stood and came quickly around the desk, hand up, signaling a stop. "Whoa! Hold it! Don't you think I deserve a better answer than that? Not interested? Not interested is not good enough. Look, you don't have to play. That's your business. I sure can't force you to play and won't try, but I really would like to know why you don't." The young coach looked confused, stung by the turn of events, and the apparent loss of a prospect.

Sam paused at the door. "Look, Coach, I really don't know if I would like to play ball or not, but I know it really doesn't make much difference. So, if it's all the same, I need to go."

Denning locked his office and searched for the superintendent and principal. He wanted to know more about Sam Prescott. Both administrators were gone. He drove to Wickmore's general store and found Irma Roush alone, sitting behind the counter.

"Hi there," he said, smiling pleasantly. "Where is everyone?" He scanned the store.

"Oh, I don't have all that many customers this time of day, Coach. Mostly home doing chores, I expect."

He enjoyed looking at Irma, just like every other man in the neighborhood. She wasn't flawlessly beautiful, but close enough; certainly the best looking woman in Wickmore; still beautiful at forty; shapely and blonde. She never wore makeup and kept her hair in the puritan bun of an Assembly of God church woman, which she was. Everyone liked Irma. She managed the general store her husband's parents left to him. The general store, gas station and garage had the good fortune of being one of the only stores still operating in Wickmore, along with the café and liquor store.

Every man in the community used Irma's store as a base of operation, and she profited. At least ten local men, the regulars, met in the rear of her store every morning, playing cards, drinking coffee, swapping lies and watching Irma the Enigma–an AG church woman in tight-fittin' jeans.

She had grown up on a sprout infested farm east of Wickmore, isolated in the hills the only child of Adam Zachariah Boone, a fire-breathing jackleg preacher. Her mother died when Irma was only five. Her daddy, a huge man with great grey whiskers and a booming voice, ranged the country with an old army tent, preaching at brush arbor revivals. He never made enough money to live on, but refused welfare and poached wild game to supplement their food supply. Irma played the piano for him at the revivals, and started sleeping with him on her fourteenth birthday. She never thought her daddy abused her. She idolized him and would do anything to please him. Anything. No man ever meant so much to her; certainly not her husband. Only one other man had ever pleased her. E Coli Bacteria from their hand-dug water well killed Zacharia and the farm went back to the bank. Irma took a job clerking at the Roush general store.

She married Edwin Roush, Wickmore's basketball coach, just before her nineteenth birthday. Edwin, a local boy, never measured up to Irma's father in any way and ended up with the superintendent's job while Irma ran the store. Irma paid her dues to the close-knit community, minding her own business and supporting the Assembly of God church with all her heart.

"What do you know about the Prescott kid?" Denning asked, confident that she probably knew everything about everyone.

Her smile vanished and her eyes tightened perceptibly. She slammed the ledger closed and carefully placed the pen aside. Her facial features hardened. Irma appeared to be annoyed and turned away. "Not much, really. Why do you ask?"

The sudden change in her demeanor surprised Denning. He pressed on. "Well, I asked him to come out for the team. He said something about not being accepted. What am I missing?"

Irma's eyes narrowed even more, fingers drumming on the counter. "Well, he's a Prescott, so you haven't missed anything. That's about all there is to know." She opened the ledger again and picked up the pen, and then reconsidered, looked up and said, "You're new here, Coach, so you wouldn't know about the Prescotts. They have cheated and schemed their way into owning most of this county. People around here despise Prescotts. Wesley Prescott is a contemptible man and all the Prescotts before him were just as bad." She noticed the coach's surprised expression. "Well, you asked."

Denning stepped back, moving away from the fire. "Wow. That bad?"

She nodded, her face a mask of anger. "Worse. Before she died, Wes Prescott's mother sued the superintendent and school.

That woman caused more trouble than you'll ever know. Oh, there ain't no love lost around here for Prescotts; you can be sure of that. If the young man feels rejected, maybe he should."

Denning tried to dilute her anger by joking. "Is that all? I thought the boy had a contagious disease or something."

She didn't warm to his humor. "He does. He's a Prescott."

He scratched the back of his neck. "Wow. I'm almost sorry I asked."

Irma laughed nervously, self-conscious about the burst of hostility. "To tell you the truth, I really don't know much about that boy. He doesn't come into the store and doesn't hang around with the other kids." She put an end to the conversation by saying, "That boy probably won't play ball for you, Coach."

"Well, that's interesting. He seems like a pretty good kid to me. We could sure use him. We need a good big man."

Irma didn't add anything and Denning departed lost in thought. She asked her daughter about Sam that evening. "Cynthia, what's the Prescott boy like?"

Irma's daughter, on her stomach on the floor, looked up from her homework. The girl had clearly inherited her mother's good looks. Cynthia was friendly and vivacious, liked by everyone; Wickmore's version of the All-American girl. "Oh, he's awfully quiet, Mother. I don't know him at all. Nobody does. He's different." She paused to think, then said, "He's the tallest boy in school. A loner, that's for sure. Too bad."

"Is he stuck up?" Irma tried to appear indifferent, rocking and knitting.

"That's what everyone thinks. He doesn't talk, so it's hard to tell. He makes straight A's in class. That's probably one reason the other kids don't like him, particularly the boys. He's just different, Mother." Cynthia smiled and cocked an eyebrow up at Irma. "He's sure pretty, though. Why did you ask, Mother?"

"Oh, no reason. I never see him hanging around the store. Just wondered, that's all." She stopped rocking and said, "Pretty? I don't like to hear you talk about boys like that."

* * * * *

"Prescott!" Coach Denning yelled down the hall the next morning.

Sam stopped and turned. "Yes, sir?"

"Got a moment?" Denning trotted to close the distance.

"I have study hall, Coach."

"Take this hall pass. Come to my office when you get a chance."

Sam lingered in study hall, thinking about meeting with Denning and about using the hall pass. He had spoken with Wes the night before about the conversation with the coach and asked Wes, "What do you think I should do?"

"Is the superintendent still coaching the team?"

"Mister Roush? Yes, but I haven't talked to him. Only the assistant, Coach Denning."

Wes clucked to himself, frowning. "You thinking about going out for the team?

"Don't know. Maybe."

"Well, Roush will sure be tough on you."

"I can take it."

"Maybe. Anyway, since you asked what I think, I think you'll just be making a hell of a lot of extra trouble for yourself. It's your call, though. Let me know what you decide." He disappeared behind the newspaper.

Sam stepped into the coach's office, closed the door, and waited respectfully as Denning finished a phone call.

"Thanks for coming down, Prescott. You can leave that door open."

"I'd rather have it closed, Coach."

Denning looked surprised. "Okay. Have a seat." He waited until Sam settled before continuing. "Hope you don't mind, but I asked around town about you last night. I think I can understand your problem. Anyhow, I'm sorry for pressuring you. Thanks for coming down." He stood and offered his hand.

Sam didn't get up. "I want to play, Coach."

Denning couldn't hide the look of pleasure. "Are you kidding? You sure?"

"Yes. I'm sure."

Denning obtained permission for Sam to miss study hall and spent the extra hour each day teaching the few Wickmore plays. Sam practiced with the team after school but learned far more at the individual practice sessions with Denning. Basketball season opened the next week with Sam sitting on the bench.

Denning commented to his wife the night before the first game of the season, "Prescott should start tomorrow. He's that good. Roush thinks the community will adapt better if he works him in slow." Denning paced the kitchen, smiling and gesturing. "Polly, you should see him! He is the real deal." He elaborated for minutes.

Polly observed her husband's excited gestures and facial expressions before saying, "I have never seen you this enthusiastic about a boy."

"Oh, he's not just good, Polly. He's a great athlete. Smart. Quick. Strong. Far better than I was at his age. You have got to come see for yourself." He pulled her up and swung her around. "God, people are going to be so shocked. Honestly, I think he can jump over the rim. I've never seen a white kid jump like he can. He's amazing."

"Are you setting yourself up for disappointment?"

"No! I'm really not imagining anything, Polly! I've been around enough good players to know one when I see one. Get a sitter. You have to watch him."

During the second half of the game, with Wickmore losing by twenty points, no one even looked up when Sam stood. Wickmore fans were busy mumbling to themselves; angered by the team's poor performance; disappointed the Ravens were not living up to expectations. Sam received a smattering of boos from a few bored fans following the PA system announcement, "Number fifty-five, Prescott in for Manes." When he stepped onto the court, the crowd finally took notice.

A damned Prescott.

They came to life in stages, a murmuring, angry undercurrent at first, then muted booing and howls of hostility. Sam's presence on the court finally yanked every Wickmore fan to attention. Some stood, pointing and jeering, anticipating the opportunity to ridicule a Prescott. They hissed and booed when he fumbled the first pass; booed louder and laughed derisively, slapping high-fives when he fouled. And then, as if wiped away by a sudden lack of oxygen, all sound ceased. An eerie, deflating hush smothered the hostile festivities and the stunned Wickmore boosters collapsed into their seats, struggling silently to come to grips with what they had just seen. Sam dunked a rebound, slamming the ball through the hoop after gathering one of his teammate's errant shots.

Coach Denning turned to Polly and winked. No one could remember ever seeing a Wickmore player slam dunk a ball, let alone while still in midair with a rebound. Polly cheered, but only a smattering of applause seeped out of the Wickmore assembly as most sat silently, dazed by feats of the interloper. Sam robbed them of something crucial to community togetherness, stripping them of a reason to hate a Prescott.

Wickmore, after mounting a furious rally, lost the game by one point and Sam gained a reason for going to school. Some freshmen and sophomore students smiled. A few even spoke the next day, but his teammates remained faithful to their creed, detached and resentful. Sam didn't care.

CHAPTER SIX

Cynthia

The old truck Sam drove to school refused to start one warm November afternoon after ball practice. He had jogged the five miles from school to the ranch on several occasions and decided to run home instead of taking the bus. A rain shower began pelting him about three miles from school, just as Cynthia Roush drove by going the other direction. Sam was running with head down to keep the rain from his eyes and didn't see her. She sped past, then turned around at the first side road and came back to drive beside him.

"Be glad to give you a ride!"

He kept jogging and waved her off. "That's okay! I don't mind the rain!"

She idled along, keeping pace, watching for traffic in the mirrors. "I just came from the way you're headed! The rain is much worse ahead!"

He jogged on, glancing over, trying to decide if he wanted to open the door of friendship to anyone from Wickmore, even for her.

"Come on! Get in!" She accelerated, drove ahead, pulled to the other side of the road and stopped.

Sam trotted on until pulling even. He stopped to analyze the situation from across the road. Cynthia had made no previous effort to be friendly.

She rolled the window down. "Get in, silly. You're already soaked."

Her smile broke the ice. He hurried across the road and got in.

"My truck wouldn't start," he said. *That's so lame.*

"Bad timing," she said, busy with the heater controls and radio volume–anything not to look at him, worried about what people would think if they saw her with Sam Prescott, regretting the impulsive decision to stop.

At the entry drive to the ranch, Sam said, "You don't have to take me all the way. I–"

She held up a hand. "No, it's okay." She turned in and continued up the private paved road to the locked gates.

"I'll get the gate." He jumped out, punched in the code and hustled back as the gates swung open. He motioned ahead after noticing her hesitation. "It's okay. You can go."

She drove on, no longer a willing participant, desiring nothing more than to let him out and turn around. The narrow road snaking through the trees permitted no "U" turn.

Sam noticed his uncle's pickup parked in front of the house. "Wes is home. That doesn't matter. Why don't you come on in. I'll show you around."

She didn't make a move to get out, just stared at the house. "No, really. I can't do that. Maybe some—"

Sam laughed. "Come on. You should see inside." He walked around and opened her door.

She protested. "No, really. Won't he–"

At that moment Wes stepped through the front door on his way out. He touched the brim of his hat and said hello to Cynthia, flashing a questioning, sidewise glance at Sam.

Sam said, "The truck wouldn't start. Cynthia picked me up on the way home."

Wes nodded. "Ah. Well, a friend in need...all that. I'll be back directly." He touched the bill of his cap to Cynthia and headed for his truck.

"Come on," Sam said, "I'll show you around."

Her eyes revealed doubt bordering on fear. "Um, no. Really, I should probably go."

He gave up. "Well, anyway, thanks for the ride."

She waved from behind the closed window, keeping her eyes straight ahead, and slipped the car into gear. He motioned for her to roll the window down. "The gate has a motion detector. It opens automatically."

She nodded and drove away over the hill.

Sam stood in the middle of the road watching, exasperated by her nervousness. After the car disappeared, he threw up his hands and yelled, "See you tomorrow, Cynthia! Nice talking to you, Cynthia! Come again, Cynthia."

When Wes returned, he said, "Well, things must be picking up at school. So, you and Cynthia Roush?"

Sam eyed him coldly. "So, nothing. She wouldn't stick around. I need a ride to jump start that truck if you have time."

Cynthia avoided him the next day. He trapped her at the lockers. "Hi. Got a minute?"

She used the open locker door as a shield, shuffling books and paperwork. "Not really. I'm in a hurry."

"I appreciate the ride yesterday. Just wanted to say thanks."

She stopped the nervous activity, hesitated, then slowly backed away far enough to regain her comfort zone. "You already said thanks. Don't make a big deal out of it, okay?"

Her defensive attitude puzzled him. He nodded and backed away. "Right. Got it." He didn't try to approach her again, lumping her in with the other kids from Wickmore–just someone else to avoid. But, he also noticed that her eyes follow him during the next game, and that she had come to a game for the first time. *Oh, she's a fraud. She's interested.*

Clyde also noticed and cornered Sam in the hall. "You got something going with my gal, Prescott?"

Sam didn't attempt to edge away. He didn't think Clyde would try anything in the crowded hall. "Didn't know you had a gal, Townsend."

Clyde poked Sam on the chest with his finger. "I catch you making a move on her, I'll kick the crap out of you."

Sam laughed. "Don't worry. Any girl of yours is safe from my attentions."

Clyde looked confused, like he had missed something. "Well, you heard me."

* * * * *

That afternoon at practice, Coach Roush blew the whistle and yelled, "Over here! Okay, men, we're gonna run a jungle rules scrimmage. One-on-one." Roush thought the frenzied, brutal, no-holds-barred practice taught players to hold on to the ball under extreme pressure. "First one to five wins. Townsend, you and Prescott start it." Roush bounced a ball to Clyde. "On my whistle." He signaled and the contest began. There would be no fouls called, no matter how violent the contact.

Sam stood between Clyde and the goal, crouching, waiting. He knew Clyde didn't have a decent shot from distance. Clyde's style consisted of slashing drives and close-in shots, relying on strength and weight. As Clyde closed the distance, dribbling leisurely, Sam gave ground easily, and, then suddenly lashed out to slap the ball away. He snatched it before Clyde could recover, drove to the basket and jammed the ball through with a resounding two-hand dunk.

"One," Sam said, grinning. "My ball." The rules, what few the coach enforced, stipulated that the scoring player kept the ball. Sam won the first game five to nothing. Clyde didn't get a shot.

Roush, scowling, blew the whistle. "Same two again. Townsend, you first."

Sam stole the ball and shot from well beyond the three point line. "One." He threw the ball back to Townsend.

Clyde threw it back, his frustration turning to anger. "Your ball, dumbass."

Sam grinned and threw it back. "It's my ball whether you have it or not." He blocked Clyde's next shot and dunked it, then stole the ball twice, each time giving the ball back without attempting a shot himself.

"It's your damned ball, Prescott," Clyde said, hurling the ball at Sam from close distance.

Sam deflected the ball. "You can't score on me, Townsend. You got nothing. Keep it." He slammed the ball into Clyde's stomach. Clyde made a fist and swung wildly.

The coach blew the whistle and rushed to separate the combatants. "Play ball, you two!" Clyde tried to back in, forcing his way using weight and muscle. Sam stopped him and blocked the shot. Clyde tried a long shot. Sam blocked it and handed the ball back, grinning.

Roush could see Clyde's frustration and blew the whistle. "Okay, next two."

Clyde shoved Sam and stalked off. Later, during team practice, he crashed into Sam, slapped at his arms, pulled his shirt and muttered threats. After the humiliation, every time they met in the hall, Clyde bumped into Sam, knocked him into the lockers, made threatening remarks and generally made Sam's life miserable.

Clyde started at point guard the next game. Sam sat on the bench. Wickmore won easily and Sam didn't get to play until the last five minutes. No one would pass him the ball. Finally, with two minutes remaining, he stole the ball and dunked it, and then blocked the opponent's next shot and dribbled through the entire team to score. He stole the ball on an inbounds play and scored again.

Coach Roush yelled, "You're hogging the ball, Prescott!"

Sam scored again off a rebound before the game ended.

Roush grabbed him by the jersey in the dressing room. "Basketball is a team sport, Prescott."

Sam couldn't believe it. "Coach, no one will pass the ball to me."

"No back talk! You hear me?"

Sam stood at attention. "Yes, Sir."

He complained to Wes the next morning at breakfast.

"Well, nothing I can do about that. Deal with it." He disappeared behind the newspaper.

Sam didn't understand. *Why is Roush so one-sided? I'll just bide my time, make the most of opportunities.* Wickmore fell behind early in the next home game against a strong Picton team and Roush called Sam from the end of the bench. "All right, Prescott. In for Justin. See if you can stop that Evans kid. He's killing us."

Some of the Wickmore crowd booed as Sam trotted onto the court. Picton relied on Jerry Evans their all state guard and the leading scorer in the state–thirty-five points per game.

Evans had already made a verbal commitment to the University of Missouri. He brought the ball down the court, noting Wickmore's tall substitute in front of him. Evans felt supremely confident, smiling as he crossed the center line. He expected to drive around the tall kid with no problem. Sam flicked the ball away as Evans tried a tricky crossover dribble and scored on an easy lay-up. He stole the ball from Evans on the next play and passed it to Clyde. Townsend lost it attempting to force his way to the goal, ignoring Sam for a wide open for a shot. Wickmore regained the lead and Roush took Sam out.

The score seesawed back and forth. When Wickmore fell behind, Sam played; when Wickmore led, Sam sat. He scored the winning basket with three seconds remaining, then sat on the bench throughout the duration of the next game, an easy win for Wickmore.

Coach Roush heard the first murmurs of dissatisfaction from the more knowledgeable Wickmore fans:

"That Prescott kid's pretty good, Coach."

"You need to let number 55 play."

"You got something against Prescott, Roush? He looks awful good out there."

* * * * *

The following day in study hall, Cynthia glanced up as Sam walked in, disturbed to find herself alone with him. He selected a desk in front of her, spun it around and sat, their knees almost touching. "Guess you know Mrs. Mitchell won't be here today," he announced, grinning, possibly because she looked almost panic-stricken.

"So?" She flipped through the book on her desk, eyes down.

He leaned back and stretched, his legs extending on both sides of the desk, trapping her.

"Just you and me, I guess. All alone. By ourselves. Yep."

"Shouldn't you be in the gym practicing?" she asked, annoyed with his banter. Sam usually skipped study hall, with permission, in favor of the gym. Cynthia tried to look busy, profoundly aware of his presence and unable to concentrate.

"Why bother? I won't get to play tonight–not against Barkley. Your dad won't put me in against a poor team."

She kept her head down.

Sam pressed on. "What is it with your dad? Why does he dislike me so much?"

"Not my problem." She looked up, then quickly back to the book, flustered to know his eyes were on her. She *was* trapped. Cynthia didn't like his boldness– so confident, overfriendly, like an old friend.

"He only plays me if we're behind." She didn't answer, so he leaned closer, his face within inches of hers and said, "Does talking to me make you uncomfortable, Roush? Am I a threat?"

She sighed and looked up, clearly exasperated. "Maybe I just don't want to talk to you."

He sat back, studying his fingernails. "Or, maybe Clyde might not like it?"

She didn't look away for the first time during the conversation. "Clyde? Whatever are you talking about?"

"He told me you're his gal."

Her face flushed with anger and embarrassment. "He what?"

Sam casually wiped his fingernails on his shirt, then looked up at her and smiled. "Yes Ma'am. That is what the man said. You and Clyde. Who knew?"

Her face lost color. "He actually said that?"

"In fact he did." Sam held up a finger to make a point. "Oh, and he's going to beat me up if I make a move on you. Yup. He said that, too." He grinned foolishly, nodding. "Well, who knew? Clyde and Cynthia."

She snapped the book closed, full attention now on her gleeful antagonist. Her nervousness vanished. "You have got to be kidding."

"Nope. So that's why you won't talk to me. You and Clyde."

She couldn't get beyond Clyde's claim. "Well, you can tell him for me...." She turned away so Sam couldn't see the threatening onset of frustrated tears. "Never mind."

"I wouldn't anyway."

She glared at him and snapped, "Wouldn't what?"

"Tell him anything."

She didn't answer. Sam stood, turned the seat back to its original position, picked up his books and took another seat closer to the door, leaning back, eyes closed, the picture of indifference.

Several minutes later, in a muted voice, Cynthia said, "I'm not his girlfriend. I have never been his girlfriend. I know he tells that around. No one will ask me out because they're afraid of him. I am *not* his girlfriend and never have been."

She couldn't see Sam's satisfied smile. He waved a hand over his shoulder, certain she was watching, and said, "Look, it doesn't matter to me. You and Clyde. Whatever."

After another long silence, in an attempt to put him on the defensive, she said, "Why are you so afraid of Clyde?"

Sam snorted but kept his eyes closed. "Not in this lifetime."

"Well, he bullies you all the time. Pushes you around. Makes fun of you. Everyone talks about it. It's embarrassing to watch."

He sat up and whirled to face her so quickly the chair screeched. "Look, I'm not supposed to.... I can't.... He doesn't scare me!"

Cynthia took delight in his dismay. She had him. "Really? Well, you sure back away from him all the time. What do you expect people to think?"

He stood and said, "Townsend doesn't scare me and I can prove it."

"Yeah, right. How? Like you're gonna fight him?"

He walked down the aisle toward her. "Better than that." He stopped at her desk, towering over her. "I'm going to ask his girl for a date. How about it?"

Cynthia would not have been more traumatized had he slapped her. She covered her mouth, stammering, "Look, I'm not his.... I'm.... What?"

He spun the desk around again and sat facing her. "Okay, I'll make it formal. Cynthia, would you go out with me?" He smiled and pointed his forefinger at her like a gun. "There, the ball's in your court."

She was too stunned to think, and would have blushed but the color had drained from her face. After sitting for what seemed like a full minute attempting to think, her mouth forming words that wouldn't come, she suddenly picked up her school work and rushed from the room.

The next day when Sam stepped into the study hall, she got up and walked out the moment she saw him. As she passed, he whispered, "Who's afraid now?"

Cynthia began attending the basketball games regularly, and occasionally sat in the bleachers with other girls during team practices. Sam noticed. Clyde noticed. Edwin Roush noticed.

After breakfast one morning, Cynthia's father said, "What's this new interest you have in sports? Don't you think you should stick around and help your mother with the store?"

"She said I could go."

"You never liked sports before."

"The team is really doing great, so I just...." She hesitated, then boldly countered his accusing glare. "Why, Daddy? Isn't it okay?"

His eyes narrowed. "You're not just there to ogle some boy, are you?"

Cynthia overreacted, confirming his suspicions. "Daddy! Well, I swear."

He shook his head, disappointed. "I'll be damned. I knew it. I knew it." He got up and walked out muttering to himself, "Better not be that Prescott kid. Tell you that. Be your last damned game."

She turned to Irma and whined, "Mother?"

Irma shrugged. "Don't you mother me. Your daddy don't miss much."

"What if I.... Anyway, what's wrong with.... Oh, never mind."

Irma's complexion darkened as anger surfaced. "Now you listen to me, girl. I know the name you won't say. It's Prescott. You best be paying attention to your father. He'll ground you forever. This is the last time I ever expect to associate your name with a Prescott.

Sam slipped a note on her desk the next day as he walked by. *The ball is still in your court.* Cynthia stopped attending the games.

* * * * *

Tad Rollins announced the weekly basketball standings. "Folks, here we are a third of the way through the season. I still have Wickmore placed number one in small schools. They lost a game early, but with the new transfer, Prescott, they're a force to contend with. For those of you who haven't seen the Ravens play, you should try to make their game at Picton tonight. Picton should give the Ravens all they can handle. I'll be there on the radio to bring it to you live, but you should join me at courtside. Take this opportunity to see Wickmore try to stop Picton's University of Missouri recruit, Jerry Evans. Should be a great game."

Later that evening, as the game with Picton began, Rollins leaned over to his associate and said, "Is the Prescott kid hurt? Why isn't he starting?"

The technician, Art Stegner, once a great player and celebrated referee, now obese and in his fifties, served as Rollins' statistics man. "Looked okay to me in warmups. Some talk about friction between him and the coach. Probably a personality thing."

Wickmore fell behind by ten as Evans stole the ball from Clyde repeatedly. Roush put Sam in for Clyde with six minutes remaining in the half. Several Wickmore fans had already started hooting and yelling for Prescott, angry with Roush for letting the game slip away.

Evans, already with eighteen points, watched Sam check in at the scorer's table and trotted over to shake hands. "You okay, Prescott?"

"I'm fine, thanks."

The Picton star smiled, supremely at home with his adoring crowd, and patted Sam on the back. "Different game tonight, big man," he said. "This time, you lose."

As they trotted to center court, Sam said, "Talk is cheap."

Picton still led at the half, but Evans had not scored against Sam's smothering defense. He couldn't get the ball, and when he did Sam forced him to pass or blocked his shot. Sam scored twelve points in the six minutes, stole the ball three times and had seven rebounds.

At the halftime buzzer, Rollins exclaimed, "Picton may win this game folks, but I'm here to tell you, the Prescott kid is phenomenal. I have never seen a quicker big man. He absolutely suffocated Jerry Evans, only the best guard in the state. The second half should be a barn burner. And now for a few messages from our...."

* * * * *

Picton's coach made halftime adjustments in the offensive patterns to help Evans get free and he scored ten points in the second half. Sam scored twenty-five, missing only three shots. Wickmore won the game.

No one on the team said anything to Sam, nor did Coach Roush. A few spectators clapped him on the back. "Great game, Prescott." "Way to go!" Some of the younger kids from Wickmore lined the sidewalk on the way to the bus and congratulated him, slapping high fives. He had noticed Cynthia watching from the stands as the team straggled off the court. *She's back.* He felt marvelous.

Evans pulled him aside at the buzzer to shake hands. "Great game, Prescott. I mean, really great."

"Thanks. The name is Sam."

"Mine's Jerry. Good chance we'll meet again." He slapped Sam on the butt. "You take care, man."

* * * * *

Rollins wrapped the broadcast up by saying, "One of the greatest high school games I have broadcast and two of the finest players I have ever watched. Folks, I'm telling you, don't miss an opportunity to watch Evans or Prescott."

* * * * *

At home, Sam noticed the light on in Wes's office and peeked in. Wes looked up from the computer and said, "Hey, good game. I'm impressed."

"You listened?" His uncle's praise surprised him, but knowing that Wes listened to the game meant more than praise.

"Yeah, I listened. Hell, boy, if you're gonna be a star, I may have to start coming."

"Don't bother next week. We have two easy games. I probably won't get to play."

Wes looked surprised. "Roush still giving you a tough time?"

Sam shrugged. "Yeah, but I can handle it. See you in the morning."

He listened? Wow. Surprise, surprise.

Sam didn't think about Wes that night, though, or the game, or Jerry Evans. His thoughts focused squarely on Cynthia. He went to sleep smiling, contented and happy for the first time in weeks.

He played sparingly the next week, as suspected, but the following week, half way through December, Wickmore played three games in a tournament. Sam didn't start any of the games, but the tournament committee selected him for the all-star team and most valuable player. Coach Roush received more abuse from Wickmore fans. The Ravens had one more game before Christmas vacation, against a much larger school from Springfield.

* * * * *

Tad Rollins previewed the game on his nightly television sports show. "The Wickmore Ravens are coming to town tonight to play Southwest. Now, folks, here's your chance to see the top rated, once beaten Ravens and their star, Sam Prescott. I consider Prescott by far the most talented player in the region, if not the entire state. Several college scouts are going to be present. Get out and support high school basketball."

* * * * *

Sam didn't start, as usual, and Wickmore fell behind. Several vocal

Wickmore fans screamed at Roush to put him in.

"We want Prescott! We want Prescott!"

"What is wrong with you, Roush!"

"What the hell's the matter with you!"

"You damned idiot! Put Prescott in!"

Roush could hear Tommy John's voice above the crowd, angry and cursing.

When Sam trotted onto the floor, part of the crowd cheered, but a sprinkling of hostile fans screamed at Roush, "About damned time, you jerk! What the hell took so long? You don't know anything about basketball!"

Sam's presence had little effect on the game and Wickmore lost. He, along with the mystified scouts and most of the crowd, recognized within moments that his teammates were deliberately keeping the ball from him. Crowd hostility increased as Wickmore fell farther behind. The game dragged on with Sam working like crazy to break free only to have the ball go to another player, or be thrown away. His only points came from rebounds and stolen balls. Coach Roush had to dodge flying cups as he ducked into the walkway leading from the gym after the final buzzer.

* * * * *

Tad Rollins, always loath to say anything derogatory, relayed to his radio audience, "Well, Prescott had an off night. Too bad." He turned to his associate after signing off. "What did we just witness? Am I dreaming or did those kids just sabotage Prescott in front of the scouts?"

Stegner shook his head sadly. "You damned sure weren't dreaming. They screwed him. Beats all I ever saw."

"Incredible. Wonder what's behind all that?"

* * * * *

Wes noticed the light on under Sam's door that night, well after midnight. He hesitated, and then knocked and entered. "You want to tell me what went on tonight?"

Sam was lying on his back fully clothed, grim-faced, hands behind his head. "I take it you listened?"

"No. I was there. I watched the whole damned thing."

Sam sat up. "You went to the game?"

"I was there. Looked to me like they wanted to make you look bad in front of the scouts. You know anything about that?"

"Yeah. They did it intentionally. Clyde told me before the game."

"He what?"

"He said the scouts would laugh at me after they watched the game. On the bus home, he said I got what I deserved."

Wes shook his head. "That's bullshit." He studied Sam a moment. "Anyway, what are you thinking?"

Sam sighed heavily and flopped back. "Nothing good, that's for sure."

Wes nodded. "Well, it wouldn't make me think any less of you if you got out. I don't see no sense in putting up with that kind of crap."

"I'll stick it out. Might salvage something."

Wes nodded. "Your call, son. Better get some rest." He closed the door softly.

Son? That's the first time he ever called me anything other than boy. Sam went to sleep smiling, but not about Cynthia.

* * * * *

Monday evening after school, Edwin Roush saw Wes Prescott's pickup sitting in his drive. He felt the churn of nausea welling in the pit of his stomach and braked to a stop. He thought about turning around and speeding away, but realized that wouldn't solve anything. He watched Wes get out and lean against his beat up truck, waiting for him, grim-faced and clearly angry.

Roush sighed and drove on, doors locked, window cracked open, and stopped beside Wes. "I figure you're trespassing, Prescott."

Wes scoffed. "Then call the damned sheriff."

"What do you want?"

"For starters? To beat the crap out of you."

Roush leaned in, away from the window. "I have a gun in here. I'll use it."

Wes laughed, ridiculing the threat. "You gutless bastard. You couldn't pull the damned trigger if I helped you." He stepped close. "I don't like what you're doing to my boy. You keep screwing with him and I'm damned sure gonna take it personal."

"I'm not doing anything to that boy."

Wes kicked the door hard enough to leave an indentation the size of his foot. "You think I'm blind and deaf, asshole? The whole damned county knows what's going on! You think I don't know what's going on? You think I don't know why you have a hard-on for the boy?"

He kicked the door again. "What's between you and me is not the boy's problem!" He took a deep breath, and then in a quiet, menacing tone said, "Now, something like that last game ever happens again, I'll be coming for you, Roush. That's a promise. And, just so you know I'm dead serious, I'll be there watching the rest of your damned games." He drove away, leaving Roush trembling in the protective confines of his truck.

* * * * *

At supper that evening, out of the blue, Wes asked Sam, "What are you planning after high school? Any idea?"

Sam hesitated, momentarily caught off balance, surprised by his uncle's question. "College, I guess. Why?"

Wes nodded, took a bite, chewed thoughtfully, then said, "Have you thought about any particular school?"

Sam nodded. "I have, but I don't think I can get in."

"Oh, yeah? Why not?" He kept his eyes from the boy, trying to appear unconcerned.

"Oh, maybe the little matter of a police record?"

Wes nodded. "Ah, that. Well, I doubt most schools would check."

"They will at West Point."

Wes looked up, taken completely by surprise. "West Point? That something new?"

"No. I got the application forms a month ago. Not much reason to bother submitting, is there?"

Wes nodded again and took another bite, chewing and thinking. "Hmmm. Interesting." He put the fork down and sat back. "Well, I'll be damned. West Point, you say? You figurin' on doing something about it?"

"I guess not. Not with a police record."

Wes wiped his mouth, nodding, his brow furled, concentrating. "West Point? Well now, let me think." He scratched his neck. "Hmmmm. Okay, let's say, just for the hell of it, that you didn't have a police record. Wouldn't you still need an appointment?"

"Yes. I know. Little problem there." Sam watched his uncle, wondering where the conversation was headed.

Wes looked up, smiling, satisfied with himself. "I know what your SATS scores and IQ are, and your grades. I know you qualify mentally and physically. Did I ever tell you who my college roommate was? Any idea?" He smiled impishly, playing mind games.

"No idea. Why?"

Wes leaned back; enjoying himself; still playing games. "Well, sir. He's presently an honorable state representative in Washington D. C., that's who." He snapped his fingers. "Zip, pop–automatic appointment."

"Yeah, but–"

Wes leaned forward. "Yeah, but nothing. Remember what I said about business? Remember me saying that I can usually figure a way to get what I want? Well, if that's what you want, it's high time you learn a little about business."

"How do I...." Sam looked confused and threw up his hands.

"How? Hell, I don't know. That's where the fun part begins. That's where you start figgerin' things out." Wes clearly enjoyed the moment, smiling confidently. "Now, if you're serious I'll damned sure get to work on it."

"I am serious. I've always wanted to go to West Point. That's my first choice. Actually, my only choice."

Wes stood, still smiling. "All right then. You get those applications ready and I'll do me some calling around." He nodded, satisfied with himself. "Yeah. Damned straight. West Point. Well, all right!" He slapped the table. "Hell yeah!"

Sam carried the dishes and helped with the cleaning even though it was Wes's night. "I still don't know how–"

"Hell, who does? It's just a problem to be solved, that's all. Whenever you have an objection to a business deal, you don't throw up your hands and quit. You find a way to solve it. We just have one problem as I see it, provided you don't go off half-cocked and hit someone and ruin everything."

"My police record?"

"That's there is the problem. Finish up here, will you. I got me some thinking to do.

"Wait. Your roomy. Is he a representative from Missouri?"

"No, from Tennessee."

"Then how-"

"He knows all the reps from Missouri. He can make a trade. Easy. Business."

CHAPTER SEVEN

Elena

She picked the phone up before the recorder kicked in. "This is Elena. What?"

"Don't you give me that what crap."

She stopped breathing. *Oh, God, oh, God, oh, God. Please, not him.* He never called unless he wanted her to do something her regular pimp couldn't get her to do. He never called with anything good.

She said, "I'm sick. I'm really sick. Please don't ask me—"

"Shut up! I'm there in ten. You better be there."

Click.

That fearsome voice, low, rumbling, angry–always angry. Elena put the phone down and rushed to the bathroom to fumble through the medicine cabinet, hands shaking, containers falling into the sink. She located the tranquilizers and swallowed two, and then bent over the sink, breathing hard, eyes panic-stricken.

What does he want? He never.... Oh, no. It's about the money. Pam ratted me out. Oh, Pam. Should never have told her. Oh, God, oh, God, oh, God.

She ran to the bedroom to get the money from the jewelry box– the money Wes gave her–then stood, eyes wide, terrified, unable to think. Finally, with no better solution, shoved the wad of bills into her bra and began pacing. Waiting and pacing. Breathing hard. *Oh, God.*

He didn't knock, just slammed through the door, shoved her away roughly and locked it. When he turned to face her, he looked mean. She didn't even know his last name. Everyone called him

Diamond, or D, for obvious reasons–diamonds–lots of diamonds on his ears, through his nose and on his fingers. Tall and slender; satin black skin; always dressed in immaculate white silk suits and Italian shoes, and layers of jewelry. Everything he owned was splashy and expensive. He always wore white from head to foot. A white fedora, long white cape coat and white shoes Everything white. His car. His women, an all white crew of has-beens and newbies.

She backed away whimpering, "Where's Petey?" She detested herself for sounding so plaintive and submissive, like a whining child. Her local pimp, Petey, usually served as insulation between Diamond and Elena. Nearly always. She started working for D after her best days, on her way down. He only showed up when he wanted something special, or to discipline.

He aimed a long diamond-studded finger at her face. "You shut the hell up. Got that?"

She nodded, arms folded over her breasts, shivering, wondering why Petey hadn't come, wishing the tranquilizers would kick in, scared witless, backing away.

D Didn't waste time. "The money! Hand it over." His extended fingers snapped.

"I don't have.... What mon–"

The blow snapped Elena's head back. Her knees buckled and the floor rushed up before her hand could stop it. The floor didn't hurt that much. She was too dazed to feel anything.

The first thing she recognized several moments later was the taste of blood. She lay on the floor blinking, trying to focus on Mister D hovering menacingly above, and then the pain came in excruciating waves.

"Get up and get that damned money. You know I ain't foolin'. I should kill your skinny, doped-up ass. No two-bit whore holds out on me. Now get the hell up!" He kicked her in the back; not too hard; he wanted her to function.

She suppressed a scream. He would be more outraged if she made a scene. After rocking back and forth on her hands and knees for a moment, she used the coffee table as a crutch and struggled to stand, wobbly and gasping for air.

"Now, bitch! I want the damned money now!" He held out a bejeweled hand, snapping those long fingers close to her face.

"I...please, the money came from my–"

The pearl-handled knife appeared like magic, almost without any motion. One moment his hand was empty, and then she heard a metallic click followed by a six inch blade beneath her nose, waving and menacing.

"No. Please. Please, don't." The knife point moved upward. Elena clenched her eye closed, afraid to watch. She felt the point touch beneath her eyebrow. "No, please don't. Please. Please."

A flick of his wrist and the razor sharp blade sliced upward through her brow. Blood gushed over her closed eye, down her face and onto her blouse. She froze, except the trembling. He moved the point to her other eye and repeated the performance. She whimpered, but couldn't open her eyes. She could feel blood soaking through her blouse.

"The Money! Now! Either I get the damned money or you get your throat cut. You got five seconds to decide. One...."

She reached in to the bloody confines of the once white blouse, removed the money and held it out. Resigned. Eyes still closed.

He snatched the wad of bills and stepped back, staring at his hand. "Bitch! You got damned blood all over.... Shit!" He tossed the bills on the couch, stared at his stained fingers for a moment, his face contorted with anger, and then lashed out viciously. The blade sliced half way through Elena's throat. D jumped back from the spray of blood and away from her collapsing body; away from the muffled, gurgling sounds of her last screams. He checked his clothes for blood spots, wiped the knife on her slacks, washed his hands in the sink, wrapped the money in a napkin and casually walked out. No one saw him enter and no one on the floor below heard anything. No one knew until her sometimes friend and roomy, Pam, dropped by and found Elena's bloated body two days later.

The cops knew what Elena did for a living. After a cursory search of city and county files, investigators located no records to indicate an Elena Dowling ever existed, other than several arrests for solicitation. Another nameless runaway. The coroner ordered her body cremated, ashes to be held as public property until claimed.

A week after Elena's death, the day Sam's Christmas vacation from school started, Pam called Wes. Seventeen years earlier, upon arrival in Boston and under the influence of drugs, Elena had told her new friend the reasons she ran away from home, where she came from and for the last time ever, shared her real name. She also wrote her home phone number and address on a slip of paper and gave it to Pam. "Just in case...you know, like if something bad happens to me."

Pam didn't forget the paper or Elena's family name. However, when investigators asked if she knew anything about Elena's family background, Pam refused to get involved. She was petrified. Mister D also controlled her life.

After Wes answered the phone, Pam said, "Do you know an Elena Dowling...um, Prescott?"

His brow furled. *Uh, oh.* "Yeah, she's my sister. I'm Wes Prescott. Who is this?"

"My name doesn't matter. Don't ask. I was Elena's friend." A long pause. "She gave me your address and asked me to contact you if anything ever happened." After a moment of silence, she whispered, "Elena's dead." She began crying and couldn't continue.

Wes groped for a chair, instantly sick to his stomach. He had always known something bad would happen to Elena. He sat, took a deep breath, and then tried to gain control of the conversation. The caller became emotional and couldn't answer his questions. He pleaded, "Please, I need to know what happened? Don't hang up. Talk to me."

Pam finally gained control. "I'm so sorry. He killed her last week. I know I should have called sooner, but I'm scared he'll know I told. He'll kill me, too. It was my fault. He made me tell about the money...the money you gave her. I don't know how he knew she had it, but he knew. He made me tell. My fault." She broke down again.

Wes was afraid she would hang up. "Wait! Who? Who killed her?"

"I can't.... He'll know it was me. I had to tell him. I didn't have a choice. I just wanted you to know she's...she's.... Anyway, I'm sorry. I have to–"

"No! No! Wait just a minute. Who? I need to know who did it! Just tell me that much."

After a long silence, she whispered, "D. He did it." The line went dead.

Wes never wept. He hadn't cried since his sixth birthday over the loss of a pet dog his father shot for killing a chicken. Even then he didn't cry for the dog; he cried out of anger. Someone took something important from him. Elena's death left him with a great feeling of loss, but also filled him with an overpowering anger. He went to the office and started calling to confirm Pam's information, using Elena's assumed name, Dowling. He called the Boston newspaper, and then talked to the police.

"No, we do not presently have a suspect. The investigation is ongoing."

Wes discovered how to claim her ashes. He met Sam at the front door after school, "I have some real bad news, son. You need to sit down."

After receiving the news, Sam left the house and didn't return until well after dark. He was sick with guilt. Sam had failed to call her. He finally asked his uncle what happened.

Wes told what he knew. He ended by saying, "I'll be taking off for a spell to see about her. Be back in a week, maybe ten days."

"What can you do?"

"I'm going to bring her ashes back and take care of her personal things. I need to see about what happened. We'll bury her with her mother."

"I want to go."

"No. It's better I do this alone."

Sam's anger flared. "Why? She's my mother! I'm going!"

"Look, boy, there are a few things I need to do by myself. Anyway, you can manage here alone. Truth is, I don't want you along, okay? There's nothing you can do." He was breathing hard. "So, no, dammit! The answer is no!"

Sam had never seen Wes confused or disorganized. "How did you find out? Who told you?"

Wes flipped his hand, annoyed by the boy's persistence. "Oh, some woman named Pam." His eyes suddenly snapped to Sam. "Why? You know her?"

"Yes. Mom's friend, sort of. I knew her. Did she know who killed Mom?"

"I'm not sure, but I think she does. She wouldn't give me a name, only an initial. I'm going to find out."

Sam stood, eyes wide. "D? Was the initial D?"

Wes looked surprised. He sprang forward and grabbed Sam by the shoulder and growled, "You know who this D is?"

Sam brushed Wes's hands away and stepped back, offended by his uncle's aggressiveness. "Yes, I know. Big black guy. He used to be her...he was her...."

Wes grabbed him again. "Tell me, dammit! Who is he? Out with it!"

Sam yelled, "Her pimp! He was her damned *pimp!*" Tears welled in his eyes.

Wes relaxed and let go, his eyes still boring in. "If you know who this D guy is, can you point him out?"

"Absolutely. Mom was scared to death of him. I would know him anywhere."

Wes stepped back, nodding, lost in thought. "All right then. All right. Good. Now I need to think. We'll talk later." He started for his office.

Sam followed. "I'm going. If you leave me, I'll just go by myself. But I'm going."

They left the ranch at two in the morning and drove straight through to Boston, arriving at three the next morning–fifteen-hundred miles in twenty-five hours.

Wes took a room at a shabby motel and they slept until noon. Wes rented a car and they drove to Elena's old neighborhood.

"You sure about this?"

"Absolutely. I lived here, remember. This is the right place. That's her apartment." Sam pointed to the second story window of an old brick building. "I used to play in the park across the street."

Wes left Sam in the car and approached a couple of winos on a park bench. For the price of a bottle of Mogen David he learned that the pimple-faced fifteen-year-old boy on the corner selling newspapers and packets of marijuana would know where D hung out.

"Hey, man, why you want D? If you're lookin' for some action, I know some hot stuff. Won't cost so–"

"No. I owe him. I need to get clean."

The kid laughed. "Owin' D? Man, that ain't no good, man. Don't say I told, but you can probably catch him at his hangout. They call it THE CLOSET."

Wes located the bar and parked across the street from D's hangout, a busy gay café bar. They waited.

At ten that evening, Sam tapped Wes's elbow and whispered, "That's him! That's him!" He pointed to a tall black man exiting a double-parked white Mercedes.

Wes moved his hand up and down to calm the boy. "Okay. Okay, just relax. We aren't going to do anything right now. Not here."

They discovered where D lived by following as he left the café near daybreak. Wes rented a ratty room across the street from the pimp's apartment, and then traded the rental car in for a panel work van. The two men moved into the room to watch and wait. Within two days they not only knew where D lived, that he lived alone, and when he left the house each evening. They also knew where he went and when he returned.

Sam grew more apprehensive. Wes hadn't told him anything, but he knew Wes well enough to know something was sure to happen. "What are we going to do now?"

"Nothing, just watch one more day just to be sure."

"Then what? Are you going to kill him?"

Wes seemed lost in thought. "Never you mind."

"Well, I do mind. I don't want to kill anyone."

Wes whirled, glaring fiercely. "That son of a bitch killed your mother, dammit!"

"I want to know what we are going to do. Are we going to kill him?"

"What the hell's this *we* business? No, I'm not going to kill him. But I'm damned sure going to leave him with a lasting memory."

"I'm going with you."

Wes studied the boy for a moment. "Forget about it. It won't be kid stuff."

Sam glared. "Kid stuff? She was my mother. I'm in, whatever it is."

Wes pondered Sam's announcement for a moment, then nodded. "Okay. I guess it is your business. You have a right."

D left after dark and Wes approached the pimp's place from the alley and searched through windows with a flashlight.

They spent the next morning acquiring supplies at hardware

and lumber stores–all purchases made with cash and never too many items from one place. That evening after D left for his nightly rounds, Wes strolled around the block, dropped over the rear fence and used a glass cutter to enter. He walked through D's apartment and unlocked the front door and crossed the street to the rented room and joined Sam. They donned white workman's coveralls with an electrical company's logo over the breast pocket of clothes purchased from a thrift store. After vacating the room and after carefully soaping away all fingerprints, they walked to the van two blocks away and drove to the front of D's apartment where they unloaded the equipment and parked the van.

Mister D arrived on schedule the next morning. He stepped inside, locked the door and turned for the living room where he found himself facing Sam in a ski mask standing behind a 45 caliber U. S. Army Colt automatic pistol. D's hands went up and he backed away, turning to leave only to come face-to-face with Wes, also in a ski mask, wielding a hunting knife.

Wes shoved D back to the living room. "You the guy they call D?"

D held his hands aloft, glancing from one masked man to the other. "What the hell is this? Look, don't do nothing crazy, man. What do you want? If it's money–"

Wes snarled, "Shut up!" He placed the knife point under D's chin. "You ever know a girl named Elena?" D, eyes wide with fright, turned toward Sam, looking for an avenue of escape, only to find the gun still directed at his forehead.

"Elena? No, man. I don't know no Elena."

Wes ran the knife blade lightly across D's throat. "You are a lying bastard. Lie to me one more time and I'll cut your damned head off." He pressed the knife point until it drew blood. "Now, what about Elena?"

"Look, I don't–"

The point pressed in. "I know what you do for a living, asshole, so lying is out. Now, what about Elena?"

"I only.... Look, okay, maybe she worked for me once, but I don't know what happened to her."

"She worked for you? Doing what?" The knife point drew more blood.

D's eyes widened. Beads of sweat popped out on his forehead.

"You know, man," he whined. "One of my girls. You know. She worked for me."

Wes had all he needed. "Just one of your girls. *Your* girls? Turn around!" Wes directed Sam to tape D's hands behind his back with duct tape. "Over his mouth and all the way around his head twice."

After Sam finished, he nodded his head and said, "Now, you piece of crap, get in the damned kitchen." He shoved, steering the pimp from behind.

D stopped. His eyes widened as he entered the room. Wes had screwed four heavy duty eye hooks into the kitchen floor, eight feet apart, forming a square, each hook with a six foot length of rope attached. D also noticed another rope hanging from a hook screwed into the cathedral ceiling–a rope hanging all the way to the floor. The duct tape muffled D's screams of protest as Wes shoved him to a position next to the hanging rope. He draped a loop over D's head and around his neck. The perspiring pimp was trembling violently, eyes wide, veins protruding.

Wes yanked on the rope, tightening the knot. "You have a choice. Either I hang your ass right now or you can lie down in the middle of the floor." He yanked the rope tighter.

D's knees folded. He wanted down.

Wes slackened the tension so D could lower himself. "On your back!" More yanks on the rope and the pimp lay spread-eagled between the hooks on the floor. Wes tied each ankle securely to a hook before cutting the tape from D's wrists. The pimp sat up and scrambled to release his feet.

"You might want to lend a hand here," Wes said dryly.

Sam grabbed the back of D's coat and pulled him down from behind. The perspiring pimp struggled desperately. Sam pulled on the rope hanging from the ceiling until D nearly passed out from lack of oxygen. Wes tied his wrists to the remaining hooks and then stood over the spread-eagled man unsheathing the hunting knife. D's eyes bulged. The duct tape barely muffled his screams.

Wes glanced at Sam and said, "Get over by the door. This won't take long. And give me that damned gun."

Sam hesitated, unsure of his uncle's intention.

Wes growled, "Don't you flake off on me now. Move it! We haven't got all day."

Sam handed the gun over. Wes jammed it under his belt. He

then cut the writhing man's trousers away from his crotch, exposing his genitals. D's head smashed against the floor repeatedly, flailing from side to side. He knew what was going to happen. He knew. His whimpering and thrashing escalated, straining the ropes.

"That should do it," Wes announced to himself, tossing the shredded clothing aside. He stood and pulled on a pair of rubber gloves. "I should kill you, but maybe this way is better." He brandished the knife. "You messed with the wrong woman, buddy."

Wes knelt between D's legs and with one hand pulled the skin of his scrotum away from his captive's writhing body. He sliced the bottom half of the scrotum off and dropped the swatch of skin on D's face. And then, one at a time, Wes jerked the testicles out, cords and all, and dropped them on the pimp's heaving chest.

Wes stood and gazed down for a moment before walking to the sink where he carefully removed the gloves and threw them into a metal waste basket already partially filled with wadded up papers. He lit the papers with a match and burned the gloves. After dowsing the fire, he leisurely washed his hands and the knife in a strong mixture of prepared ammonia and soap. He then turned again to the pimp, now writhing and moaning in a spreading pool of blood.

D whimpered from behind the tape, his eyes filled with tears. He either didn't have the strength to scream, or had given up. Wes picked up his tool box and walked around his victim cutting the restraining ropes. D cupped what remained of his genitals in his hands and rolled onto his side, folding into a fetal position.

Wes stopped at the door and said, "I expect you ought to call 911 before you bleed to death. I really don't give a damn one way or the other." He turned away so D couldn't see his face, pulled off the mask and used it to unlock the door. He ordered Sam to turn away and take his mask off. They pocketed the masks and walked out, kicking the door closed. Sam made it to the van before he threw up. Wes offered no sympathy.

They arrived at the ranch in the middle of the next night. Neither man ever mentioned the event again, other than minutes after leaving D moaning on the floor, Wes said, "That's the way my granddaddy would have handled it and that's the way my daddy would have handled it." He glanced over at Sam and smiled. "That's justice."

* * * * *

A week later, in room 23 at Mentone's motel, lying next to her partner while recovering from a passionate round of sex, Corporal Natasha Winkler said, "Hear about what happened to the D-man?" She always tried to make the pimp's name sound like demon.

Mister Clean chuckled. "Yeah. Damned shame, right? Someone nutted that slimy bastard. Talk about poetic justice."

"Not just that. Seems the D-man has lost it. Turned into a raving lunatic. Had to cart him off to a padded room. I hear he can't stop crying."

"Tsk, tsk. Aw shucks, damn. What a shame."

She murmured, "Uh huh. Any idea who did it?"

"Got a hunch. You?"

"Yup."

"You thinking what I am, Nat?"

"Probably. Like maybe some good ol' boy wearin' a cowboy hat?"

"Yeah. Like maybe someone who knew someone who got her throat cut?"

Nat propped herself on his chest and smiled. "We do think alike, don't we."

His smile changed to a look of concern. "You think we should report it?"

"I don't know. Are the dicks working it?"

"Just for show. Paperwork. Not askin' around much. Why would they?"

She rolled off and patted his chest. "Well, then I already forgot."

"Yeah, me too. I think he shudda killed him, though."

"Nah. He got it right."

CHAPTER EIGHT

Justice

S am played more during the last half of the basketball season, starring in several games. A growing entourage of college scouts attended Raven games and he received several packets of D-One university information. Most of Sam's teammates accepted that they couldn't win the big games without him. Clyde Townsend threatened to quit when the coach started Sam in his place during a crucial game. Clyde's animosity toward Sam increased, nearing the point of violence. He taunted and ridiculed Sam openly, pushing his ability and willingness to comply with the judge's edict against fighting. Sam went to the coach.

"What do you want, Prescott?" Coach Roush frowned from behind his desk, unhappy with the intrusion.

"I want to talk about Townsend, Sir."

Roush slammed his pen down. "Oh, really? Well, what about?"

"He's pushing me, Coach. Making me look bad."

Roush rocked back with a scornful smile. "And that's my problem?"

"Well, yes and no, Sir. If I defend myself, as you know, I could be thrown out of school. I'd have to go back to Boston. But if I don't do anything, I look like a coward."

Roush smiled sarcastically. "What do you want from me?"

Sam figured talking to Roush would be a waste. "I could use some help."

The coach laughed, enjoying Sam's discomfort. "And you expect me to solve your little problem with Townsend?"

Sam squared his shoulders and stood at attention, looking at the wall behind the coach. "No, Sir. I want to solve it myself."

"You mean fight him?" He snorted. "Clyde Townsend would whip your ass all over this school."

"Maybe."

"Maybe? Do you actually want to fight him?" Roush looked skeptical.

"No, but I need to face up to him. If he wants to fight after that, then so be it."

Roush rocked forward, doodling on a tablet for several seconds, then looked up and said, "You're worried I'll report you to the judge?"

"Yes, Sir. I don't want to go back to Boston–not to detention."

Roush leaned back imperiously. "All right. Do what you have to do, just not in my school. I won't report anything you do away from school. That any help?" He forced an insincere smile.

Sam had known Roush wouldn't take his side, but the "not in my school" comment was more than he hoped for. He muttered thanks and walked out.

As Sam's stock in basketball went up, so did his troubles with Clyde Townsend. Clyde went out of his way to taunt and badger, calling him a coward in front of the other students, and during lunch in the cafeteria, and in front of the entire team and most of the high school students, loudly proclaiming that Sam could no longer park his truck in the school parking lot.

"I don't want to see that piece of crap again. Keep it out of my sight." The boys laughed and the girls giggled. Cynthia turned away, embarrassed for Sam, ashamed of her interest in him. Sam got up and walked out, avoiding conflict again and bringing more dishonor.

Clyde had the Appleby boys trash Sam's truck during the next away game. They broke all the windows and lights, flattened the tires, stole the battery and crapped on the seat. Everyone in school knew about it. Clyde baited Sam the next day, "Someone crap in my truck, I'd find out and take care of 'em. I told you not to park it there."

Wes had the truck towed. He told Sam to ride the bus from then on. "You just give him another target by driving it. He'll sure have it trashed again. No sense asking for trouble."

"What about the sheriff?"

Wes huffed. "Hell, he won't do anything. Anyway, what proof can you give him? It's a bum deal. You need to let it go. Forget about it."

Sam caught Cynthia alone in the store one evening after practice. "Want to go to Springfield to a show Saturday?"

Her eyebrows raised, disbelieving. "Are you kidding? With you?"

He laughed. "Of course. Did you think I was asking for someone else?"

She wouldn't look at him. "I would rather not go any place with you."

"I'd rather you did."

She turned on him. "I don't even want to be seen alone in the store with you. You're an embarrassment." She shouted, releasing her anger and frustration, "Clyde makes you look ridiculous. You're a coward! Now leave me alone!"

He backed away. "I'm not a coward. I just can't...." He turned away and left the store and stayed completely away from her. Cynthia stopped coming to the games.

Wickmore won their six remaining regular season games. The Ravens also won the district tournament and were scheduled to play their traditional rival, Picton, in the finals of the sectional tournament to determine which team advanced to the final four and possible state championship. Throughout the long winning streak, Sam remained isolated; standing outside team huddles; never complaining about not starting; never expressing discontent that his teammates wouldn't pass the ball to him unless they had to and then only when they needed him to win.

Wes attended the games, sitting quietly above the crowd, thinking Sam seemed oddly at peace with his circumstances. He kept his thoughts to himself but could not identify with Sam's apparent willingness to accept disrespect from his teammates and coach.

After a game Wickmore won easily, a game that found Sam sitting on the bench most of the time, Wes asked, "Does it bother you that you could have easily won the state scoring championship if Roush played you regularly? Does it bother you that he has probably wrecked your chance to make All State?"

"Sure. But what can I do about it? I talked to him. He has issues with me. What goes around comes around, though."

"What the hell does that mean?"

Sam shrugged and changed the subject.

At dinner the night before the game with Picton, Wes said, "I got news from Washington."

Sam looked up, hopeful but concerned. "From your old roomy?"

"Yep. Tells me West Point is going to pass on your police record. No felony–no problem. So it looks like you're in if you still want it."

Sam's face broke into an unrestrained smile. "You must be kidding? Of course I want it."

"No, I'm not kidding. I called the judge; I called your old headmaster; I called the police. They all agreed to send recommendations. My old roomy thinks you're a great fit for West Point. The appointment is a done deal. Congratulations."

Sam jumped up and rushed around the table. He hesitated short of a hug, unable to break the barrier of familiarity. He patted his uncle on the back. "Thank you so much. God, this is great. I mean it." He danced around the room, fist raised in celebration, grinning uncontrollably. He stopped, stood still, and then slowly turned to Wes, still not sure. "I can't believe it. You're serious? This is for real?"

Wes was pleased to see the boy express emotion. "Absolutely. Now you listen to me. Keep this to yourself. Roush, and others, could still screw it up. You're still on probation. Judge Walcott wanted me to tell you that she will vacate the final year of your probation if you take the appointment. Said to tell you she's proud of you."

"I still don't know how you did it, but this is so great. Thanks again."

"Not necessary. Obstacles are just little problems to be overcome."

* * * * *

Cynthia ran after Sam as he walked to the bus after school, fully aware that everyone in school could see her. She knew they would be whispering and pointing. "Sam!" she cried. "Sam! Wait!" He stopped and she caught up, breathless. "I'm really sorry I called you a coward."

He wasn't ready to forgive. "Really? So I'm a hero now?"

"Mother told me about what happened to you in Boston. About the order not to fight. I didn't know, Sam. I'm so sorry. I'm really sorry."

He frowned, upset that Coach Roush had revealed his secret. "That's just great. Now everyone knows." He hesitated, thinking, and then said, "Why did your mom tell you?"

"I told her you asked me out. She thinks you're bad and doesn't want me to see you."

"I see. What do you think?"

"I just wanted to say I'm sorry. Oh, and good luck tonight."

"Thanks, I guess." He backed toward the bus, eyes locked on her, thinking more about the leak of his Boston record.

She waved and said, "Maybe we could talk sometime?"

He nodded. "Yeah, maybe."

Sam rode the team bus to the game to be held at a local college. He changed into uniform, packed street clothes in his gym bag, and then went to the gym early to search for Wes in the crowd. He motioned for Wes to come down. "I want you to hold on to my things, just in case."

Wes took the bag, his face registering concern. "You want to tell me what's going on?"

Sam stepped back, reluctant to enter a lengthy conversation. "Maybe nothing. I just want to be ready."

"For what?" He reached for Sam's arm. "What's going on?"

Sam pulled away and departed, shouting over his shoulder. "I'm not sure! We'll see!"

After warmups and National Anthem, the announcer made a ceremony of presenting the starting players one by one, Picton first. Clyde Townsend represented the final Wickmore player. Sam was not in the starting lineup. He walked over and tapped Coach Roush on the shoulder. When the coach turned, he said, "Either me or Townsend, Coach."

Roush looked irritated. "What did you say?"

"I said, it's either him or me, Coach. If you start Townsend, I quit."

Roush could have been looking at an oncoming eighteen wheeler, the ultimatum took him so unexpectedly. "What?" He grabbed Sam by his jersey and pulled him close, growling, "I'll put you in when I want you in, Prescott. Now sit the hell down!" He shoved Sam toward the bench. Sam resisted, stripping the coaches' hands away, standing his ground.

By then most of the people in the packed gym knew something was amiss. The background rumble of conversational noise hushed as the scene at Wickmore's bench played out. People craned their necks to see, whispering and pointing.

Sam stepped back. "I'm not kidding, Coach."

Roush looked around and realized that he was the center of attention. He stepped closer and whispered, "What the hell are you saying? Are you quitting?"

"Not yet. But I'm not going to play behind Townsend, Coach. Either start me or I am going to walk away."

Roush's face turned crimson, his jaws working. "You can't tell me to–"

Sam pulled the jersey over his head and held it out. "If you think Clyde can win this game for you, then take this jersey. But if you're depending on me, you have to start me."

Roush stepped back, unwilling to take the jersey, and then blustered, "I won't have it! What the hell! I won't have it. You can't tell...."

Sam tossed the jersey at Roush and walked off the court while motioning to Wes. The crowd began buzzing. The noise increased to a roar of confusion. He could hear Roush screaming, "Get back here, Prescott! You get back here!"

Wes met him at the door, gym bag in hand. "You sure you want to do this, son?"

"I'm sure."

Wes nodded. "Okay, it's your call, but give me a minute. I'll be right back." He marched toward Roush, now standing beside the huddle of boys in front of the Wickmore bench, looking disoriented. Roush saw Wes coming and intercepted him.

"You dumb bastard!" Wes said loud enough for half the people in the gym to hear. "You just let your chance for a state championship walk away!"

Roush screamed, "He quit! I didn't throw him out! He quit!"

"Bullshit! You have done everything possible to make him quit!" He grabbed Roush by the lapel and pulled him close. "She wasn't screwing the boy. She was screwing me." He shoved Roush away and left the court. On the way home, Wes said, "Well, you left them with a lasting memory. Damned sure cemented your name in Wickmore's Prescott hall of fame. How the hell long have you been thinking about doing that?"

Sam looked straight ahead. "Long enough."

"That figures. Well, they are sure never going to forget you." Wes patted Sam on the knee, smiled and said, "Really, it was kinda entertaining, though, don't you think?"

Sam's grim expression didn't alter. "No, that was justice."

They looked at each other and burst out laughing.

Wes pointed to the radio. "Want to listen to the game?"

"Nah. I'd just as soon forget about all of it."

Wickmore lost by twenty-five points. Picton's Jerry Evans ran free all night, scoring forty points. Picton went on to win the state championship.

* * * * *

Edwin Roush pulled into his drive at midnight after the game. He slammed the door of his pickup and looked to the heavens. He cursed and yelled, damning the empty sky. His anger didn't slacken but his strength waned until only tears remained as evidence of his wrath. Edwin's anger skyrocketed beyond human endurance a few moments later after encountering Irma sitting in the kitchen waiting for him. Irma the Christian; Irma, the long suffering wife; Irma, the torment of his life.

"Would it have killed you to start that boy?" she said, taking a sip of coffee, eyes locked on his.

"What the hell are you talking about." He hung his coat and turned, ready to level his anger at her, the always available target.

"What I'm talking about is your hatred for Wes Prescott. Hatred brought this on you, Edwin. The Devil's hatred. What did that boy ever do to you? Everyone knows he's the only reason you won anything this year. I'm surprised he stayed with you this long, treating him the way you did. You brought this night on yourself, Edwin; you and your hatred for anything Prescott."

Roush couldn't believe she would favor a Prescott over him at a time like this. His anger soared. He hovered over her, fist cocked. "He quit, damn you! He waited until we had to have him, and then he quit! He deliberately ruined our season! You saw it! You were there! What happened had nothing to do with Wes!"

She looked up at him, eyes filled with sadness, not sympathy. She spoke quietly, with no emotion, "Now Edwin, you know as well as I do that what happened tonight had nothing to do with that boy. You just can't forget about me and Wes."

"He quit! The son of a bitch quit!"

She stood, preparing to leave. "Edwin, when you calm down, you will recognize that your hatred has provoked God."

"So, now it's my fault, is it?" He lashed out, knocking a chair across the room. "So now I'm the bad guy!"

She walked to the bedroom door and stopped, tossing final words over her shoulder. "That boy was the best player you ever had. You lost tonight because you can't forget and forgive. I'm sorry for you."

Edwin watched the door close. He listened as the lock snapped. His anger evaporated, driven away by reality. Irma hadn't locked him out since the night he accused her of having an affair with Wes Prescott. She had not responded to his accusations, just shut him out for more than two years. He needed her so much. He could never sustain enough outrage or indignation to press his suspicions. He could have caught them, no doubt, but what then? She would have left home if he pressed the issue, he knew that, just as he knew his suspicions about the affair were accurate. He understood why she suffered periods of depression. *Damned Prescotts.* One had his wife's heart and the other had taken the heart out of him. *Damned Prescotts.*

* * * * *

Sam's final encounter with Clyde happened a week after the game, between classes in the boy's bathroom. Clyde had waited for the opportunity, entering the bathroom after Sam. "You screwed the team, Prescott. You're a damned quitter." He poked Sam in the chest.

Sam knew there would be no escape from a confrontation. "I'm *your* substitute, Clyde. Why didn't you win the game?"

Clyde opened his fly. "I'm going to piss on you, you yellow bastard."

As Clyde groped in his trousers, Sam grabbed him by the throat, slamming him against the wall so violently that Clyde didn't have a chance to get his hand out of his pants. Sam's fingers dug in, crushing Clyde's windpipe, shutting off the oxygen. He squeezed until Clyde turned purple, blood vessels protruding on his neck and forehead. Sam leaned close and said, "Don't you ever mess with me again." He didn't relax his grip until Townsend slid down the wall to sit on the floor gasping and choking for air.

Clyde quit school the next day.

Sam told Wes about the encounter and Wes shook his head, scowling, troubled by the news. "Ah, dammit, son. Dammit all to hell anyway! That's not good." He thought a moment, then said, "Well, I wondered if you would be able to hold out. Lasted longer than I would have. Dammit to hell. Let's hope this doesn't come back on you. What are you going to say to Roush if it does?"

"Nothing. Clyde's word against mine."

Wes nodded. "You're right. Townsend won't say anything. Too embarrassing. He will damned sure try to get even, though. Watch yourself."

Sam attended school sparingly after the Picton game, and skipped graduation ceremonies. He entered West Point a month later.

CHAPTER NINE

Loss of Innocence

Sam's life shimmered with promise, but the world Cynthia Roush knew ended during her senior year. Wickmore's veneer of heartland wholesomeness, as she had perceived it all her life, peeled away revealing her perceptions to be childish wishful thinking.

She really hadn't noticed anything more than a worrisome accumulation of little disappointments; nothing ominous to suggest the coming apocalypse. Signs of corruption had always been there, scattered details easily overlooked by a naive girl; signals and signs that gradually evolved into evidence, and that evidence congealed into a condemning indictment. Two senior boys were expelled for disciplinary reasons. Clyde Townsend quit. Four juniors lost interest and stopped attending school. Two girls, both sophomores, quit after becoming too obviously pregnant. No one said much.

"You need a diploma, Tommy," she told one of the boys, hoping he would stay.

"Ah, that's bull crap. My dad don't have no diploma. My brothers are doing okay without that dumb piece of paper. They all got good jobs at the cheese plant in Brewster."

In the end, Cynthia could only watch as the dropouts drifted away. She began to observe Wickmore more critically along the way, attempting to sort out reasons for the traditional exodus of kids from school.

Cynthia talked about her new conclusions with Irma. "It's the redneck code of conduct, Mother. They seem to instinctively self-destruct."

"Well, miss smarty, you better just keep those ideas to yourself. People around here don't take kindly to being put down."

School wasn't much fun after the boys quit, but an even more decisive event crept in a few days later to defile her last bastion of joy. The church failed her. She had faithfully served Wickmore's Assembly of God; attending the little white clapboard church every week of her life; every Sunday morning and Wednesday evening.

Wickmore's church only pretended an affiliation with the world wide Assembly of God ministries. Wickmore's church was not chartered and never had an ordained minister. The international parent organization didn't know the Wickmore AG church existed. The little church featured a hybrid brand of religion, calling themselves Assembly of God but practicing an adulterated variation of Pentecostal services including speaking in tongues and snake handling.

Arliegh Mitchell served as preacher. Arliegh had strayed from the fold as a youth, spending years sampling the wares of the pagan world, experiences that rendered him uniquely qualified to preach about the wages of sin. He knew all about wickedness.

His metamorphosis from drunken deadbeat to man-of-the-cloth seemed remarkable, even by Wickmore standards. Only months before he assumed the local pulpit, everyone in the community knew Arliegh Mitchell as a craven sinner. God's "call" came during a thirty day period of hospitalization as Arliegh recovered from an alcohol-influenced automobile wreck that by all rights should have killed him. It didn't matter to the congregation what mysterious power had summoned Arliegh back to the fold–the prodigal had come home.

"Praise God!"

"It's a miracle. God works in mysterious ways."

"It's the work of The Lord."

"Amen."

Never in Arliegh's life had amnesty for his sins come so quick and easy. His transition to the pulpit crowned the crest of a wave of adoration and congregational curiosity. As it worked out, Arliegh was pretty good up front. Emotional and sincere.

With little practice, education or experience, Arliegh assumed the duties of preacher from the congregation's bedridden minister. It felt natural. Arliegh Mitchell was home at last. No personality transformation ever happened so swiftly or thoroughly as Arliegh's transition from drunken bum to God-fearing preacher.

Jimmy Colvard paused from the chores of dehorning calves one day to take a breather and speak to his helper, Lonnie Howard, about Arliegh.

"Hey, Lon. You seen ol' Arliegh lately?"

"Nope. He don't come fishing with me no more. Hear tell he got religion."

"Tell me about it. Hell, I saw him just yesterday, awearin' a damned necktie and low-cut shoes. Keeps that hair all slicked back. He's even took to usin' shavin' lotion, or perfume–some such. Smells like a French whorehouse. Mom says he's took to visitin' the old folks home regular."

Lonnie shook his head sadly. "Damndest thing I ever heard. Arliegh damned Mitchell? You sure?"

"Yep, fer a fact. Ol' Arliegh's got religion sure enough."

That spring, Arliegh led an ill-advised attempt to have undesirable books thrown out of the school library, only to find his name splattered on the front page of the Springfield newspaper. A few weeks later he rented a carnival tent and started holding brush arbor revivals for less fortunate congregations in nearby communities. Some Wickmore people forgot about his speckled past; others waited for the collapse they felt sure would come.

Cynthia played the piano for Arliegh's services, as she had for the church's old minister. Her mother never missed a service and made sure Cynthia attended. The little church provided the substance of their spiritual and social life. Without the church and The Holy Gospel their lives would have been a waste, lacking direction and spiritual joy. Cynthia needed God, Jesus and the soothing shelter of religion.

She felt guilty about one glaring inadequacy–she could not speak in tongues. Irma could lose herself in tongues as most of the congregation could, but not Cynthia. She doubted the depth of her convictions.

What other reason could there be for such weakness?

She prayed for the ability to yield to the Spirit, to speak with divine fervor. She prayed to be one of the blessed members of the congregation who could surrender their inhibitions and celebrate in ecstasy. She failed. Some obstinate threshold of restraint always prevented a demonstration of devotion.

Cynthia thrilled to the words and sincerity of the new preacher. "He's wonderful, Mother. So sincere."

"Yes, Arliegh is a breath of fresh air. The congregation is filled with new energy."

Arliegh possessed charismatic intensity that energized even the weakest believer. His deep voice and absolute confidence carried the congregation to new heights of spiritual enthusiasm.

Cynthia never felt quite comfortable around Arliegh, though– not like the old preacher. Something about him, the way his eyes followed her–always watching. She didn't dwell on the uneasiness, for she loved listening to him, subduing the troublesome wariness that always seem to surface in his presence.

Her anxieties about Arliegh were unmasked in a blast of reality one brisk autumn Wednesday before evening services. She arrived at church early at Arliegh's request to practice music selected for the program. He stood beside her as she played, his eyes closed in a spiritual trance.

After she finished the first number he said, "Will you pray with me?"

She closed the hymnal and bowed her head.

"Not here, child. Come outside with me. Unite with God in his own realm."

Cynthia, conditioned to obedience and respect for church authority, though apprehensive, followed. Arliegh represented The Lord. He led through the back door and they stood beside the church in darkness.

"Do you *believe* I am God's messenger?" he asked, his voice a hoarse whisper.

The question made her uncomfortable, as did his hands on her shoulders.

"Um, yes, I...." She stammered, confused by his closeness.

The intensity of his voice strengthened. "And do you *believe* I am God's chosen voice in this *wilderness*?"

Her anxiety soared. The insistent urging of his hands commanded an answer.

"I do."

"Do you feel the *power* of the Lord in my hands?" He always pronounced God, Lord and Jesus with an uh. Lord-uh. God-uh.

"I...." She stammered, unable to recognize his bizarre behavior. His hands moved to her forehead.

"Then in the name of the *Lord*, I purge all sin and *guilt* from your thoughts. If you are a true servant of God, *believe*! Do you *believe*?" His voice crackled with emotion.

"I want to," she whispered, beginning to tremble, eyes closed.

His hands weighed heavily. "Do you *believe* I can purge Satan from your heart and soul?" His hands pressed more firmly and his voice strengthened, demanding.

His earnestness and passion worried Cynthia.

His hands pressed firmly against her forehead. "Do you *believe*?" he demanded.

"Yes," she whispered.

"Then I *command* the devil and his *spirit* from your body. *I command! I command! I command! I command!*" His hands moved each time he uttered the phrase–first to her neck, then to her shoulders, her arms, and then to her breasts. She froze for a moment, brushed his hands away and stepped back. His eyes were still closed, head tilted back. He appeared to be in a trance. His arms dropped and he opened his eyes as if coming out of a spell. "You are cleansed now," he said.

Cynthia spun away and ran back into the church. Arliegh never said anything to her about the incident but "accidentally" brushed against her at every opportunity. He created excuses for physical contact. He seemed to be fixated on her breasts. His eyes seldom missed an opportunity. Cynthia stopped going to church without Irma after that. Her disenchantment with Wickmore deepened.

Irma noticed. One evening as they cleaned the store she said, "What's the matter with you, girl? Aren't you happy? High school years are the best days of your life. Enjoy life while you can. These are your good times."

"Gee thanks. Is that supposed make me feel better?" She leaned on the broom, watching her mother. "I'm so tired of this stupid town. I just want to get away."

Irma stopped dusting to study her daughter. "You've changed, you know that? You are so serious. Well, maybe it's just a cycle." She went back to work. "You'll get over it."

Cynthia's enthusiasm for school and Wickmore continued to wane. Her duties at the store after school each day and weekends separated her from the few social opportunities Wickmore provided.

Irma fussed, "You worry me. You should spend more time with your friends."

"I don't want to, Mother. Sitting on the hood of a pickup on main street drinking beer does not appeal to me. That's all the boys want to do."

"There is more to the world than boys. What about Sheila and Marge? I never see you with them anymore."

"Marge is pregnant, Mother, and Sheila is going to be soon if she doesn't.... Never mind."

"Marge is pregnant?"

"She is. Not only that, two sophomore girls got pregnant and quit. The little Dalton girl and Gloria Hurd."

"Good heavens!" Irma thought a moment. "Well, some things never change."

* * * * *

Cynthia's friends noticed her disenchantment and began avoiding her. "Look at her. That stuck up nose in the air, ignoring everyone."

"Yeah, Little Miss Goody Two Shoes."

"She told Amber she can't wait to get away from Wickmore. Guess we aren't good enough for her."

"Who cares? She's so snooty."

Cynthia had always planned to leave Wickmore after graduation and had applied for scholarships at several colleges.

Irma wasn't enthused about Cynthia's plans to attend college. "I don't know where you think the money's coming from. The store went in the red last year and your father has lost money gamb.... Well, never mind. I just don't know how we can manage." She and Edwin no longer lived together, not after basketball season. Edwin was drinking again, a habit he had relied upon several times during their marriage. After he ignored several ultimatums, she moved to the upstairs apartment over the store.

Graduation day came and went with no scholarship. Cynthia's optimism wavered. Reply after reply came through the mail: unfunded; try again next year; unable to approve; no scholarship available.

She graduated with a 3.98 grade point average but barely broke into the lower 90th percentile on the national SATS test. After a visit with a counselor from a nearby college, Cynthia discovered that her test scores reflected Wickmore's inability to educate, not her ability to learn. She wasn't competitive with students from good schools.

A college placement officer told her, "You are obviously very intelligent, according to your IQ score, Miss Roush, but your SATS score and lack of AP classes isn't going to win an academic scholarship at this university. I'm sorry."

Cynthia eventually despaired, breaking into tears. "I'm useless, Mother. I feel so ignorant."

Irma, uncharacteristically, held the heartbroken girl in an attempt to console. "Maybe you're aiming too high, child. Why don't you just find a decent job in Springfield and worry about college later. Concentrate on something a little more down-to-earth."

"No! I am *not* going to spend the rest of my life working in a garment factory or waitressing at some greasy spoon restaurant. I am *not* going to work for minimum wages, Mother. I'm going to college. I have to go to college."

"Well, I think you're just setting yourself up for disappointment."

"I won't give up, Mother. I will never give up!" She wiped the tears away and took a deep breath. "Okay, I have to face facts. Tomorrow. Yes, tomorrow, I'm going to Springfield, Mother. I'll find a job. I'll make my own way, but I am going to college no matter how long it takes or how much I have to scrimp. I'm going." She walked away calmly, locked the bedroom door, fell on the bed and let the tears of disappointment pour.

Irma stayed downstairs in the store long after turning the lights out, feeling guilty for not having provided a better life for her daughter. She could escape the commonness and drudgery of her own life through God, but couldn't ignore Cynthia's plight. She sat alone in the darkness, brooding, then yelled up the stairs, "I'm going out for a spell. Don't wait up."

"Where're you going?" Irma never went out after dark except on church nights.

"I need some time alone. I'm just going for a drive."

Cynthia fell asleep before Irma came home. She had no idea when her mother returned. The next morning, Saturday, Irma's eyes looked puffy, entombed in dark, cavernous circles. She closed the store at noon and drove off again, returning near nightfall. The next day she asked Cynthia to run the store and remained secluded in her room until she had to come down to take a phone call.

Cynthia answered the call initially. "May I ask who is calling?"

"No. Just let me talk to Irma."

"Mother isn't feeling well. I could take a message."

"No, dammit, I need to talk to her."

Cynthia gave in and yelled up the stairs. Irma crept down, took the phone, turned away from Cynthia and whispered, "This is Irma."

Cynthia watched anxiously, fears mounting. Irma didn't speak again for what seemed like an eternity. She cradled the phone, shielding her face, then murmured, "Thank you. Thank you so much." She replaced the receiver gently, then patted the phone. The hint of a smile slowly crept across her face.

"Who was that, Mother?"

"Don't ask. Anyway, it doesn't make any difference." She turned to Cynthia and hugged her, uncharacteristically expressive. "I got good news for you, honey. You *are* going to college."

Cynthia pulled away, alarmed by Irma's tears. *What in the world is happening?* Irma never cried, and Irma didn't hug, and Irma never called her honey, and Irma never went off driving at night by herself, either, or close the store, or.... "Mother! What is going on? What have you done?" She began to envision terrible things: *Did she mortgage the store?* "Mother? Talk to me."

Irma brushed the tears away, smoothed the tired wrinkles from her face and forced a tight smile. "Never you mind." She straightened her rumpled dress, put on the same old apron and began stocking a shelf with canned green beans. Cynthia trailed along, stubbornly demanding an explanation.

"Mother, don't treat me this way. What have you done? Tell me!"

Irma smiled to herself, humming a tuneless song. "I got the money for your college. That's what is going on. I got it and it isn't going to work a hardship on me. I didn't do anything illegal or immoral, if that's what you're thinking. I just did something I should have done a long time ago, that's all. Past that I will not say another word. The money's in your name at the Empire bank in Springfield. You should receive a checkbook in the mail tomorrow."

"Where did you get the money, Mother?" She pulled Irma around by the shoulder and demanded, "Mother, would you please, please tell me what is going on?"

"No. I got it and that's all that matters. Now don't ask more silly questions."

Cynthia couldn't comprehend the startling news, or the sudden change in her mother. Her imagination ran wild.

"I won't take it! I know something is wrong. Did you borrow money against the store? You did, didn't you? I won't let you do that, Mother. I won't take it."

Irma stopped working and faced her daughter. "Oh, yes you *will* take it, girl! It's yours by heaven, and as Jesus is my savior you *will* take it and you *will* go to college. The money is already in the bank and there isn't a thing I can do about it now. So," she smiled reassuringly, "that's that. I'm happy for you and I'm happy for me and there's nothing you can do or say to change anything. Now, would you please just go away and leave me alone so I can work in peace?"

Cynthia could only stare. Her mother genuinely appeared to be happy. Irma's contented smile helped settle Cynthia's anxieties. She hugged until Irma pushed away, reclaiming the reserved manner that marked their stoic relationship.

"I don't know how you did it, Mother. I hope you'll tell me someday. I just can't believe it."

"Oh, it's true. Please get out of here and let me be. Just go."

"Thank you, Mother. Oh, thank you." Cynthia backed slowly toward the door, watching Irma for a sign that might help solve the mystery, only to be mystified all the more by her mother's secret smile. She started to say something but Irma shushed her. She finally left the store, puzzled, concerned, and deliriously happy.

After the door's warning bell stopped tinkling, Irma again turned back to her work. "I can't believe it either, girl. About time."

Cynthia returned shortly. The good news was sinking in and

she couldn't contain her excitement. She held the door open and said, "Mother, I'm going down to the bridge. I'll be back in an hour or two if that's okay?" Irma nodded and waved, happy to be alone.

The two-mile walk to the bridge had served her well on many occasions; a quiet time to sort out happy and sad times alike. Today the walk brought everything good about her life into focus. The world looked beautiful. Two miles of tree-lined fence rows, rolling fields of grass, herds of cattle and birds singing. She didn't see the dust and broken fences or the run-down homes.

Clyde Townsend and the Appleby brothers roared past in a beat-up hay truck on their way to town, yelling and hooting. She had less than a quarter of a mile to gain the welcome shade of the bridge and the spring-fed waters running beneath. Clyde still bothered her all the time, asking for dates, hanging around the store. She tried to avoid him but he always seemed to show up when she had the store by herself. She only spoke to him because he was a customer. He usually had something dirty to say: "I've got something for you, Roush. I'm ready anytime you are, baby. Quit being so stuck up, Roush. Live a little. Let's have some fun. Trust me, you'll like it."

Clyde didn't frighten her, but she detested being alone at the store with him. The Appleby brothers, his constant companions, took great pleasure in Clyde's remarks. Their high-pitched laughter grated on her nerves. They occasionally upset product displays with their adolescent jostling. The twins provided an appreciative audience for Clyde's off-colored comments. Their presence spurred Townsend to greater heights. He spoke loudly enough while making suggestive remarks to include them in the thrill of the moment.

"Ol' Clyde, he's sure a pistol, ain't he, Tom?"

"Yeah. Yeah. I'd sure like to look in that shirt of yours, baby. That's what he said. He's a pistol."

Cynthia reached the bridge and settled on a flat rock in the shade beneath the span. Ten minutes later her breathing slowed as she recognized the sound of Clyde's truck returning from town. She, and everyone else in the community, could identify Clyde's truck by the unmuffled sound of the engine. She listened, tensing as the truck stopped just before it reached the bridge, then sighed resentfully as three boisterous voices approached, coming down the path to the river. Cynthia retrieved her shoes and prepared to exit the scene, but too late to escape their attention.

Tom's high-pitched voice piped, "She's still here! I told ya!" They started running.

Townsend skidded to a stop on the gravel bank in front of her. "Come on, Roush! Let's you and me go skinny dipping. What do you say?"

The Applebys roared approval, punching each other as the potential for excitement blossomed. Clyde dashed over to stand in Cynthia's way as she started up the path toward the road.

"Come on, Roush. You're not afraid of a little water, are you?"

Cynthia kept her head down, unwilling to join in the banter, beginning to feel the rush of fright. Clyde jumped back and forth across the path in front of her until she finally stopped. She tried to look bored and perplexed. "You're such a pain, Clyde. Honestly."

"You're such a pain, Clyde," he mimicked. "Come on, let's go swimming." He leered, moving closer, bumping into her.

She pushed him away. "This is childish."

He mocked her again, "This is childish." He pushed back. "Okay, I'll tell you what, if you come swimming, and if you act real nice, I'll let you go, Roush."

Anger took place of Cynthia's fear. She spoke sharply, "You are not holding me here and I am not about to go swimming with you. Now get out of the way."

Her angry outburst sobered him. The cocky, boasting sneer faded and his face lost all expression. He turned his head to the side, toward the Applebys, now watching intently, but his eyes didn't leave her. "She don't want to go swimming with us. We're making her mad. What do you boys think of that? Don't you think little Miss Perfect here is getting too big for her britches?"

The brothers, sensing a new thrill, closed to stand on both sides of Townsend, forming a barrier. Cynthia began to worry about their behavior. Waves of fright washed over her, turning to desperation. She stepped from the path to maneuver around them, toward the safety of the road. Clyde pushed her back forcefully. She slipped and stumbled before catching her balance. He moved to block her way again.

The expression on his face paralyzed her. He looked ferocious, eyes cold and hateful. He appeared to be on the verge of striking her.

"I've had it with you. Damned stuck up bitch! By God, you are going swimming with me, like it or not!" He reached for her.

Her fright changed to pure panic. The situation had progressed from bad to worse in an instant. Cynthia wondered if the three men were on drugs or drunk. Townsend had never called her names before. She hardly recognized the malevolent man who seemed so determined to torment her. She twisted away from his clutching hands. The sudden movement assisted his fingers as they tore the sleeve of her blouse. She broke free, ripping buttons, exposing her breasts.

Her mind stopped racing in an instant as the seriousness of the situation struck home. She hit Clyde on the side of his face with a clenched fist. He jerked back, stunned by her reaction, then burst out laughing.

"Did you boys see that? Gawd dayum! All I wanted was a friendly little swim and she hauls off and smacks the crap out of me! I think it's about time this bitch gets what's been coming. What do you boys think?" The Applebys nodded, drool slipping from the corner of Tom's mouth.

Clyde took command. "Okay, grab her arms!" His trusty henchmen jumped to positions on either side of Cynthia. Her eyes revealed fright, providing her assailants even more confidence. Townsend's hand shot out, catching her hair while the Applebys wrestled for control of her arms. Cynthia fought against the strength of three work-hardened men. They gained control with little difficulty.

Townsend held her by the hair and led the way back to the shaded area beneath the bridge. Cynthia stumbled and tripped, dismayed that her breasts were uncovered. Clyde released her hair under the bridge. The Applebys maintained control of her arms. He stood in front of her grinning victoriously, slowly removing his belt.

Cynthia begged the brothers to let her go, but their attention was riveted on Townsend, awaiting his next command. Her pleas fell on deaf ears.

"Here," Townsend said, tossing the belt to one of the brothers. "Tie her legs together. I don't want the bitch kicking me."

The Applebys wrestled her to the ground and soon had the belt tied securely.

"Okay, stand her up!" Townsend commanded.

Cynthia noticed the growing bulge between his legs and her fright careened out of control. She knew he had gone too far. He wasn't going to stop. Clyde stepped close and leisurely unfastened the remaining two buttons on her blouse.

"I've always wanted to see what you got in here," he said. The last button snapped open.

"Please, Clyde, don't do this. Please stop. Let me go." Tears flowed steadily as she begged.

"Well, lookee here!" he said, pulling the blouse over her shoulders. "Would you look in here. She's got a whole shirt-full of tits in here, boys. And look at this–ain't this cute?"

He played with the front-opening snap of her bra. "Isn't this clever," he said, released the snap. Both cups fell away leaving her completely exposed to the eyes of her captors. One of the brothers reached. Clyde slapped his hand away roughly.

"She's mine, asshole! Hands off until I'm through."

Townsend stripped the bra away and threw it to the ground. He gazed at her for a moment and placed his hands on her bare waist, sliding them up slowly to cup her breasts. Cynthia screamed as loud as she could. She tried to bite him. Clyde didn't release her breasts. He massaged them roughly, rolling the nipples between his thumb and fingers.

"It ain't gonna to do you no good to yell. They ain't nobody to hear you. Just relax and enjoy it. You've had this coming for a long time."

Cynthia screamed until her throat ached. She tried to bite him again but one of the brothers held her by the hair. Townsend unbuttoned her skirt. She tried to drop to her knees. The Applebys held her upright, twisting her arms behind her back. The pain took her breath away. Her panic spiraled as the skirt dropped and she felt Clyde's rough fingers slide beneath the elastic of her panties.

Cynthia summoned energy to fight and scream with revitalized strength. No matter how hard she struggled, the brothers simply pressed down on her shoulders and pulled up on her arms at the same time. She couldn't move. Townsend slipped her panties down to the belt still tied around her ankles.

"Hold her, now. If she kicks me I'm going to beat the crap out of both of you," Clyde warned.

She felt the belt on her legs loosen. She couldn't see anything but the tree branches overhead as they had her head pulled back until her neck ached. She began choking.

"Don't kill her for Christ's sake! Ease up! It isn't going to hurt anything if she watches. I want her to see this."

Townsend stood in front of her and took off his trousers. She had never seen a man's erection before and jerked her eyes away. The look on his face frightened her even more. He wasn't going to stop.

"Lay her down!" he ordered. "Each one of you get hold of an arm and leg and spread her out."

Gravel scraped against her bare back. She could do nothing but scream, her voice rasping and hoarse. The Applebys held her spread-eagled, each with an arm and leg.

Townsend spit in his hand and rubbed the saliva on his erection. He held her by the throat with one hand and pried between her legs with the other. His fingers entered. She couldn't do anything to stop him. He spit again into his hand and smeared between her legs, and then dropped to his knees and moved over her.

When he finished, the Appleby brothers held her until Clyde pulled his clothes on. "You boys want to take a shot at her? Be my guest. Have at it."

Clyde walked away, his fury dissipated, to wash off in the river. The brothers seemed subdued by the experience, glancing at each other, worried that Clyde had made trouble for them.

Charlie said, "Naw, man. She's a mess."

Tom and Charlie released her and jumped away, embarrassed and ashamed to look at her. Cynthia didn't get up. She curled into a protective ball, sobbing uncontrollably. She wanted to die. Nothing seemed real except the pain–the humiliation–the loss.

Moments later she heard Townsend's truck doors slam. The engine started and the truck pulled to a stop on the bridge directly overhead. She heard Clyde's voice clearly.

"I did it my way," he sang, and drove away laughing, pounding on the truck door.

Cynthia had been a virgin.

The sheriff advised Irma to drop the charges against the boys after he interrogated them. "They all deny it, Mrs. Roush. So it's her word against theirs, and there are three of them you know. My guess is you'd probably just be out a bunch of money for nothing. Their lawyer tells me he will demand a trial by judge and a judge won't convict them on emotions alone. You don't have any proof. A jury might convict them, but no judge will."

"The medical report says they raped her, Sheriff," Irma yelled at him.

"I'm sorry, Ma'am, but that ain't exactly what the report said. It simply said she had sexual intercourse, and that's all it said."

"What about the bruises and cuts?"

"Don't mean that much. No one can prove who had sex with her. There were no witnesses and she washed all the evidence out before the doctor checked her. It's just a bad deal all around."

Irma watched as the sobbing girl steadied herself, wiped her face and walked out of the courthouse without a trace of emotion. Cynthia remained in her room for an entire week, too miserable and upset to care about anything. She lay in her room, numbed by the trauma. She didn't pray to God or Jesus during those terrible days. Not once. She felt deserted and betrayed by the same God who had sustained her for so many years.

Where were you? Where were you?

She thought a lot about God and Jesus after that, wanting to be loyal, praying to herself, feeling guilty, but Cynthia never went back to the Wickmore Assembly of God church.

She contemplated suicide, cried endlessly, wallowed in sorrow and hatred, and then with no tears remaining, Cynthia changed. She didn't get up; she didn't eat; she didn't sleep. She thought. Her emotional paralysis gradually evolved into something more, from total incapacitation to bitterness and then to a swelling, silent rage.

Irma looked up from her work late one morning to find Cynthia standing at the door, suitcase in hand.

"What in the world are you doing?" She rushed to her daughter.

"I'm okay, Mother. I can't stay here another day. I'm going to Springfield as soon as I can get a ride. I'll find a job and a place to live. I can't live here."

"I thought you were going to college."

"I am, but I'll need to save money for law school. I'll have to work and go to school at the same time."

"This is the first I've heard mention about law school."

"That's what I'm going to do. The express truck comes today, doesn't it?"

"You know it does."

"I'll ride to Springfield with him. I'll give you a call as soon as I'm settled."

Irma watched helplessly as her daughter departed Wickmore an hour later. Cynthia crossed the bridge with her eyes clenched tightly closed. She didn't return to Wickmore for many years.

CHAPTER TEN

United States Military Academy

B
east Barracks is not a place, it is a n event; an inauguration; an indoctrination; an extreme test. R day "reception day" ended Sam's life as a civilian. He stepped off the bus at West Point in front of Eisenhower Hall, there to be rudely received by senior cadets screaming, "Move it! Move it!" Nearly 1200 new cadets, a milling mass of confusion, found themselves herded and jostled into units and then rushed off to another building for shots and clothing. The new cadets would be allowed to talk to each other in public or go anywhere by themselves for the next six weeks. Beast Barracks is not a place; it is a time, a time of transformation. It is cadet basic training. Get eaten by the Beast and you are out. Sam excelled.

He didn't exactly love the marching drills and constant harassment, but dealt with it better than the ten percent who dropped out before mid-August. During Beast, every senior cadet supervises approximately eight new cadets. Upon return to West Point after Beast, there were four senior cadets to every new cadet, all hell-bent on making the new cadet's lives miserable. Sam learned to avoid upper classmen.

"Yo, Smack!"

"Yes, Sir!"

"Don't stand there, Beaner. Get over here and get your heels together. What are the orders of the day?" Pushups and verbal abuse usually followed such encounters. The torment seemed endless. The fledgling cadet's first days on the hallowed grounds on the Hudson after Beast Barracks were far worse than any civilian university's fraternity "Hell Week."

Upon return to West Point after Beast, from an all-night sweat march through the woods, the new class separated and each new cadet became part of a company, assigned to a room and team leader. Sam's team leader, a second year cadet named Tillery, had two new cadets. He called Sam to his room.

"Prescott, I hear you aced Beast. Top man in your platoon. That right?"

Sam wondered about the likelihood of more harassment. "Sir, I managed, Sir."

Tillery nodded. "Well, Prescott, here's the deal. I have two of you. Do you know Pratt?"

"No, Sir."

"Pratt is a problem. She failed to pass physical condition requirements. I have 60 days to get her in shape. If she flunks, she's out. And, if she flunks I look bad. That's where you come in, Prescott. You are going to help me get her in shape. Can you handle it?"

"I guess so, Sir."

"No, dammit! Sir, yes I can, Sir. All I want to hear from you is, I can!"

"Sir. I can, Sir."

"Good. This will happen mostly on your off time, Prescott. I'll bring her in now and get you started. Stand at ease. The two of you will be partners, not only for the physical condition tests, but for all other PT that requires a partner. And that's for the entire year. Got it? She is your permanent physical training partner."

"Sir. Yes Sir."

Tillery turned and yelled, "Pratt! Get in here! Move it! Move it! Move it!"

Sam didn't turn as the door opened. An effeminate voice announced, "Here, Sir. Pratt."

Sam turned toward the voice belonging to the cadet who could help or hinder him. Some eye-catching details about Pratt surfaced immediately: He had seen her around. She was indeed female, black and pretty, possibly one the most beautiful girls he had ever seen, even in PT gear. She took her place, looking at the wall, exuding a tired air of practiced indifference. Sam recognized another obvious detail about his partner and suffered a deflating letdown. *She's so tiny.*

Pratt couldn't have been over five-two and a hundred pounds, compared to his six-four, two-hundred pounds. She was also dark, compared to his whiter than white. No two people could have been deliberately more mismatched.

Sam had to control an almost overwhelming impulse to stare. There had been no blacks near Wickmore, not even in the county, and none at Ashcroft. The black kids he played ball with across the street from Ashcroft did not include girls. This girl didn't fit the black stereotype his experiences had conditioned him to visualize. Her facial features were sharply defined, delicate, and her hair was not frizzy. Her beauty almost took his breath.

Tillery said, "Pratt, Prescott here is going to help you with conditioning. He has my confidence. Okay, you two get acquainted. I'll be back." He left the room.

Sam extended a hand and said, "Hi. Sam Prescott."

The gesture appeared to puzzle her. Sam almost retrieved the offer of friendship before she took his hand timidly. She didn't look him in the eye, nor did she apply pressure to the handshake. Her face remained expressionless, other than the militant sulkiness he noticed initially. Her handshake revealed more to him about Pratt than she would ever volunteer: her hand was cold, and she was trembling. Her aura of indifference was a facade.

"Well, Pratt, looks like you're stuck with me. What's your first name?"

She didn't answer.

"Come on, what do I call you?" he persisted.

She tore her hand free and looked away. "Like the man said, my name is Pratt." Her chin elevated proudly.

Sam smiled and forged ahead. "All right. Pratt's good. Call me Sam."

Nothing. She acted as though she had not heard a word he said. Sam decided not to press. *Wow. She's going to be tough.*

When Tillery returned, he announced the next day's session. "You better get some rest tonight, people. Your initial fitness test will be tomorrow. The test will provide a baseline and that is going to be crucial. Okay, that's it. Have a good night."

"Guess I'll see you tomorrow, Pratt," Sam said as they walked down the passageway. She nodded and turned toward the woman's end of the barracks. He thought she looked unhappy, detached, walking slowly, eyes focused on the floor.

Sam worried about her size for himself. Such a small partner could be a major problem. He didn't understand her aloof attitude. From day-one, everyone else had gone out of their way to be friendly. Not Pratt. He worried that she could limit his chances to achieve at a high level. He sighed heavily and thought, I'll worry about her tomorrow.

He didn't notice any difference in her attitude as they gathered for the test the next afternoon. She still wouldn't look at him or smile, still remote and defensive, sequestered behind folded arms.

The test was a challenge, yet well within Sam's abilities. He passed all phases with relative ease. Pratt passed leg strength and endurance phases of the test with difficulty, but failed the entire battery of upper body strength tests.

Tillery pulled them aside afterward and said, "Okay, you two are officially on probation. You will retake the test every Friday. Pratt, if you fail at the end of sixty days, you will be administratively separated from the United States Army. Do you understand?"

Pratt answered meekly, "Yes, Sir."

"Do you understand, Prescott!" Tillery glared inches from Sam's face.

"I passed the test, Sir!" Sam protested, snapping to attention.

"You just don't get it, do you? Your *partner* did not pass! Your *team* failed! You're a *team!* That's the way things work in the Army! You are both responsible!" He stepped back and relaxed. "Now, you best do some serious training before the next test. Do you understand?"

"Yes, Sir!" they answered in unison.

The advanced cadet relaxed. "Look, I don't want to get too involved with what you do after class or weekends, but you need extra work." His voice rose again, "But if you fail the test Friday, you can believe I will be on your ass every second of every day! Got it!"

"Yes, Sir!" again in unison.

Their team leader departed, leaving the uneasy pair alone in the middle of the deserted athletic field. Pratt turned slowly and began walking away. Sam watched for a moment, totally confused by her apparent lack of concern.

"Hey! Pratt!" he yelled, and ran to catch up. "You can't go anywhere alone. You know that. Anyway, don't you think we should make some plans?"

She stopped as he pulled along side, but turned away, staring into space. At first Sam thought his presence annoyed her, but reconsidered when he noticed the tears. She didn't walk away this time, instead she took a deep breath and faced him, tears already pooled in her eyes.

"Look," she said, chin quivering with emotion. "I know you have to.... I'm really sorry you got stuck with me." She turned to leave, but paused, eyes clenched, as Sam placed his hand on her shoulder and drew her to a stop.

"Maybe you didn't understand what the man said, Pratt. We are a team. There isn't any choice. We have to work together. You are so busy feeling sorry for yourself that you forget that I am involved. Look, I can help if you give me a chance." She didn't respond. He shook her shoulder gently. "Come on. What do you say? We can do this."

She stood for several seconds, arms folded, looking at her feet. Her practiced appearance of indifference gradually changed to a troubled frown. She finally lifted her eyes. "I'm sorry. You're right. I am thinking only about myself." Pratt smiled, a thin, grim smile, but she smiled.

He couldn't stop looking at her eyes–enormous, dark, moist, sad, defeated. He caught himself staring and said, "That's all right. Okay, can we start over?"

She sighed unevenly. "I should never have come here. I didn't know what to expect. I don't think I even want to attempt any more of this. I'm sorry you got mixed up with me."

"You aren't thinking about quitting, are you?"

She looked away and shrugged. "What's the difference. I'll never pass that test."

"Never know unless you try. We have three days. What do you think? I'm good at physical stuff."

She smiled wryly. His cockiness amused her. "Yeah, I suppose you're right. If I don't try, I'll always wonder." She looked directly at him for the first time. "Okay, Prescott, what now?"

Sam breathed a sigh of relief and held out his hand. Her change of attitude pleased him. "Good. Let's start at the beginning. My name is Sam."

She took his hand, but still didn't grip firmly. "Choxie."

"Choxie? Good. Can I call you Choxie?"

"Fine. Do I need to apologize for being such a...such a–"

He interrupted. "Ass? No. Not to me. Is Choxie short for another name? Unusual. I like it."

"It's a family name."

"Are you in a hurry, Choxie?"

"Not really."

"Good. Let's walk and talk. We need a plan of action. Come on."

She remained rooted to the spot, completely confused by the dilemma created by her past. Never before in her life had she been partnered in any way with a white boy. She had to force a lifetime of reservation aside to answer, "Okay, sure. Why not."

They didn't talk on the way to the barracks. When they settled in her room, door open according to regulation, Sam asked the usual questions: "Where is home? What brings you here? Do you have brothers and sisters? What do your parents do?"

Her answers lacked embellishment. "I'm from a little town near Meridian, Mississippi. I have four brothers and two sisters, all younger. My father is a share cropper. My mother is a housekeeper. Anything else?"

"That's good for a start."

She relaxed somewhat after the exchange and told him about her hometown. Sam was surprised to learn she had been home schooled.

"Home schooling? Your folks are teachers, then?"

"No. My mother keeps house for a retired teacher. A white woman. Miss Polly. She took over my education from the third grade on. Her son is a judge. He got my appointment."

With more questioning, Sam discovered that she loved music and could play several instruments, but had spent her entire life at home helping her mother with six younger children. She had very little experience dealing with the public, and literally none with white people, except Miss Polly. No boys, and certainly no white boys. Choxie spoke with a muted southern drawl, although with evidence of social refinement from years of association with a cultured mentor.

"You come from someplace up north, don't you?" she asked.

Sam grinned and replied, "What makes you think that?"

"Your accent. I bet you went to some all-white preppie school. I bet your daddy is a doctor, or something like that. I expect your momma probably spends most all her time playing cards at snooty society parties."

Sam laughed heartily. "That's awful." He gave a brief account of his background, explaining his Boston accent. He watched her relax visibly as he revealed his recent small town, country background. After that she relaxed and spoke easily. The conversation drifted to favorite books, movies and other casual subjects. Her inhibitions had eased before they parted an hour later, as friends.

Choxie failed only two parts of the re-test, much to Sam's relief. He watched her confidence develop during the following days of strain and tension. Choxie responded positively to his enthusiasm. He was able to provide the encouragement she needed to overcome the first serious impediment to graduation. She passed all phases on the fourth week.

"I need to thank you, Sam. I was going to quit. I would have, except for you."

He held up a hand. "My pleasure, Chox."

"Chox? No one ever calls me Chox."

She trusted Sam, relied on him, and liked him far more than she would admit, even to herself. They both profited from the relationship. Their liaison was peculiar to many cadets. The odd twosome ignored the raised eyebrows and murmured comments their bond provoked and maintained a steady friendship through the trials of their Plebe year.

Choxie had a solid background in English lit and composition, Sam's weakest subjects. She dedicated evenings and weekends to him, just as he had helped her. Their friendship strengthened.

Sam, in turn, helped her with math and history as they teamed for study. The mismatched couple sitting together in the library or her room became a common scene; a spectacle inciting a continuous line of derisive comments from a few of the more racist southern cadets. The pair's superior grades provided enough reward to offset the prejudiced observations. They both made each semester dean's list.

"Sam, I would like to speak with the same accent you have. Teach me."

"Why? You know more about English than I do."

"You know that isn't true. No, I mean your speech patterns. You sound more...more what? Eastern? Metropolitan? Anyway, I want to learn."

He felt awkward, preferring not to get involved, but she insisted and maintained a positive attitude when he coached, sometimes mimicking, sometimes making fun of her. She accepted the criticism and caught on quickly.

Sam's social life at the academy consisted of rare weekends to New York City and the occasional dances arranged by the academy. He flew home over Christmas vacation and stayed at the ranch with Wes.

Choxie didn't have a social life, spending her first Christmas vacation at home babysitting. She vowed never again to return to the filth and sloth of her parent's home on vacation. She would spend her spare time at Army posts, or stay at the Point.

During the fall semester of the second year, Sam asked her to go with him to the homecoming dance.

"You can't be serious! I know you're trying to be a good friend, Sam, but some people would think we are actually on a date."

"So? Look, I'm not asking you to go because we're friends or because I don't have anyone else to go with. And I'm not asking you to go because you don't have anyone to go with. I'm asking because I want to go with you. Yes, as a date. I'm asking for a date, Chox."

They were sitting opposite each other at a library table when he popped the question. Choxie laid her pencil aside, folded her hands and examined him like she would a mischievous child. His expression didn't change. Hers did. Astonishment.

"You're serious, aren't you?" She instinctively covered her mouth.

"Damned straight. Hands down, remember. Your teeth are perfect and so is your smile. And I am absolutely serious."

Choxie sobered and cleared her throat. "You know, for a white boy, you sure are a dumb cluck sometimes." She glared accusingly.

Sam folded his papers, stacked a pile of scattered books, then stood. "Well, that may be true, my friend. I won't argue the point. But you still owe me an answer."

Choxie didn't want him to leave with the issue unresolved. "Hold it. You can't be serious, Sam," she whispered. "You're just doing this because...because..... Oh, come on. You don't really want to take me as a date."

He leaned over the table and looked her in the eye. "You have never been more mistaken about anything. I also expect you to wear something slinky, not that damned government issue gender-proof uniform. I expect to buy a corsage and I expect to dance every dance with you. And," He straightened "And, since we already know each other pretty well, you may expect that I will probably try to kiss you." He turned and walked a few steps away, then returned to the table, "And I expect an answer tomorrow. A positive answer."

"Why, Sam? Why me?"

She looked dismayed. Sam thought she might burst out in tears. "All right. Because I like you. Because I don't want to take anyone else. Because you're beautiful. Because it's about damned time. Is that enough?" He left before she could protest.

Choxie spent a sleepless night worrying about how to handle Sam, her only good friend. She didn't want to spoil the relationship. Most cadets accepted her. Sam was by far her best friend. She didn't want to alienate him but couldn't think of a graceful way to turn him down.

They met before swimming class the next afternoon. He didn't wait for an answer.

"I borrowed a car," he whispered.

"Not so fast, white boy. I'm not going anywhere with you."

"Come on, Chox. You aren't going to chicken out on me?"

"I'm not going, Sam."

The swimming coach interrupted and ended their conversation. Choxie eluded Sam after class. She didn't go to the evening meal or to the library that night, retiring to the confines of her room, insulated from Sam. She opened the door to answer a soft knock just before midnight to find him poised to knock again.

"My God, Sam!" she gasped, then recovered from shock and

pulled him inside. "You aren't supposed to be.... It's way after hours." Her roomy discreetly left the room. "You'll get us both in trouble. Good Lord! You could get thrown out for being up here. Worse than that, you could get me thrown out! What are you thinking?"

"About you, Chox."

He took her in his arms and kissed her flush on the mouth as she struggled to push him away. When he released, she stood back, eyes wide open, dazed and puzzled. When her arm came up, Sam thought for a moment she might slap him. She covered her mouth with the back of her hand and stared at him.

"I have wanted to do that since the day we met, Chox. I'm not leaving until you give me a good reason why you won't go with me." He folded his arms.

The situation completely bewildered Choxie. His unexpected behavior left her confused, frustrated, and embarrassed.

"I can't, Sam. I don't have a dress!" she said. Her eyes rolled. *God, how stupid.*

"So, get one."

"I don't know how to dance." *That's stupid, too.*

"Who cares? We'll only dance slow dances. No one cares."

She was flustered, her emotions running wild. Sam smiled the victor's smile. He knew and so did she.

"I'll be here at seven the evening of the dance, Chox. Don't make me wait." He checked the hall and slipped out.

Choxie barely spoke the next two days, averting her eyes when he approached during class. He didn't see her at the library or the evening meals. They didn't speak until late the afternoon on the day of the dance.

"Is the dress white?" he asked.

"Why?"

"I don't want the corsage to clash with your dress."

"It's white."

Sam smiled broadly. "All right! Is it low-cut?"

She answered coyly, "Well, you'll just have to wait and see, cadet." Her teasing manner initiated a drastic change in their relationship.

Sam stood impatiently in waiting room that evening, suffering the stares of women cadets speculating about who his date would be. They could not have looked more surprised by Choxie's appearance than Sam did. She floated down the stairs toward him in a long, white sheath dress that conformed perfectly to her slender body. Her hair, swept up, highlighted the graceful curve of her neck. A string of borrowed pearls dipped into the alluring vale of her breasts. The pushup bra and low-cut dress amplified more of her than he imagined. Sam took the coat she offered and held it while the speechless onlookers stared. Choxie played the part of experience perfectly.

They drove most of the way to the dance before Sam summoned the courage to look at her, to really look. "I always thought you were beautiful, Chox, but this...this...." He shook his head. "This is fantastic. You really look great."

Choxie's happiness conquered her characteristic nervousness. She smiled contentedly, feeling beautiful, and had a marvelous time that evening. For the first time in her life, Choxie Pratt felt equal, even superior.

Whispers and sidelong looks from the crowd of interested onlookers gradually subsided as the night progressed. Sam and Choxie created even more drama by seeming to be comfortably at ease throughout the evening–possibly even conspicuously familiar.

At one point, Sam said, "You lied."

"I did? About what?"

"You're a superb dancer."

"How would you know? You're so busy looking down the front of my dress I'm surprised you noticed anything else."

He laughed at her playful scolding. "I must admit, the view is tempting. Am I that obvious?"

Choxie never felt more in control than she did at that moment. She answered naturally, "If I minded, Prescott, I shouldn't have worn the dress. But do try not to be so damned juvenile. They're just glands; every woman has them."

Later, sitting in the car in front of her quarters, Sam said, "Are you going to be upset if I kiss you on the first date?"

"Will there be more?" she asked. "More dates, I mean."

He kissed her lightly on the mouth.

"More," she said.

He kissed her again with more conviction until she pushed away. He walked her to the door and she dutifully asked if he wanted to come in.

"Not unless you want to see me win the door prize," he answered.

She didn't understand at first, then burst out laughing when she understood why he held his hat over the front of his trousers. She clucked her tongue disapprovingly and said, "My, my. Aren't we naughty. You really should learn to control yourself, cadet. Really, it was just a kiss." She gave him a peck on the cheek and hurried in alone.

They didn't see each other again that weekend, but Sam called late Sunday evening and asked how she felt.

"I'm just fine. Why do you ask?"

"Oh, I don't know. I guess I thought you might be suffering from some second thoughts about the dance. Are you?"

"Not about the dance. I will admit being a little troubled by who took me to the dance."

"Why?"

"Maybe it wasn't such a good idea. I don't know."

"I had a wonderful time, Chox. I can honestly say that going with you is the best thing that has happened to me since I arrived here. Didn't you have a good time?"

"A great time, and you are a good friend. I'll never forget you for being so nice. You're different than anyone I've ever known. You are so different. Thank you for that, too."

"Why do I get the impression that you think I took you out of the goodness of my heart? Did it ever occur to you that I might have some ulterior motive?"

"Oh, don't be silly." A moment later, after reflection, she said, "You are a good friend, Sam, but...." She sighed heavily before finishing. "Maybe we weren't very smart. Maybe going out together wasn't such a good idea. Maybe the price will be too high. Do you know what I am trying to say?"

"Oh, I think so," he said, without attempting to hide the irritation. "You probably think that being seen with a white man, even at a public social function, might not be politically correct. Is that what you're trying to say?"

"No, dammit. I'm not just thinking about myself. Things are just so different where I grew up. It's hard to tell you just how different."

"I can't imagine. I don't have any appreciation for what you have lived through. But I want you to think about something else now."

"Think about what? There isn't anything to think about. I'll tell you what I think. I think we made a mistake. That's about all there is to think about, Prescott."

"Has someone been giving you a tough time?"

"Just the usual snotty comments. Nothing I can't handle. How about you? Be honest, Sam. Has anyone said something to you?"

"Nothing I can't handle. Look, Chox, I want to give you something else to think about, then I'll let you get back to your books." He paused, waiting for her to answer.

"Chox? You still there?"

"Still here. Wondering why."

"Good, then think about this: I'm not going to stop seeing you unless you stop me. No one else is going to stop me." He hung up.

Choxie stood a long time with the phone cradled against her cheek. "Damn. Damn. Damn." She hung the phone, then closed the door and leaned against it, an unconscious attempt to shut out a threat. *He'll keep trying unless I stop him.* She knew enough about him to know a plain, old-fashioned no would not suffice. *He won't give up.*

Her homework suffered. She arrived for classes the next morning with no firm idea of how to handle Sam Prescott. She didn't see him until the final class. After the instructor dismissed the class, Choxie prepared to leave.

"Just a minute, Chox. I need to say something," Sam said, tugging at her elbow.

She sat down, clutching the stack of books to her breasts. Sam waited until the other cadets were out of hearing, then sat next to her.

"Did you think about what we talked about?"

She nodded. "I did."

"Well?" His brow furrowed.

Choxie gathered courage and turned to face him. "Well what?" She spoke angrily. "What the hell do you want, Prescott? What do you want with me? Do you have a bet with your roomy? Is that what this is all about? Are you trying to change your luck? Haven't you ever had a black chick, Prescott? Do you think black girls are different?"

He grimaced. "Please don't, Chox. Do I deserve this?"

"What did you think I would do, Sam? Did you think I would flip over on my back because a white boy found favor with me?"

"You know damned well I'm not thinking black and white. What the hell is going on? I thought we were friends."

"Were is past tense, and that's good, Prescott. I don't think I can afford you as a friend. Now you listen to me. I'm going to graduate from this academy and nothing is going to get in my way–not you–not anything. So you just go find yourself a nice white girl and leave me the hell alone!" She glared at him, then stood and walked away before he could recover.

"I know what you're trying to do, Chox," he yelled as she reached the aisle. "And you are dead wrong! You are blowing it, Pratt!"

His words burned and tears clouded her vision. She didn't look back. Choxie skipped the final period for the remainder of the week and refused to accept phone calls at night. She barely saw Sam the following month, never giving him the opportunity to catch her alone.

Choxie left West Point for the summer with mixed emotions, relieved to avoid another emotional confrontation with Sam and sad because she knew his overtures were sincere. She thought about Sam Prescott all summer.

Choxie visited Army bases in Europe to familiarize herself with the Army's public relations programs. She planned a career in television as a news reporter upon completion of military service requirements. A civilian career would have to wait for two more years at the academy and five years of obligatory active duty. In the meantime she wanted to make absolutely certain that when the time came she would be prepared.

Choxie's change of attitude crushed Sam. He found her distant, haughty bearing, the refusal to talk or associate with him beyond frustrating.

CHAPTER ELEVEN

Love of Life

Sam felt a great sense of joy after discovering Choxie had returned for their final year. He always wondered at the beginning of each new year if she would come back, not that he saw much of her the second and third years. *Pratt is still here. Yes!* She barely nodded when he said hello and declined to shake hands. They maintained a reserved relationship during class and seldom saw each other during free time, always from a distance. Sam often watched her going to and from class functions. He couldn't breach her icy barrier.

One day as class broke, Sam casually said, "So, how did your summer go?"

She didn't look up from the map exercise they were completing jointly. "Is this a test?"

He persisted. "C'mon. Be nice, Chox. What did you do?"

She tapped her pencil signaling irritation, and rolled her eyes. "Nothing that would interest you. Some posts in Europe." She stopped working, still drumming her pencil on the map, appearing to be extremely annoyed. "You're bothering the hell out of me, Prescott. I don't want to make small talk, okay? Let's get finished here."

"Jesus, you're tough, Chox! Tough." He sat back, looking at the ceiling. "You've been a complete ass for as long as I can remember. Why do I bother?"

"Don't bother. Leave me alone. Get to work."

"I know you don't hate me, Chox. I think you're afraid of me."

His confident attitude exasperated her. "You really should

think about majoring in psychology." She faced him squarely for the first time in almost a year. "Okay, what do you want from me?"

He smiled triumphantly. She froze when he placed a hand on her arm. "I feel cheated, Chox. We were once great friends."

"Maybe I don't share your opinion." She didn't sound positive.

"Maybe, but you know I'm right. Give me one reason why you avoid me. Times have changed, people have changed, but not you. You're still living in the old-time South, Chox. Why do you let someone else's hate control your life, and mine?"

"You're such a wiseass. You don't know—"

"I didn't make your great grandfather a slave. I'm not responsible for what happened in Mississippi. Racial problems may be real enough where you come from, but why do they affect you here? Why volunteer to be part of another generation's mistakes?"

His intensity intrigued her and she nodded appreciatively. "Well, well. You've been thinking about this, haven't you? Nice speech. Really." She clapped sarcastically.

"God, you're tough, Chox." He sat back, disgusted with her; tired of the effort.

"You want to be friends with me? Okay, I give up. Let's be friends." She held out her hand theatrically.

He didn't think her gesture was sincere. "I'm not playing games, Chox." He smiled crookedly, recognizing a breach in her defense, but didn't take her hand. She dropped it.

"What now?" she asked, annoyed with his lingering smile.

"It's not much, Chox, but do you realize this is the first time you have talked to me in...well, so long I can't remember."

"You always were easy to please," she said and looked away. "You really should get out more, Prescott."

"I plan to."

She studied him suspiciously, knowing he had something in mind.

He leaned just-between-you-and-me closer and said, "Come with me. You haven't got anything better to do. Let's get away from here this weekend."

He watched her grope with the suggestion. Her brow creased and she refused to look up from the desk. He thought, *Now. Go for it*. "Come on. Live a little. I know you're bored silly hanging around here all the time. If we can't be friends because you're worried about what people here might think, then let's get out of here. Why not? What have you got to lose? What do you think?"

She didn't answer, but her amused smile revealed a break in their frosty relationship. She studied the pencil in her hand. Sam felt relieved. At least she hadn't yelled and picked up her books and fled, as usual. "C'mon. It's a good idea and you know it. Okay, don't say anything right now. Let me know what you think tomorrow. Will you at least do that? Please, Chox. Think about it."

"You're assuming, I presume, that the idea appeals to me and that I will actually consider it, aren't you?" Then she started laughing and shook her head. "I like you, Prescott, you know that? You're good for laughs." She gathered her books and departed, shaking her head, chuckling to herself.

The following day, Sam watched her carefully for some sign. She kept her eyes straight ahead and worked silently. After their papers were handed in, the instructor departed after admonishing the class to wait for the bell before leaving.

Choxie whispered, "So, you want to go to the big city tomorrow? Is that right?"

The question stunned him. Out of the blue. "Um, sure. What's up?"

"All right. Meet me up at the train station. Nine in the morning." She walked out.

The next morning Sam thought she looked happy for the first time since the dance their Plebe year. She talked all the way to New York City.

"Let's party tonight," he said. Have dinner. Take in a show. What do you think? We should do something."

"Okay. You're on. Dutch treat, though."

He nodded, but didn't rejoice, held back by her established wariness. "Fine." He didn't understand the change and knew better than to ask.

They took the train to the city on Saturday or Sunday every non-duty weekend for the next two months, attending ball games, Broadway shows, movies, dressing up to eat at good restaurants. All secretly. No one knew. The intrigue added spice to their weekly adventures.

They were more relaxed and natural around each other at school. The new aspect of their relationship provided more enjoyment of life in general. Their previous tensions and animosities withdrew, yet none of their friends suspected the pair were anything more than casual school acquaintances thrown together by the innocent circumstance of how their names were spelled.

The Christmas break provided two weeks of opportunity to get away from school and the monotonous routines of training. Sam borrowed a car and they drove to the city the instant class adjourned on Friday afternoon before Christmas.

"I need to do a little Christmas shopping tomorrow, Sam. I'm going to come back on the train."

"No problem. I have the car until January. You can take the car."

"You sure?" She studied his face for clues, instinct for a catch awakened.

Sam drove on lost in thought. "Yeah, but I think I'll stay over tonight, maybe take in a ball game at the Garden tomorrow. Would you mind picking me up before you leave town tomorrow?"

Choxie didn't answer immediately, struggling with a confusing new thought, a notion so alien it smothered her into silence. Sam didn't understand the silence and decided to retract his suggestion.

"It's not that important, Chox. Let's just stay on schedule."

"No. It's okay. Really, I don't mind." She retreated again into silence.

Sam glanced over repeatedly, attempting to decipher her sudden quietness. He finally broke the silence. "I hope you won't take this wrong, but.... Oh, what the hell, here it goes anyway." He cleared his throat. "Why don't we both stay over? We could get a room. Save a lot of time and driving. No strings attached. No ulterior motives. What do you think?"

Her mind raced as his suggestion converged with possibilities already running through her mind.

Don't read anything into it, girl. It's practical to stay over, that's all. The options are simple. Yes or no. Get on or get off.

They had become close again, but she sensed Sam always restrained himself for fear of upsetting the fine balance. He had been the one responsible for patching things up. She felt guilty for being so much in control of the relationship. Her thoughts raced.

It isn't a proposition, merely a way to save time and money. Why is this so damned hard?

Sam detected her distress and retreated. "You know what? Maybe it wasn't such good idea. Anyhow, it doesn't matter. Just thought it would save you a bunch of time. Let it go."

She listened from an ethereal distance as her own voice said, "No, you're right. Why not?" *How impulsive.* Her face felt hot. The abrupt answer surprised her as much as Sam. She felt a flush of excitement as the initial idea broadened to include prospects she sometimes envisioned but only on the periphery of fantasies during sleepless nights.

This is not innocent.

"I'm okay with that, Sam," she said, again barely recognizing her own voice. "Let's go someplace nice to eat first, then just hang out."

There, it's done. The reality of what they were planning slashed through her thoughts like flashing red warning lights, electrifying her. She thought Sam looked troubled. "It's okay, Sam. Really. It's a good idea."

"Maybe." He smiled. "But maybe my motives aren't pure as driven snow."

She feigned astonishment. "Sam Prescott*!* I am *shocked! Shocked, I tell you.* Don't you think we can control ourselves?" She could tell he was definitely troubled. "What's the matter, Sam? Cat got your tongue? Why so gloomy? It's no big deal, is it?"

"Look, I have to be honest, Chox. You're the best friend I've ever had, but I think a lot about being more than friends." He sneaked a glance hoping for a sign, concerned that opening up that much might be reckless and might ruin everything. "Does that bother you?"

"I'm not sure. Should it?"

He pulled to the shoulder and parked, then turned to face her. "I like the way things are with us, Chox. I don't want to spoil anything."

She stared straight ahead. "So, don't." She said it with a mischievous glint in her eyes, highlighted by a playful little smile she didn't try to hide.

Sam's confidence soared. He leaned over and kissed her. She

neither flinched or tried to pull away. After the kiss he said, "I can't tell you how much I think about you."

She didn't move. He didn't think she was too offended. Then she smiled, a satisfied smile that said everything. He started the car and drove on into the city with Choxie next to him, her head on his shoulder.

Later, sitting in the car in front of an older motel, she said, "I pay half, Sam. I think we should share. Here, take this." She stuffed money into his hand.

When he returned after registering, she said, "Let's get something to eat." She couldn't look at him.

They stopped at a drugstore for toilet articles then a clothing store where Sam bought a "T" shirt for her to use as a nightgown, and then they spent the next two hours at a restaurant, picking over food they hardly recognized, nervous, stalling, anticipating. Choxie finally broke the impasse. "Okay, let's go." She wasn't thinking about right or wrong, black or white.

They ran up the stairs, giggling, fumbling with the entry card, and quickly entered the room, pausing to catch their breath, examining the room's interior. Their glances returned repeatedly to the queen bed that might as well have been the only furniture in the room. Nothing else existed but that bed; a sacrificial altar tugging at their conscience; evidence convicting them before the crime. They couldn't look at each other.

The bed brought Choxie sharply back to reality.

"One bed?"

He looked guilty. "Well, it was twenty bucks cheaper. It's queen size."

"You should have.... I just thought.... Wow. I don't know, Sam. Let's go for a walk." Her eyes begged. "Now I'm too nervous to think. I need to think."

"Yeah, good idea. Okay."

Choxie felt relieved knowing he apparently suffered the same uncertainty. They held hands and walked around the block, seeking reassurance and trying to relax. Their bodies brushed, gently at first, then with confidence, pressing together until need pulled them to a halt. They stood in the shadows and embraced.

He unbuttoned her coat and pulled her close. The feeling of intimacy thrilled her. She had wanted him to hold her for such a long time. Sam seemed content with the embrace. She wasn't. Choxie initiated the first kiss, a tender, tentative exploration. She hungrily savored the delightful sensations and eagerly surrendered to his increasing aggressiveness. His mouth on hers felt deliciously soft and warm. Their quest for familiarity evolved from the first timid, provisional touches to demanding, searching kisses with her arms locked around his neck, on the tip of her toes to get closer.

"Whew! Okay, let's go back," she said, fanning her face, breathing heavily.

They stopped several times on the way, relishing the wonderful sensations of familiarity. Safely inside the room, Sam held her, swaying until she pulled away. "Sam, I'm getting weak."

He laughed. "Yeah, me too. Okay, you first." He pushed her toward the bathroom.

Later, he watched from the bed as she emerged, dressed only in his "T" shirt.

"This isn't much," she complained, tugging at the shirt tail.

"I like it. Get in," he said and flipped the covers back.

Choxie turned the lights off and slipped into bed. "Just hold me, Sam."

He reached for her and she nestled comfortably into his arms. She could sense his every movement, every sound, every smell and the feel of his heart beating. A neon sign outside their window cast a flickering blue-white incandescence over the room, blending everything in velvet textures.

"You're trembling," he said. "You okay?"

"Yes," she answered without conviction.

His eyes searched hers for a clue to her feelings. "Are you nervous?" he asked.

"Maybe. Yeah, a little."

They lay quietly, staring at the ceiling, holding hands, waiting, thinking, trying to relax.

"I am really nervous, Sam. I'm scared silly."

"Of me?"

"Yes. No. I'm not afraid of you, but this is all so...."

He sat up and looked down at her, then said, "You haven't done this before have you?"

"No. I... Wait." She sat up and glared at him. "What do you mean? You jerk! Do you think I sleep around?"

Sam flinched in mock terror. "No, honest, Chox, I just didn't think about it one way or another. Sorry. That just came out. Sorry."

She flopped back, arms folded, trying to look wounded. The little game helped loosen tensions. Her pretended indignation soon vanished. "Sam?"

"Shoot."

"Have you ever...you know? No, don't answer that. I don't want to...never mind."

He didn't answer immediately, then said, "I knew a girl once. We–"

"No! Never mind! I don't want to know."

"Look, Chox, there are no strings. I love being with you. That's good enough. We don't need to do anything."

Her mood changed. She no longer felt out of control. *What if I am with Sam? He's my best friend. There's nothing wrong with this.* "Sam, I don't know what I'm doing."

"You don't have to know anything. Nothing bad is going to happen." He placed a hand on her hip.

She held his hand in place. "Sam, I really don't know if I can...you know. I've thought about this, thought about you for a long time. But.... But, if it's all the same to you, I'd just as soon you don't do anything weird."

He flopped back laughing.

She sat up and glared at him. "What's so damned funny?"

"You. Do you think I'm a pervert?"

She pulled the cover up and lay back. "No. I just don't...well, you know."

He rolled toward her and placed his hand back on her hip again. Choxie thrilled at his nearness. She stopped breathing as his hand moved toward her breast. Her eyes followed his progress; heart beat accelerating perilously; every receptor in her body tingling. He didn't touch her breast, though. He pulled the shirt up. She arched her back to assist, watching, unable to trust her voice to say anything.

Her confidence suffered a setback when he threw the covers off. She had seen little boys naked before–never a man, and certainly never a man in Sam's condition. She couldn't take her eyes away. *Oh, let's just hold everything here.* She sat up and stared, then at his face, then back, a hand over her mouth, giggling. "I don't know, Sam. You just might be a pervert."

He joined in the laughter and pulled her down into a comforting embrace. He didn't rush, sensing her nervousness, although she no longer trembled. Choxie deferred everything to him. They kissed until she stirred, turning toward him, caressing, responding.

The dim light exaggerated the difference between them. Her body, small, slender and dark, opposed to his muscular fairness. The contrast provoked more sensation, heightening the moment. He pulled the covers completely away and gazed at her.

"Those uniforms sure do a good job of hiding all this," he said, running his fingers over the curves. Her skin was silky-soft, a tawny shade of brown molded smoothly over her body creating a blend of shadows accentuating her beauty. Her hips and ribs stood out prominently, emphasizing the flatness of her stomach. Her breasts, no more than average, were firm regardless of her position, swaying tautly at the slightest movement. His fingers skimmed the delicate, satin surface and her breath drew in. Her nipples hardened and distended.

Choxie lay quietly, either spellbound or too scared to move, he didn't know which. He leaned forward and kissed her lips softly, acutely aware of her breasts barely touching his chest. Her fingers slipped through his hair and she pulled him down. They kissed passionately. Sam had difficulty governing his excitement, pacing himself, caressing and stalling. Choxie shifted, struggling to slip beneath him, moaning softly, whimpering, almost pleading. He touched her breast with his mouth. Her breath caught and stopped. Her head rolled from side to side. She tugged at his shoulders, encouraging. His hand drifted down. She swallowed and tensed as his fingers slipped beneath the elastic of the bikini panties. She placed her hand on his, not to remove it, but as a form of assurance. His fingers advanced, closing, exploring. She sighed brokenly, wrapped her arms tightly around his neck and arched upward as he slipped her panties down. Her hips pressed against his in a primitive rhythm, natural and unconstrained.

Sam moved over her, lowering himself, still kissing and caressing. She submitted willingly, opening as his weight descended, then gasped and tensed, but did not attempt to delay consummation. Her previous apprehensions could not compete with the need for completion. She was beyond thought, beyond fright, beyond anything except the desire to possess him, hostage to a yearning she could not deny and had no wish to resist. Sam was gentle, but excitement had driven Choxie beyond caution.

Sam stopped moving, permitting her body time to adapt.

She felt resistance and stifled the urge to cry out, then relaxed and accepted him. They lay quietly, swept up in new sensations, then she began moving instinctively, demanding, urging. Their bodies flowed together.

Sam's mouth smothered her moans. He suddenly stopped. Choxie tugged at him, murmuring, "Don't stop, Sam. Don't stop." Every muscle in her body contracted involuntarily. She pressed her face into the hollow of his neck and a low, moaning cry escaped. Choxie, involved with her own release, didn't notice Sam's condition until his breath exhaled and the full weight of his body descended upon her.

They lay quietly, catching their breath. Tears crept down Choxie's face. A strange reaction–strange because she couldn't stop smiling.

They spent the following weekends in bed, basking in the physical expressions of love, taking little time away from intimacy to attend the public functions that had previously filled their time in the city. A deep, consuming need for each other eventually overshadowed the raw physical attraction.

"I love you" became words of greeting and good-bye. "I love you" stopped arguments, ended the blues and brought tears to her eyes. No talk of anything permanent filtered into the relationship. The potential problems of racial inter-marriage were never part of the equation.

Choxie's feelings were no weaker than Sam's, but she couldn't escape the image of bigotry and intolerance inherited from childhood and demanded their relationship remain secret. Only a few close, trusted friends had an inkling of their weekends in the city, and no one had any idea how consuming the relationship had become. He refused to answer her questions about what they were going to do about the relationship after graduation. "Time will take care of everything," he'd say, or something equally frustrating. Sam waffled. He wouldn't commit, not even to talking about it.

She accused him of quitting. He shrugged. She fumed.

His lackadaisical attitude frustrated her and she began moderating their time together. When Sam objected and pressed for more, she ended the relationship brutally, coldly and deliberately extracting herself from the confines of the liaison that controlled her life. She loved him but thought he was just playing. She wanted and needed some form of commitment.

Sam suffered, drifting through the last six weeks of school without purpose, devoid of enthusiasm, relying upon the good graces of forgiving instructors and past performance.

* * * * *

Wes came for the graduation ceremony and spent a full week at the academy. At supper the night before graduation, he handed Sam a copy of his will. "I left it all to you. No big deal. It's not like I had anyone else to give it to. Anyway, when I'm gone it's yours, lock stock and barrel. Or you can come back and take over any time you want. I expect we could work together. Anyway, whatever happens, it's yours. Just so you know."

That the ranch would be his someday didn't surprise Sam, but Wes surprised him by making it official. "I appreciate the gesture, but you must know I'm not thinking about coming back to Wickmore."

"Well, hell, I know that. It don't matter. Do what you want to with it after I'm gone."

They had a good time visiting, all the stiff formality between them gone. Two adults. Wes patted Sam on the back and told him how proud he was of his success. Their conversation eventually drifted to Wickmore.

Sam said, "I would like to know what Roush thought when I walked away."

"Oh, I heard he figured you had been laying for him all the time, just waiting for the opportunity to get even. That's what he told anyone who would listen."

"He just about got it right."

"Yeah, I know that. But, surprisingly, a lot of people blamed him for the way he treated you. I had a serious talk with him about it."

"Serious?" Sam laughed. He had an idea what serious meant to Wes.

"Yeah. Not the first time. We had a few disagreements over the years."

"Over the years? Before or after me?"

"Oh, none of what happened was ever about you. Started a long time before you came on the scene. Had a misunderstanding or two about a woman. Okay, his woman, to be honest. She always kinda preferred me. Anyway, Roush ran off with the Coker woman before school started the year after you graduated. Listen to this: Pete Hensley took his family to Disney World. Told me he saw Roush there, big as life, selling balloons."

Sam's thoughts never got past the 'she always kinda preferred me' comment. "Hold it. You and Irma?"

Wes smiled, almost happily. "Oh yeah. Irma and I go way back."

*   *   *   *   *

The next day at graduation, Pratt and Prescott were still alphabetically situated, sitting next to each other. After the President's speech, the commandant of the academy called the graduating cadets to the stage individually and presented degrees.

Sam received his degree and followed Choxie back to their assigned places. The commandant turned the class over to the cadet captain who dismissed the class. The graduating cadets threw their hats in the air and cheered. No one noticed that Sam and Choxie stayed at their seats, tears streaming. The class broke into an uproarious celebration and began seeking loved ones.

Choxie finally broke the spell. "I should find my parents." She held out her hand and said, "Good-bye and good luck, Sam."

He recognized the finality of her intention. He couldn't stop the flow of tears, but managed a thin smile. "Will you write?" he asked.

"No. I don't think we should. Let's leave things the way they are." She extracted her hand and backed toward the aisle, her eyes locked on his. "Please be careful, Sam." She turned away, head and shoulders down.

"Chox!"

The pleading note in his voice tugged at her heart and she stopped.

"Chox!" He yelled again.

She turned to see him smiling, an unfamiliar, bewildered

smile–lost and forsaken.

"I'll never forget you," he said, then turned and disappeared into the celebrating throng.

He spent a month with Wes at the ranch, then left for his first Army assignment.

CHAPTER TWELVE

The Crucible

Sam arrived late that month at Fort Bragg, North Carolina. The excitement of his first posting could not compete with the disappointing knowledge that Choxie wouldn't be there. After handing his orders in at Special Operations Headquarters, he received a permanent duty assignment from an efficient female sergeant. "You must be lucky, Lieutenant–either that or you know someone. You're the first new Second Lieutenant to be assigned Special Ops in a long time."

He held in hand the one coveted appointment aggressive young infantry officers seek. While standing at the threshold of an exciting new career, Sam didn't feel anything resembling enthusiasm. He had not enjoyed the time with Wes at the ranch, still grieving over Choxie, discovering for the first time in his life how painful it is to sorrow over a lost love. He didn't know how to cry before losing Choxie. Sam Prescott could cry with the best.   His outlook on life began to improve as he traveled from one base to another attending schools. Airborne, Weapons, Ranger School, Forward Air Control, Special Operations–one demanding school after another preparing him for the most rigorous and dangerous assignments in the armed forces. Exacting training sapped strength and occupied time, helping him through the lonesomeness. He still thought of Choxie before and after sleep. His broken heart began to mend.

The training cycle continued month after month for a year and a half, concluding with a permanent unit assignment to Special Forces Command where the training routine began again, this time with men he would serve with in combat, the men of Delta Force, the most highly trained group of specialized warriors in the American armed services.

America, inextricably engaged in secret operations against terrorists' organizations in the Middle East, needed covert presence behind enemy lines. During the coming years, Sam served in Afghanistan, Iraq and

Special Ops headquarters, constantly moving, never permanent, always involved in or preparing for another mission. He made First Lieutenant on schedule and an accelerated promotion to Captain. His career blossomed with promise, including command positions.

* * * * *

During his fourth year as an officer, Sam received orders to a secret Special Operations Command forward base in southern Afghanistan. He arrived sick and sore from a battery of inoculations, and apprehensive as always, about what came next. He stepped from the airplane at Kandahar into a stifling hot, smelly, dusty world of noise and confusion. Military vehicles sped haphazardly through a maze of helicopters and multi-engine transports, all parked indiscriminately on a flight line almost obscured by a dust storm in progress. He pulled his bags into the shade of an old mud brick building and sat to take stock of his new surroundings.

A lieutenant from the flight stopped by and asked, "Where are you headed, Captain?"

Sam looked up, mouth open from the heat, too sick to care about anything. "I haven't checked in yet. Too damned sick to care right now."

"Yeah, me too. Must be the vaccinations. This heat is too much, isn't it?"

Both men collapsed on their bags in the shade, observing the pattern of activities for several minutes. Sam finally said, "Looks like everything and everybody eventually ends up in that old airport terminal building there." He pointed. "I expect we should probably get on over and have our orders checked."

"You go on, Captain. I just can't go yet."

They shook hands and wished each other luck. Sam had a vague idea about potential duties, but his orders gave only the briefest information: Report to a SF CAMP ROYAL. He discovered that it was located near Matun, well south of Kandahar, very near the border with Pakistan.

The crusty sergeant handling his paperwork flipped through the sheaf of papers efficiently. He leaned across the counter and pointed down the flight line. "The Black Hawk with the red nose, Captain. That's your bird. Better grab your stuff and hustle on down. They been waiting all morning."

The helicopter started before he got there, then lifted off before Sam could stow his gear and take a seat. He never did get the seat belt fastened, unable to find both ends of the belt.

The crew chief grinned and yelled, "Don't worry about it, Captain!

No big deal!"

Both door gunners, lanyards snapped to their waists, dangled out of the helicopter to take advantage of the cooling wind. The crew chief closed his eyes and nodded off, as did the co-pilot. Sam was still dizzy and sick from the inoculations and paid no attention to the mountainous countryside. He would see it again soon enough.

The helicopter flew generally southeast to the camp near Matun, landing in a small clearing surrounded by mud brick huts with tin roofs. Sam jumped down and turned just in time to fend off one of his bags as it sailed out of the rising helicopter. The chopper pilot couldn't wait, lifting off immediately, executing the final indignity by leaving Sam standing in a swirling cloud of dust and sand clutching his hat. His second bag tumbled from the chopper from a height of thirty feet, flopping into the dust at his feet.

Someone yelled, "Over here! Get inside! We're taking fire!"

Sam pulled his bags into a bunker and collapsed. After catching his breath, he asked directions to the headquarters.

A dusty, sunburned soldier answered, "Headquarters? That's a laugh, Sir." He pointed. "That mud hut right there."

After the alert cleared, Sam dusted off his uniform, a futile attempt to look squared away before stepping into the building. A clerk ushered him into the commander's office where Sam snapped to attention and presented his orders. "Captain Sam Prescott, reporting as ordered, Sir!"

A balding, sweaty major sat behind the desk, eyes glued to a pile of paperwork. Sam noticed a half empty bottle of whiskey on the desk and waited a full minute before announcing himself again. "Sir. Captain—"

The major, clearly annoyed, still concentrating on his paperwork, muttered, "I heard you the first time, Prescott. Stand at ease. I'll get to you."

The major excused himself and returned moments later, his crotch spotted wet, then shuffled through Sam's orders carelessly until he opened the page with Delta Force written on it.

He looked up. "Delta, huh? What a shame. You seem like such a nice young man. Well, welcome, Captain Prescott. Your crew has the last building in the compound, up against the perimeter wall. You'll be alone, though. They're out somewhere winning the war. In case you haven't noticed, this is Indian country, so keep your head down around camp. I'm pretty much out of the loop on Delta operations so your people will have to fill you in on the details." He smiled insincerely and waved Sam away. "If you need anything, don't ask."

Sam remained at attention. "Sir," he said after the major picked up another report. "When do I touch base with the officer I'm to relieve?"

The major looked up, visibly irritated to see Sam still present. "Captain Prescott, I don't know much about your unit, but I do know you will not be touching base with your predecessor." He reached for the whiskey. "You see, Captain, he didn't come back from his last mission, and that was two months ago. That's all I know. Anything else?"

Sam snapped to attention and saluted. "By your leave, Sir."

The major nodded and presented the bottle as a salute. "Your health, Sir."

Sam studied for days until his teams returned. After conferring with his men, after researching every shred of intelligence he could find from recent missions, he carefully outlined the next series of patrols. He let the men relax and train for a week before sending them back to the field. His unit was responsible for long range reconnaissance into the mountains of southern Afghanistan, and occasional clandestine missions into Pakistan. They reported enemy movements, called in air strikes, marked targets with laser beams while attempting to stay hidden from the natives. Their missions, always extremely dangerous, always in enemy territory, usually lasted from one to two weeks.

Sam didn't go out with the first patrols, a series of road reconnaissance assignments requiring no special guidance. He received orders to report to Special Forces' headquarters in Kandahar to receive briefings on an upcoming mission.

Upon return to Camp Royal, he assigned three teams of qualified officers and noncoms to normal recon training duties and took the fourth team aside, training them for a clandestine mission into Pakistan. The operation required him to locate and assassinate a Taliban war lord suspected of assisting Al-Qaeda. The renegade war lord had, allegedly, captured, tortured and executed three American soldiers while refusing to abide by his government's neutrality policies. According to intelligence, he commanded a regimental sized independent militia. Sam's Kandahar briefing revealed that the Pakistani government had authorized American assistance to neutralize the embarrassment of the renegade war lord.

Sam received the mission orally. "Your mission is to locate and neutralize Mustafa Zahar, Captain. The particulars are in this folder. Commit it to memory and turn the paperwork in before leaving. Keep the maps and photos you need. Ask questions when you know what to ask."

Sam had troubling doubts about the mission. His conscience plagued him throughout the briefing period. *This is suicidal. I'm sure that crossing into Pakistan for the purpose of assassination is not only illegal, but will be probably be looked upon unfavorably by the Pakistan government, which will wash their hands of the entire affair if we get caught. I hate the idea of being an assassin.* He asked the briefing officer to confirm that "Neutralize" meant assassination.

"What in the hell do you think we're doing over here, Captain? We don't call killing the enemy an assassination. This is a damned war! Your assignment is to kill the murdering son-of-a-bitch! I don't know why those staff pussies want to call it "Neutralize" for Christ's sake! Don't even bother to try and figure out the morality. Just save American lives and do the damned job."

Sam couldn't escape the uneasy feeling. He planned and trained for the mission, holding personal feelings in check, desperately hoping for a last minute cancellation.

The plan to get the team into Pakistan didn't appear difficult logistically. Fly over the border at night and parachute in. *Yeah, no sweat. Just a broken leg or two.* He would find Zahar, according to intelligence, holed up near the town of Bannu, a few miles south of the border beyond the Khyber pass. Sam boiled it down to risks. *Let's see, first a night parachute drop. If we live through that, finding and approaching Zahar appears to be next to impossible. Then all we have to do is get out of Pakistan after the mission, if we manage to live through that. This Zahar character must be important.*

Sam trained six members of the team, deciding in the end to use only himself and the three best for the assault part of the mission. They would remain together after the parachute jump until locating the war lord, then split the team into two elements, one as a diversion, the other with sniper rifles attacking from the opposite direction.

They flew into Pakistan on the first clear night after receiving flash intelligence information about their target's movements, supposedly up-to-date within the hour. The parachute descent into the mountains cost Sam all chance of success. He dangled for a few moments high above the darkened forest floor after his parachute hung in the trees, then heard popping sounds of a limb breaking, followed immediately by the terrifying sensation of weightlessness. He clutched frantically at limbs brushing by in the darkness but couldn't hold on.

The impact crushed the breath from him. He rolled down a steep incline, unable to see and unable to stop the descent until he crashed into a boulder. His breath returned in gasps. He gingerly tested arms and legs for shattered bones. *Nothing broken.* After his vision adapted, Sam found loose rocks to cover the parachute, inventoried his equipment and examined the rifle for damage. Satisfied with his circumstances, he listened intently for a few moments, then flipped on the hand-held radio and waited for the other team members to check in.

Crap! Gunfire!

A small arms engagement down the mountain somewhere to the east began sporadically, then burst into a full-scale battle.

Has to be my men. Timing is too coincidental.

His radio crackled and hissed as someone on the other end keyed a mike. He listened to the sounds of explosions and hard breathing, and then, "Come on! Let's move! They're all around us!" Another voice, more distant, "Where's the Captain?"

Sam keyed his mike and whispered, "This is Fox Six. Do you read?"

The answering voice came in a terrified whisper, "Fox Six, for Christ's sake stay off the air! We're surrounded! We landed right in their damned camp. They know where we are. I've been hit. Four is hit. Three is dead."

The mike clicked off. Sam heard the battle raging, listening helplessly as the gunfire increased and then suddenly stopped. He desperately wanted to call but knew better than to try. His receiver crackled again. A high-pitched voice said, "Death to America! Allahu Akbar!" He heard other voices in the background mixed with laughter, then AK-47 shots. He could hear sounds of celebration clearly, even without the radio.

Sam moved all night in a northwest direction toward the team's predetermined rendezvous point, a hill overlooking the fork of two rivers north of their target. He waited for two days, hoping the others would join.

His team had been given six days to accomplish the mission and hike to a clearing north of the target. A helicopter would extract the team at 1300 on the sixth day. The helicopter would come back two days later if the team didn't appear on schedule. After that, the team was to go by land to another recovery site near the Afghan border.

The team didn't join up. Sam received a gunshot wound to his side just above the hip at the pick-up site while running to the descending rescue helicopter. The pilot pulled away after bullets smashed the chopper's windshield. Sam limped to trees and up the mountain, escaping by lying in a bitterly cold stream beneath overhanging tree roots. He was in and out of the water for two days and nights.

Captain Prescott walked into camp 21 days later, starving and sick, suffering a high fever feeding from infection of the festering bullet wound. The bullet had torn muscle tissue but missed bone. He received a Purple Heart and Silver Star. *Wow. A silver star for failing.* After two weeks in a field hospital, he also received orders back to the States and another hospital.

After hospitalization, Sam's next orders were back to Fort Bragg, NC. He worked at Special Operations headquarters for the next year as an intelligence information interpreter and instructor. War in the Middle East escalated. Sam continually requested orders back to combat. His commander said, "No chance, Sam. I'm forwarded your request disapproved. You are not physically ready. Sorry"

The colonel directing Sam's department developed an intense dislike for him. He envied Sam's combat experience and citations, awards no member of a support staff could expect to achieve. Sam's duties included rare visits to the Middle East to visit Special Forces' outposts in remote areas, ostensibly to provide liaison between headquarters and field units.

Doubts about making the Army a career popped up on occasion. During an intelligence gathering foray into southern Afghanistan, he arrived at Camp Matun again. By then Sam had decided to separate from the Army, sealing the decision by submitting a letter of resignation. The Army became bearable. He was in control of his own destiny. Two days later he advised the local commander, yet another sweaty, alcoholic officer, that intelligence information indicated a large force of Taliban and Al-Qaeda had moved into the hills surrounding the camp.

"Really? Well, what do you recommend, Captain Prescott?"

"Sir, maximum air strikes and an immediate request for infantry reinforcement. Either that or withdrawal."

"Do you mean to tell me, Captain, that you don't think we can defend ourselves up here? I have over 250 riflemen on top of this hill, and eight 105 howitzers. The way I figure it, Captain, we can lower the tubes of our guns and eliminate the need for infantry altogether."

The assembled staff laughed with the major. The camp, after all, commanded a hill denuded of trees for several hundred feet down all slopes.

"No enemy approach will go unnoticed here, Captain, and once detected any ground assault would be suicidal. Don't you agree?"

Sam stood. "No, Sir. The intelligence report has a good rating. There are over a thousand elite fighters out there. Probably Zahar's people. Formidable."

"Let them come, Captain. Hell, if the bastards have us surrounded, then they can't get away, can they?" He laughed at the old military axiom, adding, "Bring it on. Mission accomplished." More laughter.

The attack came at midnight. Two determined, well trained, well organized battalions attacked simultaneously, breaching the concertina wire and mud brick wall surrounding the camp

Sam stayed in the command bunker until the infantry company commander received a fatal wound and the major ordered him take charge of the infantry. As Sam arrived at the dead commander's position, the battle had evolved into a wild melee of hand-to-hand combat inside the defense perimeter. He took stock of the situation quickly, running from one defensive position to another, encouraging and instructing.

Less than an hour after the first shot, a bleeding corporal collapsed into a heap on the floor of Sam's foxhole. "Sir, the major is dead! I'm the only one left in the command section!"

"Are there any operating radios up there?" Sam asked.

"No, Sir! I got the only good radio on my back. There ain't nothing up there 'cept a shit pot full of Haji's runnin' around with severed heads. They cut off everyone's head!"

Sam thought about the dilemma for a moment before making several quick decisions. *First, this camp is indefensible. Second, reinforcements will never arrive in time. Third, I need to consolidate forces immediately.*

He ordered all elements to draw back to his position, including the wounded. It took nearly ten minutes to gather his forces, all accomplished under withering fire. He called headquarters at Kandahar and requested an air strike on the camp.

"On your position? Better be sure. We have a 130 gunship in the immediate area. Where will you be, Alpha Six?" came the amazed reply.

"We're going over the side the second I get off this damned radio."

"You better be sure, Alpha Six."

"We're going over the side the second the last flare goes out! Get that strike underway! Alpha Six, out!"

Sam spoke briefly with the collection of corporals and sergeants representing the remaining leadership. "Just as soon as the flare goes out, we go over the north side, down to the treeline!"

The tattered unit jumped off two minutes later, down the side of the darkened hill dragging their wounded. The Air Force 130 soon circled overhead, firing a steady stream of explosives into the camp.

Sam took a bullet through his left forearm, shattering the bone, leaving his hand flopping uselessly. He jammed the bleeding limb under his belt to keep it out of the way. No time to stem the bleeding; no time to worry about it; no time to think. He reloaded his weapon at least three times, firing at wildly charging militiamen.

"Captain! The men don't know who to shoot at!"

"It's simple, Sergeant! Have the men form up back to back. Shoot everyone else! Tell the men to close it up! Back to back!"

Another bullet smashed through his leg muscles just above the knee, then grenade fragments slammed into his neck and chest. Another bullet went through his helmet, knocking him senseless for several minutes.

The American perimeter of defense stretched no more than thirty yards across. Within minutes after leaving the hilltop, Sam had 64 able-bodied men left of the 250 at camp the beginning of the evening. When the firefight ceased, he contacted headquarters and reported. The air support office asked, "What are your intentions, Alpha Six?"

"What do you mean? We can't go anywhere! Keep that air overhead until daylight, and then see if you can get some reinforcement up here. Copy?"

"Roger that, Alpha Six. Hang in there."

Sam's beleaguered command absorbed only sporadic contacts throughout the night. He took morphine for the wounds and stemmed the bleeding, struggling to remain alert in case the militia command figured out where the Americans were. He had several spells of nausea and dizziness when he stopped moving. The spells always let up with the sound of shots fired. Just before sunrise, Sam ordered an end to the air strikes.

"You're calling the shots, Alpha Six, but we won't have reinforcements up there for at least an hour. You sure? Over?"

"You heard right. I want a cease fire in exactly five minutes. Copy?"

"Roger that, Alpha Six. Cease fire in five minutes. Over?"

"Exactly five minutes. Alpha Six, out." Sam called for his leaders. "Saddle up, men. We're going to take our damned hill back."

The climb back began before the circling gunship stopped firing. When Sam's little force reentered the camp, the occupying militiamen were sticking their heads out of the bunkers that protected them during air attacks. The militia were dazed and disorganized. Sam's depleted force recaptured the firebase before reinforcements arrived. He collapsed as the first American helicopter touched down.

The coming weeks fused into a sea of pain and semi-consciousness. One morning, as an orderly at a military hospital in Germany helped feed Sam breakfast, the hospital commander, an administrative colonel, stopped by and pinned a Purple Heart on Sam's pillow.

"I don't take Purple Hearts lightly, Captain Prescott. I usually pin them on but you seem to be covered with bandages, so I'll just leave it here. Congratulations and well done I hear."

"Don't worry about it, Colonel. If you've seen one Purple Heart you've seen them all."

The Colonel seldom visited the wards, except to make weekly inspection tours. Sam noticed the attending staff with clipboards seemed way too formal, standing almost at attention, and he wondered why the Colonel seemed ill-at-ease. He usually didn't inspect the ward in dress uniform. The nattily dressed Colonel motioned his smiling entourage to gather around. "I suppose you know the president is visiting next week, Captain Prescott?"

Sam eyed the group suspiciously. "No, Sir."

The Colonel squared his shoulders and unfolded a message. "I'm going to read the itinerary for the president's visit, Captain Prescott. Just one part." He cleared his throat. "1400 hours. President confers Medal of Honor on Captain Sam Prescott." He handed the message to Sam. "Congratulations, Captain Prescott." Everyone present clapped and cheered.

Sam learned later that every surviving man at the battle had given a written statement and taken part in a unanimous recommendation that he receive the Medal of Honor.

The Secretary of Defense had appealed to the President and members of Congress and to the service secretaries, to award the medal to nominated soldiers while they were still alive. The Secretary thought, and the President agreed, that the unwritten historical stinginess of giving the honor to living recipients might be affecting troop morale. No American serviceman had been awarded the medal while still alive since the Viet Nam war. Sam would be one of the first.

There had been a tremendous volume of incontestable evidence by many men, not just the two required, that Sam had risked his life well beyond the call of duty, not once but repeatedly. The most prevalent comments by the men were, "I'm sure we would have all been killed if Captain Prescott wasn't there."

"He ran through enemy fire all night, exposed all the time. I thought he was going to get killed for sure."

The Medal of Honor is usually presented by the President of the United States in a formal ceremony held in Washington D. C. The President decided to award Sam's medal while on a previously scheduled visit to Germany. All major American television networks carried the presentation ceremony.

Sam spent the next six months at military hospitals in the States. The Army conceded his request for separation, honoring a long-standing tradition of granting Medal of Honor winners any realistic wish. He had paid the price for his education. Sam planned to move to Los Angeles and find a job. His life changed again a week before discharge. A slender woman in uniform came to the room with a message from the Red Cross.

"Sam, are you awake?"

He opened his eyes and smiled at Lieutenant Leslie Grant. "Oh, Hi, Les. Yeah, just napping. Wasting time. Hey, I thought you had the duty last night?"

She smiled wistfully. "I did."

Lt. Grant cared for Sam, very much–way too much. Her heart ached at the sight of him. She loved him desperately and he knew it, as did the entire nursing corps. Sam would not permit the relationship develop.

"Sam, I have bad news. She presented the message. "I'm so sorry."

It read: Department of Army to Captain Sam Prescott: Wesley Prescott, dead of gunshot wound. Unknown assailant. For more info, contact.... Sam blinked and read it over again and again, noting the telephone numbers of the county sheriff and funeral home.

"I'm really sorry, Sam. Commander Abingdon asked me to tell you. He knows I...well, I'm sorry."

"Thanks, Les." He sighed and said, "God, this is hard to believe, but that's the way he lived." He wadded the message up and threw it across the room. "Good thing it happened when it did. I would have been out of here next week. No telling when I would have found out."

Gunshot? Who? So many people disliked him. That's an understatement. I should have gone back more often. Damn.

"I can help with all the paperwork, Sam. I'll be glad to...."

He placed a finger over his lips to stop her. "No, I'll take care of it, Leslie. My problem."

He phoned the county Sheriff, learning little more than the sketchy news in the telegram, other than Wes had been killed at the ranch–definitely not suicide. He phoned the Thurman funeral parlor in Brewer and listened to the director babble inane platitudes before interrupting. "Thanks, Mister Thurman, but I want to talk about the arrangements, that's all." He knew what Wes would want. *"Never pay a damned funeral home a dime more than you have to, or a stinking lawyer."*

"We have several nice packages."

"No! I don't need anything special, just cremation as soon as the Sheriff releases the body."

"What about services? Of course you'll want services."

"No, dammit! No services. Just cremation. Those are my instructions."

He would bury Wes himself at the family cemetery. He would dig the grave and he would place the monument and he would say the words.

"Mister Prescott, Sir. If you don't mind, this is highly irregular."

Sam's patience ran out. "Is there another damned funeral home in town?"

"Yes, Sir, but.... Oh, I see. Never mind. Yes, Sir. Just as you wish. Now, when may I expect you?"

"As soon as I get there. Good bye."

CHAPTER THIRTEEN

Wickmore

Late afternoon shadows extended nearly half way across the isolated country road intersection. The air temperature hovered near one-hundred, a brutal reminder of the Ozark's lingering summer heat wave. Not a whiff of wind stirred to relieve withering plant life and wheezing animals. The secluded farm-to-market road intersection was unremarkable, an ordinary "T" convergence of gravel and asphalt distinguished only by a smear of red dirt stain extending from the gravel road onto the blacktop.

A covey of quail exploded from the weeds in the roadside ditch, flushed by two teenage girls stepping from the woods next to the road. The oldest, a pony-tailed fourteen-year-old, exclaimed, "I swear! Those birds always scare the pee out of me."

The quail vanished into the underbrush as the girls squirmed through a barbed wire fence surrounding their father's farm. They paused to listen for evidence of traffic before completely abandoning the security of the forest. Upon reaching the sanctuary of the intersection, the girls paused again to examine each other for ticks.

The oldest girl turned away from the highway and waltzed down the gravel road. "Come on, Tammy," she moaned, agonizing theatrically, glaring back at her thirteen-year-old sister, a demonstration of characteristic sibling annoyance. "We haven't got all day, dummy. Daddy is sure to find out we sneaked off if you take your precious time."

"Oh, he doesn't care Bobbi. I swear."

"Honestly! You're so stupid sometimes! He only let us skip

school because you lied about your period. Ha! What period? He'll have a cat fit if he catches us swimming. Now, come on! He won't be in town all day."

The younger girl stood fast. "It's too hot to hurry."

"That is the most pitiful whine I ever heard. You are such a pussy."

Tammy shuffled along, the picture of indolence–head down, arms folded behind her back, swaying to and fro, selecting a humane path through the sharp gravel.

"Come on, Tammy," Bobbi appealed again, waiting, glaring, eyes rolling. She suddenly reached out and tweaked her sister's budding breast, then dodged the predictable attempt at retaliation.

"Stop it, Bobbi!" Tammy pouted, wrenching away, hugging herself.

"Itty bitty titties," Bobbi chanted musically. "You're never going to grow titties. Poor little skinny dried up thing."

Tammy appealed to the heavens, looking up, groaning. "God! Titties! Titties! Is that all you ever think about? Good grief, Bobbi, just because you look like a milk cow and have to wear a sweaty old bra. Anyway, when I get my bra, and I will," she added smugly, looking down her nose. "I won't stuff it with toilet paper like you do."

Barefoot beneath faded Levi cut-offs, each girl wore one of their father's used cotton Sunday shirts with shirt tails tied in front exposing tanned, flat midriffs.

"Well, I don't have to stuff anymore," Bobbi countered, twisting away sensually, spinning to walk backward in front of her sister, eyes closed, dancing, simulating a strip tease, slowly unbuttoning the shirt. "Show ya."

Tammy stopped. "Yeah, right. You're such a fake. Honestly."

"Fake? Watch and weep, skinny." Bobbi jerked the shirt off dramatically and tied the sleeves around her waist.

"Bobbi? What are you...." Tammy covered her mouth with both hands, "Bobbi? For heaven's sake! Well, I swear!"

"You see stuffing in here? She cupped and pushed her breasts up. Ta-DA! Nothing but the real thing, child."

Tammy glanced around nervously. "Jesus God, Bobbi! Someone will see!"

"Who? Anyway, I don't care." Bobbi danced and frolicked, and then with the haughty air of indifference, crowned the event by unsnapping her brassiere and whisking it off, twirling it overhead.

Tammy reacted exactly as her older sister anticipated. "Bobbi! I swear!" She pretended horror, and then snatched her sister's bra and dashed ahead with the garment flapping over her head. Bobbi didn't act the least concerned. So Tammy tossed it in the ditch on the other side of the road. Bobbi fluffed her hair, breasts bobbing provocatively, promenading down the road as if nothing mattered.

The instant Bobbi's bra settled into the grass, a pulsating metallic object materialized well to the south, rising from behind the crest of a hill a mile from the intersection. The device seemed to hover over the state highway, separated from the horizon by columns of vapor rising from the heated asphalt. It remained visible a few moments, pulsing and glowing eerily, then sank from sight behind a hill. The apparition reappeared moments later, shimmering just above the road, supported by an August heat mirage. It looked to be mechanical, shiny and much closer this time accompanied by an assortment of familiar terrestrial noises–a silver bus belonging to a country band.

The girls stopped, now two-hundred feet from the intersection, listening closely to the sounds of the onrushing conveyance. They couldn't see it, but both identified the sound at the same time.

Bobbi screamed, "Oh, Dear God, Tammy! Someone is stopping! My damned bra!"

They ran to the ditch and hid behind a tangle of persimmon sprouts next to the fence, giggling hysterically.

"Oh, Sweet Jesus, Bobbi! It is going to stop!" Tammy covered her mouth, peeking through a break in the leaves. "What are we going to do? Busses never stop here! This is too weird! Oh, God! Oh, God. Now what?"

They crouched behind the foliage, Bobbi struggling furiously to pull her shirt on. The bus bore down on the intersection, hissing and rumbling ominously as the driver braked for an unscheduled stop.

* * * * *

"Yo! Cap'n Prescott! Up and at 'em, Cap'n!" The bus driver bellowed the summons over his shoulder while observing the subject of his attention in the mirror. "This here's the place you want off, ain't it?"

Sam awakened, rubbing his eyes. After glancing outside, he said, "Yeah, this is it." He stood and teetered unsteadily, then pulled a bag from an overhead storage rack, paused at the door to shake hands with the driver, and then stepped out into the brilliant sunlight. The driver had taken a band to Branson's airport where they departed for Las Vegas and a special engagement. He was to meet them in St Louis the next day. The passenger door sucked into place with a resounding pop, flush with the vehicle's aerodynamic design, and the big diesel engine roared.

* * * * *

The girls breathed a comic sigh of relief as the bus accelerated. Their euphoria didn't last long. Tammy tugged at her sister's elbow and hissed, directing her attention to the presence of a tall man in a rumpled army uniform standing in the wake of the departing vehicle.

"Sweet Jesus!" she whispered. "Someone got off. Who is it, Bobbi?"

"How would I know, dummy?" Then, suddenly aware of the full scope of her dilemma, Bobbi muttered, "Oh, no. No! I can't believe this. My stupid bra is on the other side of the road!" She flopped back in the grass whimpering. "I'm going to kill you! Honest to God, Tammy."

* * * * *

Sam stood on the shoulder in rippling waves of knee-deep grass, staring after the bus until it vanished. He slowly turned to face the road intersection after the last sound of the bus engine subsided. A troubled expression marred his face–a mixture of exhaustion and dismay. He made no effort to move, content to examine the gravel road from his vantage point, safely across the highway.

He leisurely scanned up and down the blacktop, unbuttoned his uniform blouse and recovered a pair of aviator sunglasses from his shirt pocket. He wiped the glasses with a handkerchief before fixing them in place over eyes already tortured by the bright sunlight.

"Well, no sense putting it off," he grumbled. "Can't stand here all day."

"What did he say?" Tammy whispered. "He's talking to himself."

"Shhh. He'll hear you."

Sam limped across the highway dragging the luggage, discarding it unceremoniously on the edge of the gravel road. Moments later, after listening for signs of traffic, he tried to touch his toes and failed, inspiring a series of knee bends to relieve travel fatigue. More watching and listening followed by pacing back and forth across the road. The limp seemed to improve. He noticed the trash clutter in the ditches: empty pop bottles, beer cans, cigarette butts and candy bar wrappers. A psychedelic wasteland dumped in the ditches on both sides of the road. It looked like everyone passing by threw something out. And then, to the girls' dismay, he lifted Bobbi's brassiere from the tangle of weeds.

Bobbi groaned. "Oh, no. What does he want with that?"

He held the bra aloft, speculated for a moment, and then let it drop back into the ditch.

Bobbi murmured, "Whew! Thank you, Jesus."

"Come on, Bobbi, let's get out of here." Tammy had already started scooting backward toward the fence.

"Not without my bra. I am gonna kill you, Tammy. You are one dead girl."

Tammy ignored the threat. "Come on. Let's go."

Bobbi held her forefinger up. "Wait a minute. You know, I bet that's the Prescott guy, the army guy in the news. You know, the guy with the President. That's the guy dad is all bummed out about."

"No kidding? I thought he was older. Come on, Bobbi, let's get out of here. You can fetch your boulder holder later." Tammy slipped through the barbed wire.

Bobbi conceded defeat and the girls vanished into the brush and on to the river.

Sam stopped pacing and stood dead still in the middle of the road, head bowed, a model of misery, lips pursed, jaw muscles knotted, fingers alternately clenching and opening, evidence of inner turmoil. Moments later, the battle apparently lost, he surrendered, turned and lifted his gaze. His eyes settled in the direction he had deliberately avoided since stepping from the bus. A frown formed and hardened as he stared down the narrow country gravel road slicing through a solid mass of second-growth scrub oaks, sassafras and persimmon sprouts. Not a sign of life. Sam barely breathed, eyes narrowed to counter the sting of perspiration gathering to pool at the corners of his eyes. He blinked and swallowed, then turned away and limped back to the duffel bag, there to sit with his back to the gravel road.

The road intersection offered nothing of interest, nothing to alter his blank stare. A state highway department road sign some fifty feet from the blacktop provided the only evidence of civilization, other than the road and trash.

WICKMORE

4 MILES

His shoulders sagged as the sun beat down on the heavy dress uniform hanging loose from his shoulders, weighted further by a cumbersome array of military decorations and badges. Silver captain's bars glistened on the epaulets and a black plastic nameplate over the right breast pocket proclaimed his name: PRESCOTT.

The uniform bore four full rows of unit and personal citations above the left breast pocket. A Purple Heart with an attached gold ornament indicating he had been wounded more than once occupied the outside position of the top row.

He wore other distinguished awards and citations for service and valor, including the prestigious Silver Star medal. The entire collection paled to insignificance compared to the light blue, white-starred ribbon centered over the display: The Congressional Medal of Honor.

CHAPTER FOURTEEN

Homecoming

S am didn't wait long for a ride. A UPS van careened off the highway and slammed to dusty stop. The driver yelled, "Where you headed, buddy?"

He struggled to stand, slapping dust from his trousers. "Wickmore! Where else?"

The driver waved Sam aboard, chiding himself aloud, "Yeah, where else. Their sure ain't nuthin' else down this here road, now is there? Hop in, bud. Sorry they ain't nuthin' for you to sit on. Agin' company rules to give rides."

Sam gratefully entered the van. "I don't mind standing. Anything is better than melting out here. Thanks for stopping."

"The company would fire me for picking you up, but, as the big boys say, It ain't illegal if you don't get caught, right?" His voice progressively got louder as the van gathered speed. "You from Wickmore?"

"I lived here once. Long time ago."

"Well, I guess it's a good place to be from, if you know what I mean. Home on furlough, I guess?"

"Yeah, something like that."

The driver, though friendly by nature, didn't miss the unresponsive tone of his passenger's brief answers. He correctly assumed Sam wasn't seeking conversation, but conformed to his amiable nature and kept right on talking. "I see the Coker girls are skipping school." He pointed to the two girls, now walking on the road ahead, and chattered on. "Goin' swimming, I bet." The van closed the distance. "They won't take a ride. I asked them at least a dozen times so I ain't even gonna bother to slow down." He whistled. "Umm, uh! Would you look at that! That older gal sure gonna be something, ain't she?"

He waved as the van swept by, adjusting the mirror to watch until the dust blocked his view. "Man, O man. She is already something. Cute little ol' butt sticking out there. Mercy! Stacked tight for a girl that age. Gonna look just like her mamma." He shook his head and grinned at Sam. "Now that there's another story, that Candi Coker is. Whew! Wish I knew then what I know now. She run off with the Wickmore school superintendent, you know." He glanced over to see if Sam would comment. No comment.

He shook his head sadly and turned his attention back to the road. "This damned road is terrible and gittin' worse all the time. Nuthin' but a bunch of potholes and ledge rocks. The county maintainer ain't been here in months. Hateful danged road!"

Sam nodded but didn't think the road had changed at all during his absence. The sharp rocks and potholes, the washed-out sections, overhanging limbs and roadside trash. Everything looked exactly as he remembered. When they came to the bridge, he smiled for the first time that day, listening to the menacing rattle and clank of the familiar rusting old structure.

A whistled sigh of relief escaped the driver as the van crept off the bridge and accelerated east to Wickmore. He shook his head again. "That bridge. I guarantee you, someday someone is going to have to do something about that old bridge. It's fallin' through."

"Looks about the same to me," Sam countered. He recognized the sensation of mounting excitement as they thundered toward Wickmore. After the bridge, his facial features hardened as old memories rushed back. Memories he had deliberately smothered and muted. He took some deep breaths, steeling himself for the inevitable.

The van crunched to a dusty stop in the middle of the gravel road on the outskirts of town. The driver pulled the parking brake. "I gotta deliver a couple of packages here, bud." He hesitated, then turned to face Sam. "I expect it might be cooler if you wait outside in the shade." He waited for Sam to exit the van, then started briskly toward an old house partially hidden in a jungle of weeds.

"Not that I don't trust you."

Sam stood in the shade of the van scanning the city limit sign several yards up the road toward town.

WICKMORE

POP 237

His gaze shifted from the city limit sign to the shoddy dwellings indiscriminately arranged along the road. The homes, most surrounded in a profusion of battered, rusting vehicles, appeared to be on the verge of being swallowed in a sea of weeds. Dogs lay in the shade and a few chickens roamed the street. Dust and heat hung in the air. He smelled crap–cat, dog, chicken, and the unmistakable scent of human feces.

Has it always been like this? This is worse than a big city slum. Doesn't anyone ever clean anything?

The driver returned, interrupting Sam's musings. They sped on into what remained of the town's business district. Sam remembered, all too well, that the people of Wickmore didn't expect much from life. He remembered complaining to Wes about the lack of industriousness. Wes replied: "What you see is the predictable product of generations of inbreeding and welfare. Don't spend a damned minute brooding about what they think of you, and for damned sure don't let 'em rub off on you."

He now viewed the impoverished evidence in front of him from the perspective of eight years absence, and maturity. *Wes had it right*. And yet Wickmore didn't look much different from other small towns he traveled through during the day, all looking much the same: Rows of empty buildings sitting like tombstones along empty main streets. Every small town featured the scarred remains of once bustling business districts. Wes, in his finest prose, once told Sam the old buildings were "Monuments to a more glorious past."

The vacant buildings Wes once portrayed as monuments had in their heyday shared the streets with other thriving businesses. No longer. Abandoned stores lined both sides of the barren downtown streets, deserted streets lined by weed-filled cracked and heaving sidewalks and decaying buildings, all sad remnants of a common and unrecorded history. No one cared.

Sam wasn't surprised to note the absence of street lights in Wickmore. *Doubt if there were ever any.* He could see no pedestrians, other than the chickens at the far end of the town. Wickmore had changed in eight years, though. Many of the empty old buildings were gone, torn down for scrap lumber or burned, other than the general store and café. *No gas pumps at the general store now? And the liquor store is gone. That has to be the last straw. Wickmore is dead for sure.*

Sam stared. "Wow!" he exclaimed, looking up and down the street. "The town has really changed. What happened to all the old stores? The gas station is gone. The whole town is mostly gone! Wasn't this street paved?"

"You're right about that, but the asphalt crumbled. She went back to gravel. They ain't got no money to fix anything. No mayor. No city council. No nuthin.'"

Sam removed the sunglasses and squinted at the sight. "Well I'll be damned."

The driver said, "Yep, Wickmore's almost a ghost town sure enough. Only one store left open, and the café, but it don't stay open much. Town's dead as a wedge. Just old folks and welfare cases."

Sam shook his head sadly. "Isn't this something. The town just dried up. Almost makes me sad." He recovered, scolding himself for harboring any good memories. "What in the hell did you expect," he muttered to himself.

"Sorry, bud, I didn't hear what you said," the driver's voice interrupted Sam's thoughts.

"Nothing really. Just thinking out loud."

The driver braked the van to a stop in front of Roush's store. "I got to deliver here. Anyway, this is as far as I go."

"This is good." Sam had called Jim Denning, his old coach and present school superintendent, the day before and arranged for a ride home. He didn't mind the short walk to the school. He shook the driver's hand. "Thanks for the ride."

"No problem, bud. Maybe I'll see you around? Anyway, good luck." He pointed down the street and said, "Looks like the whole community is in town today. Can't remember seein' so many trucks in Wickmore at one time." He paused to speculate, then nodded toward a group of men sitting in front of one of the vacant stores. "Is that your welcome committee?" He laughed, thinking it a joke.

Sam figured the men probably, more like definitely, were not there to make him feel welcome. "I wouldn't be surprised," he replied. "Wonder how they knew?"

"What's that?"

"Nothing. Talking to myself again."

Sam stepped from the van and stretched, scanning the street, taking his time. A grim smile pulled his mouth tight. While stalling, analyzing the setting, he noticed the ritual dates of senior classes spray-painted on empty buildings. His attention soon returned to the crew at the other end of the street. Some of the men sat on a weather-worn bench in the shade of an abandoned store while others leaned against the building and some sat on the elevated sidewalk, feet in the street. About a dozen in all, strategically placed between Sam and the school, all eyes on him.

He gazed at the gathering for a moment and then stepped into the general store. Once inside he noticed Irma Roush watching from behind the counter. He thought she seemed annoyed.

I never could read her. She never looked happy. "Has Coach Denning been around, Mrs. Roush?"

Sam never liked her. He remembered Irma as a sour, unhappy woman, always bitching at the kids. She never smiled, at least not for him. Irma's daughter, Cynthia, had been in his class. He really never hit it off with her.

"He don't check in and out with me now any more now than he did when you lived here." She wouldn't grant him the courtesy of eye contact.

"Would it be okay if I leave my bag here until I can get a ride, Mrs. Roush?"

"I'm fixin' to close at six, like always. Don't intend to be responsible for it. You'll have to fetch it tomorrow if I take a notion to lock up early."

"Thanks. I'll try to be back before you close." He remembered Wes once said something about her husband taking off with another woman, and that she and Wes went way back. He remembered that the UPS driver also said the Coker woman had run off with Irma's husband.

Irma glanced at him through eyes almost clenched shut, then said, "Heard tell you were headed back this way. You been away a long time. Planning to stay?"

He didn't miss the signs of her simmering hostility, or that she hadn't called him by name. *Wonder how much her attitude has to do with me walking out on the basketball team?* "Yes, Ma'am, it has been a long time. Do you know if Coach Denning is down at the school?" He deliberately ignored the last part of her question.

"I expect he is. He ain't the coach, though. He's superintendent now. Has been for quite a spell." She began dusting an imaginary speck from the counter top. Sam no longer mattered.

He said thanks and stepped outside. Dust from the departing UPS van had settled on the array of pickups lining the street. Sam's surveyed the vehicles, all four-wheel drives with evidence of each truck's role displayed in the back, mostly hay and empty feed sacks.

Yessiree, every good ol' boy in the neighborhood is in town this afternoon.

Each truck sported at least one rifle cradled in a gun rack attached to the inside of the rear window. Every man in the community owned a gun and most owned several. The community had a fetish for firearms and shot at everything–the bridge, junked automobiles, road signs. Signs of marksmanship appeared on mailboxes, fence posts, outbuildings, trees. Everything, it seemed, wore wounds of marksmanship.

Sam faced back down the street toward the crowd of men. *All here in the middle of the afternoon. Guess it's time to get on with it. Can't keep the fan club waiting.*

He had to walk by them to get to the school. The skin on the back of his neck tingled. The spit and whittle club had the sidewalk blocked. He nodded a greeting to the men on the benches as he approached, only half expecting the salutation to be returned. He could remember some faces and a few names.

"Afternoon," he said, eyes directly on them.

Some of the men looked away, coughing and spitting, others scowled and stared.

Sam's anger boiled. *They want a confrontation, I'll give it to them.* He stopped in front of the gathering, gazing slowly and deliberately from one man to another. Allan Coker, Mitch Hensley, the Fox brothers; he didn't know the others.

Mitch Hensley spit and said, "Never thought we'd see the likes of you around here again, Prescott." He spit again, the chewing tobacco spattering the dust near Sam's feet. Mitch had dropped out near the end his sophomore year, the year Sam came to Wickmore.

"Looks like you thought wrong, Mitch."

Mitch turned away and spit again. He stared at Sam for a moment, then said, "Guess yer figgering on selling out."

Sam smiled. "That would be my business, wouldn't it, Mitch? Why? You planning to buy if I do?" He knew Mitch probably didn't have a dime in the bank.

"Just wondering if you might be gonna break it up into small farms." Mitch spat again.

Sam's gaze worked its way down the line, lingering on each man until they became restless and started shifting uneasily. "Well, I really have to run, fellas. But it's sure good to see all of you again. Yes, sir, it's sure good to be back." He forced a pleasant smile and walked away.

None of men spoke. Their eyes followed him, dripping with contempt. He smiled and thought, *Well, it isn't quite the same as a parade, but what the hell.*

Sam didn't speed up or give them the satisfaction of looking their direction again. He knew they were watching, every eye locked on his progress. The power of their voices strengthened after he passed. He could hear every word clearly, as they intended. *Just keep moving. No more games.*

"What the hell is *he* doing back here?"

"Shit, I dunno. Looks like some goddamned fag in that fancy uniform, don't he?"

"Rafe's kid had to go over there and git himself kilt, but no god-all-mighty Prescott gets kilt. The rich get richer, ain't that right?"

"Yeah, ain't that the way of it. No damned justice."

The voices faded as Sam walked away clenching his teeth, warding off an almost overwhelming urge to confront them, even if it meant a fight.

* * * * *

"Sam Prescott! By golly, let me look at you." Jim Denning had lost most of his hair and gained a creased, worried look that Sam didn't remember. His old coach smiled broadly, bounced out of his chair and came quickly around the desk to shake Sam's hand. "By golly, it sure good to see you. Let me have a look at you." He stood back, arms spread, beaming.

"It's good to see you, too, Coach. It's nice just to see a friendly face in this town. How are you? You look great."

"Oh, I'm fine, Sam, but that isn't important. And just call me Jim, would you? How are you? By golly, you sure been through hell. Are you okay?" He squinted, searching, Sam supposed, for signs of who he used to be.

Coach Denning reminded Sam of an undertaker greeting mourners at a funeral, serious and somber. "I'm doing fine now, Coach...Jim."

"Well, good. That's great. But, if you don't mind me saying so, you don't look all that good, Sam. You look a little thin maybe. You look tired, beat up and worn out, sorry to say."

"I lost some weight, but still have all my major body parts. I'm okay."

"All right, then. Sit down. Sit down, by golly, if you got a moment."

Sam laughed and took a seat. "I'm in no hurry, Jim, not any more. I have nothing but time for a while."

"Well, by golly, what do you know. It's sure good to see you back in one piece. I tried to keep up with you, Sam, but no one knew much until that deal on national TV. The news about your medal. That was a wonderful thing, Sam. I really admire what you did."

"Thanks, but things got blown a little out of proportion."

"We got to watch the president pin that medal on you. Don't try to kid me. That was a big deal. Sure made me proud to know you, Sam. Yes, sir, by golly. I'm sure mighty proud to know you." His expression sobered again. "I didn't know you got hit more than once, not until they mentioned it on the news when you got the big medal. I guess you had a rough time."

"Some. That's all behind me now. The doctors say I'll get back to normal."

"What's this I hear about you are going to get out of the Army. Is that right?"

"That's correct. Matter of fact, it will be official at the end of the month. They couldn't very well keep me, now could they?"

"No. Well, by golly I'm glad you're back, Sam." He leaned forward confidentially. "I hope you know what you're getting into, coming back here. Things have sure kinda taken a bad turn." Denning changed the subject before Sam could ask the obvious questions. "Oh, did you know Rafe's kid got killed last month? Someplace in the Mideast."

"Yeah, so I heard." Sam's thoughts were stuck on Denning's bad turn comment. "That's really too bad." He barely remembered Rafe Jones' boy and didn't want to talk any more about the war.

Denning chattered on. "Real sorry to hear about Wes. I hated that."

"Thanks. I suppose you know that's why I'm back." He leaned forward and put an end to small talk. "What happened, Jim? Do you know?"

Denning pushed back, physically separating himself from even the appearance of involvement. "Not much, really. Only that the foreman found him dead one morning. Shot in the head with a high-powered rifle, so I hear."

"Yeah, I know that much. Come on, Jim, you're in a position to know things. I need to know what happened."

Denning tugged at his necktie, scooting back, separating himself even farther. "Um, I really don't know anything particular, Sam. Anything I could tell you would be pure speculation. Sorry."

Sam had seen it before. No one wanted to get involved. Denning was part of the community now–us against them. Sam sighed, disappointed, and said, "But you have some ideas, I'll bet."

"Oh, sure, everyone has his own idea about what happened. Nothing in black and white. Just ideas."

He isn't going to help. "Okay, Coach, I won't press you. How about that ride out to the ranch?"

"Sure, I'll run you right out there."

Sam held up a finger to stop the action. "Just tell me this much, Coach, am I paranoid or was that a welcome home party I just ran into downtown?"

Denning looked embarrassed. "I heard they were going to wait for you." He shook his head. "What a bunch of jerks, huh? I heard they were all going to get together. They give you any trouble?"

"No, but I would sure like to know how they knew exactly when I planned to arrive."

Denning said, "Probably that squirrely foreman Wes hired before he.... Anyway, I think he's the one that passed the word.

That's what I heard."

Sam mentally recorded the affront, remembering that he told the foreman when and how he planned to get home, and specifically directing him not to say anything.

"How is Polly?"

"Oh, same as ever. We have another kid, did you know that?"

"No. Boy or girl this time?"

"It's a boy. Oh, and we named him after you. Hope you don't mind." He sat back with a pleased smile and waited for Sam's reaction.

"You named him after me? That's the nicest thing anyone ever did for me."

"Well, I hope he grows up to be half the man you are. He's six now. You got to get over and see him. And Polly will sure want to see you. We live out at the old Roush place."

"I'll come over soon, I promise." Sam stood and said, "I suppose I ought to get on out to the ranch. I expect I'll probably find some loose ends out there."

The superintendent clapped on an old floppy hat, stood, and then hesitated, his face a mixture of concern and anxiety. "Sam, you probably need to watch yourself out there. I don't know exactly what to tell you, but what I hear is that you're probably missing a bunch of cattle."

The comment didn't catch Sam so much by surprise as the lack of content. Denning's leading information only inspired anger. "Is that all you are going to say? Probably? Probably? Come on, Jim. I need to know more than a probably."

Denning avoided Sam's eyes, scratching his neck. "Well, I don't know anything for sure, just enough to believe you got some problems. I'm sorry, but they're pretty careful about what they say around me. They know we–you and me–got along pretty good. They remember."

"Ah, yes, the nebulous 'they.' Okay, who are they, Jim? I need to know."

"I don't know exactly, Sam. No one does. Maybe some locals. Maybe Townsend. Okay, yeah, probably Townsend." He changed the subject. "I wish things turned out different for you before you left, but I want to tell you this much, I never disagreed with what you did. You're still the best kid that ever came out of this town,

Sam. They won't admit that, but they all know it, and that's what sticks in their craw." He nodded, satisfied with himself. "Let's go."

CHAPTER FIFTEEN

Partners

D enning, an avid CB radio fan, checked in with his listening
buddies giving Sam time to think during the ride to the
ranch. He didn't listen to the truck driver conversations,
believing it comical that the completely bald Denning's CB
buddies identified him as Silver Fox. Denning's radio fixation
struck Sam as odd for a man of his professional stature.

His thoughts drifted to impending problems: selling the ranch
and the circumstances surrounding his uncle's death; everything
that had forced him back to Wickmore. Each turn in the road,
every run-down house, everything brought back memories. He had
sworn never to return.

Three miles out of Wickmore, Sam recognized the fence now
bordering the ranch. His ranch. The stately entrance didn't
materialize for another five minutes. When Denning pulled to a
stop in front of the iron gates, they found them chained and
padlocked.

"Whoops, it's locked. That's too bad, Sam. Wish I could take
you on up to the house, but it looks like this is about as far as I go."

"Thanks, Coach. This is good enough. It's less than half a mile
from here. I can walk that far easy enough. Might even be good for
me."

Denning turned the blaring CB volume down. "Well, by golly,
don't be a stranger, Sam. Keep in touch, you hear?"

"I will. Thanks again."

They shook hands and the truck clattered back toward town.
Sam slowly turned to face the gate, letting the bag slip to the

ground. He stood quietly, inspecting the enormous edifice looming in front of him. He always thought the formidable monument was nothing more than a deliberate expression of power and wealth; an ostentatious way to remind the community of Prescott status.

"My God!" he exclaimed. "No wonder they all despise us."

His vision gradually shifted through the wrought iron bars to the land beyond the gates. What lay beyond took precedence over all other thoughts. For the first time since Wes died, Sam faced reality. *This all belongs to me and I sure don't want it.* He took no pride in ownership. His thoughts skimmed over memories of the time he spent on the ranch as a teenager. Painful recollections surfaced from dark shadows where stored memories of bothersome events and people still lived. After a deep, uneven sigh, he announced to the steaming solitude of the countryside, "I am not ready for this right now."

Sam threw the duffel bag over, climbed the gate and entered the ranch. He didn't shoulder the bag again, dragging it up the smooth asphalt road toward the house. A quarter of a mile later, over the crest of the hill and in sight of the majestic house, he stopped to survey, not to admire or relish the sight, he halted because he hated to go on.

No family waiting to meet me here. No welcome home party. No friends. Nothing here for me other than some bad memories that I can do without.

Sam found food in the frig and a bottle of wine. He sat staring down the valley through the huge living room windows, waiting for the sun to go down while planning his future. He would set about inventorying the assets, and then liquidate. *Get done and get out. Nothing here for me.*

The foreman, Theo Garner, a bearded man wearing a leather frontier hat, came to the house the following morning. Sam didn't waste time. "Garner, pack your gear and move on. I want you off this ranch within the hour."

Garner held up his hands in a feeble gesture of protest. "What? What did I do? I ain't done nothin' wrong!"

"You didn't follow my instructions. The whole damned town knew when I was coming in, and that information could only come from you. And why was the gate locked? Where were you yesterday? You were supposed to be here." He followed the grumbling man every step of the way until he left the ranch.

The wall safe combination numbers Wes had given him at graduation worked as advertised. Sam found the inventory and journals Wes kept locked in the office safe. He drove over the ranch checking gates and fences, counting the herds. Denning had been correct about the probability of missing cattle. According to the journal, which Sam found to be up-to-date as of the day Wes died, at least fifty cows were missing. He reported the theft to the sheriff and moved the herds to internal locations nearer the house, and then called a commission company to make arrangements for selling the cattle. He spent the next week inventorying and preparing for a sale.

Sam's health improved. Outdoor work agreed with him. He stepped into the house well after dark, exhausted from long hours of work and felt along the wall for the light switch. His life changed in a flash of pain.

* * * * *

The Appleby twins were waiting behind the wall of the darkened living room, each with a thick hickory club. Clyde Townsend stood in the background with a pistol–just in case.

Just before Sam entered, Clyde whispered, "I hear his truck. Now, dammit, boys, I don't want him kilt and I sure don't want him to see your damned faces." He cautioned, "Just mess him up real good." Clyde had already unscrewed the light bulbs in the foyer. "Take him the second he tries to switch on the lights."

The first blow struck Sam on the side of the head, knocking him unconscious. The Appleby's, true to their nature, continued a vicious beating until Clyde called it off. "Shit, Charlie! You dumb sumbitch! I think you kilt him! *Dammit*, Charlie! Don't you ever listen to nuthin'?"

Clyde knelt to feel for Sam's pulse. He breathed a sigh of relief. "I mean, dammit all, Charlie! Don't you understand? I just said mess him up! I didn't say kill him! Jesus!"

"What are we going to do now, Boss?" Charlie asked, cringing, eyes wide, more afraid of Clyde than the idea that he might have killed Sam.

Clyde stood. "Well, he ain't dead. Not yet anyways. All right, go on ahead and mess up his arms and legs some more. I don't want him to forget and I don't want him out herdin' any more damned cows. Just don't kill him, dammit! Go on, get it over with. Let's get the hell out of here."

After the twins finished, Clyde checked Sam's pulse again. "Well, I reckon that evens things up between us, Prescott." He slammed Sam's head to the floor. "Okay, boys, let's get outta here."

* * * * *

A week after the beating; after the ambulance ride to a local doctor's office in Brewster; after walking out when the doctor ordered a hospital room, Sam's body still ached and he still had to sleep sitting up. The bruises and cuts were healing, but the pain in his swollen elbows and knees crippled him. He had forced himself to walk without crutches from the beginning, spending daylight hours patrolling with a gun and sitting in the truck at discrete places on the ranch at night.

Sam's physical condition wasn't the only thing that bothered. The county sheriff's attitude about the assault mystified him. The sheriff had listened nonchalantly, twisting the ends of his enormous waxed handlebar mustache as Sam listed complaints. The lawman didn't take a note, just gazed at Sam and nodded.

When Sam finished, the sheriff leaned back in his chair, hooking his thumbs in the gaudy, hand-made pistol belt sagging beneath his substantial belly. "I'm real sorry about all this. All right then, I'll look into it and be in touch. That suit you?"

Sam felt dismissed. "Is that it? Don't I need to fill out some paperwork?"

"Nope. That's it, partner. I'll git right on it."

Sam walked out with nagging suspicions that the sheriff had taken it all much too casually. He didn't hear for days afterward and the sheriff didn't return his calls. A week later, when Sam drove in to question him again, the sheriff didn't try to hide his irritation.

"Look, I'm working on it, Prescott. That's all I can tell you. Investigations like this take time. Anyway, you didn't see 'em and I ain't no damned wizard. Now, suppose I do my job and you just learn to be patient. I'll be in touch."

Sam had planned to start an exercise program upon return to Wickmore. The beating delayed the project. He could barely walk for a week and then at the cost of considerable pain. Ten days after the beating marked the first time he felt strong enough to try jogging. He stubbornly ignored sore muscles and struggled through a series of calisthenics and limped down the road to the gate.

He crossed the shiny cattle guard and turned down a shaded gravel road leading by the ranch and attempted to jog. Sam recognized old landmarks–fence rows and crumbling foundations once part of small farms his family had claimed over the years, some by devious methods.

Wes and the Prescott men before him left a legacy of affluence and arrogance that had never weighed heavily on Sam's conscience, at least not until the ranch fell to him. Now he was the Prescott, and now the family history bothered. He forced himself steadily down the road against common sense and pain, against rebellious muscles and faltering determination. *Better turn around. I might not make it back.*

He had returned to Wickmore with the idea of recovering his health while cleaning up the legal issues, with plans to leave as soon as possible. Now, two weeks were wasted and gone. And now he felt the stir of strange new emotions; mysterious feelings associated with emerging inklings of ownership; a sense of identity he neither savored nor desired, but it was there, on the periphery of thoughts he consciously suppressed. Sam felt something new and disturbing; an uninvited, inadvertent covenant with ownership far removed from his original plans. The realization astonished him. The strange new feeling really wasn't about pride of ownership or family allegiance. A grim resolve was gradually taking shape behind the sea of pain and anger. *What am I thinking? Am I actually thinking about…. Forget about that. Get a grip.*

He struggled on, hobbling more than jogging, spellbound by the surprising insight. *Do I actually care? What the hell?*

An anonymous caller had left threatening phone messages every day since the beating. Sam reported several acts of vandalism to the sheriff: burned sheds, torn-down fences, gut-shot cattle and other annoying and expensive crimes and malicious damage. His anger grew with each incident until he had to admit the reality of his feelings. *No one is going to run me off.*

He jogged on, each painful step a brutal reminder of the beating. He had not seen the men's faces and couldn't remember hearing voices. He remembered nothing more than waking in a pool of blood, and the excruciating pain.

The sheriff called it, "An unfortunate incident, bud. You just walked in on someone trying to rob the house, young feller. They didn't take anything, so if I was you I wouldn't try to make nothing more of it than that. I don't want you going off half cocked with some of that fancy army stuff I hear you're famous for. I'm the law around these parts."

"That's nice to hear, Sheriff. I still want to know what you're doing. What about all the missing cattle?"

"Look, son, you don't run things around here and I don't report to you. Sooner you learn that the better off you're gonna be."

Thirty-one additional head of cattle were missing. The sheriff said he would investigate. "Hell, sonny, you don't have no proof. You don't even know how many cattle you had out there before this alleged theft you're talking about. You haven't been here long enough to get a handle on things."

Sam blew up. "I damned sure do know. Wes left a complete inventory the day before he was killed and I check cattle every day. There are now a total of eighty-one head missing. I want to file a formal complaint. In writing!"

"Verbal is good enough and you just did. That's as formal as it gets around here. Anyhows, even if you could prove them cows was missin', and I doubt you can, it won't do no good. If we located some cows you think are yours, you couldn't prove they are. It would just be your word against someone else's. Wes didn't brand anything, did he? So, you see, there really ain't much I can do. I'm real sorry about all of this and wish there was something I could do, but there just ain't."

* * * * *

Sam jogged on, lost in thought, the bruised muscles in his legs warming to the task. His thoughts and the exercise stopped at the same time, erased by the agonizing pain of a twisted ankle. He gasped and hopped on the good foot until he could sit down.

"Damn! Damn! Damn!" He rocked, groaning, clutching the injured ankle tightly. "Please don't be broken." He grimaced, sucking air through clenched teeth and determined that it wasn't broken. After resting several minutes, he struggling to his feet and tested putting weight on the throbbing ankle.

Sam was too busy with the injury to notice the sound of an

approaching car creeping around the bend in the road behind him. He didn't hear it until it was on him and felt foolish, ridiculously defenseless, muttering to himself as he hopped off the road to permit the vehicle to pass. The lone occupant was a woman. He breathed a sigh ofrelief. *Damn. I'm lucky. Could have been anyone. Dumbass.*

The car stopped. A woman rolled the window down. "Are you all right?"

Looks familiar. Can't place her. "Yeah. Just turned my ankle a little bit. I'll be okay in a minute or two." He expected the ankle would limber up if he kept moving.

She didn't appear convinced. "I'll be glad to give you a lift."

"Thanks for asking, but I probably ought to keep moving." He smiled and waved her off. The car started to move away, then stopped. The woman turned to look back, apparently having second thoughts, and then drove on. He waited until the car disappeared and started limping back toward the house, angry with himself for not accepting the ride.

"You're stupid, Prescott," he mumbled, struggling to the top of the first hill with waves of pain coursing through his ankle. He heard the car again before he saw it and stood in the ditch to make room for her to pass. She stopped and got out.

"Hi again," he said. "You lost?"

She examined him from across the top of the car, her expression one of concern. "No, I'm not lost and I believe you are Sam Prescott, right?" It wasn't a question.

"Guilty," he said, losing his balance, hopping awkwardly on the good foot. After regaining stability he said, "I'm just clumsy. Don't shoot me. I'm not a horse."

She apparently didn't think he was funny and frowned while walking around the car. "You are also hurt, Sam Prescott. Why don't you get in and let me take you home?"

That's interesting. She knows who I am.

She opened the passenger side door and said, "Get in. Don't be stubborn. Your face is white as a sheet. Get in. I'm taking you home."

He didn't argue. She seemed nervous and drove with her eyes locked on the road ahead.

"You were right," he said, hoping to break the awkward

silence. "I need some help. Thanks for stopping."

She smiled wryly. "If you don't mind me saying so," she said, glancing his direction. "that ankle doesn't appear to be all that's wrong with you." She held up a warning hand and said, "Sorry. I have no right to pry."

"That's okay." He tried to sneak peeks at her without being too obvious. *She does look familiar. Wholesome. Thirtyish. Pretty. Oh, yeah, very pretty.*

He could tell his glances made her uncomfortable. "I'm sorry," he said, hoping to salvage the moment, "but you have me at a disadvantage. You know who I am and I'm pretty sure I should know you." He expected her answer would probably embarrass him.

"I didn't think you remembered. I'm Cynthia Roush."

Of course. Wow, has she ever changed. Face is thinner. Better looking than I remember. Of course. Cynthia Roush. Most popular girl in school. Maturity definitely agrees with her.

"Of course. Now I remember," he said. "You used to work in your mother's store. Sure I remember. How have you been?"

"I'm fine. I'm sorry about your uncle."

Sam nodded. "Tell me, Cynthia Roush, what are you doing roaming around out here?"

"Oh, just out for a drive. Nothing special."

"You still live in Wickmore?"

"No. I live in the county seat–Brewster." She offered a tense smile.

"Does your mother still live in Wickmore?" Sam knew she did but couldn't think of anything else to say.

"Oh, yes. Mother's a fixture in Wickmore." Her eyes rolled. She stopped at the cattle guard.

Sam remembered the time she drove him to the ranch after picking him up in a rain storm. "If you don't mind," he said, "I would really appreciate a lift on up to the house." He didn't want to lose her company. "I'm afraid I have slightly overestimated my ability. Would you mind?"

"Not at all."

Her face brightened as they drove between the rows of poplar trees lining the paved road. She no longer seemed conscious of his presence. "I was here once before, you know," she announced, taking her eyes from the scene momentarily.

"I remember. You didn't stick around long as I recall."

She blushed. "This is all so beautiful." They topped the hill and she exclaimed, "My heavens! I had forgotten how...it's just...."

He observed the house himself, trying to imagine what it must look like to a visitor. He was unable to remember ever evaluating the house without embarrassment, about what must be pretentious showiness to the locals.

"This is the most beautiful home I have ever seen," she said, pulling into the circle drive.

"Would you like to come in?" He held up his hands, palms out. "As you can see, I'm pretty much harmless."

"Oh, thanks, no. I probably should go on."

He smiled at the way her facial expression revealed exactly the opposite. "Well, suit yourself, but there isn't anyone around except me. Anyway, I owe you. Maybe something to drink?" He enjoyed watching her struggle with conflicting desires. She delayed too long, giving him more reason to think she would like to see inside. "I wish you would come in. Come on. Just for a minute. It's been years since I've talked to anyone from Wickmore. Please? Really, I am absolutely harmless."

"Are you sure? Oh, my." She grimaced and blushed. "I'm sorry. Really, I didn't mean it that way. Are you sure about me coming in, that is." She laughed. "I'm just hopeless."

Sam chuckled. "Either way," he said. "And I am absolutely sure I would like it very much if you came in. Please."

He lifted his damaged foot out gingerly and started hobbling toward the house. *Perhaps a bit theatrical, Prescott, but women are attracted to wounded animals.*

She stood by the car and said, "Can I help?"

She's coming in. "No, thanks. I'll be okay. You go on ahead. I'll meet you on the steps."

By then he knew she was not wearing a wedding ring. He hobbled along, enjoying the advantage of appraising her from behind without being obvious. *Nice legs. Nice everything.*

She walked with a bounce that attracted his attention, placing her toes down first, testing the uneven rock surface. The wary technique didn't promote a smooth, gliding gait. She bounced. Her skirt wasn't tight, but failed to conceal shapely hips and a slender waist. She turned and waited at the porch.

Sam limped onward without abandoning his observations. Her white silk blouse was buttoned to the very top with a black ribbon securing the collar. The tie communicated the impression of a career woman, or a Sunday school teacher, he thought. The blouse fit loosely, probably a size too large he estimated, jiggling delightfully.

"Go on in," he prompted, still quite content to keep her in front. "The door isn't locked."

He stepped in and pulled the drapes to furnish more light and to expose the greatest view. "What can I get you to drink?"

She apparently wasn't listening, standing in the middle of the room attempting to savor everything at once.

He watched her for a moment, then said, "Just have a seat anywhere. I'll be right back." She glided backward into a chair, her eyes taking everything in, hardly aware of his absence. Sam returned shortly, hobbling along with two glasses of soda. Cynthia was still absorbed with the scenery.

"This is simply marvelous!" she exclaimed. "The room and the view. Everything is so beautiful."

"Would you like to see all of it?"

She waved a moderating hand. "Oh, no. Not now. Maybe some other time." She finished her inspection and directed her attention back to him. "I read about your wounds and medal. We all watched the presentation on television. It must have been terrible. The war, I mean. Are you all right now?" She blushed. "How silly. Obviously you aren't. Please forgive me."

He laughed, more because her innocence intrigued him than anything humorous. Her face, her eyes, her body language, all open books betraying every emotion. *She either doesn't know how to disguise her feelings or she isn't trying.* "I'm fine," he said. "My present physical limitations have nothing to do with the war. I have just about recovered from the government's all-expenses paid visit to the Middle East."

"If you'll forgive my observation, but you don't look fully recovered to me."

"Well, I had a little run-in with some intruders a few days ago. I expect that's the reason I look beat up. Just a temporary inconvenience."

She didn't appear convinced. Sam decided to change the subject. "I started an exercise program today–maybe too soon–which brings me back to you. Do you drive the back roads for fun?"

She saw through his question. "So, you don't think I'm out here for entertainment?" She smiled, not convincingly, then added, "I suppose it's time to be honest." She squared her shoulders, lifted her chin, and said, "Mister Prescott, as you have so shrewdly concluded, my presence here is no accident. I am the county prosecutor. I came out here to speak with you. Sorry for all the deception."

Sam held up his forefinger. "Ah ha! Prosecuting attorney. Interesting, and I'm impressed."

"The title is not a big deal, Mister Prescott. Any lawyer who wants the prosecutor's job in a rural county can have it for the asking. It doesn't pay anything."

"I'm still impressed. I've never known a lawyer from Wickmore, particularly a female."

"Thanks, I guess, even if the observation does smack of male chauvinism." She smiled so he would know she wasn't serious about the remark.

Sam wanted to stop visiting and get to business. "How did you know I was here? And, if you don't mind, I wish you would call me Sam."

"All right, Sam. How did I know? My duties. I read the sheriff's daily report and your name appeared on two recent summaries. One reported an alleged break-in and the other an incident of unconfirmed cattle rustling."

His anger flared. "What? Did you say the report alleged a break-in? Didn't it say anything about assault?"

Her face registered surprise. "No. Nothing about an assault. Only a break-in that could not be confirmed by damage or missing property."

He flopped back. "God Almighty! I can't believe it. Nothing about assault? That's why I'm limping around! What about the cattle theft?"

"The sheriff's report states that evidence did not sustain your claims of theft."

"I'll be damned!" He slammed his fist on the chair arm. "Sorry.

I just can't believe this!" He took some deep breaths to regain composure before addressing her again. "Look, the reason I look pale and beat up is someone nearly killed me–right over there!" He pointed toward the front door. "And now you tell me the sheriff didn't even bother to mention the assault in his report! What is going on around here?" He limped around the room collecting his thoughts. "If you wonder if I'm telling the truth, check with the emergency room at the hospital, and the ambulance crew. And you say the theft of cattle can't be confirmed? Dammit all! I have reported eighty-one head of cattle missing! I showed the sheriff the inventory taken just the day before Wes was killed! And now you tell me it's an *alleged* theft?" He sat down across the room from her. "I'm sorry. It's not your fault. I'm having a tough time, here." Sam groaned and took some deep breaths. "Do you have any idea how this makes me feel? Do you?"

She didn't reply, waiting quietly for his anger to subside.

Sam sighed heavily. "Okay, I guess that takes us back to square one. If you didn't come all the way out here for a social visit, then why are you here?"

"Mister Prescott. Sorry. Sam, I cannot reveal the underlying purpose of my visit as it is based solely on suspicion, and I don't know enough about you to take you into my confidence. I came here hoping to learn.... Well, truth is, I want.... No. I need to know more about you."

He stood and hobbled to a chair next to her, and then with an air of determination said, "Okay, time's up. What's going on?"

She nodded approval to herself to go ahead and throw caution to the wind. "I have an idea. I am here looking for help. I need someone to help me."

He studied her for a moment before saying, "I see. And I take it you think I might be that someone?"

"Very possibly. My plan is embryonic and I need more information before setting anything into motion. I will need much more information to know if the plan is feasible. Even if it is, yes, I am definitely going to need help."

"And you think I can help?"

She smoothed her skirt before looking up. "I have several reasons to include you in the plan, Sam, not the least is your military background. I need someone who is not afraid to get involved. So, yes I believe you can help. Actually, I think you may be the only person who *can* help."

"You can find any number of ex-military types."

She grimaced. "True. However, unfortunately, I think you are already involved."

"I am?"

"I think you are, and that's all I can say right now."

Sam surveyed her skeptically. "I'm not some gun-toting redneck, Miss Roush."

"I didn't mean to imply anything like that. I think you are going to be the target of more thievery."

"How do you know that?"

"I'm pretty sure I know who the thieves are. I can't prove it yet, but have an idea how to find out."

Sam had an epiphany. She had given enough clues. He smiled and said, "Okay, I get it. I'm the bait. Is that the plan?"

"Not you, Sam. Your cattle." She stood. "I really would rather not say more at this time. Please don't mention this talk to anyone, Mister Prescott."

"Sam, please." He stood and winced, forgetting the sore ankle.

She nodded. "All right, Sam. Please do not reveal my presence here to anyone. Secrecy is and will be all-important."

"Sounds mysterious to me."

"Sorry, but I know they watch me, and believe me, that isn't some frightened woman's paranoia." She waited for his response. When he didn't acknowledge, she continued. "Is it too personal to ask if you're planning to remain in the area?"

"Why?"

"I need to know. Professionally."

"No. I want to clear the estate as soon as possible and put Wickmore in the rearview mirror."

"Oh." She looked disappointed. "I thought perhaps.... Didn't you separate from the Army?"

"Yep, I'm a civilian." He wasn't ready for her to leave. "I'd like to hear more about your plan."

She countered, "If you don't mind too much, when are you planning to leave? I need to know as my plan depends on timing."

"I don't have any idea. I haven't done much around here yet. I've been too busy trying to survive. Look, if you know who rustled my cattle, I think you probably also have a good idea about who thumped me. I want to know. As you say, I am involved."

Cynthia hadn't counted on him being so assertive. After a moment, she took a deep breath and answered, "You're right, of course. I know who is behind your rustling problems, and they probably are the same men who assaulted you. I can't prove it. Yet. I will."

Sam's interest escalated. "If catching whoever tried to kill me is part of your plan, then count me in."

She tried, unsuccessfully, to control the impulse to smile. "I'm happy to hear you say that. That's what I needed to hear, and that is exactly why I am here. I must tell you, Sam, that there is so much more to this than what happened to you. Also, these people are rough. Dealing with them will be dangerous."

"I'm still in." His voice rose angrily." I'm not going to be run off by a pack of cattle thieves. Not after all I've been through. When I get around to leaving this country, I plan to do it at my own speed." He paused to calm himself. "Sorry. I've spent enough of my life being shot at–enough to last ten lifetimes. I'll tell you this, I am angry. Unquestionably. I have never been mad in a fight, but I am now. I want to know who is doing this to me and why. If I have to fight to stop them, you can be sure I will, with or without you. This has got to stop! This is going to stop!"

Cynthia waited for him to calm before speaking. "I really must leave now. Let me think some more and then I'll get back to you." She started toward the door, hoping to bring the conversation to an end. "I can see myself out, Sam. That ankle must be painful. You really should get it looked at. Anyway, it's nice seeing you again, Sam. You have already been through a terrible ordeal and don't deserve any of this." She paused and added, "Once again, there is much more to this than you can imagine."

"Still doesn't scare me."

"Good. I really must go." She looked down and said, "I hope that ankle doesn't bother you too much."

"How did I do?" he asked.

The question halted her progress toward the door. She stopped and faced him again. "I'm sorry, I don't know what you mean."

"You said you didn't know me well enough to share your plans. Remember?"

"Oh, that. You did fine." She smiled reassuringly. "Just fine. I'm sure we'll talk again, and soon."

"Sooner the better."

"Your home is beautiful. Thanks for inviting me in. I'll be in touch."

He didn't try to delay her. A few moments later the doorbell rang and the door popped open before he could get up. She peeked inside and said, "Sorry about the intrusion. Please don't get up. I just remembered something that may be important. I'm almost certain my office phone is tapped, so please don't call me. I'll call you. Bye now." She closed the door softly.

He listened to the sound of high heels clicking down the steps, smiling as he envisioned the bouncing blouse.

Sam redoubled his efforts to protect the cattle after Cynthia's visit, seldom sleeping at night, roaming the back roads adjacent to the ranch, watching for rustlers. He carried a rifle. Late night road traffic in the local area consisted mostly of high school kids looking for a place to park. Two vehicles sped away as he approached, deliberately remaining far enough ahead to prevent examination of license numbers. His suspicions soared.

Cynthia called three days later to arrange a meeting at the ranch after office hours that evening. Sam skipped outside work, making a special effort to clean the house and look presentable himself. He was conscious of a current of anticipation. *Don't be so damned silly. She's just doing her job.*

He answered the doorbell and noticed a rusting old truck parked in the driveway. "Come in, Counselor. Nice set of wheels." He nodded to the truck.

"I borrowed it from a neighbor so no one would know what I'm up to. Secrecy is important." She appraised him critically. "You look much better. How are you feeling?"

"I am better. I don't think you could look any better." He regretted the comment the moment it slipped out. They both looked away self-consciously. She was wearing denim jeans and work boots. A too-large plaid cotton shirt frustrated his imagination.

"Sam, I need to show you something before nightfall. If you don't mind, would you please come with me?" Cynthia drove the back roads in a wide circle around Wickmore, eventually crossing the bridge heading south. She stopped the truck several miles later and reached beneath the seat to retrieve a binocular case. She handed the glasses to Sam.

"Look over there and tell me what you see." She pointed through a gap in the trees toward a cluttered farmstead half mile distant.

He focused the glasses and said, "Trucks and stock trailers. Lots of cattle. What am I looking for?"

"Read the door signs on the vehicles."

Sam toyed with the focus, and then slowly took the glasses from his eyes. He couldn't have looked more astonished. "You have got to be kidding."

"No joke. The name on those trucks is exactly who you think it is. You remember Clyde Townsend, don't you?"

"Oh, yeah. Hard to forget Clyde. How in the devil did he come up with that kind of money?" Sam paused a moment before saying, "Oh! Okay, I'm with you now. You think maybe Clyde is your cattle rustler?"

Cynthia started the truck and headed back to the ranch. "I don't think, Sam. I am absolutely certain and so is everyone else in the county. However, there is still much more. Try this. I believe Clyde Townsend is also the man responsible for your uncle's death, and your missing cattle, and I would lay odds he's the brains behind your beating. I also believe everything Clyde is doing is leading up to getting his hands on your ranch any way he can."

"Clyde Townsend? Where did he get that kind of money?"

"That's a long story. The bottom line is, he's been stealing cattle for years. Everyone knows that. I think he wants to turn legitimate, though. If he can get your ranch for a reasonable price, and by that I mean reasonable to him, he probably plans to quit rustling and turn legit." Cynthia drove without talking for several moments, and then, eyes straight ahead, her facial expression grim, said, "Clyde Townsend is the Devil."

Sam appraised her with new interest. The fierce tone of her voice and the bitterness in her eyes surprised him. "Do I detect some animosity here?" he asked.

She nodded. "Oh, much more than animosity. Townsend is easily the most despicable human being I have ever known. He has ruined more lives, committed more crimes, done more damage and hurt more people than you can imagine. He absolutely is the Devil on Earth."

Sam whistled and said, "Well, Cynthia, that sounds pretty personal to me. Has he done something to you or are these opinions an outgrowth of your professional knowledge?" He used her first name, testing for reaction.

"When it comes to Clyde, I'm just one of many victims on a very long list, and that's all I am going to say." She turned her attention back to the road. "But I am different than the others, Sam. I am going to even the score for everyone."

When she glanced over, Sam saw unmistakable signs of determination, and her eyes were moist.

"Yes, it is personal and I intend to put Clyde Townsend away forever."

"Now that does sound like bad blood."

"Something like that. I intend to stay within the law, which is more than anyone can say for him. I'm going to do it right."

He thought she had opened a private door and he wanted to keep it open. "Tell me about Clyde. Everything you know, at least since I left Wickmore."

"Clyde is a well-known fixture in the cattle business–a notorious fixture. He buys and sells, trades and hustles, and he is very good at it. He can persuade reasonable people to deal with him when they know better. Cattlemen respect his shrewdness, but most of them are afraid of him. He always has rough men working with him–the Appleby boys, some others."

"Tom and Charlie are still with Clyde?"

"Yes. I would be willing to bet they were in your house the day you were beaten. Clyde and the Appleby brothers are inseparable. He knows several more men like them–mean, vicious men who will do anything he asks."

"You seem to be well briefed on Townsend."

She smiled grimly. "I am and I should be. I have studied him for years."

"Is there more?"

"Yes. People around here suspect he is responsible for hundreds, maybe thousands of missing cattle, but the locals don't know everything he does."

"And you do?"

She nodded emphatically. "Oh, yes. I'm the local expert on Townsend. Clyde started by stealing calves and pigs as a youth, then went on to bigger and better. He devised a system of switching cattle in his pens at the Springfield stockyards, usually leaving the stockyard with more cattle than he bought." She looked at Sam and nodded. "It was simple, but it worked."

"You make it sound like past tense."

"It is. He skimmed off a ton of money with that scam, but eventually drew the attention of the feds assigned to monitor stockyard activities. They couldn't prove a huge case, but they had enough evidence to bar him from trading at authorized auctions and revoked his buyer's license for a couple of years. Clyde had enough contacts by then to change his operation. He began rustling full time and doesn't bother with the stockyards anymore."

Sam shook his head slowly. "Clyde Townsend? Hard to believe he's that smart."

"Oh, he's cunning, and contrary to popular belief, cattle rustling isn't just something out of western novels. Old time rustlers were amateurs compared to Clyde Townsend. He knows every crooked cattleman. He knows every unscrupulous auction barn and every outlaw feedlot operator in a four state area. He has wide-spread connections. And last, but not least, he has every thief in the county working for him."

"Must be a big operation."

"Huge. Clyde never moves cattle without a legal bill of sale. His paperwork can pass close scrutiny, but that isn't difficult because the government doesn't have enough people assigned to monitor the cattle business. He is well insulated from the authorities."

"How has he managed to stay out of jail?"

"We so-called authorities all know that Clyde is the power behind cattle rustling. We have not proved anything against him. Some farmers organized all-night patrols to deter the rustlers, but the endeavor failed because some of his men sat in on the organizational meeting. He has scouts to locate vulnerable cattle, either by air surveillance or from vehicles cruising the back roads."

"Air? As in airplanes?"

"That's right. Air spotters. Most of Clyde's men live in cattle country, so he has his fingers on the pulse. For instance, if a farmer has a boy on the high school basketball team, his scouts will check the gym the night of a ball game. If the farmer is there to watch his boy play.... Well, you get the idea. When he finds an easy mark, Clyde sets the operation into action. They usually have two or three strategically placed observation vehicles with two-way radios parked on approach roads to the target area. If a handy corral isn't available on the farm, his men move in and set up a mobile pen to catch the cattle just before the trailers arrive. He has trained dogs that can load the cattle quicker than you can sneeze."

"Where does he take the stolen cattle?"

"He has several outlets, but usually uses out of state auctions and feedlots. Clyde always has an alibi. Most of the time he's somewhere else during a rustling operation. He's clever."

"Sounds like a damned war."

"It is to me."

"I guess it is to me, too. I'm already patrolling my place at night."

"Clyde is buying land. I believe he eventually wants to operate a big legitimate commercial cattle operation, and, as I mentioned, I believe that's where your ranch comes in, Sam. Clyde probably thought Wes would sell out if he applied enough pressure."

"He didn't know Wes very well."

"I think Wes caught on and fired the foreman, who, as it turns out, worked for Clyde. Wes hired another foreman, and, by the way, your current foreman probably also works for Clyde."

"I already fired him."

She gave him a thumb's up. "Good idea."

They drove the remaining distance to the ranch lost in their own thoughts, arriving just after dark. His initial impression of her had changed. *She's sure no Sunday school teacher.*

"Tell me about yourself, Cynthia?" He asked the question the moment she turned the ignition off. They sat in the truck for thirty minutes. Cynthia reviewed her life after high school. She seemed stilted at first, but soon loosened and spoke freely.

"I'm impressed," he said when she finished. "I can't imagine working two jobs at once and going to school. You have done well. As I said, I'm impressed."

"Really? I live in a little town in a welfare county. I serve as prosecuting attorney because none of the established attorneys want the position. The job doesn't pay well enough to make ends meet. Grocery store clerks make more than I do. I have to do tax work to supplement my pay. Why would anyone be impressed?"

"Why don't you leave? There isn't anything keeping you here."

"Oh, but there is. I have one reason, and that is the only thing that could have brought me back to this country in the first place. And that is the reason I took the prosecutor's job. When I finish what I set out to do, I am going to leave and will never return as long as I live."

"Whew! That bad, huh?" Sam could see the hint of tears on her cheeks in the moonlight.

Cynthia swallowed, wiped her face with the back of her hand, sighed, took a deep breath and began. "I have never told this to anyone, Sam. Please don't betray me. What I am going to tell you is a very difficult subject for me. I think you have a right to know, particularly since you may become involved in something that definitely is an emotional issue for me. You have a right to know my motive." She paused a moment, then began speaking softly. "My reason for being here with you tonight, the reason I came back to this county, the reason I'm an attorney and the reason I took the prosecutor's job is Clyde Townsend."

"Hard to believe he rates such consideration."

Cynthia appeared to wrestle with inner demons. Finally, after a broken sigh, she wiped her face again and turned away so he couldn't see. "Clyde and the Appleby boys caught me under the bridge just after high school graduation. They held while he raped me."

Sam could see the reflection of her tears in the side window. He wanted to pull her close and comfort her, but kept his distance. She turned away and wept openly. Sam patted her shoulder, feeling less than useless.

Cynthia sat for a minute, wiping tears as she quieted. After clearing her throat and said, "That's the first time I've ever talked about it to anyone, Sam, not even with my mother. Sorry to be so emotional." She recovered composure, chin up, smiling grimly, and said, "Anyway, I thought you should know. Hating Clyde Townsend has sustained me for years. I don't know how I will manage without him to hate. So, yes, I am emotionally involved."

"I think your feelings are probably standard. Don't feel guilty about it."

"Oh, I don't feel guilty. I didn't do anything to deserve what he did to me. I feel guilty about the fact that I have known since the day I learned that you were coming back that I would try to get you involved. My only guilt is deliberately planning to involve you in my revenge. My motives, insofar as you are concerned, are not pure. I'm not doing this for the sake of legal justice, either. I am doing this for me, Sam. I have been planning for this moment–going to school–the prosecutor position. Everything I have done is for this moment. My life is dedicated to this moment." She looked at him, all previous emotions erased, replaced by complete calm. She looked at him a few seconds, then said, "So, now you know."

"Have you got enough on him to make it stick?"

"No, not yet. But I know how to get it."

"You and the sheriff's department?"

She thought for a full minute, holding her forefinger up to forestall him before saying, "Okay, now you need to listen carefully. The sheriff is a huge problem, Sam, and that's where things really start getting sticky. I'm pretty sure he is in with Townsend, and I mean more than just a peripheral part of the organization."

Sam sat up and slammed his fist on the dash. "I'll be damned! Is that why that son of a bitch…sorry …isn't doing anything about my stolen cattle?"

"Probably." She touched his arm. "Sam, I want you to believe that what I do from here on will be strictly professional. I admit hating him with all my heart, but that will not affect the way I handle myself. Please believe me."

"I do, absolutely. It wouldn't do any good to let your emotions ruin the case against him, would it? All right, I'm in. Now, how do you plan to get him?"

"I have been investigating Clyde for three years. I have borderline evidence that he is the head of the cattle theft ring, just not good enough for court. I can only suspect that he pays the sheriff, and I believe that is probably the reason the sheriff stays out of Clyde's business."

Sam let out a slow, diminishing whistle. "That explains a lot of things to me. No wonder no one from his office has come out here."

"Exactly. As you can see, that is the reason I cannot depend on the sheriff. That's why I need your help, Sam. I want to make it formal. Will you help?"

"You can bet your life on it."

"That really isn't funny, Sam, because that's exactly what you will be doing. We have to catch them in the act and they carry guns. They are extremely dangerous men." She suddenly sat up. "Okay, that's all. I need to go now."

Cynthia had changed instantly after unveiling the private, vulnerable parts of her life. She seemed uneasy and started the truck engine. "I really must go. Thank you or listening. Thank you for everything."

Sam stepped from the truck and stood by watching as she sped away, and then couldn't sleep for thinking about her.

CHAPTER SIXTEEN

The Trap

Cynthia also lay awake most of the night, her thoughts alternating between Sam Prescott and details of the plan that needed to advance beyond the draft stage. Her plan had always required his help. There would be no chance for success without him. *I hate to drag him in after all he's been through.*

Sam's return to Wickmore could not have happened at a better time for me, she thought, or worse for him. The window of opportunity for catching Clyde Townsend has never been so wide open. I need Sam Precott. No other way. He is the key.

The night wore on. Her thoughts continually strayed from details of the plan to her emotional disclosure of the rape, and Sam's attempt to comfort. *He's so easy to talk to. Good, heavens! Sam Prescott? A Prescott of all people.*

He was an enigma, cocky and aggressive one moment–everything she despised in men–and then humorous and comfortable.

He is different than I remember. Am I?

She forced him from her mind to review the plan only to have her thoughts return. *What changed? He is an imposing figure. Not threatening. His looks?* She smiled. The memory of his face pleased her. *Masculine? No doubt. But he seems so serious. Too serious. Why wouldn't he be? Does he think about me?* Her thoughts returned to the plan, and then back to Sam.

She sat up and screamed, "Good grief! Get a grip." She forced her thoughts back to the plan. Within minutes her concentration slipped again, centering on Sam.

His eyes are sad. Maybe he's just tired. Maybe he still hurts. Maybe he's seen too much. He must have suffered more than physical wounds.

Cynthia, throughout the years, spent very little time thinking about men. She never tried to cultivate a relationship with any man beyond formal friendships, mostly with business associates. She had spent her life at work, leaving little or no time for anything else. Deliberate isolation; a scarred victim of rape who never sought counseling; a casualty who didn't know she was broken. No man found a way through the defensive insulation. She had not met a man she liked well enough to trust, not since Clyde. College boys with adolescent, testosterone driven aggressiveness annoyed more than frightened her. A young professor tested her during graduate work. She liked him well enough, but, "I'm really am too busy. I have so much to do." No man got close, not after Clyde Townsend.

After law school, Cynthia earned a position in Jefferson City with a major law firm. The firm traditionally rotated young lawyers through its ranks with alarming frequency, providing every incentive other than advancement. Many new attorneys risked their egos trying to arrange a relationship with her, only to protest to associates afterward, "Damn, what is her problem? Is she the Ice Queen, or what the hell is it with her?"

"I take it you just hit on Roush?"

"Just asked her out for lunch, that's all. You would think I have body odor or something."

"Welcome aboard, fellow traveler. You have to be iced by Roush to become an official member of this firm. Someone should have warned you, but don't worry about it. She's just part of the firm's initiation ritual for new guys."

"That's one frosty gal, man."

"Yeah. I don't think she likes men all that much."

"You mean she's–"

"Nah. Well, hell, who knows. What a waste, though. A looker like that. Too bad."

She worked at the firm for three years before moving closer to home, to Brewster, the county seat. Cynthia lived a nonsocial life, insulated from most undesirable contacts, and from most men, other than those she had to associate with at work.

"Anyway," she rationalized to a female acquaintance who

encouraged her to circulate, "work takes precedence right now. I simply don't have time."

"John Chaffee has been asking me about you. He's good guy."

"Really? Seems pushy to me, April. Maybe when I get caught up."

Cynthia had something far better than a shallow relationship with a man. The church. She had withdrawn from religion after the rape, but eventually got over feeling betrayed and abandoned by God and returned to the safety of the church with a vengeance. It didn't matter that ninety percent of the congregation were over sixty-five, or that their idea of social activity began and ended with bingo. It didn't make any difference to Cynthia that no eligible men attended her church. She preferred it that way. She avoided an old deacon who watched her too closely and graciously tolerated the diligent matchmakers who eventually tired of meddling and left her alone. Cynthia never volunteered to play the piano or sing with the choir, not after Arliegh Mitchell. She didn't want anything from the church except the opportunity to be close to God.

The church provided all the solace and comfort Cynthia needed. She embraced the church with the same fervor her mother demonstrated throughout the years, often wondering but never asking, if Irma needed religion because of some trauma in her past.

Her thoughts drifted again to Sam Prescott. *I wonder what his relationship with God is? He is too free with bad words and rough language.* Cynthia didn't associate with people who didn't relate to God the way she did.

Dawn flooded the sky before she slept. Her hand trembled uncontrollably as she tapped out Sam's number late in the morning. She failed and tried again, fumbling through three more tries to get it correct, and then blurted, "This is Cynthia Roush. Could you possibly meet me today? I think we need to talk."

"Sure, Counselor. Say where and when."

"We shouldn't be seen together." *Good heavens. What must he think?* "Sorry. That didn't sound right. What I mean is, I don't want anyone to think we are planning something. Would the university library in Springfield be okay?"

"Sure. When?"

"This afternoon at three?" *Do I really need to meet him? I could have covered everything over the phone.*

She rushed back to the apartment early to begin preparing for the meeting, squandering an inordinate amount of time selecting clothes. Indecisiveness and disorder betrayed her mounting tensions as one dress after another fell in a heap. She paused to deal with the obvious cause of her anxiety. *Am I doing actually trying to be attractive?* She dismissed feelings of guilt and hurried to Brewster's only decent dress shop, The Rag Bin.

Later, Sam's reaction pleased her. She would have been disappointed if he had failed to notice.

"Great outfit. You look…. Ah, sorry. Really, I'm not trying to be too forward."

She thought he spoke almost as if he knew the efforts involved in getting ready. An approving smile reinforced his words. Cynthia wanted to control the meeting, to exude self-confidence that she didn't feel, but the pleased gleam in his eyes nearly destroyed her chance to be the leader. She blushed and knew the sweater-skirt outfit from The Rag Bin had betrayed her motives, along with any likelihood that she could keep the meeting strictly business. The very idea of shopping for clothes with Sam Prescott in mind was troubling, just not enough to stop her. She had deliberately drawn attention to herself and now felt giddy, almost guilty–just not quite.

"Thank you. I apologize for the secrecy. I hope you realize that we cannot afford to be seen together. I don't want anyone to suspect that we even know each other. Let's move to a less conspicuous area."

They located an isolated cubicle on the second level. Cynthia opened her briefcase and removed the contents, then looked up to find him watching her intently, smiling curiously.

"What is it?" she asked. "Is something wrong?"

"Nope. Nothing wrong. I don't mean to embarrass you. I hope you aren't offended, but I haven't been around a beautiful woman in a long time. I've forgotten how to act. Forgive me."

Any other time such a remark would have repulsed her. Not this time. She wanted the attention. She needed his attention.

"Why, thank you, Sam." She wasn't embarrassed, and that also surprised her. "I suppose we should get started."

She noticed everything about him: the old leather jacket and heavy cotton shirt; that his eyes never strayed from her; how he smiled. He hadn't smiled much until today. His hair was thick, sandy and short. She couldn't decide on the color of his eyes, gray if anything, she thought, then noticed his hand waving in front of her eyes.

"Are you there?" he asked, smiling, clearly amused, catching her in the act of appraising him.

"Oh!" she gasped. "I'm sorry. What were you saying?" She ducked her head and frantically searched through the briefcase for a pen–anything to avoid his grin and regain composure.

"It wasn't important," he said. "What now?"

His lighthearted smile lingered, distracting her, accusing and approving at the same time. Cynthia had to pause for a moment to collect thoughts. She opened a folder and began briefing while trying not to look at him too often. She finished relating her plan thirty minutes later and looked up. "That's it. What do you think?"

Sam sat back, pressing fingertips to his temples. "Wow. I'm impressed. You have been busy. When do we start?"

"Are you sure you want to do this?"

"More than ever. I think the plan is well thought out–as good as any military operation. I said you could count on me. I meant it. When do we start?"

She sighed, relieved as the major obstacle to her scheme fell away. Everything depended on Sam Prescott.

"We can start tomorrow if you have no objections."

"Sooner would be better."

"First, I'll need to coordinate with State Patrol headquarters and the Attorney Generals' office. I have already touched base with them high up. They promised to help after I polished the idea. Now for your part. You have to make sure no cattle are stolen between now and next Saturday, Sam. That would hurt the chance for success. Okay, review the plan for me."

"You want me to centralize the herds along the western boundary of the ranch near the holding pens and loading ramp. I let word slip out that I'm planning to sell the herd to an out-of-state buyer. I patrol at irregular intervals so no one can get a chance at the cattle before we are ready."

"That's important."

"I know. You set everything up with law enforcement agencies and make arrangements with the governor's office to announce a reception next Friday night in my honor. You orchestrate media coverage. Local newspapers and radio stations will carry it in the news. I hire Ted Carling to watch the place for me Friday night. Are you sure Ted works for Clyde?"

"Positive. He will be our unwitting messenger. Everyone thinks Ted is a good guy. Believe me, he isn't. Ted has worked with Clyde for years, mostly as a spotter and radio outpost. He will be more than happy to watch your place. Don't leave anything valuable lying around. He is a known thief. Okay, any questions?"

"The only thing I question is the number of law enforcement officials involved. Why so few?"

"We don't know how much of an operation Clyde will send in, or if he will even take the bait. Also, if too many people are involved the word will get back to Clyde–it always does. If we make a big deal out of it and try to catch everyone, I don't think we could keep it secret. Our primary objective is to capture Clyde and the Appleby brothers. The others are small game. If we get him, the rustling ring will break up. Above all, I want Clyde Townsend."

"All right, whatever you say." He checked his watch. "I've got a couple of hours before I have to be back at the ranch, before it gets dark. Let's get something to eat." He stood up as if matters were settled. "Not in public. I'll go to a supermarket and get cheese, apples, grape juice, some cold cuts and crackers. We can have a picnic in the truck."

"Cheese, apples and grape juice?" She looked skeptical.

"Sure, why not? Something like a picnic."

She snapped the briefcase closed. "All right. Why not?"

They ate in his truck and talked. Cynthia couldn't remember a single thing about the conversation later.

He suddenly looked as his watch and said, "Getting late. I should probably get back."

It was over and she didn't feel guilty. As Cynthia prepared to step from the cab of his truck she felt his hand on her shoulder and hesitated. *Oh, here it comes.* She didn't know how to handle what she thought would probably happen next. An inner alarm spurred her to keep moving, to get away, but she turned, ignoring the call to run. He touched her cheek first, then kissed her softly on the lips. She didn't flinch, or pull away, or blink, or even breath. She froze.

"I really enjoy being with you, Cynthia. See you soon."

The touch of his mouth, the uniqueness of the experience, left her completely bewildered. An incredible rush of emotion smothered her power to think. She forced a muffled, "I'll call," and bolted.

Cynthia drove half way to Brewster before her thoughts formed any logical conclusions. Good Lord, she thought, what is happening to me? I'm a grown woman, and I completely self-destructed over a little kiss. She touched her lips over and over that evening.

She didn't call the next day. On Wednesday morning before the Friday target date, she finally phoned to confirm the plan. He wouldn't let her be all business.

"I want to see you today," he said.

"Why?"

"Don't read between the lines, Cynthia. I want to see you, that's all. To be with you. I just want to be with you."

His voice appealed. He wasn't begging–not quite. The invitation was tempting–sort of. His voice was so earnest and so inviting. She heard a voice answer, a voice that didn't sound like her. "All right. We probably should review the strategy again."

"Same place, Counselor. Same food. One hour." The phone clicked off.

I'm going to drive all the way to Springfield so he can be with me? She scrambled madly to dress for another meeting with Sam Prescott–a meeting that had absolutely nothing to do with business. *One hour. I said I would.*

Cynthia recovered her senses before they met. *Enough is enough. I'm going to put a screeching halt to this adolescent nonsense.*

She felt cheap, her motives all too transparent and juvenile. She parked beside his truck and waited, ashamed for permitting herself to be caught up in childish emotions. His footsteps and a gentle knock on the window brought her back to the moment at hand.

"Let's eat in the truck, Cynthia. Your car is too small."

My car is too small? The only thing wrong with my car is the bucket seat. She still hadn't looked at him. "Sam," she said, speaking through the partially opened window. "Sam, I don't feel right about meeting like this. I am very uncomfortable." She looked up at him. "I hope you don't mind. I'm sorry you drove all this way just to hear that. It's my fault and I am sorry. I think we should keep the relationship businesslike."

He looked bewildered. "Shouldn't we talk?"

"Everything is on schedule. I'll see you Friday evening about five. I'm sorry." She drove away before he could protest, and before she looked at him, and before she weakened.

Sam watched until her car disappeared. *What a riddle she is.* His emotions alternated between anger and curiosity during the long drive back to Wickmore. One thought persisted: *Must be someone else. Has to be.* He tried to analyze her. *She seems vulnerable. Could still be bothered by what Clyde did to her. That was a long time ago. Has to be a man involved.* His anger ebbed. *Don't be upset. Find out what makes her tick. See what happens.*

Ted Carling arrived at noon on Friday to watch the ranch. Sam dressed formally and stepped into a state limousine with an official state license plate driven by a uniformed chauffeur, compliments of the governor's office.

Ted waved. "Have a good time, Mister Prescott. Don't worry about anything."

"Thanks, Ted. I'll see you some time after noon tomorrow."

They drove north for forty-five minutes and changed cars on an isolated back road. A state patrolman in plain clothes and an unmarked car drove Sam on secondary roads back to the rear of the ranch. Sam changed into work clothes and hiked through the woods to a small clearing near the center of the ranch and settled down to wait.

Cynthia stepped into the clearing at four-thirty, flushed from exertion and excitement. She waved and said, "There you are. This ranch is huge. Took me forever. I think everything is set. Can you think of anything?"

"Nope. I'm ready. All we have to do now is wait. How are you?" He didn't miss her effort to be businesslike; avoiding eye contact; keeping her distance.

"I spoke with the state patrol. They are ready and will be in position just after dark." She fidgeted, looking every direction other than at Sam.

"We should probably separate a couple of hundred yards and check the radios. Have you eaten?" he asked.

"Yes, and I brought some snacks for later." She patted the pocket of a baggy bush jacket.

"Me too. I still have plenty of cold cuts and crackers." He noticed that she blushed, recognizing his implication.

"I'm really sorry about Wednesday, Sam."

"Don't worry about it. That was then. This is now."

He walked over the crest of the hill, out of sight and hearing, and then spoke to her on the hand-held radio. Upon return to the clearing, he sat with his back against a tree. "Pull up a seat," he said, motioning to the tree directly in front of him. "We have an hour before dark." After she settled he said, "I'm not all that upset about what happened Wednesday, but I don't understand."

She looked off into the distance. "I made a mistake, that's all. I'm sorry. That's really all there is to say. I am really sorry."

He pondered her answer while scratching hieroglyphics in the dirt between his legs. "All right then. Would you mind too much if I talked about it?"

The question angered her. She folded her arms and replied, "Are you trying to embarrass me? Why can't we just forget about it?"

He lay on his side, head propped on an elbow. "I don't want to make a pest of myself, but did I do something wrong? Was it the kiss? Are you angry with me?" He watched as she frowned and looked away.

"I do think you presume too much."

He nodded. "That's possible. I sometimes do. Just tell me one other thing, then I'll back off." He looked up. "Is there someone else?"

She seemed surprised and took time before answering, "Why do you ask?"

"Because that's the only answer that makes sense to me."

Cynthia's thoughts raced through the risks. *No could mean a green light to him. Yes would stop his aggressiveness, but is that really what I....* Her eyes didn't waver from his for several seconds before she looked away. "No. There is no one else."

The answer surprised him. He had already decided on another man. "Well, you could have fooled me."

They both sat thinking over the situation, then Sam said, "I feel like I'm on thin ice around you, Cynthia, like we are fencing. I'm not very good at waiting for things to work out." He looked up into her eyes. "To me things are usually black and white. I am pretty open. So, in case you haven't noticed, I am attracted to you and I want to see more of you. There. I said it."

She covered her face with both hands and groaned, clearly agitated by his persistence.

"Can't we just attend to business? I don't know you, Sam. Not really."

He pressed on. "There's only one answer for that."

She dropped her hands and looked at him, almost pleading. "Sam, please. I need to concentrate. Please, not just now."

"Just now is good for me." He had a flash of insight. "Let me tell you what I think."

She looked away, distressed and annoyed. "Must you?"

"I think so. You were eighteen when Clyde caught you under the bridge. Let's see, that was eleven years ago. You never got over it, did you?"

He watched for a reaction. She countered by turning farther away.

"If that's right, then I sympathize. What Clyde did was unforgivable and unforgettable. But now I want to get close and it scares you. How am I doing so far?"

She didn't say anything.

"Come on. Tell me if I'm wrong."

She whirled to face him, angry and trembling. "My life is none of your business! You don't know me and you have no right to guess at anything. I resent this and I do not want to continue the conversation. Please stop." She turned away again, brushing tears away with a sleeve. "This is just the wrong time, Sam. Please."

He waited, giving her time to settle, and himself time to assess her reaction. He felt sure his judgment was correct. "No. I want to say a couple more things first, and then we should probably go. First, I am not Clyde Townsend. Just because I'm interested in you is not reason enough to be wary of me. If you just don't like me, okay, that's different." He got up and stood over her. "I'm not asking for a life commitment, Cynthia. I want to get to know you better, but I need some form of encouragement. Something. If we ever do have a social relationship, you will always have complete control. There. Now come on, it's time to go." He offered to pull her up. She hesitated before taking his hand. "Let's get to work, Counselor." He patted her shoulder reassuringly and stepped away to break the tension.

She keyed the mike and checked in with the lawmen to confirm their readiness. Sam and Cynthia separated and started hiking to pre-planned positions, she near one end of the road intersecting the Prescott ranch, he to a hill overlooking the corral.

Cynthia broke radio silence forty-five minutes later, whispering, "Sam! Two cars just stopped on the road below me."

"Okay. Patrol, are you on freq?"

The state patrol answered, "Affirmative."

A few minutes passed before she keyed the mike again. "Sam! I can see one car headed your way."

"Okay. Could you see occupants?"

"No. It's a car, though. It's not a truck."

"Okay, I see the lights. They just stopped at my end of the road. That means their sentries are in place. Things are beginning to roll."

Cynthia didn't speak again for twenty minutes. "Sam, a small truck just stopped here. A man is getting out. He's talking to someone in the car." Less than a minute later, she said, "There is a larger truck coming your way, Sam."

"Okay, I see it. Patrol?"

"Affirmative. Got it."

Sam noted the moon, now bright enough to illuminate shadowy forms of people moving around the barn. He could see at least three men working gates in the corral. He keyed the mike, "The truck is at the corral. They're setting the gates."

Cynthia's excited voice broke the silence a moment later. "Sam!" she whispered, but managed to convey excitement. "Sam, I can see four sets of headlights. Sounds like trucks pulling trailers. Can you hear me?"

"Yes, and I hear the trucks. Just as soon as they turn this direction you need to hustle up here to my position."

"They have all turned your way, Sam."

When Cynthia arrived, he said, "Let's move down closer so we can see."

They darted downhill to a huge stack of hay bales and climbed to a position overlooking the entire scene. One of the trailers had already backed into position at the corral. Three men led saddled horses from the trailer, mounted and rode into the pasture and began herding cattle to the corral. Cows immediately started bawling for their calves.

Sam whispered, "I'm impressed. They are really good."

Except for the noise of cows bawling for calves, the operation proceeded silently. Every man knew his job. Sam and Cynthia strained to see and hear.

"I don't think Clyde is here," she whispered, lowering the binoculars.

"How about the Appleby boys?"

"Yes. Their truck is last in line. That's Charles standing over there," she pointed to a shadowy figure by the loading chute.

"Where's Tom?"

"I think he went back to the truck. They were together a moment ago. They are both here. I'm sure of that."

"Okay," Sam said. "You need to call the patrol. They are loading the first trailer. It's time to close in."

She notified the patrol.

Sam said, "Things are probably going to get wild from here on."

They heard gates slam and the first truck pulled away. Just as the next trailer backed into position, the truck driver jumped from the cab and yelled, "Charles! The cops are coming! Come on, let's get the hell out of here!"

Charles climbed the corral fence and sprinted toward the last truck. Truck engines roared as rustlers scrambled to get away. Sam assumed a radio outpost had given the warning. He could see flashing lights of patrol cars at road intersections both directions from the corral. The rustlers were trapped. The patrol cars turned on sirens and closed the trap, soon taking men into custody.

"Sam, run down there and make sure the patrol keeps the brothers apart. I don't want the Applebys talking to each other. That's important, Sam."

The patrolmen found four empty trucks on the road and two gooseneck trailers filled with cattle. Most of the rustlers had abandoned the trucks and sprinted for the woods.

Sam spoke to the state patrol officer in charge about the Applebys, and then waited at the corral for Cynthia. He was exhilarated–the same way he felt after a battle. "Everything went just as you planned," he said. "You would make a good infantry officer."

Cynthia forced a smile, acknowledging his enthusiasm. "But I didn't get Townsend. Sam. They are taking the prisoners to the county jail. I need to get to town before the sheriff gets involved and ruins everything. Maybe I can salvage something out of this. I have an idea, but my only chance to catch Townsend now is to get the Applebys to talk. I'm going to ride in with the patrol, Sam. I'll call you later."

"Can I help?"

"No, but I really do have to go." She hesitated before saying, "Maybe we could.... Never mind," and ran to a patrol car.

Sam hung around to help unload the cattle. He walked slowly across the ranch in the darkness hoping Ted Carling would be gone when he arrived at the house. He needn't have worried.

Sam felt left out. There would be no celebration, no companionship, no feeling of accomplishment, and nobody to talk to or celebrate with.

CHAPTER SEVENTEEN

The Appleby Boys

Cynthia stepped into the jail mentally braced for Sheriff Kincaid's wrath.

He turned on her, flushed with anger. "What the hell do you mean bringing prisoners into my jail without coordinating with me? I hear you arrested these people in my county, Miss Prosecutor. I guess you think it's okay to come dragging them in here without bothering to let me know. I'm the damned sheriff around here!" The more he talked the madder he got. "What's even worse, you *deliberately* sneaked around and did it all behind my back! You cut me out! You used the state to solve a crime in my damned county! It's *my* county, dammit! I demand an explanation!"

Cynthia gained strength during his tirade. She was not going to back down. "First of all, it is *not* your county, Sheriff, and this is *not* your jail and these men are *not* your prisoners. I am an officer of the court, Kincaid, and you have no authority in this matter. You will abide by *my* directions. I have two state witnesses here who will attest to my instructions in case you decide to forget. So listen carefully. You will not allow the Appleby boys to communicate with each other. Is that understood?"

Kincaid was huffing, almost gasping for breath. "Oh, no you don't! Don't you go pulling that lawyer crap on me. I demand an answer to my questions. By, God, you have no right–"

"Kincaid, unless you pay attention, in about one minute, I'm going to slap you with a charge of obstructing an officer of the court. Now, did you or did you not understand my instructions?"

"Oh, I understand everything. Now you answer my questions!"

"No! Now I'm going to say this one more time so there is no chance for misunderstanding: no person other than a court recognized attorney legally retained or appointed by law to represent the Appleby brothers will be allowed to communicate with them at any time. Is that understood?"

"Yes, but–"

"They have already been informed of their rights by the arresting officers, Sheriff, so you have no business talking to them other than in the administration of your duties as warden. Is that understood?"

"Yes, but I still want–"

"Open the door to Tom's cell and let me in."

"You can't–"

"Sheriff, this is the last time I intend to remind you that I am an officer of the court. I said open the door, and I mean right now! And then I want you to wait for me in your office."

Kincaid weighed his options, glaring at her with pure hatred, but he also was aware of the two state patrolmen standing beside her, glaring, arms folded over their chests.

He opened the cell door. Her bold performance had taken him completely by surprise. Cynthia had never exercised such authority before and caught him off balance. He slammed and locked the door after she entered.

Cynthia breathed a sigh of relief. She had exceeded her legal authority and knew it. She had no business seeing any prisoner before their lawyer had the opportunity to talk to them. She had to gamble. The meeting with Tom would probably dictate the outcome of her case against Townsend, or determine if she even had a case. Everything depended on the next few moments.

Tom cowered, backed into a corner, scratching his arms nervously, trembling, eyes wide, drooling. His arms already bore deep red gouges from the incessant clawing.

"Do you know who I am, Tom?"

He nodded and gulped several times, then licked his lips and swallowed before replying, "Yes, Ma'am, Miz Cynthia."

"Tom, I'm the prosecuting attorney for this county and you don't have to talk to me. Did you know that?"

More nodding, swallowing, snuffling, scratching and another

almost inaudible, "Yes, Ma'am, I reckon."

"Tom, I don't want to see you go to jail. That's why I'm here. You are here because the state patrol caught you in the act of rustling. I have a duty to press charges against you. But I don't want to see you go to prison, Tom, because I don't think you are a bad person." She sat next to him and placed a comforting hand on his leg. "You don't want to be locked in a cell for a long time, do you, Tom?"

He shook his head miserably. "No, Ma'am. I ain't never been in no jail. I shore don't like it none. I'm scairt, Miz Cynthia."

She stood and folded her arms, pleased he remembered her name, but still wanted to look threatening. "Tom, if you don't tell me what I want to know, I'm going to press charges against you for rape, cattle rustling and murder."

His eyes revealed absolute panic, spit dripping from his quavering mouth. He started to cry. "I ain't never raped or murdered nobody, Miz Cynthia. I done took some things maybe that weren't mine, but I didn't do none of those other things. No, Ma'am." He trembled uncontrollably, perspiration dripping from his nose.

"Tom, Tom." She clucked accusingly. "How can you say something like that? You raped me, Tom, didn't you? You can't lie to me about that."

He shook his head even more vigorously. "No, Ma'am, that was Clyde. I ain't never—"

She interrupted to keep the pressure on. "According to the law, Tom, you are guilty of rape because you held me. That makes you an accessory. Do you know how many years you can get for rape, Tom? Rape is a terrible crime, punishable by death in some places. Even if you don't get the death sentence, Tom, you might never get out of prison. Did you know that?"

Tom closed his eyes, weeping pitifully, face twitching, body trembling, blubbering, making guttural animal sounds, rocking side to side.

Cynthia raised her voice to create the impression of anger. "And murder, Tom! I know for a fact that you are responsible for Wes Prescott's death even if you didn't pull the trigger. You are guilty, Tom, because you knew about a murder and didn't report it to the law. You could go to jail forever, Tom!" She pushed his head back and looked into his eyes. She almost felt sorry for him. "Is that what you want? Do you want to be charged with murder, rape and cattle rustling?"

Tom cried pitifully, his mouth working and drooling, unable to form words.

"Tom," she said, changing her tone of voice to a soothing level, "Tom, if I wanted to, I could take back those charges and keep you out of jail. Now, if I do that, will you help me?"

He sniffed back the mucous hanging from his nose and said, "I don't know, Miz Cynthia. I ain't supposed to say nuthin'. Clyde and Charlie will be real mad if'n I say anything. I'm real scairt, Miz Cynthia."

Cynthia reached for his hand and waited until he looked into her eyes. "I know you're afraid, Tom, but I can protect you. I can help Charlie, too." She tried to look severe again. "But if you don't help me, Tom, I will charge Charlie with rape too, and murder, and cattle rustling. I won't have any choice, unless you help. You wouldn't want that to happen, would you? You might never see your brother again. Is that what you want? You need to make up your mind right now."

"No, Ma'am. I need to talk to Charlie, Miz Cynthia, real bad. I shore need to talk to Charlie."

She released his hands and spoke sternly. "No! There is no time! You cannot talk to Charlie! You have to make up your mind right now! If I walk out of here," She pointed to the cell door. "If I walk out of here without your help, Tom, I am going straight to the judge and charge you and Charlie with rape, and murder, and cattle rustling." Her voice softened. "But, if you help me, and I mean right now, I will take away all charges and you can go free." She stepped toward the door. "Now make up your mind! I'm through wasting time with you. This is the only chance you are going to get." She turned toward the door, deliberately stalling.

"Please, Miz Cynthia."

She stopped but didn't turn to face him. "What? Hurry up."

"If I help, Miz Cynthia, will you let Charlie and me go?"

She breathed a sigh of relief and faced him. "No, Tom. I will let you go, but Charlie will have to stay in jail until the trial. But I promise you that I won't press murder and rape charges against Charlie. That's the best I can do. He might have to go to jail for a little while for rustling, but not for life. You can save your brother and you can be with him again, but only if you help me. That's the deal, Tom. You have to make up your mind before I leave this cell. It's simple, Tom, you can come with me or you can stay here and go to the penitentiary."

"I can leave?"

"Right this minute. You can leave right now with me if you promise to tell me the truth. I'm leaving now, Tom. Are you coming with me?"

Tom wiped his face on his sleeve and stood. "Yes, Ma'am. I reckon I will come with you. But I can't go back home. I can't go back because Clyde will shore enough be mad. Clyde'll hurt me bad, Miz Cynthia."

"No he won't. I have a safe place for you, Tom, but you will have to stay there and do exactly as I tell you. Is that okay?"

He nodded numbly. "Yes, Ma'am. I guess so."

"Okay. We have a deal, then?"

"Yes, Ma'am."

She shook his hand, sealing the bargain. "You did the right thing, Tom. Now follow me and keep your mouth shut. Not one word to anybody. You stay close to me and don't you say a word to anyone but me. Not the sheriff–not anyone. Understand?"

"Yes, Ma'am."

She rattled the cell door until the sheriff opened it. "I'm not charging Tom Appleby with any criminal offense, Sheriff. He is not under arrest."

Sheriff Kincaid's brain raced to understand what would surely happen if he released Tom Appleby. He knew Cynthia was up to something but couldn't think of any way to stop her.

"Come on, Tom." Cynthia motioned for the frightened man to follow.

"Where're you taking him?" Kincaid asked. He felt control slipping away. He also knew he would have to explain everything to Clyde.

"That is none of your business, Sheriff. Tom is a free man. He can do what he wants. You coming, Tom?"

She walked smartly out of the jail, Tom following closely. They got into a state patrol car and roared away before the sheriff had time to react. Cynthia went straight home, placed Tom in her car and drove to Sam's ranch. She watched the rearview mirror and prayed all the way.

She found Sam waiting on the front steps at the ranch, alerted by approaching lights.

"Cynthia? I didn't expect to see you again this soon. How did it go?" He noticed someone else in the car.

"Sam, I have Tom Appleby with me. I hate to ask, but I need your help again." She turned toward the car. "Tom, you sit still for a moment! I'll be right back!" Cynthia moved out of hearing distance and outlined her intentions.

"You want me to keep him here?" Sam said.

"No. I can't get in and out of your ranch without being detected, and that would also be far too dangerous for you and Tom. I'll talk to him here, then we have to move him."

"Okay, you're the boss."

"I need to talk to him now while he's scared and tired." She shrugged, "I really don't know how he's going to respond."

She led Tom into the house and sat across from him. "I know you didn't kill Wes Prescott, Tom. Charlie did it, didn't he?"

Tom immediately began scratching his arms again, glancing from Cynthia to Sam, pleading for relief. "No, Miz Cynthia, you got it wrong. Charlie didn't do it."

"Well, that may be true, but Charlie will have to stay in jail if I can't find out who did it. You said you were going to help me, Tom. You promised, remember? Charlie is depending on you. Now tell me. Who killed Wes Prescott?"

Tom looked miserable, grimacing, rocking from side to side. "I jes' cain't Miz Cynthia. I'll get in real bad trouble. Real bad."

"No you won't, Tom. If you tell me right now, I'm going to put whoever did it in jail. Then they won't be able to hurt you. Now tell me. You promised."

"You don't understand, Miz Cynthia. The man that done it ain't the man that's gonna hurt me. If I tell you who done it, someone else will hurt me."

Sam motioned for Cynthia and they huddled in the foyer. "Clyde probably hired someone to do it, Cynthia. Tom can tell you who, but that still leaves Clyde to hurt him, don't you think?"

She agreed and returned to Tom. "Okay, Tom, if I can get your brother to help me, as you have, and if he will tell me in front of the jury that Clyde Townsend hired someone to kill Wes Prescott, will you say the same thing?"

Tom fidgeted. "I don't know, Miz Cynthia."

"Tom!"

He cringed in face of her anger. "Yes'um, if'n Charlie says it, then I will."

"Good. Now tell me the name of the man who shot Wes Prescott and I will get Charlie to agree, and then both of you will be free of murder and rape charges. Now, for the last time, who did it?"

"Todd Pitzen, Miz Cynthia. He ain't from around here, though. He's from over in Rush County. He's the one that done it, Miz Cynthia."

"How do you know for sure, Tom?"

"Because me and Charlie had to take money to him afore he done it, an' we had to stan' guard while he done it, an we took him more money after he done it."

"Are you sure he did it?"

He nodded, eyes wide with fright. "I saw him do it, Miz Cynthia."

"How much money, Tom?"

"We took three-thousand dollars afore he done it, and then we took another three-thousand dollars more after he done it."

"Who gave you the money, Tom?"

"Miz Cynthia, I just can't say that." His eyes begged for understanding.

She raised her voice. "Yes you can, Tom! Now you tell me who gave you the money. Right now! Remember, you promised."

He started whimpering, scratching his arms until they bled.

She stood over him. "Now, Tom! Right now!"

Tom yelled, "Clyde done it, Miz Cynthia. He done it, but he won't like that I told on him. Clyde is sure going to hurt me."

She patted his arm. "No he won't, Tom. I will protect you. Did Clyde tell Pitzen to kill Wes Prescott, Tom?"

"Yes'm. I done heard him."

"And you will testify before a court that's what happened?"

"I will if'n Charlie does. Yes Ma'am."

"Good." She patted his shoulder. "Thank you, Tom. Now, where does this Todd Pitzen live?"

"He lives in a trailer a little west of where highway U and Y come together over in Rush County. His name's on the box. He is a real bad man, Miz Cynthia. Real bad."

"Tom, I want you to go with Mister Prescott now. He will take you to a safe place and see that you have plenty of food. You are not to call anyone on the phone or leave the place we are taking you. Do you understand? You have to mind me, Tom, or Clyde will find you and Charlie will have to stay in jail. Do you understand?"

"Yes Ma'am. Is there a TV there?"

"Mister Prescott will make sure there is. Now Tom, if you don't do exactly what I have told you, someone, and you know who, will hurt you and Charlie. You have to stay where we put you. If you do that, then I promise to keep you safe, and Charlie won't have to go to jail for murder or rape."

Sam and Cynthia stepped out onto the deck and closed the door.

"Whew!" she exclaimed. "That was close. I wasn't sure he would crack. I'm glad it's over. I'm going to call Lyle Bennett. He has a cabin up on Pomme de Terre lake. I'm sure he'll let me stash Tom there. Do you mind taking him up there for me?"

"Not at all. Do I need to stay with him?"

"A day or two if you can, until I get the State Patrol involved. Call me when you're settled. Tom is scared witless." She sighed, looked up and closed her eyes. "You know what?"

"No, what?" Sam could see the relief in her face.

"I'll bet I can get one of these guys to spill the beans on Sheriff Kincaid if I play my cards right."

"They might. Things are clicking in place. I'm a little concerned about the legality of freeing Tom and using him as a witness, though."

"It wouldn't have worked if I left him in jail. His lawyer could have stopped me. But I can use him as a witness since he isn't charged with anything. I believe I'm well within the law."

"How about Charlie? Will he be your witness or Clyde's?"

"Charlie's a little different. He might turn state's evidence. I sure hope he does. He will have access to a lawyer, though– probably already does–and that's going to complicate things."

"Are you in trouble with Townsend? Will he do something

weird, like maybe try to kill you?"

"That depends on how soon I can get the indictments out against Clyde and Todd Pitzen. Right now, Clyde is probably madder than a hornet and might try something stupid. You better stay out of sight, Sam, at least until after the indictments. Don't worry about me."

"You should ask for protection."

"Maybe. Let me call Bennett. I better get moving before someone can track me down."

Sam hid Tom at a fishing resort and stayed with him for two days, until the indictments against Clyde and Todd Pitzen were served and they were safely in jail. Cynthia persuaded the judge to set Clyde's bail so high that he couldn't get out.

Sam called Cynthia on the way back from the fishing resort and they met at his house the evening of the indictments. "Have you ever been a sensation on the news," he remarked as she stepped from her car. She smiled happily and surprised him by taking his arm as they walked to the house.

"I have some great news," she said. "The judge appointed a Grand Jury to investigate Sheriff Kincaid's involvement. I can almost guarantee he will be indicted because Charlie and Todd Pitzen both have incriminated Kincaid in written testimony. Charlie spilled his guts, Sam. The Attorney General's office is involved now. I have the name of every known cattle thief in four states, along with crooked cattle dealers and auction barns. Charlie told us everything." She looked up at him, beaming. "Clyde Townsend is history. Charlie also told us Clyde murdered a rancher south of Springfield. The prosecutor up there thinks he has enough evidence to take it to court. The murdered man's wife saw Clyde do it. He threatened her and she was too frightened to come forward. Charlie and Tom saw him do it, too, and they agreed to testify."

"Great. I'm really happy for you, Cynthia. How long will the trial take?"

"Shouldn't take long once it starts. The judge probably won't allow much delay. The evidence is overwhelming. Oh, Sam, I can't tell you how relieved I am."

CHAPTER EIGHTEEN

Harmony

Judge Arness reneged on the promise of speedy justice and scheduled the trial for the middle of March, giving Cynthia two extra months to prepare. An intern from the Attorney General's office helped her with the investigation, and together they compiled mountains of evidence. Cynthia not only indicted Townsend and Pitzen for Wes Prescott's murder, but turned evidence against Clyde over to another county prosecutor for the murder of a rancher. She didn't rest until the Grand Jury adjourned after binding Sheriff Kincaid over for trial, recommending charges of complicity in Townsend's cattle theft operation, and tacking on misdemeanor counts for misuse of public office.

Cynthia kept her promise to Tom. She permitted Charles Appleby to turn States' Evidence, bargaining for lighter sentences in exchange for testimony implicating Townsend, Sheriff Kincaid, the hired killer, Pitzen and eight other thieves associated with the rustling ring.

Sam called often during the weeks following their last meeting at the ranch. "How's it going, Counselor?"

"Other than being smothered with paperwork, everything is going well."

"Good. Let me take you out for dinner. Name the night."

"Oh, sorry, Sam. I really can't afford to take any time off. Not now."

He called regularly at first, then less frequently as her rejections piled up. Cynthia sensed his waning interest and agonized over some very mixed emotions about Sam, deciding to share the dilemma with her best friend and confidante, Alice Kitchell. Alice lived in the other half of Cynthia's duplex, a friendly if somewhat nosy seventy-five year old widow. She featured Ben Franklin reading glasses and a garish tint of blue on thinning hair. Alice sat in a musty, darkened sitting room filled with antique furniture, watching soap operas during the day and religious programs at night. Two enormous lighted velvet paintings hung on her walls–Jesus over the couch and Elvis over the TV. Her kings.

Mrs. Kitchell was an enigma to Cynthia–her confidante on one hand, an unfathomable riddle on the other. In addition to soaps and religion, Alice painted flowers on cheap china plates as a hobby and drank enough vodka and orange juice to stagger a platoon of soldiers.

"Alice! Are you busy? Alice?" Cynthia stepped into the murky room and waited for her eyes to adjust to the gloom.

"Heavens no, child. Come in and have a seat. It's so nice to see you."

They chatted for several minutes before Cynthia revealed her emotional quandary.

Alice listened intently, then exclaimed, "Oh, my. My, my, my. Well, I must say the young man certainly sounds agreeable to me. Intriguing. What are you waiting for, girl?"

"Oh, Alice! It's not that simple. The investigation complicates things. Sam could be called as a witness."

Alice took a drink of her "orange juice" believing Cynthia knew nothing about the vodka, nodding wisely, and then exclaimed, "Excuses, excuses. All that legal business is nearly over. Now, tell me, what is the real problem?"

Cynthia slumped, covering her face with her hands. "You know me too well. My problem with Sam is not about the trial."

Alice knew enough about Cynthia to speak her mind, "Well, I know that. Anyone with a lick of sense can see that."

Cynthia sighed and smiled helplessly at her friend. "I don't know what to do. He might not call again."

Alice nodded. "True enough, although he does seem persistent. Didn't you say the investigation is nearly over?"

"Finished as of today. I have nothing to do but wait for the trial."

"Well then, I don't suppose you will have a ready excuse the next time he calls, will you?"

"Not really. If there is a next time."

"Oh, if you only knew what I know about life." Alice clucked disapprovingly. "You wouldn't be sitting around waiting for things to happen on their own. But that's just me. Sometimes you have to give things a little push." She shook her head sadly. "It's such a shame to waste life on young people. Such a shame." She looked up and smiled brightly. "Well, I expect he will probably call again, don't you think? Oh, sure he will. But don't wait too long."

Cynthia retreated to her half of the duplex. *I don't need the problem of a relationship right now. I need to stay dedicated to the trial and he needs something from me. Ahhh!*

She awoke each morning and went to sleep at night with the words echoing through her mind. *Something. He needs something.* She thought about him constantly. Ethics of duty ruled against social contact with him, and yet the memory of his face, the sound of his voice, everything about Sam Prescott called for *Something. No calls lately. He's drifting. Something. Do something.*

She saw him several times during the investigation, secretly watching as he sat in the waiting room or on the witness stand during Grand Jury testimony, but deliberately avoided contact. She also observed him at a local café the day after she sought advice from Alice, sitting with the court recorder, Tawnee Winters.

Oh, sure. Cute, fun-loving Tawnee. Completely captivating Tawnee. Tawnee of the short skirt. Tawnee with the double Ds. That Tawnee. Ahhhh! Cynthia experienced a rush of jealousy and scurried to the rear of the room, there to sit with her back to the couple.

Later, Sam wandered over and pulled a chair out backward and sat with his arms on the back, all without waiting for an invitation. "Do you mind?" he asked, smiling and confident.

"It's a free country. You sure Tawnee doesn't mind?" She regretted the remark instantly and blushed. *You silly woman.*

The comment disturbed Sam for a moment. A puzzled frown quickly replaced his grin. "Why would she?" Actually, he was delighted. Her comment exposed everything he needed to know.

Cynthia shrugged, assumed her best I-don't-really-care look, and buried her face in the menu attempting to hide the bloom flooding her face.

Sam tarried just long enough to comment, "Well, I see you're busy, Counselor. He stood. "Maybe I'll see you around." He left the café with Tawnee. Tawnee laughing and touching. That Tawnee.

Cynthia watched Tawnee with renewed interest after that, trying to discover what Sam could possibly see in such a transparent woman. Tawnee smiled and flirted shamelessly with men, married or single, old and young, and they all responded. Men adored her. Cynthia noticed how often Tawnee touched, what clothes she wore, how she smiled, but most particularly how much she smiled. She learned envy. Tawnee was popular, flitting from one man to the next, smiling constantly. Everyone loved her.

Can men possibly be that easy?

* * * * *

"How's it going, Counselor?"

Sam's voice stopped Cynthia like a blast of wind. She froze, having just stepped onto the sidewalk after closing and locking her office door late one evening. She hesitated, grimaced, then turned to face him. Sam pushed away from the grill of his truck and closed the distance. He looked different. Levi jacket and trousers had much to do with the impression, and the western boots elevated his height yet another two inches. He towered over her.

How long has he been standing out here in the cold? The late November wind stung her face. "Aren't you freezing?" she asked.

"Oh, it's cold enough. Hope it's worth it." He bent over to deflect the wind with the brim of his Stetson. "I need to talk to you."

She panicked. *Here it comes.* "I do have office hours, you know."

"Yep, but this isn't about business. Give me a moment?"

She avoided his eyes. "Well, just a moment. I have to.... Oh, all right. Come in the office."

Cynthia unlocked and stepped in but didn't remove the shielding coat, taking a strategic position behind the desk before facing him. "Now, what can I do for you?"

He looked desperate, hat in hand, solemn, formal. "I want to see you, Cynthia."

She looked down, fidgeting with paperwork on the desk. *Here comes the yes or no.*

"I don't understand why you avoid me, Cynthia. I thought...well I thought we might.... Oh, hell!" He gestured helplessly, hat held prayerfully in front of his chest. "I'm not handling this very well am I?"

"What about Tawnee Winters?"

Sam smiled wryly. "Tawnee? Just a friend. Not my type." The crooked smile vanished before he added, "I'm not dating her. Not yet. But I sure as hell would like some female companionship. Yours, if I can get it."

She flipped through the papers, avoiding his eyes. "I'm really very busy, Sam."

"Yeah, so I've noticed." He sighed audibly and said, "Well, I hope you don't blame me for trying." He put the hat on and pulled it down over his forehead. "Okay, Cynthia, I won't bother you again. Sorry to be such a pest." He touched the brim, spun away and departed.

She sat, then collapsed over the desk, groaning miserably. Ten minutes later in Mrs. Kitchell's living room, the same agonized groan escaped as Cynthia paced in front of her patiently waiting friend.

Alice placed her paint brush aside, muted the television evangelist, and said, "I take it the Prescott fellow has been around. Anything you want to tell me?"

"Other than he probably won't bother me again?"

Alice clucked. "He said that?" Cynthia nodded. "I see." She looked over the top of her Ben Franklins and said, "Well, whatever would cause a man to do that, I wonder?"

"I don't like feeling pressured, Alice. He pressures me."

"He's a man, Honey. He is obviously interested in you, child. That's what they do if they have any male traits at all going for them." Alice smiled, adjusted the glasses, leaned over the plate and began painting. "How dreadful of him. Awful man like that."

Cynthia stopped pacing and said, "You're making fun of me." Then, more to herself, "If I say yes, it's going to lead to complications."

Alice smiled and nodded wisely. "I surely hope so. Yes Ma'am, complications most sane women would probably kill for.

That young man is a catch."

Cynthia balanced the risks of involvement and the chance of living a normal life against her deep-seated, controlling habits. "He won't call now. Not after tonight. I suppose I would have to call."

Alice concentrated on the plate. "Um huh. That's about the way I see it. But I think that's fair, don't you? Seems to me the young man has done more than his share."

"What will he think of me if I call?"

Alice looked up, exasperated. "Sweet Jesus! Who knows? I know this much, nothing is going to happen if you *don't* call, and that will be the end of that story."

Cynthia meditated while studying her friend. "This is silly, Alice, making something out of a relationship that has certainly not progressed beyond friendship. What am I afraid of?"

"Indeed. What are you afraid of?"

"I'm not afraid of him, Alice. I don't think so anyway. I really don't know him well enough to say that, though, do I?"

"No, but that's the way of it, child. I don't think I ever really understood my Walter." Alice sat back to regard her handiwork, then said, "Sit down, will you? You're making me nervous." She waved to a chair and waited for Cynthia to settle. "Now, I know a little about you, and I know something about those demons in your closet." She smiled sympathetically and continued, "But let me say this, and then maybe I'll mind my own business. Now you listen. I think your young man is already inside the castle, and I also think it's too late to pull up the drawbridge." Alice saw the stunned look on Cynthia's face. "And I think you know it, girl. Time to face facts."

Cynthia nodded. "He is always on my mind. Always. And now I don't have anything to do but think about him. Oh, Alice, am I that foolish?"

Alice painted another petal, took another drink, smiled contentedly and said, "Nope. It all sounds pretty normal to me."

"He won't call again. I know he won't."

Alice tilted her head up to look down at the plate through the Ben Franklins. "I expect that's right, but you know something? The last time I checked, the phone works both ways."

Cynthia called after a weekend of agonizing deliberation. "Sam, it's Cynthia."

"Well, hi, stranger. What's up?"

"Nothing really. It's just, I should have called sooner."

"Really?" Long pause. "What's going on?"

"My work is nearly finished, at least until the trial. Back to the old routine for me, which isn't too demanding. All the excitement is about over."

"I see. Soooo, not too much going on, you say?"

"Just sitting tight waiting for the trial."

An awkward silence followed, he wondering why she called, she working up courage to say why she called. "Sam, I would like to have dinner with you sometime, if you're still...you know."

"Well all right!" He sounded genuinely pleased. "How about tonight?"

Exactly what she hoped. "Tonight? Let's see. Tonight. I suppose so."

"Great. About six-thirty, then. Is Springfield all right? Someplace elegant?"

"Yes. I would like that. See you." She replaced the phone and leaned against the wall, eyes clenched tightly, smiling, satisfied, a little guilty and a lot elated. She hugged herself for a moment before breaking the spell, exclaiming, "Oh, my heavens! I'll never get ready in time."

Cynthia usually spent no more than twenty minutes dressing for work. A wave of anxiety swept away practiced habits. She opened the closet and frantically rummaged once again through a maze of clothes and colors without seeing anything. When the frenzy became apparent, she stood still, took some deep, controlled breaths, and then deliberately chose the only dress in the closet she considered even vaguely alluring.

Sam knocked at exactly six-thirty. She started briskly for the door, caught herself and stopped. Took some deep breaths, and then reached for the handle, pulse racing, hands trembling, forcing an artificial smile and opened the door.

"Come in, Sam. How nice to see you." She hoped the manufactured greeting didn't expose the truth of her emotions. She felt like an overanxious adolescent. He looked fresh and wholesome. A single yellow rose floated somewhere in the expanse between them. Time stopped; her breathing stopped; what little confidence she enjoyed the moment before evaporated.

"Wow. You look great," he said, smiling easily, appraising her dress.

Cynthia couldn't think or move.

"Are you there," he said, bending to look into her eyes.

She blinked and the cogs of time locked in place again. "Oh! Thank you. Please come in." She accepted the rose and stepped aside as he entered, then closed the door and escaped into the kitchen to look for a small vase. She returned to find Sam casually surveying her tiny living spaces.

"Wondered if you were ever going to let me in. Here, I mean."

"I expect you now know why I think your home is so impressive." She had decorated the modest duplex with decent contemporary furniture, a decor she designated "Early Motel." His inspection didn't last long. She thought he probably lost interest.

He said, "Your home is very comfortable."

What else could he say, she thought. Might as well have said "How interesting," or "How quaint," or any of half a dozen other platitudes employed by gentle people in similar circumstances. His eyes were on her.

"You really are beautiful," he said. "Not that I forgot, but the real thing is always better." Before she had time to blush, he said, "Get your coat, woman. Let's hit the ville."

"The what?" She laughed nervously, his compliment still ringing in her ears. "Let's hit what?"

"The ville! City lights! Let's go. I can't wait to show you off. You're going to be good for my public image."

She looked away and smiled. He bubbled over with enthusiasm. *No way to fight this kind of eagerness.* Outside at the curb sat the sleekest, blackest car she had ever seen. He held the door open.

"Sam?" Her eyes darted from the car to him, then back.

"Whatever the question, the answer is yes."

"Sam? This car?"

"Oh, this? Wes had a thing for expensive cars and fast women, not necessarily in that order. If it's too much, we can stop by the ranch and trade it for something more sedate."

Cynthia took in the lavish interior with a glance, her thoughts lingering over Sam's casual disrespect for his uncle. "Something more sedate? There are more?"

"Yep. Not like this, though. He had a sport car, a customized pickup, and a couple of trucks suitable for ranching. Traded cars whenever it struck his fancy."

Sam drove for a time without speaking. She thought he seemed preoccupied, maybe even angry. "Tell me about Wes, Sam. There were so many rumors. I don't know what to think."

He nodded. "Well, you can probably take your choice. I expect they would all be at least partially true. I never knew that much about him myself. Not really. He kept his private life to himself. Stayed out all night occasionally. Knew several women. Never drank, though." He tapped the steering wheel and thought for a moment. "We got along. That's about all there is to say. Different kind of guy."

She turned away and frowned, disturbed by his display of callousness.

He noticed and regrouped. "Oh, I liked Wes fine," he said cheerfully, attempting to recapture the moment. "We ended up being good friends. I liked him a lot."

"Let's not talk about family tonight, okay?" She wisely changed the subject. "What are you going to do, Sam, after you sell the ranch?"

"Good question. I plan to get out of here as soon as the trial is over. After that, I really don't know. I'll have to come up with something. How about you? You mentioned leaving. What are your plans?"

His intentions, even though she already had an inkling, left Cynthia with a feeling of loss. Of course he'll leave, she thought. Why would he stay here? No family, no friends, nothing but bad memories.

"I plan to leave after the trial. Kansas City or St. Louis. With any luck, join a law firm." The idea wasn't new, but she hadn't told anyone, not even Alice.

"You should be able to demand a good salary after all this publicity," he said.

Before the lights of Springfield blossomed from the darkness, Cynthia's defensive shell had softened. Her apprehensions about Sam had not diminished entirely, just slipped into the background. The thought of having a friendlier relationship with him intrigued her. She relaxed somewhat, watching the passing scenery, but Sam

Prescott's presence loomed over everything. She couldn't resist sneaking peeks at him.

He is the most interesting man I have ever known, and, of course, he's leaving. The first time I really want to know a man, he leaves. She thought about the kiss, and the night she told him about the rape and how pleasant it felt to be touched. She began to question her intentions. *Do I just let things play out?* The evening passed comfortably. Sam didn't press for familiarity.

Sam struggled all night to be pleasant without being intense. He didn't touch her, either intentionally or accidentally. He talked about current events and other mundane topics; nothing personal.

He understood far more about Cynthia than she imagined before they returned to her duplex late that night. His original impression appeared to be accurate: She didn't know anything about the refinements of dating. Her confidence blossomed, though, as the evening advanced, and she sat facing him, almost boldly, smiling more, laughing freely. He sensed promise.

"Would you like to come in?" she asked as Sam pulled to a stop in front of her duplex.

The invitation caught him by surprise. He had been thinking about a good way to say goodnight, suspecting that even a platonic kiss at the door would probably be too venturesome. He thought the best method would probably be to ask her out again and set a date, never thinking she might invite him in.

"Sure. I would like that."

They sat on opposite ends of the couch, almost like starting over, grappling with polite conversation, each reluctant to initiate an end to the evening or take the next step to familiarity.

"I'm keeping you up too late, Cynthia," Sam finally said. "I should probably go." He waited a moment, then accepted defeat and stood.

"Please don't go, Sam. Not just yet."

He noticed signs of distress in her eyes and a puzzling urgency in her voice. He sat. She appeared to be upset about something not apparent to him. "What's on your mind, Cynthia?"

She did look bewildered, but faced him bravely and began speaking. "Everything you said to me that afternoon in the woods is true, Sam. I haven't done anything socially since...well, truthfully, in all those years. Okay, really, not ever." She took a deep breath and said, "You were right about everything."

He didn't say anything, though she waited for him to carry the moment. He didn't want the evening to end on a sour note and decided not to pursue the issue. Instead, he said, "I had a good time tonight, Cynthia. I probably should have said good night at the door." He stood and pulled her up. "So I'm going now—not that I wouldn't like to stay. I want to see you again, and I don't mean six weeks from now. Soon. The sooner the better." He didn't release her hand nor did she attempt to remove it.

She gazed directly into his eyes, pretending confidence, then said, "Day after tomorrow? You call it."

A triumphant smile spread across his face. "Great. I would leave, but not without my coat." He nodded toward the bedroom. When Cynthia returned with the garment, he said, "Wear your jeans, woman. We'll go someplace less formal."

She nodded. Her expression solemn. "The answer is yes, Sam."

He looked puzzled. "Okay, I'll pick you up at six-thirty."

"That's not what I mean. Remember what you said about wanting something from me?' The answer is yes. This is my something."

"You didn't have to say anything." He smiled mischievously. "I figured it out."

"I needed to say it."

At the door, Sam touched her lips lightly with his fingers. "Soon," he said and stepped smartly into the darkness.

They dated often after that. Sam discovered that she would not show affection in public. He kissed her on the cheek or forehead, almost brotherly—on the mouth only in private, and then not to stir passion. He followed her lead, allowing everything to happen at her pace.

"How would you like to go someplace quiet tonight; someplace with good music; someplace quiet where you can order an excellent steak and talk without interruption?" He asked the question as they started another evening together near the end of the second week of dating. Sam felt secure enough by then to begin exploring her limits.

"Sounds good to me," she said, scooting across the seat, so close he had to put his arm around her. Cynthia didn't seem troubled when he drove directly to the ranch, other than he noticed that she stopped talking. He could almost read her thoughts. *What's he up to?*

They listened to music for an hour before he busied cooking steaks and building a fire in the fireplace.

"My, you have been busy today," she said, the signs on her face accusing him of conspiracy. She was well aware of the table in the candle-lit dining room, already set with china, crystal and polished silverware. Soft music and subdued lighting added to the setting.

* * * * *

He cooked on the deck. After finishing the meal they sat on a bearskin rug in front of the fireplace, basking in the warmth, leaning comfortably against each other. Sam kissed her on the mouth–not an insignificant kiss–but received an anemic response. He didn't detect evidence of panic, though, nor did she discourage further exploration, so he kissed her until she reacted. She began responding in kind, following his lead. Her hesitant, uncertainty provided ample evidence of an inner turmoil.

She suddenly stiffened and pushed away. "Sam, I just need–"

"Shhh," he whispered, a fingertip on her lips. "Relax. You have control. I won't press for more than you give." He wanted to kiss, but recognized resistance. He sat up and moved away. "Okay, what would you like to do?" He really wanted to say something to imply disappointment but checked the impulse.

"Let's just talk."

"Talk?" *She wants to talk?* He felt a surge of impatience bordering on anger. *Okay, slow down, Prescott.* His thoughts raced, ending with, *Slow down my ass.* "Talk? Look, Cynthia, to be honest with you, closeness is a vital part of a man-woman relationship, at least it is for me. It's all I can do to keep my hands off of you. I am not indifferent to your charms."

"Sam, if you're making fun of me, I wish you wouldn't."

He sobered. *Okay, that's her limit.* "Sorry. You're right. Okay, you want to hear some good music?"

"I'd rather not. Tell me something about your religion. What do you believe?"

Sam wasn't about to become involved in a religious discussion. "I'd rather kiss around on you." He leaned close, inhaling the perfume on her neck.

"Please, Sam." She held him away. "I want to know. I need to know."

He rolled away, frustrated once again, thinking, picking at the rug. He had a pretty good idea how she felt about religion and was also pretty sure his lack of belief would have a devastating effect on their relationship, possibly lethal. He decided on a measured approach. "My beliefs are not ironclad. Maybe nothing more than I really don't have a religion." He saw instant distress in her eyes. "It really doesn't get any deeper than that for me." He stood, hoping to bring the conversation to an end. "Now I'm going to turn on the music."

"Not yet, Sam. What about life after death?"

"If there is life after death, it will find me on my knees begging forgiveness, or raging mad for the lack of...never mind. I really don't dwell on religion, Cynthia. Let's dance."

Her brow furrowed. "Oh, Sam. Such flippancy. I cannot understand you."

He didn't ignore her signs of concern. "Are you sure you want to?"

"Yes. I want to know what you believe."

"Okay." He sat beside her again. "Let's talk about life everlasting, Cynthia. I cannot imagine infinity, and I'm sure I never will, and I'm not going to waste time thinking about it."

She started to protest and he held his hand up for silence.

"Let me finish. Let me have my say before you walk out and slam the door." She started to protest again.

He touched her mouth. "Please, let me finish. I am not hedging my bets here on Earth hoping for a hereafter. I believe in death–absolute, permanent, final, inevitable death, and I'm not saving anything. I want to spend the rest of my life loving–a woman preferably–not some figment of someone's else's imagination." He wanted to end the conversation, satisfied that anything more definite would drive her away. "After what I have seen, I don't believe there is a merciful god. Couldn't be. Too many perfectly innocent people killed, and I killed way too many of them."

Cynthia sprang to her feet in one movement. "I want to go home. Now, please."

The sudden announcement really didn't surprise him. "What? Was it something I said?" He laughed. He knew exactly what prompted her reaction. "We could change the subject."

"Please, just take me home."

He decided to surrender without a fight. "Okay, let's chalk this off as a learning experience. What about tomorrow?"

"Not tomorrow, Sam. I need time to think. I'll call." She didn't call. Two weeks passed. She spoke to Mrs. Kitchell about the dilemma, finishing by saying, "His views on religion are so alien to me. I have thought about never seeing him again. I have spent days and nights praying about it, Alice. I'm sure he doesn't believe. He doesn't have a religion."

"It is a problem, child, as religions usually are. Maybe he has reasons. He has been through a lot. Try to see what he has seen. Might help you understand."

"That's what I decided."

Alice looked surprised. "Well, that's a start, right? So, what now?"

"I think religious differences could be important to our relationship. Don't you agree? But he doesn't have a religion. He won't call, I know that, so I will call him again. It worked the last time." She bounced to her feet, arms extended triumphantly. "So that's it then. That's what I'm going to do."

Mrs. Kitchell agreed. "Good thinking. Nothing much to lose."

* * * * *

"Sam, would you come to church with me Wednesday evening?" She asked the question immediately after he picked up the phone.

"Well, it's good to hear your voice again, stranger. Sure, I'll go to church with you if you come dancing with me."

"You know I don't do that." Her heart sank.

"Don't or won't?"

She didn't answer, but breathed a sigh of relief when he said, "Let's both make a concession."

His willingness to negotiate arrested her initial overwhelming flood of disappointment. "How do we compromise, Sam?"

"I'll pick you up at six. Let's go to Springfield."

"No. Tell me the compromise."

"That's easy. I forget about dancing; you forget about church."

She felt somewhat better. The thought that he might discard her completely receded. Getting Sam to attend church had been a shot in the dark anyway. *No sense making an issue of it.* "Okay."

She told Alice, "At this point nothing appeals to me more than finding out about Sam. That's what I have learned these past days. There, I said it out loud. I feel good for the first time in days, Alice. I'm going to study Sam Prescott. I want to know everything about him."

"Is he really that important, or just the idea of him?"

Cynthia had already spent hours thinking about it. "Maybe he is. I'm not sure. I tried to put him out of my thoughts and failed miserably. I have decided to deal with his lack of religious convictions when the time comes–if the time ever comes. We might not get that far."

The days of searching thought brought one almost staggering fact home with force. She had not been to church more than five times since she met Sam Prescott. *Who am I to talk? How strong is my faith?*

Cynthia's spirits soared. She hummed and smiled until he rang the doorbell at six. Sam didn't ask to come in, nor did he try to make small talk. He didn't open the car door for her and drove much too fast. He seemed different–reserved, distant, distracted, possibly angry. His glowering mood and somber expression worried her. She tried to engage him but received one word answers or grunts.

"Pull over here for a moment, Sam. I need to take care of something."

He stopped the truck on the shoulder. Cynthia scooted over and kissed him soundly on the mouth. "There. Now stop being so stuffy, will you?" She was secretly satisfied with her performance. "I'm sorry for not calling, Sam. Please forgive me. I needed to think. I have and that's that."

He remained wary of her erratic conduct and unwilling to accept the impulsive exhibition of affection as genuine. "I take it you reached some conclusion?"

"Yes." She nestled close and pulled his arm over her shoulder.

"Are you going to share the finding with me?"

"When the time is right."

"I don't know. What are you thinking? "Do we need to talk?"

"Not now, Sam. We can talk later."

The significance of what she planned to reveal held a prominent place in her thoughts during the evening; more like an ominous foreboding.

"I'm sorry about the last two weeks, Sam," she said, finally opening the subject as the city lights dimmed in the rearview mirror.

"Well, don't worry your pretty head about it. It was nothing to me, really, just two more lost weeks that can never be recovered. Jerk."

She smiled, but understood. "Things were going too fast. Forgive me?"

"Oh, probably. I am notoriously weak, most particularly when dealing with beautiful women. And most particularly you."

They stopped at the ranch and sat in the truck on a cleared hilltop watching the stars. Cynthia pulled her feet onto the seat and sat with her back against him. Sam soon tired of the arrangement and pulled her head down on his lap. They enjoyed the intimacy, muted voices merging with peaceful night sounds. The soft undertone of conversation gradually faded to quietness.

Cynthia could not remember exactly how it started–perhaps an innocent touch, some subliminal signal. Perhaps the impetus came from the awakening of arrested biology, but something happened when he kissed her. She didn't mind–not in the least. No shrinking or pulling away. She would have been disappointed had he not tried to kiss her. After a long, demanding kiss, her inhibitions remained dormant. The sensation of his mouth ignited a surge of stimulating impulses. Cynthia thought he was deliberately pressing her, almost angrily.

It had taken two weeks to decide in favor of what she knew would probably become an emotionally challenging relationship with him. Countering thoughts had assailed her waking hours: guilt barriers, religious background, the traumatic memory of Clyde Townsend all weighed heavily. Two weeks of rationalizing and balancing. *Is it a sin to think what I'm thinking?*

Cynthia recognized the attraction existing between them, an appeal she had never experienced–primal temptation. Thinking about Sam tormented her. She ached. Her heart literally ached. Hurting attended her thoughts about him. She could not stop thinking about him and didn't want to. She desperately wanted to be with him. And finally, right or wrong, decided to find out; to venture; to push aside restraint. Watching stars and kissing Sam

Prescott was no accident.

Cynthia deliberately vanquished her doubts and gave in to the craving for him. Her fingers and lips explored. Each daring touch ripped down another barrier, opening the way to yet another path, leaving her yearning for more. She gave no thought to the possibility that she might lose control, desperate for more, moving closer, testing emerging new sensations, experimenting with the hungers his nearness ignited. She didn't feel powerless to stop him. She didn't want to stop.

"Whew! This is sudden," he said, catching his breath, apprehensive about her startling transformation. "Is this what you've been thinking about the last two weeks?"

"Yes, and much more. I wish I could go back, all the way to high school, and start over. I don't know how much I have missed, but I want to catch up."

"Are you using me?"

"Am I? Maybe. Yes. I don't think this could happen with anyone else. I suppose I am using you. Do you mind?"

He laughed. "Are you kidding? I'm a guy. A little uneasy, though. You must know that this is a pretty amazing transformation. Dramatic, actually. Do you know what you're doing?"

"Honestly? No."

"Then at least tell me what you think is going on." They moved apart, eyes searching eyes. "Is this a test, Cynthia? Will I blow the whole thing apart if I make a mistake?"

"I'm not testing you. This is experimental for me, but you can't make a mistake. Just be who you are. I'm counting on that."

"Well you can make a mistake if you shut me out again. Our relationship has been torture."

"I want to tell you something, Sam, and please don't panic." He didn't say anything, so she went on. "I have never really loved anyone, but I suspect something like that might be happening." She immediately regretted the confession. The announcement clearly took Sam by surprise. His puzzled expression concerned her. Cynthia recovered her senses before he did. "Sorry. I just.... Just forget what I said."

Sam's grim smile cast light on his reservations. He shook his head, clearing his mind. "Yeah, like I'm going to forget that. Oh,

Cynthia. All this since the last time I saw you?"

"No. I've known something was different from the moment I met you that first day on the road. I don't have any idea what happens next, if anything. I don't know how this works." She turned away, murmuring, "I'm sorry. I shouldn't blurt things out."

He put a hand on her shoulder and turned her toward him, then said, "Let me see if I have this right. You want to learn to play, and you want me to keep the game in bounds. Is that it?"

She nodded, eyes cast down. "Correct. I don't know the rules. You get to lead."

"What makes you think I can do that? Remember, I'm the guy who said you flip my switch. I don't think you should count on me to be noble."

She held his hand against her mouth. "I'm a lifetime behind, Sam." She covered her face with her hands. "Sorry. I've already said too much, haven't I?"

"Come here." He pulled her close and kissed the tears away. "Well, this sure opens up an entirely new world, doesn't it? Anyway, I'm glad you told me."

"Does that mean you will do what I want?"

"If humanly possible."

She held him at arm's length, gazing into his eyes, then nodded and said, "Good. Then make love to me." *There, I said it.* The thought of making love with Sam had lingered just beneath the surface of her conscience for weeks. If she could get beyond memories of that day beneath the bridge, maybe the years of torment and guilt would go away, along with the anger and hatred. Maybe her life could be normal. Maybe she could learn to trust. Maybe she could cast out the pain and cleanse the stain of shame. Maybe she could start over.

The candid request surprised Sam. He questioned her emotional state and how to handle what came next. She worried him. "Have you really thought this out, Cynthia?"

"Yes. I know what you must be thinking, Sam, but I have never been more serious about anything. Don't overthink. Just do. Please?"

He wrestled with the astonishing magnitude of her change. "Are you serious? If you are, this whole thing strikes me as being more than just a little bit impulsive."

"I'm thirty, Sam, old enough to make my own decisions. I know what I'm doing. Make love to me. Tonight. Right now."

The worried expression on his face deepened. He was profoundly troubled.

She turned away, embarrassed. "If you don't want to, Sam, that's–"

He held her face between his hands. "No, I want to! More than anything. But what will you think tomorrow? Will you hate yourself? Will you hate me? Will this kill my chances with–

"No. I won't hate you no matter what."

"You think you're in love with me?"

"I'm not sure. I really don't know what much about love, but if it's not being able to sleep for thinking about you, if it's feeling a thrill every time I see you, if it's chilling each time you touch me, if it's hurting because I'm not with you, then maybe. Do you feel anything like that?"

"Everything you said."

She smiled to reassure him. "Then we aren't going too fast." She kissed his hands. "I have taken forever to gain this kind of courage, Sam." She kissed him hard on the mouth. He didn't kiss her back. She pressed against him, tugging, whimpering.

He stared at her, frowning, uncertain, unable to subdue his doubts. She was suddenly a stranger. He could not understand the unfamiliar aggressiveness, or her peculiar, agitated expression, or the primitive fierceness of her mouth, the tears, or the moaning, whimpering pleas.

Cynthia's eyes locked on his mouth. She kissed him again and again, more ardently each time. The strength of her behavior pressed him against the door. She was on her knees on the seat, pushing, mashing his lips until he tasted blood. An alien, keening sound came from the depths of her body. She became a feral creature, almost frantic, tearing at him. Sam felt the warmth of tears and pushed her back, holding her away as she struggled to get to him.

"Don't push me away, Sam. Please."

He held her at bay until she suddenly went limp, then pulled her to his chest, rocking as she wept. The intensity of her emotions startled him. Some time later, he said, "You know what? I'm taking you home."

She slumped against him on the return trip to Brewster, listless and defeated. Sam held her at arm's length at the front door and said, "I'm sorry, Cynthia. I am really sorry, but I don't know what to think of this. You should probably take some time to think, okay? Because there is only one way what you were doing is going to end, and I don't want to be sorry for it."

She smiled weakly and placed her fingertips on his mouth. "You don't need to say anything. I'll be okay."

"What happened is no deal breaker, okay? I'm still in. You need to take a break."

She smiled more convincingly. "It's not your fault. Good night, Sam."

He waited until she locked the door. Her sudden change disturbed him greatly. At the ranch, he sat in the darkened living room a long time, thinking about her conduct, and then fell into a troubled sleep on the couch.

The click of the door latch woke him. He bolted upright as the lights flicked on.

"Do you think you could ever love me, Sam?"

"Cynthia? What...?"

"Do you?" she demanded. "I need to know." She looked exhausted. Her eyes didn't waver from his.

Sam moved toward her and said, "I think we have exactly the same feelings, but...." Then he noticed the overnight bag at her feet. "What are you doing? Have you lost it?"

"I'm not crazy, Sam, and unless you insist, I don't want to leave. I want to stay with you tonight."

He cast away all pretense of restraint and kissed her eagerly until she broke away, breathless and weak. "I won't stop this time, Cynthia. You can't expect me to stop." He read her eyes for signs.

"I won't let you stop," she said. "Not this time."

They eventually made their way to the bedroom, after several stops along the way to embrace and kiss. She didn't try to disengage. He knew she had to feel the firmness of his erection.

"You better be sure," he said, stopping at the bed.

"Stop talking."

He stepped back and unbuttoned her sweater. The process stimulated them profoundly. She extended her arms to assist. He stood behind and pulled her close. She covered his hands with hers as he traced slowly over the contours of her stomach and hips. They swayed gently from side to side, the dance of ages, the dance with no steps. The rocking motion captivated her. His mouth brushed against her neck and she tilted her head aside to promote more sensation.

"Please don't stop," she begged when he paused.

He moved a hand to her breast, half expecting resistance. She murmured softly and lay her head back on his shoulder, eyes closed, smiling luxuriously, enjoying the intimacy. Sam's concern for her emotional condition slipped away as passions took control. He whispered, "I won't stop, Cynthia."

"Good. I'm okay."

He unbuttoned her jeans and pushed them over her hips. She nudged her shoes off and stepped away, almost naked in front of a man. Cynthia unbuttoned his shirt and pulled it over his shoulders, surveying his body with unconcealed curiosity–until she saw the terrible evidence of his wounds.

"Oh, Sam," she whispered, touching the scars with trembling fingers, passions of the moment forgotten. "Oh, Sam." Tears welled and she bowed her head against his chest and wept.

He held her and said, "That's all in the past."

"I should have…. I'm so sorry." She held him, tears washing down his chest, swaying gently until he broke the silence.

"I'm freezing," he said. "Let's get under the blanket." Sam sat on the bed, his back to her, and took off his clothes. They joined beneath the covers and lay close, gazing into each other's eyes, touching and caressing. Sam resisted the craving to rush.

Her sadness gradually diminished, replaced by a timid smile. "This is all so strange, Sam. One minute I'm scared to death, and then I'm not."

"There is no hurry. Anyway, I like what we're doing. I could look at you all night."

His fingers brushed her mouth and face. She stopped breathing, then relaxed and answered his kisses, permitting his explorations without resistance.

Sam released the snap on her bra, pulled her to a sitting position and slipped it over her arms. Her breasts surged free, breaking the spell. She folded her arms, suddenly timid.

Sam gently moved her arms away. "You're beautiful, Cynthia.

Please don't hide from me."

She closed her eyes, took a deep breath, and let her arms drop.

He said. "I have never seen anything so perfect." He pulled her down and knelt over her body, pinning her wrists to the bed, kissing her breasts. She shuddered, breath drawing in sharply. Sam could feel her heart racing. He caressed her hips to break the pattern. She strained toward the touch of his hand. Her eyes popped open and she stopped breathing altogether as his fingers slid beneath the band of her panties. She didn't hold back. Her hips arched to assist as he removed the last barrier without a sign of resistance. He wedged his leg between hers, pausing to let her adapt to the new vulnerability. She relaxed, legs easing apart, yielding, answering his kisses, pulling fiercely at his shoulders, abandoning all pretense of reserve, writhing beneath him.

"Now, Sam," she murmured. "Please."

He teased with his body until her hips surged against him and then pressed cautiously and pulled away when she whimpered. A moment later she stirred again, tugging at his shoulders, arching against him.

Each movement created a wave of stimulation. She peaked almost instantly. A series of involuntary contractions rippled and shuddered through her body. "Oh, Sam," she said, gasping for breath, "That happened so fast."

After her heartbeat and breathing slowed, he moved again, merging in rhythmic, primeval impulses until her fists clenched and unclenched on his back and it happened again–the same intense, wondrous experience, much stronger.

Later, still clinging, Cynthia murmured, "Can anything be more perfect?"

"Not for me."

She smiled and pulled him closer. *I'm not ashamed and I'm not sorry.* She laughed out loud. "I hope you're not exhausted, because I plan to stay up all night. Oh, Sam, I'm so relieved. I was scared to death of.... It doesn't matter. I'm free."

CHAPTER NINETEEN

The Trial

At three in the morning, Cynthia lay wide awake, listening to the comfortable, steady rhythms of his sleep, thinking about the changes he brought to her life. While still resting securely in his arms, she alternated feeling some reservations about the incredible change and exulting in swells of incredible happiness. A torrent of thoughts raced through her mind as she stared at the ceiling. At dawn, while Sam slept, she slipped from the haven of his arms and dressed in the dark.

"Are you okay?"

His voice startled her. "Yes, I'm fine. Didn't mean to wake you."

He switched on the bedside light just as she finished dressing. "Are you leaving?"

"Yes, I need to go, Sam." She didn't understand exactly why it seemed so urgent to leave, only that she needed be alone to deal with what happened in more familiar surroundings. "I just can't sleep. Please don't get up. I'll let myself out." She returned to the bed and kissed him.

Sam wasn't satisfied and sat up. "I'm not going to question your reasons or beg you to stay, but I am going to worry." He wrapped a sheet around his waist and followed her out. "Do you have to go?" he asked as she opened the car door.

"I think so. Don't worry about me, Sam. I just need some time. We are not in trouble, so please don't worry."

He placed his hands on her shoulders, looked directly into her eyes and searched for clues. "You need to think? I've heard that before. Scares me, Cynthia. Don't think too long this time. I want to be part of whatever it is you have to think about. You won't shut me out, will you?"

Cynthia didn't think she would ever forget the hurt and confused look on Sam's face as she drove away. The guilt she felt for defying her moral principles and fundamentalist religious past had seeped in during the night, as she knew they would, threatening to smother the joy. That was bad enough, but nothing compared to the remorse she now felt for leaving Sam to worry. Self-reproach for the night of passion didn't fill her thoughts as much as the pained expression on his face.

Once in the secure confines of the duplex, her thoughts wavered between guilt and Sam's disappointment–shame and Sam–on and on. A procession of guilt-ridden condemnation measured against memories of the night.

She stood at the bathroom mirror talking to herself. "What about Sam? This didn't happen to me alone. What must he be thinking?"

She called him before eight o'clock. His voice seemed lifeless.

"Did I wake you?" she asked.

"No. I couldn't sleep. You okay?"

"I'm fine. What are you thinking about, Sam? Why can't you sleep?"

"You, Cynthia–only you. I'm worried sick. Have I ruined everything?"

I should have known. He isn't thinking about himself. He's worried about me.

"Sam, I love you. Stop worrying. You can't lose me. I wouldn't change what happened last night for anything. Now get some sleep." She replaced the receiver gently and slept soundly until after noon.

Cynthia closed the office and drove to the ranch. Sam wasn't at the house. She found the door unlocked and stepped inside to wait. He arrived just before dark, dirty and wet with sweat from hours of loading cattle.

"I hope you don't mind," she said. "You left the door open."

He laughed. "Believe me, I will never mind. I left it open for you."

"How did you know I would...oh, never mind." Cynthia hadn't

known until a few moments before closing the office that she would drive to the ranch. "Sam I want to know something." She moved closer.

He stepped back to avoid contact. "I'm filthy, Cynthia. Let me clean up first, then we can talk." At the bedroom door, he turned and examined her intently. "Am I in trouble?"

"No." She smiled and added, "I've never felt this good about life. Hurry."

A few moments later, dressed and clean, he imprisoned her in his arms and kissed her affectionately. "There, that's better. Now, what's on your mind?"

"Last night is on my mind," she said. "I couldn't work today for thinking about last night. Tell me your thoughts about what happened. I don't want applause for what we did or how we did it, and I don't want to know if I'm good or bad compared to someone else. I don't need to know any of that."

"Then what?"

"Did something special happen last night? I want to know if what happened to me was just the usual, or did something extraordinary happen?"

"If you felt what I did, then something special happened. I can tell you last night was perfect. I can also tell you there probably isn't a more exciting woman on the face of this planet."

Cynthia's smile faded quickly and she looked disturbed. "I'm thrilled that you feel that way," she said, "But, at the same time, it makes me sad." She kissed him to arrest the onset of an unwanted question, then continued, "Just think about all the wasted years–of how much I missed. I feel so cheated, Sam."

He curbed the urge to kiss her and said, "Well, look at it this way–maybe you wouldn't feel the same if last night happened years ago with someone else. Maybe what happened is special because you waited. Maybe the lost years prepared you for last night. Let's just make every minute count from now on."

They made love after dinner and again before Cynthia left for work the next morning. A week later he asked her to move in. She wasn't ready to alter her life that much, but shamelessly spent every spare moment with him. They became inseparable friends and lovers–at least until the alarm went off each morning at five.

Sam groaned, "Oh, God, Cynthia! Why five? Five is

inhuman." He rolled over and collapsed after mashing the alarm switch. "I hate that damned alarm!"

"Oh, you'll live. You don't want everyone in Brewster gossiping about me, do you?"

"You are completely wrong, Counselor. I do. I absolutely do. I want everyone to know."

They spent hours and days recounting memories of their previous lives. Neither tired of hearing about the other's favorite songs, poems, foods, movies, celebrities, cars, jokes, and making love.

"You're a changed woman. What a surprise you turned out to be. You're a better woman than I am a man. I can't keep up with you."

"Is that so bad?"

"No. I wouldn't change anything. I like unruly women."

"Sam, do you know how much I suffer at work each day? I actually suffer during our separations. My heart aches for you. That's a country song, isn't it?"

"I know the feeling. It's mutual."

When apart, every phone call, every knock at the door, every footstep seized her attention.

Sam?

"My entire life has changed, Sam. I wonder how I existed without you. A month ago, I knew almost nothing about you, and now you're so much a part of me that nothing matters except you. Is that crazy?"

"Crazy is good. I feel the same way."

She smiled and hugged him. "It is scary, though. You are so much a part of me."

Sam helped her with legal preparations for Townsend's trial, mostly running errands. Cynthia would have let the work slip without his penchant for discipline. She lost interest in Clyde Townsend. He no longer mattered. Nothing mattered except Sam.

He chastened her about lack of effort. "You have him right where you want him. Concentrate. Don't let him slip away."

The defense asked for and received a change of venue. The trial date slipped to April. Cynthia didn't object, quite content to spend another month with Sam before they each had to make a decision about what to do with their lives. They began spending weekends away from prying eyes and the gossips of Brewster and Wickmore, traveling to Hot Springs, Arkansas, a shopping trip to Kansas City, visiting theaters and fine hotels in St. Louis.

A day before the trial, Sam drove her to the Barry county courthouse in Cassville where the trial would take place after the change of venue.

"Why do you think it's necessary to waste a morning looking over the courtroom, Sam?"

"You will be more relaxed if you're familiar with the field of battle. Trust me on that, Counselor."

Cassville is a bustling little town deep in the Ozarks; the only town of any size in the county. The old, graying stone courthouse sat in the middle of the city square, a municipal design common to many Missouri county seats. They went directly to the courtroom and stood at the entrance to survey the chamber.

Cynthia whispered, "It's so...so...."

Sam whistled softly and shook his head. "Yeah, I know. Looks like you will be performing in a pit. Reminds me of a Roman amphitheater with Christians and lions. Actually, that's almost fitting, you being the Christian."

"No! Wrong! Not this time. This time I'm the lion. It's so small, Sam, and look, only one table for the lawyers. I will be sitting right next to the defense lawyers. This is so unusual."

The courtroom featured several huge cast iron radiators along the walls and numerous old fashioned overhead fans. She counted six church pews for spectators in the balcony and six rows on each side of the lower center aisle. An ornate oaken bannister separated the pit from the spectators. The judge would sit on an elevated dais with the jury, hovering over the performers, looking down into the pit.

Jury selection began the next morning. Cynthia didn't exercise her right to challenge even one juror. The final jury consisted of nine men and three women. The men, with one exception, an eighty-year-old, all looked to be about fifty. The men wore either bib overalls or cowboy boots, and none had any misgivings about recommending the maximum sentence if the defendant was proven guilty. The women were also positive, leaving no doubt about their inclination to render justice. Ken's attorney challenged his full complement of prospective jurors, complaining bitterly to the judge later, "Where did you get these people? Is everyone in this county a fire-breathing fundamentalist? This is a hanging jury if I ever saw one."

"Poor Ken isn't going to find a friend on that jury," Cynthia told Sam on the return trip to Brewster that evening. "Those people are mad at the world, cattle rustlers in particular. He'll never–"

"I'm tired of Townsend, Cynthia. Marry me."

Her mind locked as his words sank in. She stopped breathing, then covered her eyes, peeking through her fingers to see if he was joking. "Did you just say–"

"Yes! Yes! I don't want to go another day without you. I'm begging. Please, Cynthia Marry me."

"Oh, yes! A thousand times, yes!" She smothered him with kisses, tears flowing uncontrollably. Cynthia had known since their first kiss how she felt about him, but never once permitted herself to dream about this moment. She broke from his embrace and covered her mouth

"Oh, my God! Sam, I...."

"What's the matter?"

"How am I going to tell Mother? Oh, my heavens! I'm planning to be married and she doesn't even know I'm seeing you. And a Prescott." She started laughing. "A Prescott! She is going to flip."

He was astonished. "What? You haven't told your mother?"

"No. If she knew about us...if she knew what we.... No. She is so inflexible, Sam. If she had any idea how much you mean to me. How close we are. No one except Alice knows about you, and not that much, really. No one knows." She added, "Oh, mother will have a cat fit."

"I see. Well, I hate to say it, but your mother has always seemed a wee bit peculiar to me, Cynthia. She can't be that old fashioned, can she?"

"Old fashioned isn't even close, Sam. She is so straight-laced and righteous that even God would have a hard time believing it. Webster invented the word "pious" to describe my mother."

"Well, everyone gets married. Doesn't she believe in marriage?"

"Oh, sure, but she has a little teeny problem with men. My father really never understood her. Did you know he quit the school and ran off with the Coker woman?"

"Yeah. Denning told me."

"Mother despises men. All men I think. My experience with Clyde sure didn't improve her outlook that much. She will be so shocked."

"Well, that hardly matters as we aren't depending on your mother for approval."

* * * * *

Cynthia gave her opening statement–a brief outline of Townsend's offenses, assuring the jury that they would find the evidence indisputable. One morning during the trial, Sam drove to Joplin and bought a diamond. He gave it to her on the final day of the trial, just before her closing argument.

"The jurors must have thought I was supremely confident, Sam. I couldn't stop smiling. This is the most beautiful ring I have ever seen." She made the comment gazing at the ring, sitting in the hallway of the courthouse waiting for the verdict. "I'm going to call Mother." She walked away and returned a few moments.

"What did she say? How did she take it?"

"Well," she admitted sheepishly. "I didn't actually tell her. I said I would be home tomorrow with a big surprise. I'm sure she probably thinks it will be something about the trial."

"That's all? That's it? She still doesn't know?"

"Sam, really. A woman simply doesn't tell her mother something this important over the phone. Anyway, I want to see her face when I tell her. Oh, I do wish the jury would hurry. The wait is driving me crazy."

"Relax. They've only been out a couple of hours."

Another hour passed before the bailiff opened the courtroom door and shouted, "Jury's in!"

"Sam, help me up. My legs don't work."

Cynthia was sure the assembly of reporters and onlookers could see her knees quaking as she stood to await the ritual reading of the verdict. She had to lean forward to grip the table for support, thoughts racing back through the week-long trial. Townsend's attorney had tried to discredit her primary witnesses by attacking their character. He accused them of being, "Confessed thieves and liars." Charley and Tom performed well under brutal questioning, supporting each other's testimony.

Pitzen, the hired killer, realizing the Appleby brother's testimony would convict him, had previously turned "States Evidence" in hope of less than a death sentence. He provided the crucial evidence to convict Townsend by admitting that Clyde paid him to kill Wes Prescott, and his bank account supported times and influx of Clyde's money.

Townsend stared at Cynthia throughout the trial. She tried not to look his direction for fear of encountering his eyes. In one unguarded moment, she met his stare and recalled what he did to her beneath the bridge. She never looked again.

The judge protected her strategy from the defense attorney's objections and her case unfolded in an orderly manner. The defense attorney failed in his attempt to damage her witnesses. His defense, as it evolved, depended entirely on his ability to discredit the Applebys.

During closing comments, Cynthia declared, "The defense has failed to establish a defense. The defense had no alternative other than to present a clearly transparent attempt to discredit prosecution witnesses. Ladies and gentlemen, the state did not deny the previous activities of prosecution witnesses, nor will I attempt to convince you that they are upstanding members of society. However, you know Tom and Charlie Appleby did not lie about Clyde Townsend. Why would they? They have far more reason to fear the defendant by testifying *against* him than they do for lying in his favor. No, the Appleby brothers didn't lie to you. They are simple, uneducated men who, when faced with the opportunity to right a wrong, chose to do right. Todd Pitzen's motive for turning "State's Evidence" is not so honorable. Nonetheless, without once varying his testimony, Mister Pitzen agreed exactly with the Appleby brothers. You must not be persuaded by the defense's obvious intent to lead you from the truth. Ladies and gentlemen, the truth is, Clyde Townsend hired Todd Pitzen to murder Wes Prescott. You *must* find him guilty."

The jury foreman's voice interrupted her mental review. "We have, Your Honor."

"And how do you find?"

"We find the defendant guilty as charged."

Cynthia's eyes clouded. She took a deep breath before turning to seek Sam's face in the audience. He winked. A wave of elation swept over her.

The judge announced a date for final sentencing and mashed the gavel down concluding the trial. Cynthia closed her briefcase and turned to leave just as two officers led Townsend from the defendant's chair. Clyde braced against the officers and stopped in front of her, his face contorted in a storm of anger. Cynthia had seen that same look beneath the bridge.

"It ain't over, Roush! You'll pay for this you snooty bitch! It ain't over!" He lunged, struggling in vain against the two burly officers.

Cynthia stepped into the aisle so the officers could not steer Clyde around her. When Clyde stopped resisting, she stood directly in front of him, a thin smile accenting the triumphant look on her face. The smile faded as she addressed him. "This time, Clyde, we did it my way."

CHAPTER TWENTY

Kinship

Cynthia remained at the courthouse for more than an hour, answering questions for a flock of newspaper reporters and television news teams. She was flushed with excitement but could find no escape from the clamoring demands of the media. Sam watched from the distance. Their eyes met on occasion. He smiled and nodded encouragement. She paused to answer the final barrage of questions on the way down the front steps.

"What does this trial mean to your career, Miss Roush?"

"A lot less than you might imagine," she said with a deliberately devious smile.

"Wait a minute, Miss Roush. What did you mean by that? Did I detect a hidden meaning there?"

"You will just have to wait and see," she replied.

Sam hugged her proudly as they drove away. "You were wonderful. I'm happy for you. I have never done anything to compare with what you did this week."

"Of course you have, but it was exciting, wasn't it?"

"Like a movie."

"Sam, I'm going to resign the moment we get back to Brewster."

"I thought you might, and I think you should. Oh, there is something I haven't told you. Something I have kept on hold all week."

"It's not fair to have secrets, Sam."

"I didn't want to clutter your mind with the trial going on. I don't get legal control of the ranch until it clears court, so I can't sell it yet, but my real estate agent has rented the ranch to a cattle outfit from Arkansas. Just the land. All I have to do is sign those papers and I will be free. I want to leave just as soon as possible. This week works for me."

His announcement pushed her to the edge of the inevitable dilemma, and she wasn't prepared to jump. "So soon?"

"Can't happen soon enough. How quick can you wrap things up at the office?"

"Sam? You can't be serious? So soon?"

"Why not?"

"Where would we go? What will we do?"

He laughed. "What difference does it make? You make it sound like you won't come if I choose the wrong place. So, you choose. Anyway, that part is not important."

"I think those are fair questions, Sam. What are you planning to do?"

"We, Cynthia. We. I won't know where or what until we get there. I think the first thing we should do is get married, though. Then maybe California. A real honeymoon. Maybe a cruise. After that, who knows? We have plenty of time to plan what comes after that."

"How much time do I have to pack?"

They laughed. Her answer wasn't impulsive at all. She desperately wanted to leave.

"When can I see you tomorrow?" he asked as they approached her duplex in Brewster late that evening.

"I need to do laundry and then see Mother. I'll go to Wickmore tomorrow afternoon and bring her up to date. I'll see you at the ranch early in the evening."

* * * * *

Cynthia drove slowly from Brewster to Wickmore the next day, an ominous sensation of dread toying with the harmony of her life. Meeting her mother would be an unpleasant ordeal. No doubt Irma would close the store and predictably ask the precise questions Cynthia dreaded to answer. Irma would want to know everything, but most of all how a secret romance could advance so far without her knowledge, and with a Prescott.

Cynthia envisioned the conversation:

"A Prescott? When did you start seeing him? A Prescott? That

Prescott boy?"

"He's a man, Mother."

"Isn't this awfully fast? How can you possibly know enough about him in such a short time? What will people think? I'll tell you what they'll think, they will think you are pregnant. That's what they'll think. And a Prescott? Of all people, Cynthia. You haven't known him long enough."

Cynthia concentrated on possible answers to her mother's theoretical questions until the clattering of the bridge jerked her thoughts from the impending meeting to the present, and inevitably to the past. Not once during the years had she crossed the bridge without dreading it. The bridge didn't seem so menacing this time; holding none of the familiar terror this time; just another bridge this time. She imagined no shadowy figures. The horror of Clyde Townsend had been banished.

The doorbell tinkled as she stepped into her mother's store. She hadn't been to see Irma in months, since before Sam. They had talked on the phone–monotonous conversations revealing few details about her personal life, and certainly nothing about her love life and Sam Prescott. Irma never asked about Cynthia's social life.

She yelled, "Mother?"

"Back here in the stock room! Just a moment!"

Irma appeared, wiping her hands on the soiled Calumet Baking Soda apron. She looked old and tired. "Have a seat, girl. Let me have a look at you."

They didn't hug and kiss or exchange loving touches. There were no joyous smiles. The two women could have been strangers fencing with other, searching for something to say. Their greetings always struck Cynthia as a peculiar mother-daughter relationship. This time she looked at her mother from different eyes, and once again felt cheated.

Mrs. Kitchell is a better friend. And Sam? No contest.

"You look good, Mother," she lied.

Irma responded with a grim, thin smile. "Yeah, sure I do." She placed the apron on the counter in a wadded heap. "Well, I hear you put Clyde Townsend away. I suppose he probably deserved it."

Cynthia felt a rush of anger, suppressing the desire to snap back by flashing an empty smile. Probably? He probably deserved it?

You know he deserved it! "

Yes, Mother, he probably deserved it."

"And I suppose that's your surprise. Well, you could have saved yourself the trip. Lord knows that twenty-five miles between here and Brewster must be an awful chore.

Cynthia frowned. "Please, don't start, Mother. Need I remind you, it's the same distance from Wickmore to Brewster, coming or going." Another pretend smile.

"Well, aren't we huffy today." Irma turned away and tried to look hurt. "Anyway, I already heard all about the trial on the news. Everyone around here knows about it. That's all they talk about. You have been all over the news, even on the national news. Everyone asks me about you."

Their eyes settled on each other for longer periods as the conversation progressed. Irma almost smiled as the initial tension began drifting from their customary hostilities.

"Lord knows, I couldn't tell them anything more than they already knew. No one ever calls to tell me anything." Irma appeared to be on the verge of tears.

Cynthia cringed and waited for her mother's familiar "Poor Me" performance to run its course, from neglected mother to pitiful victim, and then ultimately to anger or conciliation, depending.

"I'm sorry, Mother. I didn't get home until late. I thought it would be better if we talked today." She suddenly brightened, yearning to change the gloomy atmosphere–anything to coax Irma from her melancholy mood. "Aren't you happy for me?"

"I don't mean to be sour, Cynthia, but you haven't stopped to see me in weeks. How did you expect me to act?"

"Happy, Mother. Be happy for me. I have just completed the most important case of my life. I'm thrilled. Come on, this is a happy occasion. Happy! Happy! Smile! Come on. I put Clyde Townsend away for life and he deserved it. "

Irma cleaned imaginary specks from the counter top. "Well, now that you're here, I suppose I better take advantage of it. Lord knows there's no telling when you'll be back."

Irma took her traditional place on the stool behind the counter. Her facial features softened as she examined Cynthia critically, and she finally smiled. The fencing was over. Their visits always seemed to begin the same way. When Irma took her seat, it was time to talk. Cynthia took her long-established place, sitting on the counter facing her mother.

"So, how have you been? You look tired, Mother."

"Oh, I'm fine. Maybe a little tired. The kids from school are stealing me blind. It's a madhouse in here when they come in after school. Decent people won't come in when that mess of kids is in here. They steal more than they buy."

"Can't you catch them at it?"

"I catch them, but it's just a game. It only makes the game more interesting when I catch them. I'm getting too old for this."

"Why don't you sell out and leave?"

"Maybe I will. Just might do that."

Cynthia recognized the conversation. The same subject always surfaced to serve as their initial discussion topic. She knew Irma would never leave the store, or the Assembly of God church, or Wickmore.

"Would you like to hear the surprise now, Mother?"

"Do you mean there's something else? My, aren't we just full of surprises."

Cynthia's smile faded. Time had run out.

"Let's have it, girl. Don't be so mysterious. You know I hate surprises."

"I'm going to be married, Mother."

Irma looked irritated. "Oh, be serious. If you've got a surprise, just tell me. You know how I hate to play games. Now, out with it. I need to get back to work."

Cynthia had mentally prepared for her mother's astonishment, just not total disbelief. Her brow furrowed at the unexpected complication. "I am serious, and I am going to be married."

Irma's skepticism changed to suspicion. She frowned, and then rejected the announcement. "Yes, well that's nice, dear," she said, dismissing the news nonchalantly. "Now go ahead and tell me what's on your mind."

Cynthia slipped from the counter and took her mother's hand. "You're not taking me seriously, Mother."

Irma pulled her hand away, still skeptical yet beginning to be guarded.

"Okay, Mother, let me try it this way: I resigned from work

today. I'm no longer the prosecutor. I resigned. I quit."

Irma's perpetual frown deepened. "You didn't."

"I did. I'm going to close the office, give the key to my duplex back after storing my household furniture. All that tomorrow, Mother. And then on Sunday I will rest. On Monday, I am going to California with Sam Prescott and we are going to be married. See?" She held out her hand out to show the ring. "Ta DA!"

Irma's eyes blinked repeatedly. The corner of her mouth twitched, as it always did under stress. Her lips pursed and her jaw muscles knotted. She appeared to be unable to speak.

Cynthia shook Irma by the shoulders. "Look at me. I'm serious, Mother." She didn't recognize her mother's expression. She had never seen her so bewildered. Irma just stared, then turned ashen white. Her mouth moved silently, eyes filling with tears.

"Mother? Are you okay?"

Irma's eyes rolled upward and she fainted. Cynthia caught and eased her to the floor, then ran to the medical section and snatched a box of smelling salts and brought Irma quickly back. After color returned, Irma struggled to a sitting position on the floor, leaning against the counter.

"Mother?"

"Oh, I'll be all right. Close the store, girl. Turn that closed sign. Do it right now before someone comes in." She shooed Cynthia away.

Cynthia complied and then helped her wobbly mother up the stairs to the meager apartment over the store. Irma sank into a kitchen chair and motioned Cynthia to sit.

"How long has this business with the Prescott boy been going on?"

"He is not a boy. We have been close friends since he returned from the Army, Mother. Let's see.... Well, last fall. Did you know he won the Medal of Honor?" She felt foolish for offering the tidbit as a diversion.

Irma's mouth faded into a thin, wrinkled slash. "You can't tell me anything about a Prescott that I don't already know," she said, eyes cold and angry.

"I just did, Mother. I'm going to marry Sam Prescott. You didn't know that."

"How did you ever get messed up with the likes of him? Have

you been...." She snapped her eyes away. "No, I don't want to know."

"Mother, I didn't expect you to be overjoyed, but I don't understand the need to be so hateful." Her anger surged and she struggled to govern an almost overwhelming desire to strike back. "Sam helped me break the rustling ring and catch Clyde Townsend. I don't consider that to be messed up."

"All right! Enough is enough! Now, come on. You simply cannot be serious about running off to get married? And a Prescott!"

"Oh, but I am serious, Mother." She desperately wanted to rescue the encounter from what she knew would be destructive if not contained. "I'm so happy. He means everything to me. I know what you think about the Prescotts, Mother. I've heard you talk about them enough over the years. But Sam isn't like that. He's a wonderful person. He is decent and kind. He isn't like Wes, or any other Prescott."

"What do you know about Wes Prescott anyway?" Irma snapped.

"I know no one from Wickmore cared much for him. I know he didn't do much for the community or anyone around here. I know more about Wes Prescott than you do, Mother. Sam isn't like his uncle, Mother."

"You have no idea what you're talking about! Wesley Prescott has done a lot for at least two people around here." She spat out the words, glaring at Cynthia.

Cynthia could not comprehend her mother's venomous hostility. Her voice literally dripped bitterness and hatred.

"That's right, girl. You heard me right. Wes Prescott did a lot for you and he did a lot for me. He brought you into this world and he put me through living hell. He put you through college and he put me through hell."

Cynthia stopped breathing. She couldn't see for the sudden sting in her eyes. The roar in her ears could not blot out her mother's voice.

Irma got up and stood in front of her daughter. "Now you listen and you listen good." Her fingers dug into Cynthia's shoulders. "Wes Prescott came back to Wickmore the summer I was seventeen. I was a weak, foolish girl; never been away from home;

didn't know right from wrong. He pestered around until I finally gave in and went out with him. Then he left the country and went off to play baseball."

"But–"

Irma snapped, "No! You had your say! Now let me finish!" She closed her eyes, sighed, and then said, "I came up pregnant." She glared defiantly. "I guess any fool can figure out that's what Wes Prescott did for you, girl. So don't you tell me I don't know anything about the Prescotts! What you have done is a sin, girl– worst kind of sin. Now, you get shet of that boy and fall down on your knees to beg forgiveness. You didn't know, so maybe the Lord will forgive you."

A violent wave of nausea swept over Cynthia as the words crashed into her thoughts. She stood, gripping the cabinet top with one hand, clutching her stomach with the other, and stumbled across the kitchen to the waste basket and vomited. She collapsed, sitting with her back to the wall, the sound of blood flooding through her ears. All other sounds came from a dreamlike void, like the hollow tick of a clock in a barrel. She slumped against the wall and stared at Irma's distant face.

"I don't understand, Mother," she said weakly. "What about my father? I always thought...I just–"

"Well, you thought wrong. Your so-called father couldn't father anything for a woman, not after he started drinking. Anyway, the truth wouldn't have done you any good. Every little girl needs a father. Yours just happened to be off playing baseball." Irma's face bore no sign of compassion–only disgust.

"It can't be true, Mother. Please tell me it isn't true."

"Oh, it's true all right. I've kept the disgrace of it secret near thirty years. It's true."

Irma didn't recount her relationship with Wes, a relationship that began in high school and ended with his death–a thirty year love-hate relationship. She didn't tell Cynthia, or anyone, that she would meet Wes any time he called, disregarding the church's commandment against adultery, or that she tried to kill herself when she found out he married, and again when she discovered he wouldn't come for her after his divorce, other than for an occasional spree of sex. She hated him until he called, and then she always went, despising her weakness, unable to let him go.

Cynthia's eyes begged, entreating her mother to take back the devastating disclosure. She found no comfort in Irma's eyes; eyes harboring years of frustration and shame; eyes hiding memories of an obsessive affair that didn't end until the day Wes Prescott died; eyes with memories of the lover she would not give up and could not have.

Cynthia struggled to her feet, staggered down the stairs and out of the store. Hours later, well after dark, after driving aimlessly over miles of back roads that she neither saw or remembered, Cynthia parked in front of Irma's store and sat in the darkness. Her eyes were empty and dry by then, staring straight ahead, thinking about the magnitude of Irma's incredible announcement. Two inescapable facts arrested her thoughts: foremost, she shouldn't see Sam again, and she needed to talk to her mother again.

Irma was sitting in her cane-back rocker knitting, needles clicking steadily keeping time with the rhythmic motion of the creaking wooden rocking chair, which in turn creaked in harmony with the grandfather clock.

"Have a seat, girl. I been waiting on you." She didn't look up.

Cynthia slumped into a threadbare easy chair, leaned back and closed her eyes. "What am I going to do, Mother?"

"You don't have any choice. Oh, I know what you been thinking out there all by yourself. Believe it or not, I can sympathize. I know how you must hurt. But you have to face facts. Forget all the foolishness. Forget the evil choices I know you have been thinking about tonight. You have to do what's right and the answer is as plain as your face. Anything else is against God's rule." She didn't look up and the needles clicked nonstop.

Cynthia spoke quietly, without emotion. "You know, Mother, I always knew something wasn't right between you and Daddy."

"I take it you have come to believe what I told you is true?"

"I want to see my birth certificate. And something else–the money for my college."

Irma didn't seem surprised by the demands. She signaled with her eyes and a nod to a small lamp table between their chairs. "Certificate won't do you no good. It's in the drawer there, and yes, Wes gave me the money. About the only decent thing he ever did. He owed us that much."

Cynthia rummaged through a pile of snapshots and greeting

cards until she found the envelope.

Father of record: Edwin Roush.

"This doesn't say Wes Prescott, Mother." She waved the certificate, almost triumphantly.

Irma nodded. "What was I supposed to write down? I married Edwin before I started showing with you. I didn't lie to him about Wes, but then he never really pinned me down. Oh, he knew about me and Wes all right." She nodded. "He knew."

"Do you mean he married you knowing you were pregnant by Wes?"

Irma sighed and closed her eyes. "It was a little more complicated than that. He wasn't sure about–"

Cynthia's incredulous expression distorted into disbelief. "Are you saying what I think you are? Were you seeing both of them at once?"

Irma's chin lifted proudly. "I never lied to your father about Wes. He just never asked." Her lips turned white and the needles clicked faster to match the accelerated motion of the rocker. The clock remained constant, though, resisting her need to hasten beyond the moment. "Anyway, none of that matters now. What's done is done."

"And that's why Daddy hated the Prescott's so much. And that's why he treated Sam so poorly. It all makes sense. You and Wes Prescott, and Daddy knew it all the time. You pretending to hate Wes. Wes was the reason you fought with Daddy and Wes is the reason Daddy left, isn't it?" Through it all, Cynthia didn't open her eyes to look at her mother. "It all makes sense now. I feel sorry for you." After another long silence, she said, "So, what does that make me to Sam–cousins?"

Time passed before Irma broke the silence. "Maybe not." She closed her eyes, sighed heavily and then said, "I never wanted to tell this to another living soul, but I suppose there's no other way." She rocked, frowning and thinking, and then said, "So I'm just going to say it." She stopped rocking, but didn't look at Cynthia. "Sam Prescott is probably your half brother. He probably is." She held up a hand to stop Cynthia's objection. "Now let me finish. Elena and I were best friends. Wes used to bring drugs when he came home. I know what you're thinking, but we were just kids. I don't like to remember some things we did with Wes. Not just me–

Wes and Elena, too." She buried her face in her hands. "I just can't go on. I suppose you can figure out the obvious. That's what I'm saying. I'm saying you are probably brother and sister. I know what went on between those two after they learned that they were adopted. They were not blood kin, so things changed." She shrugged.

Cynthia stumbled to the bathroom and threw up again. When she returned to the chair, her face was a pasty white and she trembled uncontrollably.

Irma's eyebrows raised. She said, "Oh, he called while ago."

Cynthia's pulse quickened. She sat up. "What? Tell me!"

"I told him you were out."

"What did he say, Mother? What did he want?"

The needles stopped and the chair gradually slowed. "I expect he probably wanted to see you, girl. Don't you imagine?"

"Of course he does. I'm hours late. He must be frantic. I'll have to see him." She really wasn't asking, just stating the obvious to herself.

The synchronous rhythms of the chair, the clock and the knitting needles began again as Irma settled back to work. "I expect so. It never does much good to avoid inevitable things. Has to be done. Sooner the better."

Cynthia stared at nothing, listening to the knitting needles for a long time, and then got up and walked out without a word.

* * * * *

Sam had driven to Irma's store just before dark, two hours after his first pang of uneasiness about Cynthia's tardiness. He didn't see her car in Wickmore and drove to Brewster to knock on her door, then raced back to the ranch, fully expecting to find her there. He decided to call Irma and breathed a sigh of relief at Irma's announcement, "She left here a while ago." At least he knew she had been there, but found little solace for his worries about her extended absence.

Irma continued, "I'll tell her you called." She hung up before he could ask, leaving him with nothing to do but wait by the phone. He held off until he couldn't tolerate the stress, and then sped recklessly toward Brewster. Nothing there. He raced to Wickmore, turning onto the bridge just as another car entered from the other direction. He honked impatiently and forged ahead, powering his way across the bridge. The oncoming car stopped and backed up.

He recognized Cynthia and vaulted from the truck. "What in God's name has been going on?" he asked before she could say anything. "Are you okay?" He opened the door and pulled her out, opening his arms to sweep her into an embrace.

She backed away, holding him away. "Oh, Sam. No, I am not okay. We are not...."

Her eyes were hollow and sad. She appeared to be sick, white and shaking. His momentary sense of relief faded. "What's wrong? What happened? I've been going crazy."

"We have to talk," she said, leading him onto the bridge.

Sam, more puzzled than ever, pulled her around roughly. "For God's sake, Cynthia, don't...." He stopped talking the moment he noticed her tears. "Cynthia? What's the matter? Is it your mother?"

"No, Sam, it's us." She twisted away and walked toward the middle of the bridge.

"You're talking in riddles. Will you just stop and tell me what is going on!" He stepped in front of her, panic-stricken about her alarming condition.

Her voice faltered when she spoke. "We can't marry, Sam." She covered her face and wept bitterly.

He waited, confused and frightened by her emotions, then pulled her hands away and forced her to look at him. "You aren't making any sense. Look at me, Cynthia. For God's sake. Talk to me. Tell me what happened."

She clutched his shirt, shaking him fiercely, and then cried out, "You're my brother! My brother! Wes and Elena. Wes and my mother...." She backed away, heartbroken, wrenching away from his grip.

Sam fought off her feeble attempts to get away and pulled her close. She finally collapsed in his arms, weeping uncontrollably. He felt helpless. Her announcement was not incomprehensible. Wes and Irma went back. Wes said so. He held and soothed, waiting while her tears flowed in endless torrents. He wasn't sure yet exactly what happened, but sensed that everything was different.

"That's ridiculous." When she quieted, he said, "That just can't be true."

"It is, Sam. Mother explained everything to me. Wes came back to Wickmore a lot during his senior year at college. She and Wes were lovers. They have always been lovers. They never stopped being lovers."

"But you said brother. That doesn't make me your brother."

They stood together, rocking gently, comforting each other, but the shadows of impending doom spread. Cynthia said, "Wes and your mother were also...."

"This whole thing is ridiculous, Cynthia. Irma is mistaken. Not with his sister."

"No mistake, Sam. Mother has no reason to lie. She never lies. Elena was not his blood sister. They were both adopted."

"No! She lied, Cynthia. This all sounds like a lie to me. Let's just take our time and sort things out. Tell me exactly what she said."

"It's awful. Everything is so mixed up. God will forgive us. We didn't know. But we can't go on. Not now. Not with what we know."

"We don't know anything for sure."

"You have to accept that we can't marry and have children. You're my half-brother. I am your half-sister. That's all we can ever be. There is no other way."

Her words burned into his mind. He understood the threat to their relationship, if what she said was true. "Let's take time to find out for sure, Cynthia."

She disengaged suddenly, pushing him away. "I have to go, Sam. Let me go."

"No. Please don't leave this way. We can–"

"Please, Sam!" She stepped back and held him off.

"Cynthia, no! Wait!"

"I think it better for both of us if we don't see each other for a while." She cupped his face in her hands and said, "Please, for the sake of everything we have been to each other. Please, just let me go tonight." She turned and ran to the car.

"I won't let you do this!" He stopped her. She broke away, struggling toward the car. "Please, Cynthia. Please!"

She fought against his hold. "Let me go, Sam. Let me go! You're hurting me!"

"Where will you go?" he asked. "You can't just run away." He released her.

She turned to face him upon reaching the car, her sadness now a mask of anger. "It doesn't matter, does it? Don't you understand that? It's over! Nothing matters anymore! Please try to help me the only way you can. Let me go!" Her face glistened with tears.

He had never seen anyone look so heartbroken and instinctively reached for her.

"No!" she screamed, fighting his hands away.

They stood face to face, tears shimmering in the moonlight. Cynthia recovered first. "I'm so sorry, Sam. I'm sorry for both of us. Now I have to go." She ducked into the car and locked the door.

Sam stood by helplessly, watching her slump forward over the steering wheel. He could see her body heaving as she wept. Moments later, Cynthia started the engine and backed away with him hanging onto the door handle, running alongside. She shifted gears and the car gathered speed. Sam fell awkwardly, sprawling on the gravel road. He scrambled up in time to see her slow and look back. He started running again as she sped away and disappeared around the turn.

*****

Sam remained in the area for weeks, attempting every possible way to find or contact her. Cynthia either refused to answer the phone or wasn't home. Irma's store remained closed. No one in Wickmore knew where Cynthia was, or wouldn't say. Mrs. Kitchell worried. Sam couldn't find out anything from her neighbors. Her secretary didn't know anything. He searched everywhere, talked to everyone, and then one day at Wickmore he found the general store open for business again after a month's absence. Irma looked terrible, dark circles sagging under her empty eyes. She had aged ten years.

"She's gone, boy. That's all there is to it, and that's all you're going to learn from me. She's gone! Forget about her. Pray for forgiveness and thank the Lord for sparing you the Devil's abomination you were caught up in. I don't ever want to see you in here again. And she doesn't want to see you. Now get out! Leave me alone!"

He searched the country by day and waited through the nights in front of Cynthia's duplex, or down the street from Irma's store.

He badgered a deputy sheriff for answers.

"Well sir, her mother tells me she ain't missin', Mister Prescott. So we ain't been looking."

"Look, we were going to be married. I have to find her. I know something is terribly wrong."

"That may be, but Irma is her mother, bud. Now look, I know you're upset, but you got to quit houndin' Irma. The way I see it, she don't want to be bothered, an' she's got a right. Listen to me now, 'cause this here is official. The judge says you have to stay away from her. Miz Roush don't want you hangin' around. It's a legal thing now that she's got a restraining order. I'll have to run you in."

Sam searched. Weeks drifted into months. He checked with law enforcement and hospitals. He covered back roads around Wickmore and Brewster, asking everyone. And then, confused and despondent, he finally concluded that Irma wasn't his problem, Cynthia was. She obviously didn't want to be found. He hired a young couple to stay in the house, packed some clothes and drove across the bridge heading south. He drove two days and nights without stopping–through Memphis–through Knoxville and Tallahassee–always southward, stopping in Key West only because the road ran out.

CHAPTER TWENTY-ONE

Key West

S am checked into a peeling, shabby clapboard motel on the waterfront and slept twelve uninterrupted hours. The tourist season had concluded in Key West and local residents were in a semi-relaxed state, still open for the last remnants of business and starting to connect with their neighbors for the first time in months.

He didn't care about any of it: the tropical weather, the bizarre collection of humanity, the blue-green water, Hemingway's cats, feral chickens, or Key West. Sam settled into the listless routine of walking for hours until too tired to walk, and then sitting on the same rock jetty staring out to sea. He learned to drink, drinking too much, sleeping too much and remaining completely isolated from human contact. He drank and slept to counter the ravages of depression, but depression spiraled out of control anyway, ruining the first half of each day which found him tired and sleepy and still sick from last night's hangover.

And he cried. Sam could not control the weeping, breaking down often. Mostly the tears flowed when the influence of alcohol wore off, leaving no protection from agonizing memories of Cynthia. His state of mind vacillated wildly, leaving him listless at times, angry and violent the next moment, and always sad. Sam cared about nothing during the heartbreaking, lifeless moods, and then for no reason his mood would shift to anger. He confronted complete strangers over something so trivial as incidental body contact on a sidewalk.

"Watch where you're going, buddy!" he growled, ready for

battle, craving a fight.

"Hey, man. Back the hell off. You got a problem?"

Sam usually collected himself and apologized. The next day, dependent on circumstances, something just as bizarre would happen, always without provocation. Rare flashes of drunken laughter would suddenly turn to tears.

He called Irma often. She always hung up the moment she recognized his voice. One night, during one of his more destructive binges, she surprised him and listened.

"Please, Irma, tell me how she is. I have to know something about her. Not knowing is killing me. This is too hard."

"I wouldn't tell you anything if you were the last man on earth. Now stop bothering me!"

"Please, Irma. Anything. Something. Please. I'm going crazy. I have to know how she is. I'm begging you."

"There's nothing to tell. She doesn't live around here, I will tell you that much. I hear from her occasionally. That's all I'm going to say. She's as happy as she can be under the circumstances. I've said more than I should and I only told you that much so you won't call me again. I'm going to get an unlisted phone number if you call again. I don't want to be out the extra money, so leave me alone!" She slammed the receiver down.

Sam flew back to Missouri after three weeks in Key West. Cynthia's apartment and office contained new occupants. Mrs. Kitchell didn't know anything, other than some movers had taken Cynthia's things to Irma. Sam believed her. Irma locked the store when she saw him coming. The new sheriff didn't know anything. No one knew anything. He hounded the only sheriff's deputy he knew.

"Have you heard anything, Wally? Anything, man. I'm desperate."

"They ain't nothing I can do for you, partner. Miss Roush isn't missing as far as we know. I checked it out myself after you mentioned it the last time. Her mother says she just wants to be left alone. You probably ought to try and forget about her. Now, dammit, you best not be bothering her mother again. She called and reported you."

Sam roamed around the area for a week until he ran out of ideas. No one had seen her, or they were all liars. He thought about hiring a private detective. *Maybe she doesn't want me to find her.*

He recalled her ultimatum on the bridge. "Please help me the only way you can. Let me go."

He called the Missouri Bar Association. They didn't know anything and still had her old address in Brewster. "That doesn't mean she isn't working somewhere else, Mister Prescott. All that means to us is that she hasn't contacted us with a change of address."

Sam conceded defeat again and flew back to Key West to his truck and clothes, back to drinking alone during the day and pacing the beaches and jetties at night. He lived much the same way the derelicts frequenting the bus station and sleazy bars just down the street from his motel did–detached from all human contact. Sam lingered in Key West into the summer, washing all signs of ambition and enthusiasm away with alcohol. His faithful companions helped: alcohol, walking and reading, sleep an hour or two, and then do it all again. Sam was exhausted but couldn't stop. If he stopped, he thought, if he thought, he wept.

He sometimes walked until daylight, and then bought another book and substituted reading for the sleep that wouldn't come. He drank and read by day and read and drank at night until his health began deteriorating. He recognized the worsening condition, but couldn't stop. His face thinned dramatically, eyes receding into dark, vacant sockets. The hollow stare of emptiness deepened and became a part of his character. Regulars on the waterfront recognized him by the look in his tortured eyes. He felt exactly the way he looked–terrible.

Late in September, eyes temporarily fogged from reading during a long night stroll under the street lights, Sam strayed by the fishing boat docks. He looked up from a paperback just in time to avoid colliding with a sign newly positioned in front of a charter boat. An older wooden fishing vessel rocked against the dock behind the sign. He matched the boat's name to the sign advertising for a deck hand. Sam wasn't aware of the sign's effect until he walked by again on the return trip an hour later. He closed the book and stared at the sign, and then went directly to the barbershop for a haircut and shave. He didn't take a drink that night for the first time in weeks and looked fairly fresh when he talked to the captain the next morning.

"Is that job still open?" he asked, pointing to the sign.

"Reckon so," said the leather-skinned, gray-headed man Sam estimated to be about sixty. "You ever worked a boat?"

"No Sir, but I would like to give it a try."

The captain stopped working on some snarled fishing tackle, looked up and gave Sam his full attention. "What makes you think you can do the job?"

"What makes you think I can't," Sam replied, smiling amicably.

The old man laughed. "Well, by George, come on aboard then and let me have a peek at you." He appraised Sam skeptically for a moment before declaring, "You don't look none too healthy to me. You on drugs?"

"No. I never use drugs."

"Are you an alcoholic?"

Sam hesitated. "I don't know. Maybe. I wasn't before this spring. I have been drinking too much lately, that's for sure, but you don't need to worry about it. I absolutely won't drink while working for you."

"You got personal problems?"

"Yeah, but that won't matter, either. I need the work."

"You got a handle on your problems, then?"

"Not really, but I'm ready to work. I'll do a good job."

"Okay, if you can stay off the booze, I'll give you a try. You look like a decent sort to me, no matter what the mayor says."

Sam grinned, offered his hand and they sealed the bargain. "I'll stay clean. That's a promise. My name is Sam Prescott."

"Dan Grady. Welcome aboard, Sam. You got a place to stay?"

"Yes. Been here all spring."

"Yeah, I've seen you around. I have a charter tomorrow, Sam, and you have plenty to learn. We should probably get started. He led the way toward the pilot's cabin. "This here is the Peggy Sue, Sam. Don't ask me why. I inherited the name when I bought the boat and just never changed it. She's fifty-four feet long and sleeps six. We don't often stay out overnight, though, so you can keep your gear below and stay aboard if you like. I don't do party trips anymore, only serious fishing. I've been doing this for thirty years, mostly the same people year after year. It's a good life. You meet lots of nice people in the charter business and they generally come back if you treat them right. How are you with people?"

"I'm a fairly sociable type. Do we run the show by ourselves?"

Dan shook his head. "Nope. It takes five of us to do it right. My brother and his son do most of the fishing work. I'm the navigator and pilot. My wife does the food. You to do the rest, mostly clean up–dirty work and maintenance." He watched Sam intently, looking for signs of dissatisfaction about the duties, and added, "Gopher stuff, you know–go fer this, go fer that."

"I don't have any romantic ideas about going to sea, Dan. I expected to do menial work."

Sam and Dan Grady developed a solid friendship. He worked steadily until the tourist season ended late that winter, only occasionally lapsing into depression. The episodes were short-lived.

Captain Dan learned to recognize his new friend's emotional state. The two men spent most of their off-duty time together fishing as they didn't get the opportunity to fish during the charter trips. Dan provided everything: an outboard motor fishing boat, all necessary fishing gear, two six-packs of beer and enough crackers and bologna to last all day. They talked more than they fished and enjoyed relaxing in the out-of-the-way inlets far from civilization. Sam never talked about Cynthia but Dan gradually accumulated details by comparing bits of information. He had a good idea what the Sam's depression was all about.

Dan usually steered Sam away from bouts of depression by engaging in conversation when he observed the growing moodiness and brooding. One late March evening, he noticed Sam standing on the stern alone, watching the sunset as the Peggy Sue approached home from the west.

He decided to join him. "We aren't going out tomorrow, Sam."

"Did you cancel? I thought that bunch from New Jersey wanted to go out again."

"I gave that charter to *The Wharf Rat*. You and me are going fishing tomorrow."

"No thanks, Dan. I think I'll just lay around."

"No way. I gave up a charter for you. I'll see you at the dock come sunup."

They pulled into a mangrove inlet the next morning on the south shore of the mainland. Dan threw the anchor out, capped a beer and leaned back and said, "You ever going to talk to me about whoever or whatever is bothering you?

Sam looked surprised. "That why you cancelled?"

"Yup. That's it. Been watching you, Sam. I've seen you go through bad spells before and my guess is that you are headed for tough times again, and soon. I wish I could help, but the only thing I know how to do is listen. So, talk to me."

Sam contemplated his friend several moments before answering, "You're right, she's been on my mind lately."

Dan threw the can of beer as far as he could and raged, "Shit! I knew it was a she. Dammit to hell! I knew it! Look, it isn't my business and you danged sure don't need to feel pressured to tell me anything, but I am worried about you, Sam. Seems to me like you are maybe bordering on some serious emotional problems. I see too many signs. I think you may be headed for some serious trouble if you don't get straight." He capped another beer, took a long drink, and said, "Crap! A dang woman. I...oh, hell, never mind. Dammit all!"

"Why don't you just say what's on your mind."

They both laughed.

Dan didn't let the subject drop. "I know what I said is a hell of a thing to say to a man. And I wouldn't say it for anything if I wasn't so damned worried about you. I'm seeing too many things to stew about."

"What do you see, Dan?"

"I see a young feller in the prime of life who ends up crying when he only started out to laugh. I see a man who is smart and friendly watching sunsets all by himself with tears in his eyes. What I don't see is you smiling very much. I have watched you suffer since I first knew you and managed to keep my damned mouth shut. But now I'm really worried, and I'm taking a ration of crap from the wife. She sees it, too, Sam. Talk to me."

"I don't know if I can." He took a deep breath and stared at the horizon. "Well, okay. Cap me a beer and let's see if I can get through this."

They didn't wet a line or bait a hook that day. Sam took his time and the story spilled out just as it happened. Both men had tears in their eyes on more than one occasion.

"That's terrible, Sam. That's the toughest thing I ever heard. I don't know how you stand it. That would be too much for me."

"Do I stand it? Not sure I do. The toughest part is not knowing anything about her. I lost her, Dan, in the truest sense of the word. I lost her. I can't even grieve properly because I don't know what happened to her. If I could just talk to her; if I knew she was okay; if I knew anything. She's out there somewhere. Sometimes I don't think I can stand the frustration of not knowing. Sometimes I think.... Well, if time cures pain I wish to hell it would get started. Time does not bring relief. That's a poem, and she sure had it right."

Two weeks later, when Sam announced his intentions to leave, Dan said, "I've been expecting this. I wondered how long you would stay. Never figured you to stay this long, Sam. Where you headed?"

"I've got some unfinished business up north. Can I come back when it gets too cold up there?"

"You always have a job here. I guess you know that, though. Stay in touch."

They clasped hands and looked directly into each other's eyes, sealing a lasting bond.

"I will write," Sam said. "Thanks for everything. You've been a good friend when I needed one most."

The drive back to Wickmore took three days. He used the time effectively, making notes and planning.

First things first. Make the rounds and learn anything I can about Cynthia.

He planned to research the Prescott family history, to go through family records as far back as possible–all the wives, including Angeline, Wes's ex. After a week at home, he had learned nothing about Cynthia. Irma refused to talk and no one knew anything, or so they said. He opened Wes's office safe and gathered information from his files. He even searched through old boxes in the attic. Sam also retrieved everything from a lockbox at the bank, records from dentists, the hospitals and doctor offices. He asked to read the sheriff's records where he found a rich history of incidents, mostly assault, all the way back to his great grandfather. Thing began to sort out in his mind.

He discovered a letter from Wes's ex, Angeline Pierpont of Nashville, Tennessee. The butler intercepted his call. He confirmed that she still lived there. Sam left for Nashville immediately, arriving that evening. He drove to a motel and took a room after deciding not to bother the Pierponts so late in the day. His initial euphoria about doing something positive gradually changed to hopelessness during the long drive.

Probably another dead end.

He ordered supper and ate in front of the television, idly flipping channels. The late news came on and Sam settled back to watch, only to bolt upright, astonished, staring. He rushed to kneel in front of the television to see better, his attention riveted on the anchor woman sitting between the weatherman and sportscaster. The attractive, businesslike threesome were waiting for the station's self-promoting hoopla to play out before delivering the late evening news. When the news delivery began, the words meant nothing to Sam. He wasn't listening. His eyes never moved from the woman in the middle.

"Good evening," she said, as the camera zoomed in, isolating her from the men. "I'm Choxie Pratt. Tonight's lead story features...."

He didn't hear another word. Sam stood in front of the television set and smiled until the news team signed off. He couldn't stop smiling.

Choxie. After all these years. She hasn't changed. Prettier, if anything.

He remembered her ambition of working in television. She left the Academy after graduation with orders to Germany, to an assignment with The Armed Forces Network.

She did it. This is what she wanted.

He thought of her often through the years, even thought about locating her, but resisted for fear of interfering with her life.

She's still beautiful.

Sam grabbed his phone and called the station to ask for her. He had second thoughts before the front desk operator answered and hung up..

Tomorrow will come soon enough. Tomorrow.

He couldn't find her name in the Greater Nashville area phone directory.

No surprise. A news personality wouldn't be listed. I'll go to the station in the morning.

He slept little that night, showered and shaved before six the next morning, then walked for miles, returning to the room to shower again, arriving at the station well before noon.

The cheerful receptionist said, "Miss Pratt usually doesn't arrive until after noon. Would you care to leave a message, Sir?"

"No thanks. I'll wait." He took a seat in the only chair in front of her desk.

The secretary began demonstrating signs of nervousness. She too often had to deal with crackpots. "I'm not sure exactly when she will be in, sir. Perhaps if you–"

Sam waved her off and said, "It doesn't matter. I really don't mind waiting. We're old friends."

He wandered around the receptionist's office until she finally asked that he wait in the lobby. The lobby provided a better view anyway, and more room to pace. Sam's thoughts traveled back to their years at the academy. He had plenty of time to think of a dozen reasons why she wouldn't be happy to see him.

The receptionist dialed management. A burly woman came down to observe. After a few minutes observation, she shrugged and left.

So much time has passed. She's probably married.

He thumbed through a stack of sports magazines, but found it hard to concentrate, not with Choxie so close. He looked up anxiously each time the entrance door opened.

Finally, as the clock in the lobby struck one, the front door opened and a boisterous group of technicians carrying cameras and sound equipment entered. They were laughing and joking. The petite black woman carrying a briefcase seemed to be the center of attention.

"That's it, guys," she announced. "Good job. Get it ready for the evening news. The mayor is expecting to see himself tonight. I expect the network will probably want a copy. Thanks again for everything. You're the best."

She turned and marched toward the news offices. And then, as if seeing a ghost, she suddenly stopped and turned slowly, looking across the lobby. Choxie Pratt, the consummate professional, dropped her briefcase and reached blindly for the paneled wall seeking support. The crew noticed the sudden change in her behavior and one by one their eyes followed the direction of her eyes, toward Sam.

"Oh, my God!" she whispered. "Oh, my God."

Two of the technicians perceived Sam as a threat and maneuvered quickly to get between Choxie and the smiling stranger. She pushed them aside. "No! It's okay. It's Sam." She squeezed through the bewildered group and ran. "Sam! Oh, Sam! I can't believe it!" She flew into his arms.

The amazed crew watched as their very professional business associate lost herself in a carefree exhibition of the most unusual behavior. She laughed and cried, kissed and embraced, and then stepped back to look at Sam and did it all again.

Finally, with happy tears streaming down, still holding tightly to his hand, she led him across the lobby to her companions and announced smugly, "This is Sam, everybody. This is my Sam." She beamed proudly, her eyes never leaving his face. "This is my Sam."

A deep, reverberating voice from the hallway entrance drew everyone's attention. "I suppose this means I'll have to prevail on Ted to fill in for you tonight." The voice boomed from a fiftyish, balding man casually leaning against the receptionist's counter.

Choxie smiled radiantly. "Oh, Phil, could you do that? Is there any way I can have a couple of days off?" The smile disappeared and she looked at Sam. "Are you.... I mean, will you be–"

"As long as you like, Chox."

The balding man approached Sam and offered his hand. "I'm Phillip Spencer and I know exactly who you are. I am supposed to be the producer here, but, as you have probably already determined for yourself, I don't have much control of anything. Sam, it's an honor to meet you. I have known about you for years, my man. I have to be honest, though, we would all appreciate another picture. I, for one, am damned tired of that same old photo she keeps on her office wall. Okay, two days, Choxie. Then you owe me. I mean to collect."

Choxie's friends shook Sam's hand and the little group drifted away, mercifully leaving them alone.

"This is too much for me, Sam. I don't know where to begin. What are you doing here? Where did you come from? There are so many things. Where have you been? Can I keep you?" She looked away instantly, embarrassed by the impetuous stream of questions, particularly the last one. "That's not exactly what I meant to say. Can you stay for a while, Sam? Will you stay?"

He hugged her and said, "I'm not on a schedule, Choxie, if that's what you mean. Yes, you can keep me." He laughed. "I take it you're free for the day?"

"Yes. Let's get out of here. We have been a spectacle long enough. Come on."

"Oh, Miss Pratt," a musical voice sang out from the receptionist's desk. "Would it be a reasonable request to know just when I might expect you back?"

Choxie winked at Sam and spoke without a trace of humor. "I don't know, Joy. I honestly don't have any idea, but you don't need to expect me at all. You can check with Phil. I'll be in touch with him."

Sam already knew the answers to two important questions. She wasn't unhappy to see him and she definitely wasn't married, either that or he was terrible at reading signs. Choxie appeared to be even more beautiful than he remembered, more mature, and far less inhibited.

"How did you find me?" she asked.

"Watched the news last night."

"Is that all? You found me by accident?" She pretended disappointment.

"Maybe it wasn't an accident. Maybe destiny?"

"That's a good one, soldier. You didn't come to Nashville just to see me, did you?" She looked wounded.

"I won't lie to you. I didn't know you lived here. Now, will you let me say something in defense?"

"It better be good."

By then they were standing on the sidewalk beside his truck. He held her shoulders and looked directly into her eyes. "I have never been so happy to see anyone in my entire life." He whirled her around, kissing and laughing.

Phil Spencer, observing the scene from his office window, turned to his male anchor, Ted Dent, as Sam drove away. "If I am any judge of people, Ted, it is my educated guess that you are going to be doing the news by yourself for a spell. Choxie is in another galaxy."

Ted shook his head and said, "No doubt about it. I can't believe

I actually saw Little Miss Professional blow apart the way she just did. Wouldn't have believed it."

Phil smiled and clucked to himself. "She really has a case for him, doesn't she. Hard to imagine her so taken by anyone. So, that's Sam Prescott. He isn't a female fantasy after all. I'll be damned." He shook his head. "Well, I hope Choxie's Sam is still everything she thinks he is. You won't mind filling in for her, will you, Ted?"

"Does it matter if I do or don't?"

"No. And I'm pretty damned sure she doesn't care if either of us exist right now. I want this to go smoothly for her, Ted, so let's pull together. Drop your personal animosities and get on with the job. Help her out for a change. It isn't her fault that she's black, female, beautiful, smart and network bound."

*****

Sam and Choxie spent most of the afternoon in a small, out-of-the-way café, sitting alone in a secluded, glass-covered greenhouse room featuring cascading rivulets of manufactured rain. They held hands, touched, kissed, and briefly reviewed their lives.

Choxie told him about her three year marriage to a professional musician. Sam knew all about her husband and his band, just not that Choxie had been married to him. He had followed her husband's career until drug abuse destroyed his talent.

She told him that drugs also terminated their marriage. "He had trouble dealing with my success," she admitted. "He came from a poor suburb in Chicago and didn't understand me, my job, my friends, or my way of life. He hated my job and the time it demanded. He wouldn't adjust, or maybe he couldn't."

"So why did you marry him?"

"Made a mistake. There really isn't anything else to say about it. He was attractive...." She shrugged and shook her head sadly. "Fortunately, no children."

"You have changed, Choxie. You seem more confident, more...? What? Peaceful?"

"Maybe I grew up. That's all there is to it." She reached across the table to hold his hand. "I have always regretted the way we parted, Sam. I missed you more than you will ever know. More than I can tell you. You didn't deserve what I did. I was too young to know what we had. I couldn't see anything but problems ahead for us. I'm so sorry." She looked sad.

"And now?"

"I have come to believe that I probably threw away the one chance I will ever have for true happiness."

The confession elated him. "I never forgot about you, Choxie. Do you have someone?"

"Oh, I get out occasionally. Mostly to events associated with my job, but I'm not seeing anyone. My time for socializing is extremely limited."

"What about the network? You mentioned the network several times."

She smiled and said, "It looks good. They use me regularly. I have been advised to prepare for a network offer."

"Would you like that?"

"That's what I have lived and dreamed and worked for. I have spent years preparing for the opportunity. I am ready." She studied him for several seconds. "What about you? What are you up to?"

Sam told her about Wes and the ranch, about his time in Key West, but not his reason for being there. "Just bumming around, waiting for something to appeal," he told her. His tan suggested an outdoor life. He looks marvelous, she thought, much thinner than before. His facial features were more refined and mature. His hair was sun-bleached, a color that magnified the difference between them. Many people did a double-take upon seeing them together. Choxie didn't worry about the difference, or how people stared. She knew Sam had never cared.

"You have asked me about the men in my life, Sam. Now it's your turn. Be fair. Tell me about your love life."

"Never been married and nothing in the works." He smiled, but sadly.

She thought he had answered too quickly, and that her question seemed to bother him. She also noticed an undercurrent of sadness surfacing when he fell silent. She could still read the expressions on his face, just like old times.

"Okay, I'll buy that for now," she said. "But there has been someone."

"Yes." A slight frown.

"You don't want to talk about it?"

Sam gazed at her reflectively. "Not really. Talking about it won't serve any purpose. Certainly not right now."

Choxie wanted to know everything and couldn't resist the temptation to press. "I think what happened must have been important, Sam. Your eyes say it still is."

Sam eventually said, "Maybe. I guess you really never fall out of love. I have always loved you, Choxie. Still do."

She smiled and said, "And I never stopped loving you. But?" She inclined forward, eyebrows raised, encouraging him to confess.

"I'll always have feelings for her, Choxie. She's gone. That's it. She's gone. Okay?" His eyes begged for relief.

"Okay, I won't ask again. Maybe sometime you can…never mind. But I want you to tell me about her sometime, if you want to. It's just that I want to know everything about you." He clearly did not want to continue with the topic, so she said, "Okay, I'll stop being nosy."

He sighed and relaxed. "Maybe someday. It's not a pretty story, Chox, and certainly nothing we need to talk about right now. Let's concentrate on now. I have missed you, Choxie. This is too good to be true. So, now what?"

"Now that I know you are free and healthy and pretty much the same as ever, I want you to stick around. Any objections?"

He laughed and pulled her close. "No. I like that. Do we pick up where we left off, or do we need to spar?"

"Your choice."

"Nothing has changed for me, Chox. I don't think I ever disconnected."

Choxie helped carry his belongings up three flights of stairs to her apartment. They leaned against the door gasping for air when the last of his luggage lay on her living room floor.

Choxie said, "Don't move," and disappeared into the bedroom and returned a moment later to place two keys in his hand. "The fat key is to my apartment, just in case you have any doubt about my purpose. You're free to come and go as you please. The other key is to my car."

That night, after hours of conversation and touching, they made love, and then again upon awakening. Neither would deny the other's hunger.

Choxie believed Sam had always contained himself and

responded to her needs during their previous affair. She wanted their love to be equal this time and consciously threw herself into the partnership.

She returned to work two days later, tired and happy. Her associates made good-natured sport of the circles beneath her eyes, and the silly smile she couldn't hide.

"God, you look terrible, Choxie. Didn't you get any sleep?"

"Jesus, Choxie, would you cork that silly smile."

"How is he doing, Choxie? Better than you, I hope."

The friendly banter gradually slackened and her working relationships returned to normal. Choxie didn't spend extra time at the studio after Sam's arrival, though, and Phil mercifully kept special assignments to a minimum. She couldn't get enough time with Sam. He drove her to work and picked her up each day. He went on special assignments and stayed by her side at the social functions she had to attend for the station. They were inseparable. Late dinners, dancing, off-Broadway shows, ball games, hiking, drives into the country and a whirlwind of other activities drained their strength. Choxie couldn't remember being so happy.

*****

"Miss Pratt! If you please, a moment of your time." Phil never called her Miss Pratt. He beckoned from his doorway as she scurried past on the way to meet Sam after work. She stepped into the office and he closed the door.

"Take a seat, Choxie. This will only take a moment. I want you to see something I consider very interesting." He flipped on a television monitor and they watched the early evening local news that she had just broadcast.

He switched the monitor off and spun his chair to face her. "Notice anything different?"

She frowned. "I'm not sure what you mean. I thought it went okay, Phil. Is there a problem?"

"Oh, the program was satisfactory, but you were not. Look, Choxie, I hate to be the bearer of bad news, but you are exhausted and the camera sees it. Your face is too thin and you have circles under your eyes. Truthfully? You look like hell." He leaned close. "Let me give you a piece of advice. You can't make up for lost time, Choxie. What is gone is gone and you can't make it up. You need to get a grip. I think you need to slow down."

She stood, anger flashing from her eyes. "Okay, I get the picture, Phil, and I'm not too terribly angry with you for meddling. I will even admit that you are probably correct, but you, sir, are in fact, meddling. I'll try to do better, okay?"

He waved her away, growling, "Get the hell out of here. You're hopeless."

*****

She sat quietly beside Sam as he navigated through going-home traffic. Several blocks and several minutes later, she declared, "He's right, you know."

"Who is right?"

"Phil. He called me in this evening to watch a re-run of the news. He thinks I look tired. He thinks I'm trying to make up for lost time, or something like that. Maybe we should stay home tonight, Sam."

He pulled her close and nuzzled her ear. "I hate to say anything, but it sure isn't the time we spend away from home that makes you look tired. Maybe we should do something else in bed occasionally–like sleep."

They both thought for a moment, then simultaneously declared, "Naah!" and broke into peals of laughter. The impatient horns of irritated motorists reminded them that the light had turned green.

They had lived together for two weeks by then. The attraction wasn't tapering off. Choxie felt more captivated by him each day. "Am I promiscuous, Sam?"

"Oh, yeah. You are a bona fide trollop. Why?"

"Everything about you excites me. I'm worried that you might conclude that my interest in making love is too much. Maybe extreme. What do you think?"

"I don't want to change anything."

They shared an emotional closeness that Choxie was sure she could never attain with another person. Sam appreciated her viewpoints, as she did his, and she knew he understood her as no other man ever had, or probably would. She couldn't think of a single objectionable aspect of his personal qualities, physical, mental or emotional. They lived together easily.

"You couldn't be more perfect if you were a god," she told him after making love. "I forgot it's possible to love someone so much it hurts."

"I know. I'm afraid of waking some morning to find this has been a dream. "

So much happiness, she thought. How can it be possible to love someone this much? Nothing in the world can compare to how important he is to me.

"I love you, Sam. I know other people use those words to express their feelings and I despise them for it. I want to be the only human on earth with permission to use those words. I want those words to be my original thoughts so you know how I feel. I wish there were better words, but there aren't. I love you more than anything. More than I thought possible."

They made love again that night and the next morning. Phil clucked and shook his head sadly as Choxie arrived for work looking worse than ever.

"Still honeymooning, I see."

"Hi, Phil. Isn't it a wonderful day?"

CHAPTER TWENTY-TWO

Choxie

The ensuing weeks fused into a fantasy world of happiness. "I was never happy without you, Sam." They hoarded time, protected time, budgeted and stretched time. Time was everything.

"Time with you is so important, Sam. I can't stand a moment without you."

Choxie's dream of a network position receded into the background.

"My goals have changed. I don't think about the network anymore. For the first time since I can remember, my job is no longer important. Nothing is important to me. Just you."

And then it happened. The terror of her insecurities rose from the sea of happiness and spoiled everything. A crack in the foundation of their relationship popped up one evening and Choxie's fairytale castle began crumbling. The opening fracture wasn't entirely unexpected; she had noticed it coming for days. She wasn't surprised or indignant when the final clues fell into place. The most obvious signal of the impending breakdown had become apparent shortly after he arrived. Choxie said nothing. The signs of the approaching doomsday seemed innocent enough at first–nothing major. The dam of contentment cracked open one afternoon when Sam failed to meet her one afternoon after work. Simple as that.

She waited for him in the lobby several minutes before calling, hoping he was at the apartment. As his phone rang, she prayed he would not still be there. He answered the third ring. She wasn't surprised. Disappointed, but not surprised. The insidious sensation of impending doom probably would not have affected her so much if he had a good reason. He didn't. She could have accepted anything else, sickness, a flat tire, an incoming call–anything but the truth.

"Oh, damn, Choxie. I forgot. I'm sorry. Time just got away. I'll be right there."

"Don't bother. I'll take a cab." She replaced office phone softly. Choxie Pratt, sophisticated television personality, captain of self-control, collapsed against the desk and a primal moan issued from the depths of her soul. A prolonged, agonizing, "Oh, God, noooooo, please, nooooo." until no breath remained.

A hundred thoughts fought for her attention during the long taxi ride home. She had already identified and acknowledged the signs–nothing more than a collection of little things. The evidence had been there all along, masquerading behind way too many unanswered questions.

Why hasn't he started work? Why isn't he going to school? How can he sit around doing nothing? Why is he sitting around doing nothing? Has he grown more distant or is that my imagination? Is he going to leave?

Sam apologized profusely. The oversight wasn't intentional. Choxie knew he would never deliberately hurt her and would have given anything if he had intentionally stood her up, for any reason. She could easily understand and forgive him for losing track off time, if he had a reason. He didn't.

"What would you like to eat tonight?" he asked.

"I'm not hungry. I'd rather drink."

He surveyed her suspiciously. Choxie never drank at home. "Whoa! I don't think my forgetfulness is cause to celebrate."

"That's not it, Sam. We need to talk and I expect to communicate more freely under the influence."

"Uh oh. That serious?"

"I think so. Make mine strong. I'll be back just as soon as I change."

She returned a few moments later wearing faded jeans and a West Point sweatshirt. Half an hour later, after two drinks and several transparently uncomfortable attempts at pleasant conversation, Choxie said, "Okay, let's do this."

"Thank heaven. It's about time. I don't think I can stand much more of this. So, what's bothering you?"

"Sam, I love you enough to do almost anything for you. I can give anything, be anything, do anything, but there is one thing I cannot and will not do for you. I cannot and I will not live with your ghost."

Sam grimaced as she dropped the bombshell. He sighed, then nodded and said, "I presume we are now going to talk about the woman in my past?"

"Yes. Our life together has been perfect until recently, Sam. Today's forgetfulness is really meaningless, unless you consider everything else–like the things that have not happened."

"Give me a for instance."

"What have you done to make me believe you are planning to stay, Sam? The truth is, you have done nothing. I think you are, consciously or unconsciously, mentally conditioning yourself to leave. I have begun to think that I am the only one in love here. You have changed, Sam. You are drifting away and I don't think you even know it. Are you preparing to leave, Sam?"

"No! Come on, Chox! Nothing has changed. I just lost track of time, that's all. It's no big deal."

"It's not about what happened today, Sam. You know there's more to it than that."

He recognized the preliminaries were over and he was in for a lengthy conversation. He settled back. Choxie looked sad–sad but determined. He surrendered with a sigh and said, "Go ahead, Choxie. Let it out."

She drained the glass again and placed it aside, then pulled her legs against her breasts, hugging her knees. She sat that way for several seconds, chin resting on her knees, eyes fixed on him.

"I love you to distraction, Sam. You know that, don't you?"

"Beyond a doubt."

"I want you in my life, always and forever, but not just part of you. I won't take just part of you."

"I take it you don't believe I'm all here?"

She shook her head sadly, eyes already wet, her lower lip and chin quivering. "No. I don't think you are. So, no. There is something...." She covered her face and groaned. "Oh, I hate myself for being so weak." She smoothed her face and resumed.

"I'm not going to cop out and start bawling. Okay, here it goes. Not something, someone still owns a big part of you–maybe all of you. I'm not sure. But I do know that you are not all here with me, Sam. You have and are drifting away. I can't deal with a ghost controlling you."

"My, God, Chox! I don't feel anything like that. I don't understand this."

"I am not imagining. I can see and feel, Sam. You are just treading water, waiting for something to happen. I wonder sometimes if you realize that you never finish anything important. Do you know that?"

"A for-instance would help, if you don't mind."

"All right. I know all about your life, Sam. Let's start with the prep academy. You got thrown out. I think you wanted out. I think you made sure that they would throw you out, and I think that was a form of quitting. You quit your mother. Not that I blame you. You turned in your basketball jersey. You quit the relationship with me–okay, more my fault than yours, but somehow we never got together again. You quit the Army. Can't say I blame you there, either, but it's part of a pattern. You ran away from the ranch, maybe for good reason, I don't know. And you apparently didn't finish...." Choxie threw up her hands. "Her. Metaphorically, you turn in your jersey every time something or someone threatens to tie you down. What have you ever finished, Sam? Nothing!" Anger broke through her control.

"Is that the way you see my life?"

"Yes! Yes, dammit! Can't you see it?"

"Not exactly." He leaned closer. "Where is this going, Choxie? What do you want me to do? What do you expect?"

"I want you to start by finishing something." She held out her glass and said, "But first, Play this again, Sam." She held out the empty.

After he returned with the drink and took a seat, Choxie said, "Now, in case you think that was all I have–here's the killer. I asked you to tell me about her once, Sam, and you put me off. Again, you didn't finish. Now I need to know. No, I have to know about her." She took a long drink, leaned back and closed her eyes. "Okay, sport, your ball. Go."

Sam stood, picked up his glass and exhaled expansively. "Well, now I need a drink." He went to the kitchen again and returned with the bottle and stood in the middle of the room downing the remaining contents in two swallows, then held up the empty and said, "Here goes something."

"What do you mean by that?"

"That means, I don't have a clue how to say what I'm going to tell you." He returned to the couch, leaned back, rested his legs on the coffee table and gazed at her for several moments. "I do think you're probably right, though, about the talk part. There have been some things on my mind lately."

"Some things? Things?"

"Okay, she has been on my mind. My feelings about you have not changed, not in the least, but...." He sighed. "Oh, Choxie, this is going to be so hard."

"If it's too painful, Sam, perhaps we should wait. I don't have to know." She sensed an ominous change in his behavior and wanted the discussion to end before he told her something she didn't want to know. Maybe, she thought, it would be best to leave well-enough alone. Maybe he will come back to me in time. This is not good.

His voice broke in. "Have you ever really loved anyone else, Chox?"

"No. I can say that honestly, now that you have returned to my life. I once thought I loved Von, but I know now that I didn't–not really. Only you."

Sam deliberated for several moments before answering. "Well, I can say without a doubt that I have loved someone else. Before I tell you about her, I want you to know that my love for you is not incomplete because of her. If anything, I can love you more because of her. I love you, Choxie, and need you in my life now more than ever, but...." He gestured helplessly.

"But you can't forget her, can you?"

He nodded. "No. and I never will. I don't think it's possible to love more than I love you, but you're right, I can't stop thinking about her. I cannot forget her."

"Don't you think time will–"

"No. It's been almost a year. She is as much on my mind now as the last time I saw her. No, time does not bring relief."

"What will help, Sam?"

"I don't know. Maybe nothing. Sometimes I think I must be destined to go through life worrying about her. I sometimes think–

"Okay! Okay! You don't have to tell me about her, Sam. I can see how much this conversation bothers you." She noticed moisture forming at the corner of his eyes.

"No, you deserve to know." He left and returned with another drink. "This will be the most difficult thing I have ever done– telling you about her, and I probably won't handle it well. Bear with me."

He swallowed the drink and began. "Her name is Cynthia Roush. We were schoolmates in high school. Graduated together. We didn't have a close relationship then. Hell, that's a laugh. We barely knew each other. You already know that after I separated from the Army I ran head-on into that gang of cattle thieves. What I didn't tell you makes all the difference. I didn't tell you that Cynthia was the county prosecuting attorney."

"Really?"

"Yes. We worked together to catch the rustlers and Wes's killers. One thing led to another and...." He shrugged. "We fell in love. I know that's extremely oversimplified, but no purpose is served by more detail. Cynthia came from a strict religious background...perhaps I should say fanatic, at least it would be to most of us. You need to understand that about her, Choxie. She had to make an almost impossible break from her moral principles and religious background to get to know me. She did, and ultimately brought total commitment to the relationship."

He paused and Choxie said, "Just for curiosity's sake, Is she pretty?"

"Yes. Exceptionally."

"Damn. This is going to be more difficult than I thought, Sam. I wanted to know, but now I'm not so sure."

Sam stared at the empty glass for several moments, apparently deciding if he needed another. "No, let me finish."

His eyes sought permission, but she countered, "What more could there possibly be? She exists. You know she does and you still love her, don't you? What else can there be?"

Sam shook his head slowly and said, "Oh, there is more, Choxie. There is, unfortunately, much more."

Choxie chilled as she glimpsed the cloud of grief in his eyes.

"I'm so sorry I asked. Really, I know enough. All I want now is to stop. I know something terrible happened and I don't want to hear about it. Please, no more."

"I asked her to marry me," he said, eyes closed.

Her head flopped back on the chair back and she exhaled. "Well, I sure didn't need to hear that. So?" Choxie knew Sam needed to finish. "So, did she turn you down? Is that what happened? Finish it, dammit! I'm not enjoying this."

He spoke softly, "No, she accepted. Her mother stopped the wedding."

Choxie's face wrinkled into disbelief. "What! Do you mean to tell me two competent adults couldn't get married because her mother said no? Come on, Sam!"

He waved her off. "What neither one of us knew, and why her mother objected, is because she is my sister."

Choxie covered her mouth and stared. "Oh, my God."

Sam held his hands palms up. "We didn't know. It's a long story, but her mother revealed the truth the day Cynthia told her about our plans to marry." He leaned his head back on the couch and stared at the ceiling. "Can you believe that? My sister!" Tears began seeping. "We had no idea. Wes was my father and her father."

"Oh, no," Choxie whispered, then rushed to him, rocking, stroking and soothing as he wept. "I'm so sorry, Sam. It must have been terrible."

He wiped his eyes, sat up and sighed heavily, and then said, "Yeah, it was bad, but that's not the worst part. She disappeared and I can't find her. I looked for weeks. Her mother won't talk to me. The police won't talk to me. No one knows anything. She is gone and I can't stop worrying. It's killing me. That's what you see, Choxie. I have not lost interest in you."

"So you just took off and haven't stopped running."

"Yeah, something like that. I suppose it's like you said, I didn't finish. I quit again. That's what I do, like you said."

Choxie cleared her throat and announced, "Well, you have to find her, Sam."

"Yeah? What if I did find her? Then what?"

"What happened is not so terrible, Sam. You aren't guilty of anything dreadful. You were innocent. Don't you know that?"

"Even so, it sure changed everything. We were both so sure." He stared vacantly.

"There has to be a mistake. Maybe that's it? It's all a terrible mistake. There must be a way to...."

He shook his head. "Don't you think I have thought of everything? She left before I got a chance to discuss anything. Something must be terribly wrong, Chox. I know it. I feel it and I'm worried sick. She was so distraught that night. Well, you can imagine, with her background."

Choxie stood at the window looking out at the glittering skyline. She heard Sam go to the kitchen and mix more drinks before returning to his chair.

She got up, took the drinks to the kitchen and dumped them. Upon return, she said, "I know how painful it must have been for you to share that with me, and I thank you, but I cannot tell you how sorry I am that I asked. It was none of my business."

They sat silently for several minutes before Sam spoke. "Choxie, would you marry me if I asked?"

The question stunned her. "That's not fair, Sam. That's like hedging your bet. Anyway, why would you ask such a question now?"

"Because it's important."

"Then the answer is no. Not now."

"Why?"

"Because now I know there is a ghost. Because now I know the problem isn't going to disappear. Because–"

Sam interrupted, "Wait just a minute! If the ghost weren't there, then would you marry me?"

"Is this all hypothetical, or are you really asking?"

"Just answer the damned question and quit fencing."

She whirled to face him. "You're the one fencing. Without the ghost, yes, damn you! Yes!"

"Well then, I guess that makes it your business. Now, what do you want me to do?"

She fell back into the chair. "Christ, Sam. I feel as if my entire life is in the balance. Can I think about this?"

"I expect we both better sleep on it. I seriously doubt if either of us can think clearly right now. Probably won't sleep, either."

The next evening, after Sam picked her up from work, Choxie

pretended cheerfulness.

"Did you have a good day or something?" he asked, puzzled by her good humor. "I have been on needles and pins all day, Chox. I had a lousy day. What makes you so damned happy?"

"I'm going to put my life back in order, Sam Prescott." She looked confident, and if not quite content, almost.

Sam pulled out of traffic and parked so he could watch her face as he talked.

"Okay, suppose you take some time, right now, and tell me what's going on."

She smiled lovingly and smoothed the tired circles under his eyes. "Sam, I love you and I would marry you in an instant if you were free. I think we could be very happy together–if you were free. But you are not free. You may not know that, but I do. You belong to a memory. I will always love you, Sam, but I'm not going to marry you. Not under these circumstances. I won't share you–not even with a memory."

Sam started to speak but she restrained him with a wave.

"I took the job with the network today, Sam. I'm leaving tomorrow for a six-week orientation tour of network facilities, and then on to special reporting worldwide. I know you didn't really ask me to marry you last night. You only asked if I would, if. So, if the circumstances are ever different, the answer will always be yes." She smiled at him adoringly. "You get your life straightened out, Sam Prescott. When you do, if you still want me, I'll be there."

"Just like that?" he said.

"Bingo. Just like that. There can be nothing gained by avoiding the truth. We will never have a complete life together unless you're a whole person. I want you, Sam. All of you. Find yourself or leave me alone."

"What do you expect me to do?" He seemed puzzled by the sudden change.

"I don't know what you're going to do, but I am going to work. My problem is simple compared to yours. I'm going to do the only thing I can to help you. I'm going to let you go. Go, Sam. Find her. Find yourself."

"She's my sister, for Christ's sake! What can I do?"

"Do what you have to do! I wasn't there, remember. I don't

know what to tell you, except you have to do something. Now let's go home. We both have to pack."

The ultimatum stunned him. "You're putting me out?"

Choxie yearned to comfort him. He was the last person in the world she wanted to hurt. "You got it, Jack. I'm leaving. The lease is up next week and I'm not going to renew. There is no point in wasting our lives living a lie. Life is too short and I love you too much. You have to find her and sort your life out. If you can't, then don't come back. If you do come back, I'm for sure going to take you. In the meantime, I have a plane to catch."

"How long will you wait?"

"Oh, probably forever. I don't think I will ever even want to love anyone else."

Sam closed his eyes, shutting out the world, coming to grip with her ultimatum. He nodded and said, "Okay. I got it." He started packing the minute they walked into her apartment. Choxie slipped out before he finished and watched him leave from a store across the street.

Good-bye, Sam Prescott.

*****

He drove across town to the southern suburbs of Nashville and took a motel room. He would see Angeline Pierpont the next day, and then head back to Wickmore.

Sam really never expected to learn anything specific from Angeline, or even what he would say to her. He would get a night's sleep, then pop in on Mrs. Wilson Pierpont and let the pieces fall where they may.

He drove straight to the Pierpont address in the exclusive Berry Hill community near the governor's mansion the next morning. PRIVATE ROAD the sign read. He stopped between the enormous brick columns on either side of the grand threshold to the Pierpont manor, massive ornate pillars defending a concrete drive leading down the hill to the estate. From the distance, the house looked old to Sam. *Old and stately and enormous.* The light-gray granite had weathered with age until it matched the dismal, rainy sky hanging over the affluent section of the city. The Pierpont mansion was only one of many proud estates in the neighborhood.

Sam parked, pulled on a light jacket and ran up the steps to a sheltered spot in front of a massive door. Everything about the house and grounds reeked of money and status. The ornate cast-iron door knocker beckoned, but Sam chose the anachronistic electric button to announce his presence. He was nervous.

The door creaked open slowly. A formally attired butler stepped into the opening. After spotting Sam's truck, and with ill-concealed displeasure, he said, "All deliveries are made to the rear."

"I'm not making a delivery."

"Really? I'm not aware that we called for you."

"I am here to see Mrs. Pierpont."

The butler's nose lifted perceptibly, as did one of his eyebrows, "Indeed? Do you have an appointment?"

"No. Please. just tell her Sam Prescott is here." Sam took pleasure watching the butler's haughty expression change to uncertainty.

The courtly man cleared his throat. "I'm afraid that will not be possible, Mister Prescott. Mrs. Pierpont is not receiving callers today."

The butler's imperious demeanor irritated Sam beyond patience. "Look–whatever your name is."

"Hughes, sir."

"Hughes. Thank you. Just tell Mrs. Pierpont that I'm here, will you? Whether she sees me is not your decision to make. This is a family matter."

The butler half-bowed and stepped aside, making a grandiose sweeping gesture through the door. "Won't you please step in, Mister Prescott." He didn't lift his head until Sam passed.

The butler left him alone in the foyer. Several minutes later, Sam heard a side door open and Hughes reappeared. "Follow me, Sir, if you please." His previous condescending manners were conspicuously missing. Hughes appeared to be somewhat chastened.

They entered a small, dimly lit sitting room at the end of a long hall. Hughes motioned toward a straight-backed chair sitting in the light of the room's only window. "Please wait here, Sir," he said and departed through yet another door.

Sam had entered the room by one door, the butler left by another. A third door opened noiselessly and an incredibly beautiful woman stepped in. Sam automatically stood in deference to her presence. She smiled pleasantly, pale blue eyes sparkling in the sunlight, and Sam forgot to breathe.

"Won't you sit down, please," she said, her voice musically soft and clear.

Everything about her struck Sam as beautiful. She wore a long, flowing silk dress with a high collar, very little jewelry and little or no make-up. Her hair was the most captivating color of silver he had ever seen. She was probably in her fifties, but her hair was pure silver.

"Hughes tells me you came to see me," she said, sitting gracefully in the chair opposite Sam, smiling pleasantly.

He stammered, "That's correct. Did Hughes happen to mention who I am?"

A puzzled expression crossed her face, then quickly receded. "He did, Mister Prescott. You favor Wes perfectly, but I suspect you must know that. Is this about Wes?"

"Yes, Ma'am. If you don't mind."

She smiled warmly. "Not at all. Please, tell me about Wes. It has been such a long time."

She doesn't know. Why would she?

"I'm sorry to say, he was murdered. I didn't come to tell you that, though."

She covered her breast. "Oh, my heavens! What happened?"

He told her, which only made things worse. She took it much harder than he imagined she would. "I'm sorry," Sam said after giving her time to choke back what appeared to be sincere grief. "I'm truly sorry, but I really did not come here to tell you that."

She dabbed her eyes and said, "Then perhaps you will be kind enough to say why you *are* here." She smiled to excuse the brusque question.

"I'm here to find out what I can about the Prescott family. It's really for extremely personal reasons. I'm afraid your private life may be exposed, but I need to ask some questions."

"I see. Then perhaps you wouldn't mind sharing your reasons for asking."

Sam briefly told the story, ending with his relationship with Cynthia.

"You poor man. How tragic. What can I say or do to help?"

"What do you know about my mother? Elena."

"Not very much, really. I never met her. She was gone before I arrived."

"Do you know anything.... I'm sorry. Would you mind sharing anything Wes told you about her?"

"Of course not. He loved her, I know that. He really never talked much about her, other than to lament her lifestyle. I am aware that he hired a private detective to find her, then had the same detective keep track of her."

That's all?"

"Forgive me, but there was no one to talk to about Elena but Wes. His parents died in a terrible car wreck, along with the boy. Too bad."

They talked for almost an hour. Angeline didn't trash Wes but admitted she had been unable to tolerate Wickmore, that and Wes had some peculiar ideas about fidelity. "If there is no more, Sam, I really must attend to some pressing matters." She stood and offered her hand, then turned and spoke softly toward the door, "Hughes."

The side door opened immediately. The butler stepped in and bowed.

"Hughes, would please show the gentleman out." Angeline Pierpont glided through the door and out of sight.

Sam thought, *Hard to believe a woman like that ever saw anything in Wes.*

The sensation of yet another door slammed shut on his past.

CHAPTER TWENTY-THREE

Cynthia

The solitary cross-country drive provided plenty of time to think. The pain of Choxie's proviso receded along with distance from Nashville. Her precise dissection of his unwillingness or inability to commit served as a ringing indictment of his entire life. By the time he crossed the Mississippi River, Sam was determined to bring order to his life, beginning with Cynthia. He concentrated on what he had to do while speeding across southern Missouri.

I need to take care of things at home. Home? Really? Home?

Possible courses of action had formed long before he clattered across the old bridge, its rickety rods and planks still popping and screeching a grudging reception. Curious emotions surfaced at the bridge–emotions that puzzled him initially, before he conceded a victory for familiarity. He thought, as the truck bounced off the bridge, The fact is, Wickmore is the only real home I ever had. That's crazy. Crazy is yet another "C" word.

I let everyone down and never finish, just like Choxie said. I never finish anything. This time I will. Didn't finish with Cynthia. Ah, Cynthia, a C word. Choxie, a C word. My life is full of C words. Commitment is a C word, almost a curse word. Curse is.....

He began the quest for satisfaction in earnest the next morning, giving the young couple engaged as caretakers of the ranch house double pay and releasing them. He then called the Kinglsey Detective agency in Boston and asked him to locate Elena's friend Pam. He learned that Pam, by now a social worker, was married and happy and ready to talk about Elena. She opened by saying,

"How strung out will you be if I tell you some really personal things about your mother?"

"Not at all. That's what I need to know."

"Okay. First things first, then. Did she ever tell you who your father is?"

"No. She never talked about that."

"Brace yourself, then. She got pregnant by her brother. Wes."

The sound of blood rushing through Sam's ears was deafening. "Excuse me? Say that again. I need to know that for sure."

"I'm absolutely serious. That's exactly what Elena told me. Said her parents told all the kids that they were adopted one day when Wes was home after baseball season. She told me she had always loved Wes, that they had a thing, you know, even as kids. Wes protected her from their father. I guess the old man really disliked her for being so independent and rebellious–drugs and stuff. She always had trouble with drugs, right to the end. She definitely was in love with him, though–Wes, that is. She and Wes were thrilled when they found out they weren't blood kin. That's when they started…well, you know. That's about all I know. Hope that doesn't mess you up too much. She never talked about another man like she did Wes."

He thanked Pam and hung up, then sat perfectly still reviewing his life.

Things fit together. Things make sense. That's why Mom ran off. It all starts to makes sense.

After the initial shock, Sam's thoughts raced back through his life. *That's why I look so much like Wes. And that's why he started calling me Son.* He also remembered, as a small boy, asking his mother, "Why is your last name Dowling and mine is Prescott?" She had smiled proudly and said, "Because you are a Prescott. It's a better name to have."

He found the adoption papers of the Prescott's three children, and his grandfather's will leaving the entire ranch to Wes. Nothing to Elena. It took a week to finish researching his family's records again. Everything:, medical and dental records, courthouse records, attorney records, police records. Once finished, he drove to Wickmore after dark and parked down the street from Irma's store. He waited in the truck until her last customer departed before stepping into the store. Sam glanced around to make sure she was alone, and then locked the door. He ignored her angry protests and turned the business hours sign to "CLOSED."

She sat behind the counter glaring. "What are you doing here? You got no right to–"

"Enough!" He blocked her into the space behind the counter. "You know what I'm here for, Irma."

She wiped her hands on the same soiled apron she always wore and slammed the cash register drawer closed. She locked it and placed the key in her apron pocket, irritably brushing an unruly string of hair away from her forehead. They surveyed each other like animals thrown together in a cage.

"Well, I wondered when you would come nosing around again," she said. "You got some nerve coming back here. That's all I got to say."

Sam said, "We are going to talk, like it or not."

Her facial muscles knotted, nostrils flaring, eyes barely open, poised to attack.

"I don't want to fight you, Irma."

"Don't you now? Well, what made you think anything is changed around here?" Her eyes were cold, hostile. Her folded arms served as a barrier.

Sam figured anything he might say would only add fuel to her anger and decided to wait; hoping she would soften; hoping she would take the lead.

Irma took the apron off and marched directly to the front door, hesitated, hand on the reversible plastic sign. Sam thought she was going to flip it back to "OPEN." She left it "CLOSED" and leaned, he forehead against the door, sobbing quietly. When she regained control and faced him, Irma looked beaten, her eyes pleading. She looked sad and old, her shoulders slumped, arms dangling. Irma's face was drawn and hollow. Tears welled at the corner of her eyes. She looked defeated.

"Come on upstairs," she said softly. "I expect we ought to have that talk."

Sam followed her to the meager apartment and sat across, waiting for Irma to open the conversation. The change in her attitude puzzled him. He didn't know what to expect. His plan to raise hell if necessary, to threaten, rage, anything to find Cynthia, seemed premature.

"Would you take something to drink?" she asked, almost like an old friend, almost pleasant.

"No thanks." Sam was confused and suspicious of her surprising metamorphosis.

"Well then, I'll be back in a minute and we can get on with it. There ain't no sense putting off what's got to be said. I need to wash up."

Sam had expected determined resistance. After she left the room, he used the opportunity to look over the apartment for evidence of Cynthia. He saw her high school graduation picture and instinctively picked it up, heart pounding, tears threatening. Irma returned, but detoured into the kitchen.

"I'm going to find her, Irma! You can call the sheriff if you feel like you have to, but I'm not going anywhere until you tell me how to find her. You can have me thrown in jail. I'll just come back. I'm not leaving until I find her."

Irma stepped back into the little living room and straightened some crocheted doilies on the arms of a stuffed chair and placed a stray magazine aside, delaying the inevitable.

"I have to find her, Irma," he declared again, his eyes following as she walked from one piece of furniture to another, idly touching and straightening.

She finally collapsed into her rocking chair and sighed. "So much has happened," she said. "So much to say." Her mouth began to quiver.

Sam thought he had seen signals that forecast a breakdown in the store below. Irma now covered her face and wept pitifully, so forlorn and beaten that he almost wanted to comfort her.

"I'm sorry," she said, wiping her eyes on the back of her wrists. "Give me a moment." She took a deep breath and blinked to clear the tears. "I'm a poor Christian and the Lord has punished me for my sins. It was all my fault. All my fault. Everything." She shook her head and stared, lost in thought, rocking.

Sam didn't want to hear apologies or confessions. "I came to find Cynthia, Mrs. Roush. That's all I care about."

She stopped rocking and said, "I know this will be hard to believe, but I prayed you would come. I knew you were coming." She rocked again, smiling contentedly. "Cynthia needs someone. She's in bad trouble and so am I...I.... We. We don't have anyone.

No folks. Edwin is gone. My people are gone. You're the only person who can help us. I prayed you would come back." She faced Sam for the first time, smiling amiably. "And you're here. My prayers are answered."

He felt a rush of excitement and his heart beat accelerated. *Finally.*

"What about Cynthia, Irma? What trouble?"

"I can't go to her anymore. I'm not physically or mentally fit. But I'll fix it so you can see her. You will be the only one they allow in."

Sam felt sick to his stomach. *I knew it. Something is terribly wrong.*

Irma's chin came up and she smoothed the deep creases in her face. She looked resigned and sad, the muscles around her mouth and chin still trembling, hands kneading the apron in her lap, but she smiled.

Sam couldn't help feeling sorry for her. "What trouble, Irma? Where is she? Tell me! Right now. Tell me!"

Irma closed her eyes and nodded. "She's at a mental rehabilitation center in Springfield. Has been since you last saw her."

His heart sank. "Why? What happened?" Sam's voice broke. He could barely control his voice.

"She had some sort of a mental or emotional breakdown the night you last saw her. Hasn't talked to anyone since."

Sam couldn't stay seated. While pacing he said, "I need to know everything, Irma."

Irma folded her hands, rested her head on the chair back, and then reached for her knitting–a partially finished afghan lap blanket. She started knitting. "I suppose I should start at the beginning. Okay. Well, she didn't make it back here that night–the night she told me you two were going to be married." The clicking sounds of the knitting needles lapsed and Irma appeared to lose her train of thought, staring straight ahead. "Did she tell you what I said about you two being...you know...being related?"

"She did. Then she drove off and I couldn't find her."

Irma sighed and the needles started clicking again.

Sam took a seat, hoping to reduce the pressure. "How is she, Irma?"

"I'll get to that!" She spoke sharply, and then collected herself and smiled. "Her mind must have snapped. Anyway, I got a phone call in the middle of the night from Claude Belcher down at the sawmill. He told me her car was sitting in the middle of his yard. Figured she must have missed the turn or something. Said she wasn't hurt. Just sitting there. Staring. He thought she might be drunk. Anyway, I brought her home. She wouldn't talk to me, just sat there, right where you are now." She nodded toward Sam. "Just staring. That's all she has done since. Sits and stares."

Irma began sniffling and the conversation lapsed. Sam was desperate for information, impatient for Irma to regain control of her emotions and finish.

She blew her nose and picked up the knitting. "Well, I took her to the emergency room at Cox hospital in Springfield the next morning. They transferred her to a stroke clinic, and then to rehab."

"How is she, Irma?" *Come on, come on!*

"I'll get to it!" she snapped, then winced at her outburst and forced a smile. "I didn't have enough money to afford a good private doctor, so she's been there all this time. They haven't helped her that I can see. She just sits and rocks. Never says a word. The doctors tell me she might have had some kind of stroke. Can't remember the exact name for it. Caused something like amnesia, though. They thought she would eventually come around on her own. Now they're doing a lot of talking about chemicals and other therapy–stuff I don't understand. I don't understand much about her condition."

Irma stopped and closed her eyes. Sam got up to leave. He wanted to run, to scream, anything to get away from the truth.

Irma's eyes opened as he headed toward the stairs. She looked terrified. "No! I'm not finished!" She relaxed only after Sam returned to his chair. "I try to get up there to see her. She won't talk to me either. I don't think the poor thing knows who I am. They don't know why she won't respond. I don't think she even knows where she is. Just rocks and stares out the window. Never seen anything like it."

Irma shook her head sadly, ignoring the flow of tears, but stopped rocking and gazed at Sam intently. "You say she did mention that the two of you are related?"

Sam shouted, "Of course she did! What do you think this is all about?"

Irma recoiled slightly from his outburst. "Well, she needs someone now. I can't do it anymore." She wept softly, fumbling with the knitting. "Truth is, I got cancer and it's spread all over me." She pointed to her head. "Worst is up here. Doctors say I'm dying. Tell me the cancer is not treatable. Too far gone. Going to shut my mind and organs off sometime soon, just like an electric light. He gives me three months at the most. Most likely less. I'm closing the store. Get dizzy and pass out all the time. Never know where I'm going to find myself when I wake up. It's the Lord's punishment. I have to accept it."

She placed the knitting aside and turned her full attention to Sam. "But he answered me when I prayed you would come back. Cynthia needs someone to see after her. I can't do it anymore, but there's another reason I prayed."

Irma pulled the lamp table drawer open and retrieved an envelope. "Here. You'll need these legal papers making you guardian. Her birth certificate's there, and other stuff." She leaned forward and handed the envelope to Sam. "Read it now. We still have more talk. Read it."

Sam scanned the certificate. His face lost all color even before he finished reading. Never in his life had anything confounded him so much. His head and eyes lifted slowly. "Is this right? Cynthia told me you said Wes was her father. Is this right?" He tapped the document.

She pointed at the paper. "That there is the truth. Don't doubt what I say for a second. I know what I told her was the wrong thing to do, and the Lord is punishing me for it. Yes, Edwin Roush is her natural father." She noticed Sam's look of disbelief. "See, Wes was off playing baseball when I got pregnant, so he can't be the father. You can check it out. No way was he her father. They got tests now. You can check it out."

"I would have checked a long time ago if you told me where she was! Why, Irma? You told Cynthia–

"I know what I told her! Do you think I have thought of anything else since that day! I know what I said! I know what I did!" Her face was contorted in distress.

"Why, Irma? Why?" Sam suffered the most incredible sense of

301

disbelief. "For God's sake, why?" he whispered.

Irma stared straight ahead and the ever-present frown deepened. "Why? Because he always hurt me and I wanted to hurt him back. I never loved anyone else."

Sam was confused. "Who are you talking about?"

"Wes Prescott!" she screamed, tears washing down her face in an instant. "That's right. He took advantage of my feelings and I sinned for him."

"I thought you said Edwin was her father."

"I know what I said, and I meant it, but now I'm talking about Wes Prescott. He kept after me. I never could turn him down. I never loved another man. Then he up and married that uppity society girl. I never stopped believing he would come back to me, though. And he did after the divorce, just not to marry me. I was such a fool. Always gave in. Always thought we would...."

Sam didn't care. "If Wes was not her father, then why did you lie to Cynthia?"

Her face distorted with anger. "Because you're just an extension of him, that's why! You even look like him! You *are* him! God forgive me, but I wanted to hurt you just like you were Wes. I wanted to get even for all the times he made me sin." She held up a warning finger. "Don't you be too quick to judge. You don't know everything."

"Those are not good enough reasons for all the pain you caused."

"I got pain, too! No one will ever know how he used me. I never loved anyone else." She looked away, chewing her lower lip. "But I never wanted to hurt Cynthia. That wasn't what I wanted."

"You did all that to get even with Wes? For Christ's sake, Irma, he was dead!"

"Oh, you don't know how he led me on. Wes Prescott was the Devil on Earth." She lowered her head, sighed deeply, then said, "But I loved him so much. He just played with me. Wicked man. Corrupted me." She glared at Sam and said, "I put up with it for years, but the tumor has changed me. Made me mean. I never lied to anyone in my life before the tumor." Her eyebrows lifted and she said glibly, "I know I sinned, but God forgives. You're here."

The rocking chair, the grandfather clock, and the clicking needles slipped back into a synchronized rhythm. The conversation ended after she said, "The key to my bank box is in that envelope. I will have your name put on the list of people who can open it. Your engagement ring is there."

Sam stood shakily. "I will take care of her, Irma." She nodded and Sam thought he detected a trace of a smile. She didn't look up again from her knitting. He heard her humming a religious tune as he staggered down the stairs.

* * * * *

Sam crossed the bridge again early the next morning on the way to Springfield, arriving at the hospital well ahead of visiting hours. He had to wait for the physician with overall responsibility for Cynthia's case.

"Mister Prescott?" The doctor, baldest man Sam had ever seen, entered the waiting room and offered his hand. "I'm Fred Harald." He wore the traditional white medical smock over a gaudy orange turtle neck sweater. A pair of red basketball sneakers protruded from beneath what appeared to be military camouflage trousers. "I hear you're here about our Miss Roush. I'm the ward doctor. I expect you already know her mother called us last night. She has also called lawyers to make arrangements for your status as Cynthia's legal representative. I'm glad Cynthia has someone."

"How is she?"

"Oh, physically healthy enough. Mentally and emotionally, somewhat limited, I'm sorry to say."

Sam was afraid to ask what somewhat limited meant. "What happened to her, Doctor?"

Harald gestured helplessly. "We really don't know for sure. All indications point to a stroke and then amnesia. There has been no indication of organic problems, though. No signs of chemical imbalance. We believe it might, not sure here either, be early Alzheimer's disease. No way to know for sure right now. She lives behind a shield we have been unable to penetrate. There are some pretentious medical terms to describe her condition, but let's just call it what it is, amnesia."

"Will she recover?"

Doctor Harald smiled grimly. "I suppose it is only natural for those close to her to assume she might recover. I wish it were reasonable to share such hope. Honesty usually serves best in cases like this, and the honest truth is that we have observed few signs to warrant such hope."

"But people do recover from stroke, right?" Sam desperately wanted to fend off the sensation of losing the war before the first battle.

"Indeed, some do, and Cynthia eventually might. Might being the operative word. I must advise you that prospects for her recovery decrease as amnesia lingers, and we are already dealing with a lengthy absence."

"Can I see her?"

The doctor scratched his neck and looked down. "Perhaps. Since you have been absent for an extended period, I'm going to recommend a short visit. You should meet with the medical team on her floor first, though. I will go with their decision. Follow me, please."

* * * * *

"I'm Doctor McFall," a fresh-faced overweight female intern announced. "Cynthia is presently my team's responsibility." She introduced Sam to the three other members of the team. Sam received a brief review of Cynthia's medical history from everyone assigned to her case. They asked many personal and intimate, questions about his relationship with her, and then left him alone. Sometime later, Doctor McFall returned and announced, "I'm happy to inform you, with positive recommendations from everyone," her motion included the white-clad members of the team, "that we believe you should be permitted a short visitation. Cynthia will be right out."

Sam felt giddy and said as much.

Doctor McFall cautioned, "I am fairly certain she won't recognize you. She doesn't react to her own mother. It's best if you do not expect too much. I believe, in cases like this, expectations may lead to disappointment."

Doctor McFall chattered on as she guided him to the waiting room. "Cynthia is one of the most difficult cases I have witnessed. Almost no response to therapy. She lives in a secret place, safe from the reality of her past."

"Doctor Harald told me she never speaks."

"Ahh, the good Doctor." She smiled blandly. "I'm afraid he may be too busy to read every report. Cynthia does talk on occasion, only to herself, and then only when she's alone. We tape her conversations but she does not respond later to the information we tape. Now, that said, she has demonstrated no evidence of recognition, other than the person she talks to in her fantasy world." Doctor McFall studied Sam's face for evidence of understanding.

Sam frowned, and then his expression lifted. "Fantasy world? Who is she talking to? Anyone in particular?"

The entire team of doctors and nurses froze; all eyes locked on Sam. Doctor McFall finally said, "Yes, her someone is you, Mister Prescott. She smiles and murmurs your name." She placed an arm around Sam's shoulders. "So you see, Sam, you are a welcome sight. We didn't know if you were real or imagined."

"I hope I'm not too late."

Doctor McFall sobered. "We're grasping at straws. Our treatment inventory has been depleted. You may be our last practical chance. I wonder if you would mind if we observe through the one-way window?" McFall directed Sam's attention to a simulated medicine cabinet on the wall of the waiting room.

"We?" Sam replied, glancing at the crowd of medics.

"We are not voyeurs, Mister Prescott, just concerned. We are naturally interested in the patient's response to a stimulus we consider hopeful. We hope you will understand."

Sam consented and the team left him alone in the small room. He could hear the clock ticking and the blood rushing through his temples. He paced the length of the room several times, too nervous to remain seated. The doctor's warnings left him with a sickening premonition.

The door opened and Sam murmured to himself, "Please. Please. Please." He took deep breaths, like preparing to lift a heavy weight, forcing himself to watch the white-clad orderly backing into the room pulling a wheelchair through backward. The door closed of its own accord after the conveyance bumped through. The orderly turned the chair toward Sam, smiled antiseptically and politely stepped back.

Time stopped.

The room seemed to brighten.

Background noises subsided.

The ticking of the wall clock faded.

Sam could hear nothing but his heartbeat.

The orderly motioned him forward and left the room.

My God. She's so pale.

Her hair was straight and oily. She stared blankly to one side, mouth open, eyes dull and listless. His breathing slowed as the evidence of her condition settled into a crushing weight on his hopes. She began a rhythmic rocking. Saliva drooled, stretched, hung for a moment before separating to blend with the wet spot spreading on her dress.

Sam took a deep, faltering breath and knelt before her. Her eyes were dull, listless and unfocused. She appeared to be looking at something light years away, away from him.

"Cynthia?" he whispered. "Cynthia, it's me. It's Sam."

Nothing. No sign of recognition. Sam seized her shoulders to arrest the incessant rocking.

"Cynthia!" He panicked. "Cynthia! It's me!"

Nothing. The team watching exchanged nervous glances.

Tears clouded his vision, and then spilled, trickling down over the corners of his mouth before he brushed them away. He touched her cheek softly, nudging the hair away from her face. She didn't blink, even as his hand passed over her eyes. He kissed her tenderly on each cheek.

"Cynthia," he begged. "Please look at me. It's Sam. I'm back."

She began rocking again. Sam couldn't bear to watch and slumped to his knees, resting his head on her lap, surrendering to the terrible reality of defeat.

* * * * *

"Oh, damn, this isn't at all what I hoped for," Doctor McFall whispered behind the mirror.

Jill White, the ward head nurse, said, "She doesn't even know he's there. So sad."

"Alert the orderly, Jill. This isn't doing either of them any good." The doctor sighed and stepped back from the mirror to scribble her observations in Cynthia's medical record.

A moment later the nurse exclaimed, "Doctor McFall!" She motioned to the mirror.

"What is it, Jill?"

"Look! Look at her eyes!"

McFall looked through the one-way mirror. "Well, well. We may have something here. She appears to be focusing."

Cynthia's head had moved, almost imperceptibly at first, but the nurse noticed. Cynthia looked around the room, as if seeing it for the first time, and then stared down at Sam. Her hands moved, poised over his head. She appeared to be confused by the object in her lap.

"Do you think she knows who he is, Doctor?"

"Shhh. Let's watch, Jill. This could be something. Just watch."

Cynthia's hands moved, tentatively closer, framing his head, almost touching, and then pulling back, and then closer, and then contact.

"Look, Doctor! She's comforting him. Look at her face! Oh, my God! My God! Oh, my God!" The nurse burst into tears.

"Get a grip, Jill. This room is not completely soundproof you know." She patted her shoulder and smiled. "Just watch."

"Oh, I hope, I hope. She has been waiting for such a long time."

They watched Cynthia stroke Sam's hair, the entire staff weeping silently as the blank stare into forever vanished and Cynthia made cooing sounds. Sam suddenly sat up, gazing at her with the most incredible look of astonishment.

Cynthia blinked several times. A smile formed at the corners of her mouth. She reached for him.

Everyone held their breath. Their hopes collapsed as Cynthia frowned and pushed him away and started rocking, eyes blank again. No expression.

An orderly watching said, "Well, crap!"

"What?"

"She really has no idea who he is. I have seen her do that to the cats."

The clinic allowed three cats free access to the wards. Most of the patients liked them. Cynthia always pushed them away.

The orderly came in, propped the door open, motioned for Sam to leave and turned the wheelchair away.

Cynthia's head turned to follow Sam as he departed. She smiled and waved weakly just before the door closed behind him.

The stunned team heard her speak to the orderly. "That was Sam. Did you see him? Sam came to see me. I hoped he would. I look awful. I need to wash my hair."

CHAPTER TWENTY-FOUR

The 'C' Word

Cynthia improved steadily and left the rehab center with Sam for an experimental field day two months after his return. He drove directly to the ranch with instructions not to excite her in any way, but rushed back to the center three hours later. She had become confused and distraught. Cynthia continued to improve and the facility moved her into a private apartment on the upper floor. She speaks and thinks clearly. Sam visits regularly and they have become a good friend. The doctors are delighted and encouraged by her progress, believing she will soon be independent. Sam is devoted, though the team told him she may not come return to the intensity of their previous relationship.

Sam called Choxie with the news shortly after finding Cynthia. He didn't tell her everything, leaving out the fact Cynthia didn't always know him in the beginning.

"I'm happy for you," she said. "Now what?"

"I'm not going to leave her, Chox."

"As in, ever?"

"Ever."

She sighed. "Well, I am happy for you, Sam Prescott, I guess. Let's stay in touch."

"Can't do it, Chox. I'm committed."

"Can't is a really strong word, Sam."

"I know. So is committed. Goodbye, Choxie."

She put the phone down slowly. *Well, good for him.*

* * * * *

Sam paid a nurse to stay with Irma until she died. He took care of her funeral and burial expenses.

He hires only local men to help with the ranch, people he knows who need work, not men from outlying communities. He bought a herd of cattle and has become a working cattleman.

It took time to locate and apologize to every member of his old Wickmore basketball team. One after another the men said nearly the same thing: "Oh, that business is all done. Anyhow, I expect we deserved it. I probably would have done the same thing in your shoes. Hell, just forget it." Each man offered his hand.

Sam has detractors, people who will probably never forgive him for being a Prescott. The people he cares about sympathize with his reason for quitting the team and value the support he gives the school, and how much effort he devotes attempting to be a good neighbor. The board of education asked him to run for a vacated position. He refused, thinking his name would create problems.

Sam occasionally stops to play cards with the good ol' boys down at the general store. They give him a tough time, the same way they treat each other. He is recognized as part of the community.

His best friend is the great ball player from Picton, Jerry Evans, now a family physician, the only doctor in Picton. They see each other often, usually at games during basketball season. Jerry is Sam's only confidant. The two men have become great friends. Doctor Evans knows everything about Sam and Cynthia. He arranged DNA tests to verify that Sam and Cynthia are not related.

Sam has many friends other than Doctor Evans. He is not a lonely man. He recently bought yet another farm at auction, adding to the ranch. Sam enjoys life, ranching, the cattle business, the land and the hills, but mostly he cherishes the comfort of belonging.

Cynthia is always happy to see him and they have a solid relationship that has flourished beyond friendship to dating. Cynthia demonstrates ever more consistent signs that she remembers how close they once were. She is comfortable being touched and hugged, no longer pulling away when Sam kisses her. Cynthia is practicing pro bono law for the rehab center and has purchased a car.

The rehab director recently told Sam that the team of doctors and nurses have planned an intervention to urge Cynthia to move away from the facility and rejoin society. They believe she is ready to fly by herself.

* * * * *

Cynthia phoned Sam late in the afternoon a day after the intervention.

"Sam, do you still grill steaks?"

"Yes. Yes I do."

"Good. Are you too busy to grill a steak for me this evening?"

"Nope. I will gladly drop everything for you."

"That's great, Sam, because at this very moment I am standing at your front door with steaks. And, if you don't mind too much, I would like to stay over tonight."

Sam Prescott is home.

About the Author

Larry Cunningham retired from the Marine Corps, a Lt. Colonel, fighter squadron commander. He wrote the USMC plans for the evacuation of Vietnam, Cambodia and Laos. He flew many combat missions and served as Air Officer during the siege of Khe Sanh. He is an ex-cattle rancher, high school science teacher,  college fiction writing instructor and poet. He often speaks at writer's meetings and conferences.

Other books by Cunningham:
Choices
The Inevitable Man
The Velvet Scar

Check the author's website
https://jameslarrycunningham.com

www.ingramcontent.com/pod-product-compliance
Lightning Source LLC
Chambersburg PA
CBHW031249170626
46807CB00001B/58